T0284809

COLD TRAIL

Also by Taylor Moore

Down Range
Firestorm
Ricochet

COLD TRAIL

A GARRETT KOHL NOVEL

TAYLOR MOORE

WILLIAM MORROW
An Imprint of HarperCollinsPublishers

COLD TRAIL. Copyright © 2024 by Robert Taylor Moore. All rights reserved. Printed in the United States of America. No part of this book may be used or reproduced in any manner whatsoever without written permission except in the case of brief quotations embodied in critical articles and reviews. For information, address HarperCollins Publishers, 195 Broadway, New York, NY 10007.

HarperCollins books may be purchased for educational, business, or sales promotional use. For information, please email the Special Markets Department at SPsales@harpercollins.com.

FIRST EDITION

Designed by Kyle O'Brien
Title page art © Pi-Lens/Shutterstock

Library of Congress Cataloging-in-Publication Data has been applied for.

ISBN 978-0-06-329246-8

24 25 26 27 28 LBC 5 4 3 2 1

To the good stewards of the earth, I dedicate this novel

COLD TRAIL

PART ONE

Innocence, once lost, can never be regained.
Darkness, once gazed upon, can never be lost.

—*John Milton*

1

Kohl Ranch
Texas High Plains

It had been at least a week since Garrett Kohl had spotted the trespasser's tracks on the ranch. The first time he'd seen them hadn't rung any alarm bells. But with the second occurrence came a trail of blood. He had no problem if a deer was taken in hunger or desperation. In this case though, the poacher had killed three bucks, cut off their antlers, and left the meat there to rot.

As a former Green Beret, DEA special agent, and, more recently, an undercover operative for the CIA, Garrett had spent the better part of his life hunting people who didn't want to be found. For that reason, and a natural instinct for tracking, he was damn good at finding them. He'd hoped those days were behind him, but apparently he wasn't done just yet.

His new area of operations was the place his forefathers had settled back in 1893 and his family had lived on ever since. His particular piece of heaven was seventeen thousand acres of ranchland, roughly twenty-six square miles of prairie that ran north of the Canadian River and beyond the majestic ridgeline that towered above their farmhouse.

This two-hundred-mile stretch of caliche cliffs, known as the Caprock Escarpment, spanned from New Mexico to Oklahoma and jutted up from the vast plains over a thousand feet high in places. It divided the ranch nearly perfectly, marking upper and lower grazing areas of windswept heights of open savanna, and river bottom pasture plentiful with cottonwoods.

Garrett turned to his son, Asadi, who was riding beside him on a red roan quarter horse named Scamp, and pointed at the footsteps in the snow. "Well, what's your assessment, Outlaw? When were those tracks made?"

Asadi dropped from the saddle and led the gelding up to the trail. He knelt and studied the prints for a good ten seconds. "Late last night or early morning hours."

"And what makes you think that?" Garrett always pressed for a reason that would rule out any lucky guesses. "Seems like kind of a narrow time frame, don't you think?"

Asadi took off a glove, reached into the divot, and let his fingertips glide along the powder. "We got a few inches of snow yesterday afternoon. But there's a light dusting on top of the tracks. Probably from what blew in today before dawn. Means he was here in between then."

"And how do you know it was a *he*?" Garrett had never heard of a female poacher, but that wasn't the point. The point was never to make claim that you couldn't back up. "Sounds like you're weeding out about fifty percent of the population without any evidence."

Asadi eyeballed the tracks for a moment and then turned back. "Boots are at least a size twelve. D width. And the tracks are deep. Whoever made them was big and heavy."

"I've met some big ol' gals in my time." Garrett shot his son a wink to let him know that he was having a little fun. "Some of them wearing clodhoppers too. Maybe it was one of them?"

Asadi rose from his crouch and stuck out his hand to shake on it. "Wanna bet?"

Seeing dollar signs in Asadi's eyes, Garrett moved on from a wager he was sure to lose. "So, where do you think he or *she* might be headed?"

It was a bit of a difficult question. Whoever made the tracks had clearly tried to hide them. They'd taken a circuitous route back to the barbed-wire fence that separated Kohl property from the neighboring Mescalero Ranch. The poacher was more than likely hunting deer from a vehicle. But given all the oilfield traffic in the area, there was no way to narrow it down.

Garrett hadn't expected to catch anyone in the act. Rather his end goal of the outing was a little uninterrupted father-son bonding. If he had broached the idea of a heart-to-heart talk, his increasingly aloof teenager would've certainly balked. But a sunrise mission to hunt down a poacher on horseback had all the makings of a really badass time.

Since starting up his own oil and gas exploration company nine months earlier, Garrett had been preoccupied at best, and borderline absentee. Asadi wasn't neglected by any stretch of the imagination. His surrogate grandad, Butch, was a constant fixture in his life. And the kid was just plain busy like most his age. Between school, ranch work, and the rodeo team, Asadi had his own thing going. In fact, he seemed to love his newfound independence.

A recent breakup, however, with this girlfriend, Savanah, had left him a bit on the mopey side. Garrett wanted to visit with his son one-on-one uninterrupted, just to make sure he wasn't trying to hide his pain.

As Asadi climbed back into the saddle, Garrett eased over on Sadie, a buckskin mare he'd trained the year before. He flashed a guilty smile that forewarned a ruse. "Want to talk a sec?"

Asadi looked over, clearly skeptical of the overture. "Talk about what?"

"Nothing specific. Checking in, that's all. While it's just you and me."

A slow nod came from Asadi, who was probably terrified it was going to be a follow-up to *the birds and the bees* conversation they'd had a couple of years ago. "Okay . . . I guess."

Garrett feigned nonchalance. "Anything pressing on your mind these days?"

Asadi glanced back at the footsteps in the snow. He was either totally uninterested or pretending to be uninterested. Either way, it was a solid showing. "Ah, no. Not really."

"Nothing at all?" Garrett pressed. "You can talk to me about anything, you know."

Asadi looked up and narrowed his eyes. "You mean about Faraz?"

The mention of that name hit Garrett hard, although it probably shouldn't have. It was only natural that Asadi would bring up his brother in Afghanistan, who they'd once falsely believed was executed by the Taliban at the same time as his parents. Where Faraz was located or what he was doing was anyone's guess, and the *not knowing* made it a whole lot worse.

Asadi could neither give up and grieve nor dare to dream of a day when they would be reunited. It was an odd purgatory. Although it wasn't the topic Garrett had been aiming for, it was obviously on Asadi's mind. So, he decided to fake it and keep going.

"Still think about him a lot?"

Asadi looked out at the blanket of powdery white plains, seeming to stare at the nothingness on the baby blue horizon, with its sunrise streaks of pink and orange. "Every day I think about Faraz. My parents too."

"That's good," Garrett reminded him. "You should always keep them close to your heart."

"That's the problem, I guess." Asadi turned back. "I'm starting to forget everything. How they looked. How they talked. And I'm worried that one day there'll be no memories at all."

Garrett had also lost his mother tragically at an early age, but he at least had his father and brother with whom to reminisce. Even his sister, Grace, bore a striking resemblance to Mena Kohl. But Asadi had none of that. There was no evidence that his family even existed. He'd fled his village in the Hindu Kush with nothing but the clothes on his back.

"Well, don't give up. Keep Faraz in your prayers. Because he might still be out there."

Asadi brightened. "You really think so?"

Garrett didn't really believe it to be true, but this wasn't the time to admit it. The kid needed a little lift in his spirits, even if it came from false hope. "You remember what Kim said?"

Asadi didn't miss a beat. "That she'd never ever stop looking for him. *Ever.*"

"That's exactly right. And that woman is a bloodhound. Once she gets on the scent, she won't let go. We just need to give her some more time. Okay?"

If anybody could track someone down to the far ends of the earth, it would be CIA operations officer Kim Manning. But Garrett hadn't heard from her in months. He only knew that she was leading a task force to track down a network of Iranian Quds Force operatives. Having done his share of deep cover work with Kim and her deputy chief, a paramilitary officer named Mario Contreras, Garrett suspected it would be a while before the duo resurfaced again. With no real idea if they would ever get resolution on the Faraz situation, Garrett opted for a subject change.

"Aside from all that, everything else okay?"

"Why?" Asadi looked a little nervous. "Did Butch say something?"

It was actually Garrett's girlfriend, Lacey, who had spilled the beans. "Nope. Just noticed you haven't been spending as much time with Savanah as you used to."

Asadi's face fell. "Well, we're not together anymore."

"*Really?*" Garrett feigned surprise. "What on earth happened?"

There was a moment of silence before Asadi answered. It was as if he were still thinking through it, struggling to come to an answer that made sense. "It's like we started talking less and less. And now we don't talk at all. Or she doesn't want to for some reason. I just don't get it."

Savanah had lived out at the Kohl Ranch a few months prior. But when her dad, Ray Smitty, was offered a job as foreman out at the Mescalero, they moved and she started going to a new school.

Although vast and expansive, the Texas Panhandle could be the smallest of worlds. Garrett would never say it, but he suspected that she'd found a new boyfriend.

"Well, sometimes things sort of fizzle out. You'll find someone else though. I'm sure of it."

Asadi shrugged. "But I don't want anyone else."

Garrett was just gearing up for the *old plenty of fish in the sea* conversation when a thundering *BOOM* came from behind. His thoughts turned to the obvious culprit—the poacher on the prowl. But this was no crack of a rifle. It was the rumbling thunder of an explosion. It was on a scale that he'd not heard since his war zone days in Iraq and Afghanistan.

As his horse tried to bolt, Garrett pulled the reins to bring the spooked Sadie back under control and turned to the horizon, where a plume of black smoke rose into the sky about a half-mile away. Although he couldn't see the origin, for the line of mesquite brush on the fence blocking his view, he knew what it was.

Asadi, who was working hard to get Scamp settled, stared in awe at the billowing cloud. "That from the Kaiser place?"

The Mescalero Compressor Station, which pushed natural gas through pipelines across the surrounding ranches, had become a permanent fixture and largely went unnoticed. But accidents at places like these happened on occasion, and when they did, they could spark an inferno straight from Hell. It was rare for anyone in the near vicinity to survive that kind of blaze.

Garrett didn't even want to mention the first thought that came to mind. But his best friend's son worked there. "Yeah, that's on the Kaiser side." After a few seconds of contemplating a plan, he turned back to Asadi. "This is gonna be real bad. We need to get over there now."

ALTHOUGH ASADI HAD BECOME A capable rider since his transition from Afghanistan to Texas, he was still nowhere near the skill level of his dad. Trailing right behind Garrett, he was in awe at how deftly he maneuvered Sadie through and around clumps of mesquite brush at nearly a full sprint. Fortunately, there was no guess-work as to where they were headed.

Beyond the billowing black cloud rising high into the ice-blue sky, he could hear the hissing shriek of the gas leak, even over the rumbling four-beat pattern of Scamp's hooves as they pounded the earth. Asadi broke the line of mesquite trees to find the pumping station in worse condition than he'd imagined. The facility, which was a football-field-sized hodgepodge of silver tubing, industrial machinery, and steel tanks, wasn't only spewing flames from a rup-tured shaft, the fire had spread to the main building that housed the control center.

By the time he was at the back exit on the security fence, Gar-rett was already off his buckskin and kneeling beside someone on the ground. Looking away from the horribly burned body, Asadi locked eyes with his dad. "Is he still alive?"

"Barely." Garrett pointed to a dip in the terrain about forty yards back. "Need you to move him out of here. Could be another big explosion coming."

Asadi nodded but couldn't really wrap his head around the ca-lamity. It was almost too much to process. It wasn't the first time he'd been near a fire of this magnitude, but it was the first time he'd been so close to one that was being artificially fed by an unlimited supply of fuel. It reminded him of the footage of the *Hindenburg* disaster he'd watched in his social studies class.

"Wait, what are you going to do?" Asadi followed his dad's gaze and saw the familiar red Toyota Tundra that belonged to a close family friend, then looked over at the building, which was engulfed in flames. "You think David's inside there?"

"I don't know. But I couldn't live with myself if I didn't try to find out."

Garrett removed the lariat from his saddle, shook out the loop, and slid it over the unconscious man. He tightened it beneath his underarms, yanked out the slack, and handed the rope to Asadi. "Okay, now dally it off on your saddle horn and pull him away from here as gentle as you can."

By the time Asadi was mounted again and had the rope secured, his dad was already loping onto the facility grounds. Asadi
nudged his horse onward but they had made it no more than a few
feet when heard the *WHUMPH*, and then felt the shock wave of
another thundering *BOOM*.

2

Garrett maneuvered through the compressor unit compound around burning piles of rubble, pulse racing, as his thoughts turned to the charred body he'd seen only seconds before. He had experienced his share of life-or-death situations, in some of the most dangerous places on earth. But those were not nearly as frightening as the wall of flames that now hemmed him in.

Spying a tiny gap in the blaze as he spun in a circle to the left, Garrett eased the reins to the right and aimed at an opening in the barrier. Sadie sprinted through the scorching heat of the tiny breach, where they found safety on the other side. Garrett pulled the reins, brought the mare to a halt, and did his best to survey the grounds through the wafting smoke, stinging his eyes.

Psyching himself up for another charge into the flames, Garrett spun Sadie around, pointed her at the front door of the control center, and gave her a little prod with the spurs. She went from a walk to a lope until building into full-on sprint. But within thirty yards of the burning structure she balked, came to an abrupt halt, and slid a few feet across the melting snow.

Between the suffocating smoke, leaping flames, and a howling shriek from the busted lines, every bit of the disaster was an assault on the senses. As Sadie stomped, stamped, and snorted, Garrett suspected that she'd done all she would do. He dropped from the saddle, wrapped the reins around the horn, and gave a slap on the rear. In a matter of seconds, she was at the front gate and bolting toward safety in the wide-open pasture.

Garrett turned and sprinted to the office, but nearly ten feet from the front door his arms shot up reflexively to shield his face from the scorching heat. Reasoning that if it were too hot for him to handle on the outside, then there was no way anyone was alive within, he decided to escape while he still could. He was getting ready to make a run for it when something caught his eye. On the ground, at the front door, just breaking the threshold, was what appeared to be a hand.

Garrett twirled around in search of something that could help him to withstand the heat. But between the flames and smoke, he couldn't find anything of much use. Then he noticed several sheets of corrugated tin that had blown from the rooftop during the blast. It wouldn't be perfect, but he reasoned that the three-foot by four-foot panel could work as a makeshift shield.

After sprinting back to the parking lot, Garrett grabbed the thin metal pane and flipped it over. Using the shattered beam still attached as a handle, he raised it in front of his body and hurried to the door. Garrett felt the same blistering burn, but he persisted, pushing through a heat so intense that he cried out in pain.

Reeling back, Garrett hid his face behind the tin and forced himself onward. He was about to look around the side when he slammed into the outside wall of the office and the armor slipped from his grip. He threw his hand to his face and clamped his eyes shut, as he dropped to his knees, grasping and groping for his shield in a pure state of terror.

A quick look back at safety, and Garrett rose to flee. But a glimpse of the hand caught the corner of his eye. He dove for the threshold and gripped the wrist tight. Rare, if ever, was there an occasion where he would've spouted the merits of panic or losing control. But his body's desperation to escape the burn seemed to have given him what felt like a supernatural strength.

One swift tug and the body was through the door. Another hard yank got him some relief. And a third big pull got them far enough out where he could breathe. A giant inhalation of smoky air and Garrett rose to his feet. He didn't think. He just hauled. Over and over again, he dragged the body until they were in the middle of the open parking lot, where he collapsed in the frozen mud.

Lying prostrate on the snow-covered caliche ground, Garrett turned back to the inferno to find he'd made it at least forty yards. Mustering what little strength he had left, he rolled over to check on the one by his side. Although he had unfortunately been overseas for most of the big benchmark moments of his godson's life, he recognized David the instant he saw him.

As the sirens grew close, Garrett leaned over to check for a pulse. But if there was any sign of life, it was too faint to detect. What wasn't hard to find were the severe burns from the blast. As he did his best to wipe the soot from David's face, his heart broke for Tony and his family, and at the thought of what horrible suffering was still yet to come.

3

Asadi arrived back at the barn with the horses a half hour later, still feeling a bit numb. The stranger, whose hand he'd held while he died, didn't pass on to the next world in any memorable way. His breathing just stopped and that was that. But for some reason, Asadi just couldn't shake the image of that burned body. He saw it everywhere. Even when he closed his eyes.

"You okay, sonny?" Butch called from the porch. "Would've met you out there, but I figured by the time I got saddled you'd already be back." He marched from their farmhouse to the barn and took Sadie's reins. "Looks like I was right. You made it here in record time."

"I'm fine, I guess." Asadi could see a look of genuine concern in Butch's eyes and thought he'd better reassure him there was no need to worry. "Once I knew Garrett was safe, it wasn't too bad. Just took a couple of minutes to find Sadie. But she came right up to us."

A soft smile raised on Butch's face. "Guess you got a little more than you bargained for when you went looking for that poacher this morning, huh?"

Butch was the kind of man who was all business. Although as goodhearted as they come, the old rancher was as rough and tough as the land he'd worked his entire life. The softened demeanor made Asadi wonder if there was other bad news. "Is David going to make it?"

"Don't know yet. He's in the ICU up in Canadian." Butch shook his head. "Time will tell."

Asadi hated expressions like "time will tell." It had always been that way when it came to his brother. While he appreciated Garrett's attempts to keep his hopes up, he suspected there was no real chance that he'd ever see Faraz again. "When is Dad coming home?"

"Don't know for sure. Said he didn't want to leave until he got a chance to talk to Tony." Butch grimaced. "I expect that's going to be a hard conversation. Maybe one of the hardest. And that's saying a lot for someone like Garrett."

Asadi didn't know exactly what that meant, but he suspected it had to do with the war in Afghanistan. Garrett had made references to a big loss over there that had sent him spiraling. Of course, he never revealed much about his time in Special Forces beyond the most general details, but it was obvious he'd experienced something that he'd not gotten over.

Before Asadi could ask any more questions about his dad or David's condition, Butch offered a hand to help him down from the saddle. "How you feeling about what happened?"

The question about feelings was rarer than the gesture of helping him down. The old man was all about self-reliance in every sense. Of course, he'd had to be. He'd run the whole ranch alone for most of his life. Independence for him meant survival.

Asadi followed behind Butch, who was already pulling Scamp back to the barn. "Really wish we could've done something for that guy. The one who died. But I didn't know what to do. Just held his hand. Talked to him."

Butch spoke as he walked. "You did more than you think. Won't be easy for his family. But it'll be no small comfort for them to know you were with him. To know that he wasn't alone in the end. Believe it or not, it'll help with their grief."

Asadi didn't see how that would make any difference but didn't feel the need to argue. "Who was it? I'd never seen him before."

"Sounds strange to say it, but maybe that's the good news. Wasn't from around here. Was an inspector out of Houston just visiting from out of town." Butch glanced back and gave a shrug. "Wrong place at the wrong time it seems."

Asadi wouldn't exactly classify it as good news, but he knew what Butch meant. Somehow it was less painful if they didn't have to watch the family mourn. But someone somewhere was living a nightmare. And "wrong place at the wrong time" wouldn't ease their pain. Like his parents and brother, this inspector was just another poor soul who would also be forgotten.

AFTER GETTING A THOROUGH CHECKOUT from the doctors in the ER, Garrett was cleared and free to go. Having been in a lot worse before, he'd assumed as much. But to make his girlfriend happy he succumbed to a full overview. Despite a few coughing fits and an unquenchable thirst, he was feeling back to his old self. At least physically speaking. The fact that Tony's son, David, was hanging on by a thread cast a dark shadow that he just couldn't shake.

Garrett suspected that much of it had to do with a favor he owed his best friend from a couple of years past. When a foreign rare earth minerals mining company had set the ranch ablaze and attempted to gun down his family, his best friend, Tony Sanchez, a Hemphill County sheriff's deputy, had put his own life on the line to save Asadi.

Now that there was an opportunity for Garrett to return the favor, it was starting to look a lot like he'd failed. He had enough of ghosts haunting him without adding yet another. Of course, feeling sorry for himself was pointless, especially when Tony was heartbroken. Garrett had just walked out of the ICU and rounded the corner in search of him when they came face-to-face.

It was clear from Tony's puffy red eyes that he'd been crying.

And it occurred to Garrett that in all his adult life, he'd never seen this battle-hardened former Marine get emotional. He cleared his throat, buying a little time to try and think of the right words. "Hey, man, I was just coming to find you. Can't tell you how sorry I am. Just don't even know what to say."

"It's all right." Tony raised his hand, looking as if he was about to break down. "Is what it is, I guess."

Garrett found it difficult to meet Tony's eyes. "Just wish I could've found him sooner."

"Wouldn't have mattered," Tony answered, his voice sounding a bit raspy as he fought to compose himself. "Most of his burns came from the first blast." He reached out, gripped Garrett's shoulder, and squeezed. "If you hadn't gone in after him, he'd have no chance at all. Whole building collapsed, they told me. Came crashing down in flames."

At risk of taking the conversation to a gloomier place, Garrett moved on to a subject that they might be able to do something about. "Do they know what caused the explosion? Heard the one who didn't make it was an inspector. Assume he was out there for a reason."

Tony shook his head. "Inspection was on the books for months. This was just a routine visit."

"So, it was just an accident."

Tony's face tightened. "I don't know about that."

"What else could it be?"

Tony looked over his shoulder to make sure that no one else was around, then turned back. "Before David went into surgery, he regained consciousness for a couple of minutes. And he told me that they saw someone else out there."

Garrett looked over his own shoulder too, although he wasn't sure why. "Like who? You mean another employee?"

"No. It was no one he knew. Big guy, he said."

"Was he wearing a uniform? Maybe he was a contractor. Was there a vehicle around?"

Tony shrugged. "He didn't say."

"Well, I need more details. What *exactly* did he see?"

"I don't know, Garrett. My son wasn't exactly in good enough shape to interrogate just yet."

Garrett threw up a hand, palm out. "Sorry, man. Sorry. Just an old habit of the trade. The fact that he was able to get that out says a lot. But that intel takes this to another level. If there was someone out there trespassing before the explosion then we need to know who it was."

Tony gave a nod. "That's why I'm telling you this."

Garrett didn't need any plea for help. He was all over it. "It's got me thinking. We've had someone sneaking onto our ranch, poaching pretty close to the compressor station. Doesn't mean there's a connection between the two, but it's at least a place to start."

Tony glanced around again, this time as if he was expecting someone. "Look, Silvia will be wondering where I am. She's a mess. Kids are too. I just can't leave them right now. But knowing this information I feel the need to—"

"Tony, you just be here for your family. Don't worry about anything else. I'm on it. I'll head over to the Mescalero and track down Smitty and Bo. Maybe they've seen something around the ranch that doesn't fit. Someone who shouldn't be out there. They keep a close watch."

A weak smile raised on Tony's face. "Knew I could count on you, brother."

As his friend turned and walked back toward the ICU, Garrett's stomach dropped at the thought of what the Sanchez family was going through. Even if David survived, it wouldn't be an easy recovery. He'd known quite a few soldiers who'd gone through that long and painful process. One had even told him that if he had to go through it again he'd rather just die.

Garrett had just made the move to leave when he felt the buzz from his phone. He pulled it from his pocket to find a text from his business partner, Vicky Kaiser. It was fortunate since he was heading out to the Mescalero Ranch anyhow. But the reason for her to reach out was more shocking than the explosion, or even Tony's revelation that there could be foul play.

Her message was right to the point. And it involved a person, whom he thought he might never see again.

Your sister is here in my office. We really need to talk.

4

Ray Smitty didn't know much about environmental activists beyond what he'd seen on the news. But apparently they were out in full force, loud and proud, protesting in front of the burning rubble that was once a natural gas compressor station. According to his boss, Vicky Kaiser, owner of the Mescalero Ranch, the *trespassing hippies* were to be removed at once.

She'd added the words *by any means necessary*, which Smitty had hoped, but wasn't certain, was all just bluster. On top of being ranch foreman, he was Vicky's oil scout. It was a title that meant many things to many people. To her, it meant spy.

Strong-arming had never really been Smitty's forte, but the passenger in his pickup was born for the task and looked eager to put his skills to work. Bo Clevenger was the head of Mescalero security, a title that Vicky treated more like mafia muscle than privatized law enforcement. Fortunately, given his appearance, he rarely had to get physical. The old rodeo bulldogging champ still looked the part of a man who used to dive from a running horse onto a five-hundred-pound steer. Add in the shaved head and prison tattoos and you had a modern-day desperado.

Smitty, on the other hand, was slight as they come. No matter how much he ate, he stayed as rangy as an antelope. Unfortunately, he had none of the animal's vigor. Like Bo, he maintained the look of a cowboy, wearing boots, blue jeans, and pearl snap denim. He'd always been told he had a warm smile, which he'd used on more than one occasion to talk himself out of trouble.

As they drove up to the smoldering rubble of the compressor station, Smitty took in the scene. Although most of the fire was put out, the facility was still swarmed by fire trucks, state troopers, and sheriff's deputy vehicles. To the side of the caliche road were nearly fifty or so protesters. Luckily, the TV news crews were gone.

Smitty turned to Bo, whose eyes looked hungry for a fight. "All right now, take it easy. Don't want to make anything worse than it is. Just going to ask them to leave."

Bo was bird-dog focused on the scrum of intruders. "And if they don't?"

Smitty eased his boot on the brakes and slowed the pickup. "Hell, you've seen the forecast. We've got a damn blizzard coming in tonight. Supposed to get down near zero. And you know how these people are. They'll stick around awhile. Get cold and hungry. Then head on home."

It wasn't until Smitty pulled around one of the fire trucks that he saw the retrofitted Greyhound, and about two dozen cars, vans, and SUVs, few of which looked any friendlier to the environment than his own one-ton Ford. There were fires scattered about their encampment, and at least fifty shelters, lean-tos, and tents of every shape, size, and color. They *were* home.

Given the wide assortment of pennants from around the world, there were representatives across the globe. But anything beyond the Union Jack and Canadian flag, he was pretty much stumped. Bo turned to Smitty but didn't say a word. A look said it all. *This is gonna get ugly.*

Smitty softened his tone to take it down a notch. "You're gonna be cool, right?"

Bo turned to face the protesters and narrowed his gaze. "Uh-huh."

Smitty pulled his truck up to within twenty-five yards of the group and put it in park. He wanted a little distance in case things got physical and they needed to get away. He'd seen footage of nutjobs jumping in front of vehicles and blocking roads. But in the wide-open space on the High Plains, it would take a lot more than a few dozen bodies to stymie their exit.

As Bo opened his door, Smitty clutched his coat sleeve. "I'll do the talking."

Without reply, Bo jerked away and made a beeline for the group. Smitty made his own hasty departure and kicked into high gear to catch up with his partner. A quick survey of the protesters revealed a lot of ponchos and hoodies. A few were even wearing brightly covered beanies with flaps over the ears. Most carried signs, with varying messages of disgust for Mescalero Energy.

They were met halfway by one of the protesters who broke from the pack and made his way over. Unlike the others, who looked kind of wormy, this guy was beefed up and assertive. His blond dreadlocks were pulled into a ponytail, and he wore a week's worth of stubble. In cargo pants and a blue goose down jacket, he looked a lot more mountain climber than rabblerouser.

Dreads launched in with a "Can I help you, gentlemen?" before Smitty could get a word out.

Bo was quick to respond. "We'll be asking the questions."

Smitty threw up a hand to Bo and turned back to Dreads. "Well, sir, as a matter of fact you can help us. My name is Ray Smitty and I'm going to be in charge of the cleanup and reconstruction around here."

Dreads gave a nod. "I'm Kai Stoddard." He tilted his head at the group. "And that's Cosmic Order. We're out of Austin."

Smitty fought off a grin. He was almost disappointed when the guy's name wasn't Moonbeam or Sunflower, but Cosmic Order certainly scratched the itch for joke fodder. Dreads hadn't needed to mention Austin given the Texas license plates on the bus. *Where the hell else?*

"Fine-looking group of folks you have here."

Stoddard wasn't buying the nice-guy routine. "What can I do for you, Mr. Smitty?"

"Well, we want to get our operation here back up and running soon as possible. Once the firemen clear out, we're going to get a repair team and a construction crew in here to work."

The guy glanced back at the facility and shrugged. "What does that have to do with us?"

"Nothing," Smitty answered. "And I guess that's the point. There's going to be a lot of blowing and going. Dozers. Cranes. Semitrucks. Could get dangerous with vehicles moving in and out. So, if you're done with what you're doing, we'd appreciate you taking your leave."

The guy smirked, clearly not believing a word. "You could give a rat's ass about our safety." He peered around Bo to check out their truck. "See the Mescalero logo on your door there. My guess is this has more to do with our message and how it might affect your company's image."

The banner hanging on the side of their old Greyhound read: *Mescalero = Enemy of the Earth.* The funny thing about it was that Vicky Kaiser couldn't care less about the company's image. She had given up on public relations a long time ago. But what she did care about was profitability. Getting the compressor station back online was her primary concern.

Smitty flashed a warm smile, which would hopefully take the tension down a notch or two. "We're probably not going to agree on politics. But we can agree that the law is the law. And you're breaking it here by trespassing."

"That's where you're wrong." Stoddard fished an envelope from his pocket, took out a typed letter, and handed it over. "The property where we're set up, on the other side of the county road, belongs to Garland Porter. And as you can see, we have his permission to camp here." As almost an afterthought, he added, "His number is in the letterhead. Feel free to give him a call."

Damn. Smitty had known the feud between Vicky and Garland would come back to bite them in the ass. He just didn't think it'd be this soon. And there'd be no convincing their neighbor of reconsidering this deal. Garland had hated the Kaisers for years.

Smitty shook off the offer. "Got Garland in my phone already."

He looked over at the sign. "But you have to understand that it's not just our natural gas coming through this pumping station. Comes from all over. And your message is focused on us. Do you mind telling me why?"

Stoddard seemed confused. "Because of the new pipeline."

Smitty looked to Bo. "You heard anything about that?"

Bo shrugged. "Above our pay grade, maybe."

Stoddard appeared eager to fill them in. "Our lobbyists in Austin tell us that the state is looking to approve a major pipeline deal called the Trans-Palisade, running from the Texas Panhandle down to the Permian Basin. Connecting somewhere around Midland and Odessa."

Smitty took a second to process the information but came up short. "What does that matter? There are pipelines running across the whole damn state."

"This one is different," Stoddard shot back. "It'll be delivering natural gas to facilities down on the coast near Brownsville. From there, it'll be put on tankers and hauled to Europe. Which means, once again, *we'll* be the ones responsible for polluting the rest of the world."

"What about that monstrosity?" Bo pointed to the Cosmic Order Greyhound bus. "Reckon it runs off butterfly farts and Mother Nature's goodwill to humanity."

Stoddard looked a little ashamed, but not enough to back down. "We do whatever we have to do to get the job done."

"So do we." Bo stepped forward. "And you're about to find that out the hard way."

Smitty reached out and grabbed Bo's sleeve again. "Hold on there." He looked up at his partner and nodded in the direction of the protesters. More than a few were holding up their cell phones, recording the whole scene with their cameras. "Let me talk to Mr. Stoddard for a minute. *Alone.* Don't want to end up with any more eyes on this than there needs to be."

Bo remained focused on Stoddard. At first he looked loath to relent, but eventually he unclenched and lumbered back to the truck.

The only man Smitty knew who had ever put the giant in his place was Garrett Kohl. And to this peacenik's credit, he hadn't backed down, even when Bo threatened violence. In fact, Stoddard looked downright ready to rumble.

As soon as Bo was back in the truck and cameras were focused elsewhere, Smitty continued. "I don't have anything against you or your cause. I'm just doing my job. Trying to keep things running. And I got a wife and a kid to provide for. Surely you can understand that."

Stoddard's face softened and he dropped his shoulders. "I don't wish you or your family any ill will, Mr. Smitty. But we're here to stay. And until this pipeline deal is over, you, Mescalero, and whoever else comes against us, should consider yourselves at war."

5

Before heading down to his meeting with Vicky at the Mescalero Ranch, Garrett swung by the house to pick up Asadi, who was more than a little rattled given the day's sad and unexpected turn of events. Not only had David Sanchez been a constant fixture in his life, but the fact that Asadi was present when the visiting inspector passed away had naturally hit the kid doubly hard.

Hoping that Savanah might offer some much-needed cheering up, Garrett dropped Asadi off at the horse barn, where she worked, and then drove to Vicky's office in her mansion home. At the top of the ridge, he parked between her white Range Rover and a silver Mercedes AMG.

Garrett had just exited his black GMC pickup when he saw a very familiar face coming out of the front door. It wasn't just familiar because it was his sister. It was familiar because she was the spitting image of his beautiful mother. Same silky black hair, high cheekbones, and slender frame. In fact, Grace was probably around the same age now that their mom was when she died.

It should've made for some warm feelings, but seeing the woman who'd abandoned their family when they'd needed her most produced a shock wave of emotional pain. Garrett was about to start the conversation with some trite saying like *you've got a lot a nerve* when she beat him to the punch with a wallop of kindness.

"My baby brother." Grace's eyes twinkled just liked their mom's. "Handsome as ever."

Garrett didn't believe a word of it but smiled anyhow. He still wore the same look as he'd had during his days undercover with the DEA. It was a rodeo rogue kind of style that included Howler Brothers pearl snaps, Twisted-X cowboy boots, and Lone Star Dry Goods trucker hats. With his sleeve tattoos, thick beard, and long dark hair that fell well past his collar, he could blend in with ranch hands, rig hands, and modern-day outlaws of every sort.

Grace, on the other hand, had always been into high fashion, even when the Kohl family barely had the money to make ends meet. Garrett didn't know anything about *couture*, as his girlfriend, Lacey, called it. But he'd run in enough wealthy circles during his days with the cartel to recognize a few iconic patterns and emblems on Grace's outfit, like Burberry and Chanel.

Disarmed by her dewy sweet charm, Garrett softened as she brought him into a full embrace. "Hey there, sister. How are you?"

Grace stepped back and took him all in. "Your timing couldn't be better. I was just about to call you."

Garrett glanced over at Vicky, who was standing at the front door with a drink in each hand. The martini no doubt belonged to Grace. That had always been her drink of choice, even in high school. Whenever everyone else was drinking Natty Light and Boone's Farm, she was preparing her palate for a more sophisticated lifestyle.

Before Garrett could ask what was going on, Vicky walked out and handed him a highball of bourbon. "A little Garrison Brothers Balmorhea?" She added in a throaty whisper, "Think it's time we celebrate."

Given the circumstances surrounding the explosion and the protesters, Garrett had naturally assumed Vicky would be in the foulest of moods. But cocktails before noon meant something was up. Something big. Of course, she would take almost any occasion to clink glasses, he'd learned. In fact, she'd once had him make a toast on Boxing Day. *Whatever the hell that is?*

• • •

AFTER THEY MOVED INSIDE TO the office, their conversation un-folded in the most pleasant of ways. Come to find out, Vicky's happy disposition was prompted by the fact that Grace had returned home bearing generous gifts, which centered on a pipeline connecting major petroleum-producing fields in the Panhandle to the Permian Basin, which would ultimately be converted into liquefied natural gas, or LNG, at a facility on the Texas Gulf Coast.

"To be clear, this isn't just *any* pipeline," Grace explained. "It'd be a major artery. The biggest in regional history." She stood and walked over to an easel, supporting a large map of Texas. There was a legend indicating which pipelines were in existence, and which were proposed. "We'd link up around Midland and run southeast to Brownsville, where it will be converted to LNG for the European market."

Garrett had so many questions he barely knew where to start. The Kohl Ranch was sitting above the Anadarko Basin, one of the largest natural gas formations in the United States. But the Perm-ian oilfields were flush with it too. He found it unlikely any min-eral owners or operators working exclusively in that area would ever want to spread the wealth. The devil was always in the details, and he was sitting in an office with two of the dark lord's most devious minions.

Garrett cocked his head and turned to his sister. "Why do you need us? The Permian should be covered on delivery."

Grace looked to Vicky and back again before speaking. "This is no ordinary deal we're making. This is bigger than just us. We'll need to pool our resources to meet demand."

Given what he knew about the vast natural gas reserves in the Permian Basin, Garrett doubted that was true. And he suspected she had an ulterior motive. "Well, that'd be a big deal for sure. What are we talking about here on terms?

"This is a fifty-year contract, Garrett. With the loss of Russian natural gas, the European Union is looking for a long-term stable source to replace it. Obviously, they're moving toward renewables, but they're not going to get there overnight. This would bridge that gap. We're talking tens of billions of dollars in contracts for LNG. And that doesn't even cover the infrastructure investment, also in the billions. This deal is going to change everything."

Garrett looked to Vicky, who couldn't seem to contain her grin.

There wasn't much to think about in terms of the financial upside. When he'd partnered with Vicky's Mescalero Energy, they'd come up with an arrangement whereby his company, Savage Exploration, would share in the profits from any drilling in unexplored zones. In exchange for resources from Kohl Ranch, such as groundwater, frac sand, and road materials, he could participate in joint operating agreements on any oil wells considered new production.

The bottom line was that the more they drilled, the more money he made. The downside was that it further depleted his land's natural resources. And they were dwindling already. He knew though that beggars couldn't be choosers. And he still owed Vicky for getting him out of debt.

Doing his best to only see the upside, he replied, "Well, I think this would provide a permanent market. No worries about price fluctuation. We'd lock in a deal that would keep Mescalero Energy and Savage Exploration in operation for at least two generations."

"*Savage?*" Grace asked, looking confused.

Garrett had once overheard one of Vicky's henchmen, an on-the-payroll local sheriff named Ted Crowley, refer to him as "the offspring of a savage." It was an ugly dig based on his Comanche heritage, which didn't faze him in the least. In fact, he took it as a compliment.

Garrett shrugged. "Just thought it was catchy, I guess."

"Well, it's sure to become a household name. Assuming we have your full support."

"Support for *what* exactly?"

Grace pointed to the map again. "Here on our ranch is where we'd want to put in a connecter. It's right in the fairway of the best natural gas fields around. Perfect nexus for other pipelines around the Panhandle. We'd have to beef the Washita Compressor Station but that won't be a problem. Crews will be out here anyway getting the Mescalero unit repaired."

There were three things in her statement that didn't sit well with Garrett. He was all for letting bygones be bygones with Grace, but she'd used the term *our ranch*. Sure, she was family, but she hadn't stepped foot on the place in years. Her plan also meant there would be more trenches and construction. There was already enough activity given the drilling operations. And lastly, there was still the chance of an accident, as they'd only just witnessed.

The Kohl Ranch had only recently recovered from the damage done by a rare earth minerals mine and a devastating wildfire. *How much more could the land possibly take?*

Garrett further wondered what Grace's official role would be in all this. Her husband owned a bank in Midland-Odessa that had several locations around West Texas, which were filled with oil and gas money. He suspected that Grace was sent up as some sort of Permian Basin envoy to the Texas Panhandle since she was an acquaintance of the Kaisers and a member of the Kohl family. Before he could inquire about that, Vicky changed the subject.

"And don't worry about those filthy hippies, Garrett. Smitty and Bo are seeing to that."

Garrett braced for impact when he asked, "Seeing to *what* exactly?"

He hadn't seen the "hippies" yet, but Garrett had gotten an earful from Ray Smitty when he'd called about the trespasser Tony Sanchez had mentioned at the hospital. Apparently, some protesters were blocking the road leading up to the compressor station and chanting slogans in front of news crews that were there to film the fire.

Vicky smiled, looking coy. "Oh . . . I sent them over to see what all the fuss was about. Make sure there wouldn't be any more *accidents*."

Garrett's first reaction was to put an immediate stop to whatever schemes she was hatching, but her comment took him by surprise. "Sounds like you think these protesters were behind it."

"Ecoterrorism," Vicky stated with confidence. "These people are getting more and more radical every day. You should see what they're doing over in England."

Garrett had to admit that some of these groups were doing some disturbing things to get their messages across. But he doubted Smitty and Bo had the skills to do a thorough arson investigation. With Tony's revelation of a trespasser on the site before the explosion, they couldn't rule anything out. But Vicky's plan, particularly now that she thought this was an act of environmental terrorism, had corporate scandal written all over it.

"Call off Smitty and Bo for now and let me do a little digging. I'll see what I can find out."

Vicky seemed reluctant but didn't argue. "Okay . . . I've got another job for them, anyhow."

Garrett looked to Grace. "So, are you headed back to Odessa?" As soon as he asked, he regretted it. It was meant to be idle conversation. But he should've known better.

"Was planning on sticking around to hammer out a few of the finer points." Grace looked to Vicky. "What's the best and nearest hotel around here these days?"

Garrett hoped Vicky would chime in with an offer of one of the seventeen extra bedrooms on the Mescalero grounds. But when no invitation was forthcoming, he was left on the hook. With nothing short of herculean effort, he rallied to smile.

"Well, of course you're welcome at the house, Grace. Just, me, Dad, and Asadi these days. The boy took your old room, but I'm sure he wouldn't mind camping out on the couch."

His sister's face beamed in a way that looked like genuine gratitude. "If it's not a bother, that'd be wonderful. I think it's been years since I've been home."

As they wrapped up the rest of the meeting, Garrett didn't know what to fret about first. The fact that they were potentially a target of ecoterrorism was one thing, but breaking the news to Butch about their new houseguest was going to be a helluva lot worse.

6

As Asadi walked around the massive show barn, he couldn't help but envy the Kaisers' impressive setup. He'd never admit that any of their quarter horses could match the bloodline they'd developed over decades on the Kohl Ranch, but the training facilities on the Mescalero were hands down among the best around. Garrett and Butch had lost more than a few big rodeo, cutting, and ranch horse clients and customers to Vicky over the last couple of years.

The Kaisers had a world-class, state-of-the-art equestrian center. The Kohls had a few stalls and a tack room. And after a wildfire had destroyed much of the ranch two years prior, and left them on the verge of bankruptcy, they were lucky to have even that. But the Mescalero-Savage Energy partnership, formed nine months earlier between Garrett and Vicky, had saved the ranch. Now their energy and agriculture-related businesses weren't just surviving. They were thriving. Grit and determination were fine, but the truth was that money makes the horse world go round.

Asadi's pride was also hurt by the fact that Savanah worked for the Kaisers part-time—taking all the skills she'd learned from the Kohls to the competition. Their actual breakup hadn't been messy, just a subtle drifting away. But before any of that, the two had been best friends. She'd taken him under her wing when he first arrived in Texas and until recently, they'd been inseparable.

Somehow though, the distance after she'd moved had put a gulf between them. She had an entirely new life that slowly but surely no longer included him.

As he wandered around the barn, Asadi wished he'd never come out there. Not only did it bring up the sting of losing Savanah, but it also reminded him of what small potatoes they were compared to the Kaisers. But his dad had wanted to check in after the incident that morning and make sure everything was okay. Asadi was about to get out of there when *she* walked in.

Savanah looked more annoyed than surprised. "What are you doing here?"

The simple question for some reason cut deep and Asadi certainly didn't care for the tone. Savanah didn't own the place. Her dad, Ray Smitty, just worked there.

Asadi worked hard to play it cool. "Killing time while Garrett meets with Vicky."

Savanah moved over to the wall by the tack room, picked up a plastic bucket by the door, and scooped some Purina Ultium pellets into it from a white plastic bin. "Oh. That's okay, I guess."

"Yeah, I know it is. Garrett asked Vicky on the way over and she said it was fine."

"Well, I can't stop and talk now." Savanah continued her scooping without looking back. "Got a lot of work to do before the storm comes in."

As always, Savanah's mousy ringlets were pulled back into a messy bun. Nary was the occasion when she wasn't in boots and jeans. And she pulled it off like a champ. It bugged him terribly that he was still so attached. But what could he do? The heart wanted what it wanted. And he was having to pretend really hard that it *didn't* want her.

"Don't mind me." Asadi kept on the move. "I'll just pretend like you're not even here."

"Good." Savanah turned her gaze to him and flashed one of those *I know something you don't know* kind of looks. "*We* will do the same."

Asadi gave a confident nod, having felt as though he'd scored a few cool points with his frosty response. But then it dawned on him she'd used the word *we*. Before there was a chance to follow up, he saw why.

The sight of Duke Newhouse made Asadi's blood run cold. And it wasn't just the surprise of seeing someone who'd been shipped off three years ago to the New Mexico Military Institute (NMMI) in Roswell. It was also the fact that Duke was nearly the spitting image of his departed uncle, Preston. Until Vicky took control of Mescalero Energy, her brother had been at the helm.

On top of being a world-class jerk, Preston had worked with a vicious Mexican cartel in a drug trafficking and money laundering scheme until Garrett, Tony Sanchez, Ray Smitty, and a few other fed-up locals had taken him out. According to gossip, Duke was going down that same dark path as Preston. Not only was he using drugs, but he was selling them. There was an even juicier rumor that Duke had barely avoided arrest in New Mexico for doing just that.

Just like his uncle, Duke was tall and muscular, with a blond shock of perfectly coiffed hair that totally fit the Hollywood stereotype of an arrogant rich kid. And his bad-boy reputation had raised his profile with more than a few of the girls who were into the *dangerous thing*.

Doing his best to fake a greeting, Asadi called out a greeting in a voice that sounded strained, like he was trying too hard. "Hey, Duke! When'd you get back?"

Duke squinted. "One of the Kohl kids, right?"

"Sophie and Chloe's cousin," Asadi replied. "They introduced us. A few times, actually."

Savanah stepped up and stood beside Duke. "He's living back home now."

"*Home?*" Asadi asked. "What home?"

Duke never really had an actual home in the traditional sense. He was the only child of a divorced, self-described bohemian mother, Miriam Newhouse, who tended to *vacation*, when she wasn't focused on her art. She had a place in Canadian but split her time between the historic district of Charleston, South Carolina, and an exclusive resort in California near Laguna Beach.

When Duke had gotten too difficult to handle, Miriam sent him to NMMI to get straightened out. Now, apparently, he was Vicky's problem.

Savanah sounded defiant. "He's been living here at the ranch with Vicky for over a month now and doing quite well."

Doing quite well? Asadi was tempted to call her out but fought to hold his tongue. Savanah didn't talk like that. When he met her, she was living at a trailer park in a rusted-out Airstream. And why on earth was she defending Duke? Was he a wounded animal she'd taken into her care? Asadi remembered that at one time, it was he who had been the recipient of her affection.

Duke jumped in. "Look, kid, I know my aunt said you could poke around here, but playtime's over. Hate to see you get hurt."

Is this guy for real? Asadi knew more about taking care of horses than Duke Newhouse would ever know. He was about to say as much when Garrett's GMC pulled up to the open double doors at the opposite end of the barn.

Duke spoke again. "Looks like your ride's here." He gave a friendly wave to Garrett like a parent might do, then locked his gaze back on Asadi. "Better skip along now."

This was almost too much for Asadi to take. *Kid? Playtime? Skip along?* Of course, there was the very real possibility that Duke was actually trying to be nice. But that theory was shot when he moved in, lowered his voice, and added, "Probably best you don't come back."

Duke donned a fake smile and squared off. His fighting posture was subtle enough to hide it, but obvious enough to drive home the point. Although the menacing message was clear, the reason for sending it wasn't. *Is he after Savanah?*

7

As Garrett drove up to the Kohl Ranch he was shocked to see that the entrance was blocked by a crowd of about two dozen protesters. He was about to stop and see what they wanted, but since Asadi was riding shotgun, Garrett decided that they'd better just drive around them and keep on going. But before he could make the turn, a few angry activists jumped out in front of his GMC and started slapping on his hood. The others fanned out and closed in around them.

Most of their chanting, other than the words *greed* and *pipeline,* Garrett couldn't make out. But it was clear that the message was directed at him. He looked to Asadi, who seemed more amused than scared. Garrett's first impression was that this group was more bark than bite. And if push came to shove, they'd be out of danger with a mash on his accelerator. But phones were out, and cameras were rolling, which meant it was likely that he'd look like the antagonist.

Opting for the back entrance to the ranch over the main gate, Garrett threw the shifter in reverse. He'd just pressed the gas pedal when he heard a few gasps and screams. Slamming his foot on the brake, he glanced into the rearview mirror, finding half a dozen activists had moved in from behind to block his escape. "You've *got* to be kidding me."

Apparently, his aggressive maneuver had riled the crowd. And what had once been palms slapping the front and sides of his truck turned into banging fists.

Garrett turned back to Asadi, who was no longer amused. His eyes were wide with fear. "It's okay, buddy. They'll move out of the way."

Garrett hoped that was true, but the reality was that the activists looked like they were just getting started. Given the circumstances, he figured he'd better involve the law. The mob was out on a public county road but there was no way it was legal to stop him. And their belligerence was starting to feel like a threat. Unable to call Tony Sanchez for obvious reasons, Garrett did the unthinkable and pulled up Sheriff Ted Crowley's contact info.

The Hemphill County lawman was *almost* the last person in the world he'd want to call for help. But part of him reveled in the idea of making him get off his lazy ass to come do his job. Garrett was just about to hit the number when he was interrupted by a *thwack* to his windshield that caused him to look up. Spying the baseball-sized rock atop his hood, he turned to Asadi.

"Who threw that?" Garrett looked back at the crowd but there were no obvious culprits. "Where'd it come from?"

It was evident from his son's blank expression that he didn't know either. And it didn't really matter. The crowd was getting rowdier and their shouts more obscene. The banging on all sides of his truck turned into a subtle rocking back and forth. Garrett had just turned back to comfort his son when a rock pelted the passenger door, and another banged the passenger side, just below Asadi's window.

"*Dammit!* Enough is enough." Garrett threw the truck back in drive, laid on the horn, and was about to jam his foot on the accelerator when he saw a familiar face. To himself, he whispered, "*Stoddard?*"

The guy with blond dreadlocks, in a puffy blue coat, was the spitting image of someone he once knew well. And it seemed there was a mutual recognition in his old counterpart. Even in the special operations community, Kai Stoddard had always marched to the beat of his own drum, but Garrett never dreamed he'd be marching along with anyone in this group.

As an avid outdoorsman and rock climber, Kai had been a natural fit to lead a quick reaction force (QRF) made up of Army Rangers in Afghanistan, who'd worked with Garrett's mountain warfare unit hunting down high-value terrorist targets. Growing up in the redwoods of Humboldt County in Northern California, Kai was a little more granola than your average *batboy*. But when it came to mountaineering, he instructed the instructors.

Kai threw up his hands to the other protesters and shouted at them to halt. It took a few tries to get them subdued, but eventually the rocking stopped, the vulgarities subsided, and the mob backed away from the truck. He stepped around the hood and made his way around to the driver's-side door, pushing any stragglers who were slow to get moving.

Garrett rolled down his window, working hard to cool his temper. "Thought Rangers were supposed to be kind of stealthy." He forced a smile. "You're about as subtle as a garbage truck with cinder-block wheels."

Kai shook his head. "When I heard Kohl Ranch, you came to mind. But then I thought, there's gotta be a jillion cowboys in the state of Texas with that last name."

"A jillion and one." Garrett pointed to his busted windshield. "I'd ask for reimbursement, but it looks like the villagers spent all their money on pitchforks and torches."

Kai surveyed the crowd, then turned back to Garrett. "They're just passionate about what they want to protect."

"Know the feeling." Garrett tilted his head at Asadi. "We gonna have a problem?"

His follow-up gesture of patting his shirt around the belt buckle wouldn't be lost on Kai. He'd know there was a pistol under his clothing. And more importantly, he wouldn't hesitate to use it if he thought his son's life was in jeopardy.

Kai looked over at Asadi. "Didn't see him there."

Garrett wasn't smiling anymore. "Yeah, well, now you do."

Kai turned around slowly and batted a hand at the mob. "Everybody back away! Give him some room!"

The crowd grumbled but moved away from the truck, looking disappointed that their fun had been spoiled. Most of them mulled off, but a few stood guard, keeping their focus on Kai.

"Looks like you've got some well-disciplined soldiers." Garrett added, "Sort of."

Kai ignored the barb. "Bet you're wondering how I ended up here?"

"Hell, I didn't know if you were still alive. Lost touch after Panjshir Valley."

Kai looked off into the distance. "After all that, I decided to get lost for a while."

Garrett was the only survivor of a mountain warfare unit made up of indigenous forces and Americans operators who were pinned down for thirty-six hours in the Hindu Kush. There were a lot of excuses as to what went wrong: bad communication, horrible weather, and dithering top brass. But the bottom line was that Kai's team dropped the ball and got there too late.

After a survey of the protesters, Garrett could see that these men and women weren't your twentysomething-year-old deadbeats, looking to smoke weed and avoid getting a job. They were a hardened bunch, out braving the cold and his grille guard for their cause. He lowered his voice to make sure the protesters couldn't hear him.

"Listen, Kai, I don't know exactly what you're up to, but I'm worried that there might be some folks who'll get the wrong impression about why you're here."

"Oh yeah?" Kai smirked. "Who might be getting this *wrong* impression?"

"Well, me for one. Guess we can start there."

Kai got serious. "And what impression might that be?"

"That this isn't just some friendly freedom of expression going on. There's something more."

"Garrett, there's nothing friendly about this. We're here for one reason and one reason only. And that's to shut down the Trans-Palisade pipeline."

"I wouldn't expect you to know this, but pipelines are running all across the whole damn ranch. In fact, we're probably sitting on top of one right now." Garrett shifted a little in his seat. "I'm not one to tell a man his business, but if you're here to stop oil companies from moving hydrocarbons beneath the ground then you're about a century too late."

Kai leaned a little closer and lowered his voice also. "This connector you got to the Permian will affect global energy policy for the next fifty years. We're talking next level here." He crossed his arms. "We're not leaving until this project is dead."

Garrett found it odd that Kai was learning the news about the pipeline deal at nearly the same time as him. The fact that this group of protesters had made it up to the compressor station so fast was also fishy. Vicky's theory about ecoterrorism had seemed a bit far-fetched until now.

"Well, Kai, it looks like this won't be our last meeting then. A lot of people with money and influence want this to happen. Your fight is a helluva lot bigger than me."

"Like it or not, this is ground zero. First skirmish. This won't be the last you see of us."

His words were said in a way that sounded a whole lot like a declaration of war. Garrett didn't want to believe that anyone he'd served in combat with would later become an enemy, but if there was anyone capable of sabotage, it was the man standing before him. As a platoon master breacher in the Rangers, Kai knew explosives. And now he had clear motivation to use them.

If Kai wanted to fight the good fight, then he'd get one. But before levying any threats of his own, Garrett just offered up a salute in jest, mashed the accelerator, and drove off the battlefield. He had a feeling that it wouldn't be long before he and his old friend faced off again.

8

There were so many things going on at the kitchen table during dinner that Garrett didn't know which to focus on first. The fact that a violent mob of protesters had nearly torn them apart was somehow trumped by the sudden appearance of his long-lost sister, who would apparently be staying with them for the next couple of nights.

For the most part, Butch had been on good behavior. However, he did make a mumbling comment about how the ranch wasn't a *home for strays*. Grace pretended not to notice, marching into his house and stowing her Louis Vuitton luggage in her old bedroom like she'd never left.

Dinner around the kitchen table had been forced. The silences were mostly filled with Garrett getting Grace up to speed on what he'd been doing the last few years. Since his dad, brother, and Asadi already knew, he admitted to her that he had spent the last few years as an undercover narcotics agent, but left out his more recent exploits as a black bag operator for the CIA.

After dinner was over, everyone moved into the living room, just as they had back in the old days. The television was tuned to the Weather Channel, but no one was really watching. The awkward lull in conversation was filled by a documentary on the world's most destructive hurricanes. Butch had been mostly silent. At least until now. He eased back into his La-Z-Boy recliner looking a little unhinged.

"So . . . after all these years, Grace, you finally came back?"

Garrett jumped in quick to head off a fight. "Daddy, not now. Let's at least get a night of sleep. Between everything that happened with the explosion at the Mescalero Compressor Station and dealing with that mob today, I know I could sure use a good one."

In true Kohl fashion, Grace sat erect, looking eager to tangle. "You don't have to defend me, Garrett. If he's got something to say, he can say it."

"Better believe I can." Butch turned red. "This is my house. I'll damn well say what I want."

"Some things never change. *Your* house. Say what *you* want." Grace looked to Garrett. "Ever wonder why I left this place and didn't come back?"

In fact, Garrett had wondered exactly that for years. He'd only been a boy when their mother was killed in a car accident and Grace left for college. Squirming a little, he shifted position, buying a little time to search for the right words to bring the temperature down a notch or two. But there were a few burning questions that needed to be addressed.

"I'm glad you're back, Grace. Really, I am. But I know what Daddy is getting at."

Grace looked incensed. "Oh, you too then, huh?"

"Well, the timing of it all raises some suspicions." Garrett looked between his father, who was seething, and Grace, who was little better. "You can understand that, right?"

Grace recoiled. "You think I'm just here about the pipeline deal?"

"Damn straight," Butch interjected. "There's an opportunity for you and your husband to make a fortune and you don't want to miss out." He added with clear disdain, "That *banker* wouldn't pass up a chance to grab at a nickel if it was floating in outer space."

Grace turned to Garrett. "So, that's what you think too?"

Garrett hated confrontation of any kind, especially when it had to do with matters of *feelings*. He was equally standoffish in conversations about money. Now he was wrapped up in both.

"Don't know what to make of that outer space comment." Garrett cut eyes at his dad. "Not even sure what that means." He softened his voice as he turned back to her. "But I do see his point. You've been MIA for a real long time. I think you owe us an explanation."

"Garrett, I've built a life for myself down there. You can't blame me for moving on."

"We don't blame you for that." Garrett lowered his gaze and stared down at the floor, struggling again for the right words. "But I mean, after Mama died, you just left. Abandoned us. We were hurt by that."

"I didn't abandon *you*. I went off to college. It's what kids do when they graduate from high school. And I'm not going to apologize for my success. Making something of myself. I worked damn hard to get where I am in my career."

Garrett looked up. "I'm not asking you to say you're sorry. Especially not for your success. I just—" He cleared his throat, feeling a bit of emotion welling up. "It just felt like you wanted nothing to do with what was left of our family. Like we weren't even worth your time."

She stared daggers at him. "Is that what you think?"

"It's not what I think," Garrett answered. "It's what I saw with my own two eyes. I kept waiting for you to come home, but you never did. I missed you, sister. I needed you. We all did."

It looked as if Grace might argue, and then her bitter defiance seemed to wash away. "Trust me, it wasn't that I didn't miss you. I did." She looked over at Butch. "All of you. With everything in me. With all my heart."

Butch's temper seemed to have cooled. "Then what was it?"

Although kind and generous as they come, Butch was as rough around the edges as the business end of a handsaw. Despite all his talk of not caring about Grace and whether or not she came or went, the old man had clearly missed her.

When she didn't answer, Butch followed up. "Why didn't you come home to us, Grace?"

She shook off the question. "Garrett's right. We all just need a good night's sleep."

Butch got red, his body tensed, and he gripped the armrests of his La-Z-Boy like a vise. But then something happened. He closed his eyes, let out a breath, and unclenched, as if he'd mentally, physically, and spiritually let go. It was the look of a man who'd once lost everything.

Butch opened his eyes and smiled. "No, let's settle it now. Too much time has passed already." His gravelly voice turned to molasses. "Let's talk all night if we have to. I can't lose you again."

Grace took a breath and replied softly, "Just because I look like her doesn't mean I am her."

Garrett leaned forward, unsure if he'd heard her correctly. "What are you talking about? Look like who?"

Grace locked on to a photo of her mother on the end table. "Everybody always said it. Especially after the funeral. You look *just* like her." She shook her head. "But me and Mama were nothing alike. You all know that."

"What does your looks have to do with anything?" Butch asked.

It was in that moment that Garrett's perspective of her changed. After his mother died, he'd lived for years battling the same ghosts. Having survived the car crash that killed her left an awful scar, a guilt that although he knew now was baseless seemed no less real in the wake of the tragedy. He'd always felt that it should've been he who died, instead of the beloved Mena Kohl.

When Grace didn't answer, Garrett spoke for her. "No, I get it now. Mama was the hero nurse. A living saint. Adored by everyone who met her. Those were impossible shoes to fill. Not only for you. Impossible for anyone. It was too much pressure."

Butch stared back at him with a look of disbelief. "Nobody would've expected that. You were just a young girl. Still grieving your own self."

Garrett intervened before she could answer. "Yeah, we would've, Daddy. We'd have wanted someone to fill that void and it would've fallen to the daughter. You, me, and Bridger were equipped to run a ranch. But Mama was the one who made this place a home. Grace wasn't ready for that responsibility back then."

Butch gave an understanding nod and turned to Grace. "I understand that you might've had those feelings at first. Right after everything happened. But after all these years?" He paused a second, looking a bit confused. "What took you so long to come back?"

"I was embarrassed. *Okay?* And the more time that passed, the harder it was to return."

"But you did," Butch countered. "And it all has to do with this pipeline." He raised a hand when it looked like Grace was about to argue. "Hold on now, I'm not accusing you of anything. But you can see how we might be leery about your motives."

"I get it," Grace admitted. "But can't you see that it finally gave me an excuse. A valid reason to come back here. Without it, I'd have had to—"

"Admit you were wrong," Garrett filled in.

"I'd have to come crawling back with my tail between my legs. This was a way to come back with my head held high. With something to offer."

"Stubborn pride is a damn terrible trait," Garrett replied, "but you come by it honestly. Kohl DNA just is what it is. Not a damn one of us is quick to back down. I've done my own self-flagellating before making that long trip home. So, you'll get no judgment from me."

Tears welled up in her eyes. "I'd like to get to know you again. Make up for lost time."

Garrett looked to Butch, who just stared at the television. There was a scene of a massive cleanup taking place after the devastating aftermath of a storm. Something about the image seemed fitting. He gave her a quick glance before returning his focus to the screen.

"This is your home, Grace. No matter what, you're always welcome."

There probably should've been a group hug or some celebratory toast to acknowledge the truce. But in true Kohl family fashion the whole incident that had involved a lifetime of pain and sorrow pretty much just came and went. The past seemingly in the rear-view, Grace turned her attention on Asadi. She wiped away a tear and offered up a kind smile.

"So, tell me, young man. How's life out here on the ranch?"

Asadi looked relieved that the standoff was over and seemed to welcome the change of subject. "Life here is great. I ride horses almost every day."

Grace looked to Garrett. "Sounds like someone else I know when he was your age."

Butch perked up. "This boy is as good a horseman as I've ever seen."

Garrett had learned over the years not to be offended by a compliment that clearly knocked him out of the running. His dad thought Asadi was the second coming of Roy Rogers.

Grace's eyebrows rose. "Now that's an endorsement. Did you ride back home?"

Asadi shook his head. "Learned here."

"Do they even have horses over there?" She looked to Butch and furrowed her brow. "I'm thinking Afghanistan is more of a camel country, but social studies was never really my thing."

"They've got horses," Butch interjected. "Good ones too. But none as good as the ones here on the ranch." He shot Asadi a wink. "Ain't that right, sonny?"

"That's right." Asadi beamed with obvious pride. "No quarter horses over there."

Garrett chuckled to himself. Asadi had become as fiercely proud as Butch of the breed and particularly their remuda, which the boy had worked hard to train since he moved to the ranch.

Grace smiled and looked over at Butch. "I see another thing hasn't changed."

Butch wore a curious expression. "Yeah, what's that?"

"You're still brainwashing everyone on the merits of those big-butt cow horses."

Butch batted off the comment. "Don't tell me you're still push-ing Thoroughbreds."

"You mean the breed of kings?" Grace jokingly put her nose in the air. "Better believe I am."

Garrett could tell that the conversation was winding up into a spirited debate on equine superiority, a conversation that if left unchecked could lead to another multi-decade family dispute. But the discussion was interrupted by a call on their landline.

Garrett picked up the cordless from the end table and answered a call from Ray Smitty, whose number registered on the caller ID. "What do you mean *another* explosion?"

Grace was the first to ask. "Out at the Mescalero?"

Garrett cupped his hand over the receiver. "No, this one happened on our place. Pipeline blew out in the west pasture."

Butch moved from his chair. "Anyone hurt?"

"Thank God, no," Garrett answered. "It was off the road a ways."

"Anyone know what caused it?" Butch pressed.

"Not yet." Garrett could feel his blood boil. "But I know the first person I'm gonna ask."

9

Kunduz Province, Afghanistan

Kim Manning couldn't help but think that the only thing worse than driving through Taliban country was staring into the menacing gaze of Asadi's older brother, Faraz Saleem. He looked so much like Asadi but showed none of the same sweetness and charm. However, Kim also knew that looks could be deceiving. As a petite blonde, who'd made her bones working counterterrorism in the CIA, she didn't exactly fit the image of a seasoned warfighter.

It was a quality that she had used to her advantage. And it worked particularly in a place run by religious zealots who viewed women as unintelligent and weak. Being underestimated had typically played in her favor, but it was a dangerous game. In Afghanistan, offenses as minor as wearing the wrong garment could result in imprisonment or even death.

For that reason, in addition to her flowing black robe, on the streets Kim wore a *niqab*, which covered her hair completely and left only a narrow slit to see. Inside the vehicle, she'd shed the head covering but shrugged low in the seat so as not to be noticed by passersby.

The Taliban's promise of safe passage from the Iranian border to Pakistan meant little in a place where no one accepted rules beyond Islamic sharia law, which meant her life was at the mercy of the highest bidder, a fact that wasn't lost only on her. It was all too clear to the other man she'd rescued, a former CIA asset turned true-blue American named Reza Bayat.

Unlike Faraz, a criminal, Bayat had been taken hostage and used as leverage over his son, Liam, whom the Iranians had blackmailed for access to a U.S. nuclear weapons facility. With Garrett's help, their plan to steal five nuclear warheads was thwarted. In exchange for one of the high-level Quds Force operatives he took prisoner, Kim brokered a spy swap that included Faraz.

Given the fractured relations between the United States, Iran, and Afghanistan, the deal was brokered through a third party, a powerful Waziri tribal leader named Omar Zadran. But the terms of the agreement extended no further than the exchange. Once it was made, all bets were off. Kim and the others were fair game for anyone who was willing and able to take them down.

Kim, Faraz, and Bayat rode in the back of a maroon Toyota Corolla, virtually in complete silence. Bayat was in poor health, weak due to torture and malnourishment from his monthslong incarceration at the notorious Evin prison in Tehran. Although beyond grateful for rescue, there was little this shell-shocked grandfather could do but fight off sleep, which always turned fitful.

Conversely, Faraz, in his early twenties, was fit as an ox and keenly alert. His head was always on a swivel in search of lurking danger, a skill that had probably kept him alive in a land where life meant little. It wasn't lost on Kim that the narrow streets and crowded sidewalks hemmed them in. It would be a perfect place for an ambush as there was little room to escape.

All attempts at conversation with Faraz had been a bust, but Kim gave it another try. "You look almost just like your brother." She smiled, hoping to generate a little softness in return. "Except for the five o'clock shadow, of course."

Unlike most men in Afghanistan, who wore traditional garb, Faraz looked every bit the part of someone in the international drug game. Beyond the slicked-back hair and stubble, his outfit was almost comically cliché. He wore linen slacks and a black and gold satin shirt, no doubt a Versace or Gucci knockoff he'd picked up in a place like Istanbul or Algiers.

Faraz kept his eyes trained out the windows. "I don't have a brother," he refuted calmly. "Everyone in my family is dead."

Kim was impressed with Faraz's English. He had first learned it working as a contractor on a NATO military base. The rest he'd probably picked up in the drug trade. But she was amazed how Americanized he'd become, having never been to the States. He even had the Western inflection and used pop culture lingo. Of course, after two decades in Afghanistan, many of the locals, particularly those who had fought alongside U.S. soldiers, had picked up many of their traits. Wearing baseball caps, blue jeans, and dipping snuff, they were nearly indistinguishable from Kim's own American CIA paramilitary officers.

"Your brother is alive," Kim kindly corrected. "He escaped with the help of an American who was at the village during the massacre. I wouldn't lie about something like that."

"An American?" Still looking out the window, Faraz scoffed. "Was he CIA as well?"

Kim had never mentioned anything about the Agency, but it wasn't that hard to figure out. Who else but the CIA would be brokering a deal with Iranian Quds Force?

Ignoring the question about Asadi's rescuer, Garrett Kohl, she pressed on with her case. "Your brother desperately wants to see you. Wanted that for years. I want to take you to him."

Faraz whipped around, looking a bit frantic. "To the United States?"

Kim wasn't sure why that had gotten such an animated response, but she decided to play on it. "We'll fly out from Islamabad, make a couple of stops. But ultimately, we'll end up in Texas."

"So, I'm being extradited?" His nervousness morphed into outrage. "Is that it?"

And there it was. Extradition was a word drug traffickers feared most. Unlike other places in the world, there'd be no bargaining, no bribery, nor escape. In America, when you went away, you went away for good. No doubt, he thought he was being set up for prison. His Iranian drug kingpin boss, Naji Zindashti, had likely taught him to avoid American capture at all costs.

Kim quickly shot down the notion. "No, it's completely the opposite. You're being given an opportunity for freedom. A life where you can do whatever you want."

"Not interested." Another sneer came from Faraz. "Already have that here."

His reluctance didn't surprise Kim at all. Orphans who grew up in organized crime knew that nothing ever came easy or for free. And if it sounded too good to be true, then it probably was. The problem was that she had to convince him to go along. He wasn't her prisoner. If he wanted to stay in Afghanistan, he could stay. But coming back to Asadi empty-handed was unthinkable.

"Faraz, I know you don't trust me yet. And I don't expect you to fully believe me anytime soon. But at least think of your brother. Consider this opportunity for him, if not for yourself."

It was clear by the look on his face that Faraz wasn't buying a word of her offer. In his world, fanciful stories that tugged on the heartstrings were a way to get someone to let down their guard or lure them into a place of vulnerability. He'd probably used that very technique himself.

Kim continued. "What if you talked to him?" She fished out a satellite phone from her backpack. "Would that change your mind?"

Her plan was to put them in contact only after they'd safely crossed into Pakistan and were back on Omar Zadran's home turf. But Kim could tell that Faraz was looking to escape. In a bustling city like Kunduz, he could bolt into the crowd and never be seen or heard from again.

Faraz dropped the tough-guy façade as he stared at the phone. It was clear he'd never wanted anything more in his entire life. "I can talk to Asadi?"

Kim gave a single nod. "It'd probably be around dinnertime over there. Maybe we could catch him at the house."

Faraz paused a moment, still staring at the phone, and shook away the offer. As he repositioned himself in his seat and again stared out the window, Kim couldn't help but notice he'd glanced down at the door handle. At any moment, he could make a break for it and there'd be nothing she could do. With that terrible outcome in mind, she made another desperate appeal.

"Please, Faraz, talk to him once. And if you have no interest in coming with me to America, I'll let you out. Wherever you want." Kim opened the bag again and fished out a fistful of Afghanis, about a thousand U.S. dollars by rough estimate. "I'll even give you some traveling money. No questions asked."

Faraz turned back and eyed the wad of cash. He was hungry for it. "For a stupid phone call?" He looked up and eyed her as if she were a total fool. "Hand it over then."

Kim didn't know if he meant the money or the phone, but she opted for the latter. It was a hell of gamble for so many reasons, but it was one she had to take. After pulling up the contact info for the Kohl house, Kim pressed the number and keyed the speaker function. With the number ringing, she held her breath.

Part of her was desperate for Asadi to answer, and the other had no idea what to say if he did.

After the seventh ring, Kim was about to give up when she heard that unmistakable voice. It had only been a single word *hello*, but Faraz instinctively knew it too. His body lost all its rigidity and he seemed to melt back into his seat.

There was no need to coax or prod him. His expression said it all.

As tears welled in Faraz's eyes and ran down both cheeks, his voice cracked as he whispered, "Badih, is that you?" His hand shook and he nearly lost his grip of the phone. "That really you?"

Kim had never heard Asadi mention the word *Badih*. Must've been a nickname that by happy coincidence sounded a lot like *buddy*. There was a pause on the other end of the line and then she heard it click, the recognition of a missing piece of Asadi's soul.

Asadi said his brother's name like a child, grasping for a lifeline in the dark. *"Faraz?"*

The young man beside her smiled wide, looking as if he could burst with joy. "It's me, Badih! It's me! It's your brother!"

Asadi cleared his throat and stammered a little, clearly resisting the urge to cry. "Is that—is that really you?"

"Of course, it's me! Who else?"

"I—I don't know." There was a pause on Asadi's end before he stammered out the rest. "Is this real?"

Kim wrestled back her own tears, but this reunion was almost too much to bear. She was about to take the phone off of speaker to allow them some privacy when their car came to a sudden halt in the middle of the road. Expecting yet another mundane impediment like a stalled rickshaw or an overturned fruit cart, she looked ahead to find their lead vehicle was blocked by a black Toyota Hilux with a Dushka machine gun mounted in the back.

Kim ordered Faraz to duck, just as two men rose up from behind the bed, crewed the heavy-caliber weapon, and turned it on the convoy. As he opened fire on the Nissan passenger van carrying Zadran, her driver threw their car in reverse and mashed the accelerator. But before they'd made it more than a few feet, the gunners set their sights on the Corolla and let loose with a flurry of rounds that punctured the windshield and ripped through the interior.

As tempered glass from the rear window shattered and rained down atop them, Kim threw her body over Faraz, who was beside her on the floorboard. With their driver most likely dead, they could either flee the vehicle or try to get it going. The only option that wasn't viable in any way, shape, or form was staying in the kill zone. They had to move. And they had to move fast.

10

Smitty blew into his hands to warm them and watched as Sheriff Ted Crowley barked orders at the fire chief while they stood before the pipeline inferno on the Kohl Ranch. It was a wild scene for sure—as if God had sliced open the earth and let the shrieking fires of Hell spew forth into the night. Smitty turned to his partner beside him, who was clearly in an awful mood.

Not only was Bo agitated about having to wait around in the cold, but he also resented the fact that his plan to rough up the protesters was thwarted. Proof or not, he'd made up his mind that the "enviro whack jobs" were responsible and punishment should be dealt.

Smitty had to admit that it was a strange coincidence, but accidents *did* happen. They just usually didn't happen in such close succession. But he also knew that they couldn't start levying accusations without any evidence. As an oil scout for Mescalero, it was Smitty's job to sniff out any threats. And it appeared that they might just have a big one with Cosmic Order.

It wasn't just the explosion that had Smitty worried. It was the fact that their spokesman, Kai Stoddard, had used words like *enemy* and *war*. Vicky was going to want some answers. And at the moment, there weren't any. Given enough time, she'd draw her own dangerous conclusions.

Bo turned to Smitty with a look of disgust. "Told you we should've taken care of them hippies earlier, the way I wanted to handle it. Put an end to all this."

"You don't know it was them," Smitty shot back.

Bo turned toward the fire. "And *you* don't know it wasn't."

"No. I don't," Smitty admitted. "But we got to be smart about this."

"Smart don't work these sorts." Bo's eyes reflected the flames. "Gotta put the fear of God into them. Make it hurt."

Smitty could see that Bo was getting all worked up again, which meant he needed to talk him down. And that could usually be done with a little talk of the scriptures. The old drug runner had found religion in prison and altered his ways, to a small degree. But men like Bo could change only so much. He was the sort to sin first and repent if he felt like it. Which he usually didn't.

Smitty figured if he couldn't calm Bo, then maybe he could distract him. "These folks are just trying to do what God said to do, aren't they? Take care of the earth and all that crap."

Bo proceeded to instruct Smitty on the scriptures, with no less authority than a Harvard Divinity School graduate. "Bible says be a good steward. Means use our resources wisely."

"Well, maybe they think we're *not* using them wisely. Ever think about that?"

Bo scoffed. "If these nutjobs had their way, we'd all go back to riding dinosaurs instead, filling up our tanks with them. You can't preach sense into hippies. Brains too fried on dope."

Smitty didn't know whether to start with the historical or scientific fallacies on oil and gas that Bo had apparently derived from watching *The Flintstones*. "All I'm just saying is that it wouldn't hurt to sit down and have a beer with them folks. Hear them out. That's all."

"I wouldn't sit down with them Birkenstock-wearing beatniks if you put a gun to my head."

"Jesus wore sandals," Smitty reminded him. "Bet you'd knock back a Pearl with him."

"First of all, Jesus didn't drink beer. Drunk wine. And he wasn't guzzling down no damn pruno like some jailhouse junkie. He drank the good stuff. Like that kind you get down at the *fart and fetch it* with a kangaroo on the bottle."

Smitty had never tried *pruno*, a prison liquor that inmates made in their toilets. And it wasn't just the *King of Kings* who'd take a pass on the stuff. His plan was to keep Bo distracted by further pontificating about what you'd find in Jesus's liquor cabinet when Sheriff Crowley broke away from the fire chief and marched over.

Crowley looked directly at Bo. "Suppose you know who's behind this, right?"

A single nod came back in return. "Want me to take care of it?"

"Not just yet." Crowley wagged a finger. "Think I got a way to hide our hand."

Uh-oh. Smitty knew exactly what that meant. Since Vicky had teamed up with Garrett Kohl's Savage Exploration Company to secure oil and gas dominance in the Texas Panhandle, the sheriff, a silent partner in her company, had been doing what he did best— monetizing the law. Crowley hadn't broken any statutes, but he'd certainly abused his authority to feather his nest.

Any outfit that wasn't Mescalero or Savage seemed to have a tough time *following the rules* in Hemphill County. Crowley used the sheriff's office resources to ensure the competition was monitored, pretty much around the clock. Somehow, somewhere, at any given time, Vicky Kaiser's competition was getting ticketed or jail time. In some cases, it was both.

It had become bad enough that some drillers and energy services enterprises had signed over their leases to Vicky, or just hauled off their equipment and boarded up the doors. Smitty had kept Garrett in the dark about all Crowley's shenanigans, since they fell on the shady side.

Smitty suspected that he had better keep tabs on what the sheriff was cooking up next. "What you got in mind, Ted?"

"Well, Cosmic Order has permission to set up camp where they are. Can't do nothing about that. But if there's one thing I do know, it's that these types are partial to drugs."

"I was just saying that." Bo turned to Smitty. "Wasn't I just saying that very thing?"

"Might smoke a little weed. But there ain't much of a penalty in that these days."

"Nope." Crowley flashed that campaign poster smile. "But a stash of heroin has a big one."

"*Smack?*" Bo shook off the idea. "Hippies don't mess with that stuff."

"No, but they might sell it. You know, to further their cause and what have you."

Smitty had no love for the protesters, but he'd never wish prison on anyone. "Kind of steep, don't you think? Hate to ruin anyone's life over it."

The sheriff pointed to the blaze as the firefighters worked to contain it. "One man is dead, and my deputy's got a son in the hospital over what they've done."

"*Might* have done," Smitty corrected. "We still don't have any proof yet."

"No, but I'm working on that."

Unexpectedly, Bo chimed in. "Think I'm with Smitty on this one. Don't mind whipping some asses, but I know the consequences of what'll happen if they get busted with smack."

Smitty knew that Bo was talking about his son, whom he'd lost custody of when he was doing prison time. His partner might be a risk taker but in a rare show of vulnerability, Bo had confessed that losing Sam had nearly done him in. Smitty knew the same pain, having nearly lost his own family after running afoul of the law had landed him behind bars twice.

Crowley donned a look of disgust. "You two are supposed to be looking after Vicky's interests. The tip of the spear for Mescalero. More like a couple of butter knives, I'd say."

Bo was about to counter when Crowley continued. "Don't need to worry about anyone going to prison. I already got it figured out."

Smitty's curiosity got the best of him. "How you gonna make sure of that?"

"These snowflakes don't want no real prison time." Crowley seemed to soften a little. "You've seen these greasy bums. Probably haven't had a real job in years. If ever. My guess is they're bankrolled by one of them big environmental outfits that fly around in private jets."

"So, what are you getting at?" Bo asked.

"I'm getting at the bad press that will haunt anyone who gives money to a drug trafficking organization that's masquerading as some sort of do-gooder philanthropy. See how that affects donor contributions and political support. But it won't go public if everybody just packs up their signs and shanties, gets on that bus, and slinks out of town. It'll be their choice."

Smitty couldn't help but admire the sheriff. He was as devious as he was cunning. But this was a bridge too far. It was one thing to use a heavy hand, but quite another to fabricate evidence. And he wanted no part of it. The best thing he could do for the moment, though, was play along. Too much resistance would raise flags, which meant he'd be left out in the dark.

Smitty nodded in phony agreement. "Long as no one gets in trouble, I don't see a problem."

Crowley seemed content with the fake enthusiasm. "Good to hear you're on board because I'll need you to plant the dope."

Before Smitty could protest, Crowley spun on a heel and left. So much for turning a blind eye now. Like it or not, he was the lynchpin in a major hatchet job on Cosmic Order.

11

Despite the sudden dropped call, which were common in Afghanistan, Asadi was on cloud nine after talking to Faraz. He was bursting at the seams as he drove out to the Mescalero Ranch, wanting to shout it from the rooftops, but there was no one around with which to share the news. The only one who would value the report as much as Garrett and Butch was Savanah.

Despite their differences, they'd been there for each other through thick and thin. She'd been his confidant on the issue all along. And since there was no way to reach her out in the barn, Asadi decided to drive over to tell her about Faraz in person. Of course, taking Butch's old flatbed Ford pickup was liable to land him in some hot water, but Garrett had said, "Sometimes it's better to ask forgiveness than permission." And this seemed like one of those occasions.

Asadi had been strictly forbidden from driving off the ranch onto the highway since he didn't have a license, barring a life-or-death emergency. While learning about his brother was a huge deal, it didn't constitute a crisis. But with the others inspecting the pipeline disaster, he was certain he could make it to the Mescalero and back before anyone knew he was gone.

Asadi pulled up to the barn to find the John Deere Gator that Savanah used to get from the house to the barn. It was parked next to a red and black Turbo Polaris RZR. It was the same sport utility task vehicle (UTV) that Duke had used to rip and thrash over the nearby sandhills—the massive grass-covered dunes that reached two stories high in some places on the ranch.

Asadi understood the temptation because it looked like a blast. But it had scarred the land severely and it would take years to recover. Not only that, he couldn't help but wonder if Duke was behind the poaching on their land. There was no proof of it yet, but anyone with such disregard for nature might be capable of such a despicable act.

It was a theory and nothing more, but he'd definitely circle back to investigate. With more important issues at hand, Asadi shoved his anger aside, put the truck in park, and flew out the door. He was about halfway between the truck and the barn when lo and behold, Duke marched out the front door and stopped abruptly, putting his hands on his hips like Superman.

"Thought I made it clear earlier that this place was off-limits." Duke flashed his fake grin. "Like I said, don't want to see you get *hurt*."

Asadi responded with equal boldness. "Just need to see Savanah. Will only take a minute."

"Well, she's on the clock right now. Bringing horses in from the pasture before the storm. Doesn't have a minute to spare."

Duke's reasoning struck a chord with Asadi, who knew how devastating a blizzard could be, particularly when you had live-stock. High winds, subzero temperatures, and whiteout conditions were all possibilities. Butch had told him that back in the 1950s, a particularly harsh storm on the High Plains had killed eleven people and decimated around 20 percent of the cattle.

Asadi and Butch had already made sure their own herd had plenty of hay near their windbreak panels where the animals could hunker down and hide. But it'd still be a fight for survival. Forecasts were predicting wind gusts of up to fifty miles per hour. Given that harsh reality, it wasn't a great time for a friendly visit.

Asadi reluctantly conceded. "Okay, I won't stay long. Just need to tell her to call me later."

"Nope." Duke shook his head. "I'll do it."

Knowing she'd never get that message, Asadi marched right ahead toward the barn. He had nearly made it by when Duke grabbed his shirt at the buttons beneath his chin and yanked him so close that Asadi could smell the beer on his breath. To the unskilled fighter it might've been a problem, but to the trained martial artist it was manna from Heaven.

Asadi simply reached up and dug his thumb into the pressure point at the base of Duke's index finger, which caused him to yelp and immediately let go. Freed from the trap, he could've turned and fled. But adrenaline and wounded pride was a dangerous combo. In a lightning-quick motion, Asadi twisted Duke's arm behind his back and shoved him toward the wall.

It all would've been without much consequence had it not been for the slight rise in the concrete. The lip caught the toe of his Duke's boot and sent him tumbling face-first into the door frame. He wobbled a moment on weak knees and then crumpled. It looked as if he might collapse to his side, but he managed to stay upright where he sat, leaning against the wall.

Asadi dashed over to find a three-inch gash on Duke's forehead. He pulled a handkerchief from his coat pocket and handed it over.

Duke took the bandanna and just sat there in stunned silence, gingerly dabbing the wound. His glassy eyes connected with Asadi's and he spoke a bit groggily. "Does it look bad?"

Apparently the trademark Kaiser vanity superseded everything else. Rather than tell Duke the truth, Asadi opted for a change of subject. "I'll go get help."

Sprinting through the open double doors at the back of the barn, Asadi made his way across the empty corral to the planked fence on the opposite end. A quick clamber to the top and he spotted Savanah walking in beneath the glow of the moonlight. She was leading four grown horses and a couple of rambunctious colts. The little ones were turning in circles and kicking up their back hooves. Every so often Savanah rattled her feed bucket to keep their attention.

Asadi called out to her in a loud whisper, "Hey, Savanah, it's me!"

"*Asadi?*" She looked up startled. "Is that you?"

"Yeah, I need your help."

"Can this wait?" There was a clear edge to her voice, and it would've been much louder and angrier had she not been afraid of spooking the horses. "I'm kind of busy."

Asadi didn't quite know how to explain what happened. He eased up closer, careful to make no sudden movements. "Duke is hurt. Might need a doctor."

Savanah's face scrunched with her confusion. "*Hurt?* I just saw him a few minutes ago. How did he get hurt?"

Asadi cleared his throat before the confession. "Well . . . I . . . sort of pushed him."

"Great, that's all I need." She pointed to the corral. "Shut the gate behind me and help me get the horses inside. Once they're safe and sound we'll tend to Duke."

Asadi was debating when to tell Savanah about Faraz when he heard an angry mechanical roar and turned to find Duke racing up on his Polaris. And he wasn't slowing down. Asadi sprinted to the gate, ready to close it the moment the horses were inside the corral. But it was already too late. They nickered, then turned, and bolted toward the darkness of the pasture.

Asadi tried to catch them but couldn't stop the stampede. Within seconds, all he could hear was their thundering hooves, as the horses tore off into the sixty-eight thousand acres of the Mescalero Ranch— and over a hundred square miles of frozen wilderness.

12

Garrett hated to admit that his reason for driving out to confront Cosmic Order had more to do with an axe to grind than anything else. It wasn't that the group had busted up his truck and potentially blown up the pipeline; it was the fact that Kai Stoddard was involved. In truth, his old friend didn't owe him anything. But there was a bond between soldiers, particularly when they'd served together in battle. And that superseded a whole helluva lot.

As they pulled up to the protesters' encampment near what was left of the Mescalero Compressor Station, Garrett stopped the truck about fifty yards away. Their bivouac was a half a football field in length, sprawling across an open prairie flooded with moonlight. It looked like a cross between some postapocalyptic outpost from *Mad Max* and a music festival after party.

Garrett turned to Butch, who was sitting in the back seat of the GMC. "Just hang tight for a minute. I'm going to try and get a word with Kai alone."

Butch's face mirrored his outburst. "Have you gone nuts?"

Grace, who was in the passenger seat, looked equally stunned. "Seems like a bad . . . idea."

"Maybe it is," Garrett admitted. "But I've gotta have a conversation, at least. Get to the bottom of what's going on around here."

"You want to talk to them carnies?" Butch leaned forward. "After what they did earlier?"

Garrett noticed that his dad had quit calling the members of Cosmic Order protesters and was for some reason referring to them as *carnies*. Although a complete misnomer, he couldn't help but agree there was somewhat of a carnival atmosphere around the camp, especially given that their larger shelters looked like circus tents.

"I think if I can talk to Kai one-on-one, I'll get somewhere." Garrett shrugged. "Can't disagree that his bunch is a bit too enthusiastic. But he was reasonable once. Maybe he still is."

Grace pointed to his cracked windshield. "That what you call enthusiasm? 'Cause I call it vandalism. Might even call the folks who did it a few worse things if I'm not being ladylike."

"Not happy about it either," Garrett replied. "But we've had two explosions in one day. And I don't want to make it a third." He chinned toward the encampment. "Hoping I can get some answers. Find out what the hell is happening around here."

"Then let us go with you," Butch suggested. "They'll be less likely to stir up any trouble."

Garrett could only imagine how *that* would go down. With the ghost of John Wayne and a *Real Housewife of the Permian Basin* along for the meeting, détente would break down before it even got started. First sign of granola, lava lamps, or a naked Matthew McConaughey banging on bongos and Butch would start blasting away with insults like the cannons at Verdun.

"Daddy, I've got my pistol. Anything gets ugly I'll shoot in the air." Garrett looked to Grace. "Sit up here in the driver's seat. You get the signal, come a flying in there to get me."

Grace looked to Butch, as if seeking permission. It was a funny sight to see this grown woman waiting for her father's approval. But some things never changed. A nod of confirmation from their dad and his sister moved forward to crawl over the console.

Garrett opened the door, stepped outside, winced at the frigid bite of a cold north wind. He turned back and wagged a finger. "Now y'all don't be cranking up the Jerry Garcia while I'm gone. Need you two all ears and on alert. Got it?"

Both Grace and Butch's faces resonated with the same look of confusion. The joke about the Grateful Dead's fabled frontman was completely lost on the two of them. Rather than explain, Garrett decided he'd let them figure it out. The riddle would hopefully keep them occupied, and preferably out of any trouble, while he was gone.

GARRETT WALKED UP BOLDLY, EVEN making an extra effort to clomp his boots as he trekked across the powdery snow. Showing no fear was a no-brainer in any kind of negotiation situation, but he especially didn't want to spook anyone, suspecting him of a sneak attack. By the look and sound of their sprawling encampment that would've taken up a city block, there was a party going on.

There were bonfires, loud music, and a dull rumble of voices peppered with an occasional burst of laughter. Apparently, this was how radicals unwind when they weren't making trouble for him. Within fifteen yards of the perimeter a sentry appeared from the darkness.

"Stop right there." The guard moved closer. "What do you want?"

Garrett couldn't nail down the sentinel's accent, but it sounded Scandinavian. The way the moon was shining, it kept a shadow over his face. It was obvious that he wasn't a little guy.

"Want to talk to Kai." Garrett kept marching forward, despite the order to halt. "Tell him to get out here. Right now."

"He's turned in for the night," the guard shot back. "He'll see you tomorrow."

When Garrett finally saw the watchman's face, it didn't disappoint. If there was ever someone that God put on the earth to scare away trespassers, this was him. With his heavy rust-colored beard, bushy hair, and leathery skin, he looked like a Wildling from *Game of Thrones*.

Garrett stopped and shook his head. "Tomorrow might be too late."

The Wildling looked curious. "Too late for what?"

"I don't know." Garrett shrugged. "Seems like a lot of things going boom lately. Hang around long enough and this place might be next."

The Wildling took a couple of steps forward. "That a threat?"

"Nope. Just a very unfortunate reality since you all showed up."

The Wildling bristled and was about to move when a voice sounded from behind him.

"All right, that's enough." Kai walked up and waved off the guard. "I've got it from here."

The Wildling looked as if he wanted to argue but knew better. Without a word, he went back to his post in the shadows. He was hidden but watching.

Kai stepped up and looked Garrett in the eye. "Surprised to see you here."

"Shouldn't be," Garrett shot back. "Unlike you people, I live here."

Given his expression, the comment seemed to catch Kai off guard. "What can I do for you?"

"Guess that depends on what you can tell me about that explosion on my ranch."

Kai looked as if he were making an extra effort to play coy. "Don't know anything about that."

"Well, that's what I'd hope. Especially seeing as how we were friends once."

"*Friends?*" Kai scoffed. "We both got a paycheck from the American taxpayer, but that's where it all ends."

The remark hit Garrett the wrong way. It wasn't only that they'd both worn the uniform. It was that he had always felt like they'd shared a special bond because of their ancestry. His Comanche roots meant a lot to him, and he'd shared that connection with Kai, whose mother's family had grown up on the Yurok Reservation near California's North Coast.

Garrett gave a nod. "I've always considered anyone I shed blood with to be more than a casual acquaintance. But that's my system of beliefs. Won't hold you to that."

"If I shed any blood now, it'll be for a worthy cause."

Garrett's philosophy on military service had always been based on a biblical verse. *There is no greater love than to lay down one's life for one's friends.* Sacrificing yourself for the sake of another was a tall order, even for the most gung ho. But he lived by it faithfully.

Garrett could feel the heat rising on his neck. "This kind of talk makes it hard to believe your presence and these explosions are a coincidence. Hope you'll convince me I'm wrong."

"Maybe it's *you* who needs to do the convincing, Garrett."

"What's that supposed to mean?"

"Means that energy companies run by people like you and Vicky Kaiser are the problem. Not us. You're a hell of a lot more dangerous than we are."

"Kai, people need fuel, and we supply it. Got a problem with the rules in this country then take it up with the legislators. They make the laws. We're just following them. Simple as that."

Kai looked to grow more agitated as he gathered his thoughts. "That the way you see it?"

"That's the way it is." Before Kai could rebut, Garrett continued. "You think I want all this crap out on my place? Drilling rigs everywhere you turn. Tank batteries. Frac pits. Semitrucks running up and down the road all damn day and night. Think again."

"You let it happen."

"Nope. That's where you couldn't be more wrong. The oil deal on our property was signed and put into effect three decades before I was even born. I do what I have to do to keep the ranch going. Keep our heads above water. If it were up to me, I'd dial back the clock to when the bison roamed this country by the millions. But that's a dream. Not a reality."

"Excuses," Kai rejoined with venom. "This is all about money. Justification for greed."

The cold, hard truth for Garrett was that it *was* about money. Without the oil and gas deal they were bankrupt, foreclosed on, and the ranch was completely sunk. It hurt bad enough without being reminded of the fact he'd not saved the place without making a compromise. And the biggest one of all was having to forge an alliance with the Kaisers—their family nemesis.

It stung to have had to partner up with Mescalero Energy, which he'd held responsible for his mother's death. After failing to claim responsibility for one of their oil trucks that ran her off the road, the company's lawyers skirted liability by saying it was her fault. Although it had been different leadership back then, his current partnership was a painful reminder of a horrific past.

"Yeah, I've compromised," Garrett admitted. "But I did what I had to do out of necessity to keep our way of life. To leave something behind for my son. The ranch is our legacy."

Kai snickered. "So, you rolled over and gave up for your ego and an inheritance."

Garrett fought to censor himself, but questioning his motives for leaving the land behind for Asadi was way over the line. And it spewed forth in the ugliest way.

"Tell me, Kai. Is that any worse than leaving your brothers up on a mountain to die?"

The insult came out so quickly and easily that he couldn't believe he'd said it. And the words weren't taken lightly by Kai, who ducked his head and came in a rush. Garrett failed to move in time and took the full brunt of the assault. His head slammed to the ground, and he tried to rise, but it was much too late. Kai had already climbed on top of him and let loose with a right hook.

The fist landed solid enough to make Garrett woozy, but not so lightheaded that he didn't take notice of the other Wildlings, who were sprinting up from the camp. A burst of adrenaline and Garrett shoved Kai off of him, buying just enough time to reach for his gun. But he was about a half second behind, which allowed one of the attackers to rip it from his hand.

Garrett struggled to a knee, but a swift boot to the head sent him back to the ground. One hit followed another, until the flurry of fists crescendoed into a lights-out final blow.

13

Kim rose with a lull in the automatic weapons fire and slithered over the center console into the front seat. She kept her head below the dashboard, reached across the dead driver, grasped the handle, and pushed the door open. After shoving the body out onto the road, she maneuvered behind the steering wheel and jammed her foot on the gas. The engine revved and the tires spun, blasting up a spray of pebbles that *thunked* and *tinged* in the wheel wells beneath the car.

The smell of burnt rubber filled the cab as they rocketed backward and smashed the fender of a green Suzuki pickup about twenty yards to their rear. Kim had just shifted into drive when a round punctured the center of the windshield and then two more bullets followed in quick succession. She jammed her foot on the gas, cut the wheel left, and fishtailed onto the sidewalk.

Plowing into a *Kabuli Pulao* stand that slung mutton, rice, and vegetables across their hood, Kim redlined the speedometer, dodging motorized rickshaws and commercial flatbed trucks, careening down a one-way street in the wrong direction. Some distance between her and the machine gun allowed Kim to rest easier, but they weren't out of danger just yet.

The powerful tribal leader, Omar Zadran, was the whole reason they were given *so-called* safe passage across the country in the first place. Without him as a chaperone, she was at the mercy of the

Taliban. And Afghanistan was still home to ISIS and Al Qaeda, who may have been tipped off that CIA was in town and didn't want to miss an opportunity for revenge.

It was tempting for Kim to let her mind wander on all possibilities, and as an intelligence officer, it was part of the job. But none of that mattered at the moment. The only thing she really needed to concentrate on was what to do next. With Zadran likely dead, the deal with the Taliban was over. Which meant she, Faraz, and Bayat were now on their own.

At that thought, Kim glanced back to see if Bayat was awake. Between the gunfire and stunt driving, he'd finally regained consciousness. Faraz unscrewed a bottle of water, raised it to Bayat's lips, and held it there for him to drink. Other than the earlier phone call with his brother, it was the only sign Faraz had shown of tenderness, which was one of Asadi's hallmark traits.

Kim had just turned back around to find yet another impediment, not unlike the first. A second Toyota Hilux, this one silver, careened down the street right toward them until skidding to a halt and lining up parallel to block their egress. Two gunmen wielding AK-47s rose up from behind the sides of the truck bed and opened fire.

Certain that more bad guys were chasing from the rear, Kim dared not turn around, lest she end up sandwiched between the enemy trucks. Spying an alley, she jerked the steering wheel left and veered across the street toward the opening. With 7.62 rounds raking across the passenger side, she punched the gas a little too hard and the vehicle skidded out of control.

Kim mashed her foot on the brake, but it was already too late. They slammed into a wall inside the narrow passageway. With their car too wide to continue, she put the car in park and looked to Faraz, who leaned forward and grabbed the M4 rifle from the front seat. After jacking in a round, he threw the back door open, jumped out, and let loose with a full auto burst. Before the two approaching gunmen had even gotten off a single round, Faraz dropped them both. This wasn't a *grip and rip* kind of job. He had picked his targets and made them count.

Fully aware that enemy reinforcements were on their way, Kim leapt out the driver's-side door, moved around to the back, and pulled Bayat out of the car. She put her arm around his waist and took on most of his weight. Faraz moved around the trunk of the Corolla with his M4 at the low-ready. He didn't stop to talk, just continued on past them farther into the alley. He was about thirty yards ahead and pulling away from them, gaining more ground with each step.

Kim took the risk of revealing their position and called out to him. "Faraz, wait!" She shot a quick glance back at the Corolla, desperate for her satellite phone, which was probably on the floorboard beneath the seat. "Faraz, please! I can't move him that fast on my own!"

Faraz either hadn't heard her or didn't care. He just kept moving forward, checking doors every so often, trying to find a way inside. He yelled something in Dari, probably a profanity, and then turned back and charged up the alley.

Faraz spoke on the move. "What the hell are you doing?"

"We're trying to follow you!"

"Then don't." Faraz stopped and shooed them away. "Go somewhere else!"

Kim glanced over her shoulder and turned back to him. "But I don't know where to go."

His face was more of fear than frustration. "And you think I do?"

Kim took the opportunity to catch up to Faraz. She tilted her head at Bayat, whose woozy eyes were starting to close. "He can't go much farther on foot."

"How is that my problem?" Faraz asked.

Kim thought a moment for a good answer and came up with zilch. "We won't make it without you."

The honesty seemed to calm Faraz. "Just call up one of your CIA black helicopters and have it fly you out of here."

Before she could respond to his sarcastic remark, he turned toward the end of the alley, looking eager to move. "And why should I help you anyway?"

Kim wanted to launch into everything she'd done to help save Asadi. That she had used every bit of leverage to come back to Afghanistan, risked her life, purely out of the desire to reunite him with his brother. But if talking to Asadi earlier hadn't sparked enough of a desire to help her, then maybe one other thing would.

Kim blurted out, "Because I'll pay you."

Suddenly Faraz seemed less anxious to flee. "How much?"

"I can't give you an exact figure right now. But you're a smart guy. Clearly, we have someone here that the American government desperately wants back." Kim put the emphasis of importance on Bayat, unsure if Faraz would see him as hindrance and want to ditch him if all that mattered in getting his money depended on rescuing her. "It'll be enough to last you a really long time. At least six figures. Maybe more."

Two words. One reaction. Faraz could barely contain his smile. "Follow me."

He'd just said it when the screech of tires and the rev of an engine echoed through the alley. As the black Hilux lined up with them, Kim looked to Faraz, who raised the M4 to his shoulder and fired at the handle of a locked door. Following up with his boot, he kicked the broken frame, and then gave a couple of bumps with his shoulder until it busted open and he was inside.

Close behind, Kim pushed a shaky Bayat through the entryway first. Thankfully, Faraz took the brunt of his weight and eased him down the hallway. She dashed into the building and trailed the other two into what, at a glance, looked like the back entrance of a warehouse.

Kim turned a sharp corner, past row after row of crates full of vegetables to find what appeared to be a storeroom. It didn't take long to see what had stopped Faraz in his tracks. The look of surprise coming from the armed men probably matched her own. She'd gotten out of one problem. *Thank God.* But apparently now they were into something that was a whole lot worse.

PART TWO

By God, life is cheap up here
on the Canadian River.

—*Larry McMurtry,* Lonesome Dove

14

Old Executive Office Building
Washington, D.C.

It wasn't Mario's first late-night meeting with someone at the National Security Council (NSC), but it was his first time doing it alone. Kim had always taken the lead on the political side of operations. She was the scalpel, while he was the bludgeon. Mario didn't necessarily mind crossing the Potomac, but as a former SEAL and a current paramilitary officer with the CIA, he preferred an enemy who wasn't glad-handing one minute and kneecapping him the next.

Over the years he'd found that the backstabbers on Capitol Hill were as cutthroat as any he'd faced on the battlefield. His NSC counterpart, however, Conner Murray, had proved to be a partner he could trust. As the president's go-to for all things off-the-books, Murray typically fell into the category of risk-averse. But when push came to shove, he'd put it all on the line.

And the job of *covert action*, more specifically *paramilitary operations*, was an interesting one. In fact, it was Mario's stock in trade. And it had been Garrett's as well, until he forsook them all by settling down and becoming a real human again. Although he wished his friend was still on the hunt, Mario didn't begrudge the DEA gunslinger a normal life, especially on nights like this. No matter how many times he'd done it, bad news never got any easier to deliver.

After a long, lonely march down the dark hallway, Mario passed the empty receptionist's desk, stopped outside the open office door, and gave it a soft knock.

Murray looked up from the overhead imagery spread across his desk and pointed to a leather chair. "Hey there, Mario, have a seat." He offered up one of those close-lipped sympathy smiles that you see at funerals and then rubbed his bloodshot eyes. "Can I get you some coffee?"

Mario declined the offer, sat as instructed, and focused on Murray. It was rare to see the Beltway veteran rattled, but the news of Kim missing her check-in calls was taking its toll. For once, he didn't look like he was hiding an ace up his sleeve.

Murray winced before asking, "Any new news from our girl yet?"

Mario looked down at his watch. "She's missed three check-ins and we're about to hit number four." He looked back up and shook his head. "That's not like her. *At all.*"

"But it's Afghanistan." Murray looked hopeful. "Comms issues aren't out of the norm."

Since Kim had been declared to the Taliban before entering the country, she had taken a few items your average operations officer trying to fly under the radar wouldn't have considered—a satellite phone, for one. "Can be a problem over there, for sure. But I think something's off."

Murray narrowed his eyes. "What makes you say that?"

"Well, they're in the city right now, for one. Her phone might be down, but Zadran isn't responding either. And neither is any of his lieutenants. I should be able to contact someone in the convoy, even if those phones are offline."

"Maybe it's a satellite issue?"

"Maybe." Mario shrugged. "But she'd get on a landline to call. Hit me up on a pay phone or go to an internet café. That was our deal. Three missed check-ins and I sound the alarm."

Murray rubbed his chin. "And Zadran's usually pretty reliable, right?"

"Typical warlord." Mario gave a nod. "*Very* reliable when money is involved."

Any look of hope on Murray's face vanished. "So, what do we do now?"

This time it was Mario who winced. "Maybe it's time we reach out."

To *reach out* meant that the White House would have to make official contact with the Afghan government, which would entail admitting to the Taliban that the U.S. needed their help. Although Kim's prisoner swap was authorized, Kabul would only assist in finding her to gain leverage, trading their help for financial assistance or lifted sanctions. And there was also the chance that they might not help at all. If Kim was still alive and they found her, it was possible that they might execute her for retribution against the CIA and just blame someone else.

Murray stared blankly at the wall for several seconds. "What are our *other* options?"

Mario didn't want to suggest it just yet, but it was possible to put together his own team. The Agency still had friends over in Afghanistan. Of course, activating them wouldn't be easy. And it would certainly be dangerous for everyone involved. That said, working in coordination with the Taliban butchers was nearly unfathomable. And Kim, no doubt, would feel the same.

Mario let out a breath. "Want me to head over there and see what I can find out?"

Murray looked a little surprised. "You don't want to wait? See if she calls?"

"There's no time. If Kim has been taken, she'll have hours, not days." Mario was pissed at himself for trusting Zadran. "Probably should've been with her in the first place."

Murray looked squeamish. "Then who would go after you?"

The obvious answer was Garrett, but Kim had insisted that he know nothing about the risky mission until it was all over. She'd even made Mario swear on his mother's life that he would not reveal the status of Faraz Saleem or Reza Bayat until they had safely arrived on U.S. soil.

"I'll head over to Tajikistan and cross the border. Still got some friends over there." Mario looked down at his phone again to make sure he hadn't missed a call or text. "If Kim checks in, that's great. I'll turn around and come home. If not, then we'll know we did all we could."

Those somber words *did all we could* seemed to hit home with Murray. "It's that dire?"

Seeing the dread in Murray's eyes, Mario answered gently. "Kim's brilliant. And a survivor. If I had to bet on anybody in the entire world to get out of a bind, my money would be on her."

"Can't disagree with you on that one." Murray wore a look of sad confusion. "It's just that Afghanistan is beyond my understanding now. It's completely lost."

More commando than consoler, words of reassurance weren't Mario's strong suit. But he did his best to inspire confidence. "You know what they called me over there, Conner?"

"What's that?" Murray asked.

Mario chuckled, remembering all the fun Garrett had with his nickname. "The Puerto Rican ambassador to Afghanistan."

Murray laughed too. "A master negotiator, huh?"

"Well, let's just put it this way. I know how to get things done in that country. Understand the people. Always did. And I've still got a good network, particularly in the north. People who love us. Guys who will jump at the chance to help." Mario hesitated before making the vow he knew he couldn't keep. "Don't worry. I promise, I'll find Kim, and bring her home safe."

He rose from his chair and walked out of the office before having to tell another lie. The harsh reality was that most of the people he knew over in Afghanistan had either been airlifted out or were already dead. And those left behind probably hated him with a fiery passion.

Mario racked his brain searching for someone—*anyone* he could think of over there who wouldn't shoot him on sight.

15

If Duke's high-speed approach on the Polaris was meant to intimidate Asadi, it had certainly done the trick. Drunk or not, the driver handled the machine masterfully. A few feet before impact, he slammed on the brakes and turned left into a skid, kicking up a spray of powdery snow that billowed into a frozen white cloud and glistened in the moonlight.

In a fit of laughter, Duke dabbed the bloody gash on his head with the bandanna. "What's your problem, kid?" He flashed a boozy grin. "You crap your pants?"

Savanah responded first. "*You're* the problem." She marched over to the driver's side and killed the motor. "Do you even know what you did?"

It was clear by the look on Duke's face that he didn't like being dressed down. He shifted in his seat, looking half-angry, half-alarmed. He finally mustered up a response. "You can't talk to me like that. You work for me." He jabbed a thumb into his chest. "Not the other way around."

Savanah shook her head. "No, I work for your aunt. And she's going to be super pissed to learn that her prized quarter horses are not in the stalls when the storm hits."

Duke's facial expression registered a big *uh-oh*, but his ego responded, "Who cares? They're freaking animals. Supposed to live outside."

"Maybe that's true." Savanah's retort came out as smooth as silk. "But did you know Star Dancer Cat is out there?" When Duke didn't answer, she continued. "Tell Vicky that *she's* just an animal and we'll see what happens."

Asadi knew that the prized three-year-old bay filly was valued at three-quarters of a million dollars. The others ranged from seventy-five thousand to a hundred and twenty-five thousand apiece. Price tags meant nothing to Savanah. She gave each animal the same love and attention she showered on her cherished rescue horses. But Vicky *would* care about their worth.

Duke feigned indifference. "Money doesn't mean as much to us as it does to people like you."

Savanah wasn't fazed by the insult. "Does the name Stratton mean anything?"

Duke swallowed hard. "*Senator* Stratton?"

A nod came from Savanah. "Star Dancer Cat belongs to his wife. It's her baby. Vicky told me that whatever I do, keep that horse safe. Protect her with your life were her exact words."

Duke's boldness faded. "Well, all we have to do is go out there and get them again." He turned and stared into the darkness. "Pasture gate is closed. Probably just bunched in a corner."

Savanah looked out into the black nothingness. "Let's hope so."

Asadi knew what Savanah was thinking because he was thinking it too. When horses were badly startled, they weren't always easily stopped. At night, it would be easy for them to bust through a barbed-wire fence and keep on going.

"I'll help you bring them back," Asadi offered, "but we have to hurry." He turned and surveyed the moonlit landscape. "Once the storm rolls in they'll be hard to move."

Savanah looked to the Polaris. "Duke, I need to borrow this."

Duke whapped the passenger seat with his palm. "All right, hop in."

"No way." Asadi tilted his head at Savanah. "Let her drive."

Duke looked as if he might protest, but then thought better of it. "Fine. Free me up for better things anyhow." He pulled a Coors Light can from the cupholder and took a long swig.

Savanah looked down at the feed bucket at her feet, then to Asadi. "I don't think coaxing the horses in is going to work now. We're going to have to push them from behind into the corral."

It was a riskier option with the horses now agitated, but he couldn't disagree. They'd have to fan out and drive them back to the barn. Once the horses were safe, he could head back to the house—hopefully before his dad or Butch knew he was gone.

THE AWKWARD DRIVE TO THE back side of the pasture was made in near-total silence. The alcohol had made Duke drowsy, and Savanah was fuming mad. Asadi was thankful that her anger was directed at the guy in the passenger seat. Apparently, Duke wasn't *mister perfect* after all.

Trying to resist a huge smile at the thought, Asadi zipped up his Carhartt coat and pulled the hood over his head. The wind was starting to burn his ears. He rubbed them with frozen hands, then leaned forward as their headlights met the horrific sight. It wasn't only the busted fence posts that turned his stomach, it was the bloody horsehair that was caught in the barbed wire.

Savanah was the first to muster up a response. "I can't believe it. I just can't believe it."

Asadi looked out into the frozen nothingness of the plains, where the horses were injured and suffering—maybe even dead.

Duke spoke in a panicked voice. "What are we gonna do?"

"We're going to find them, you idiot!" Savanah's voice billowed into rage. "Right. *Now!*"

Asadi couldn't disagree that time was a critical factor, but he was due back home hours ago. He was about to suggest they turn around and go back when Savanah jammed her foot on the gas and maneuvered the Polaris through a gap where the wires were cut.

Asadi leaned forward and stared ahead at where the headlight's beams met the trail of hoof tracks. He glanced at Savanah, but her gaze was fixed ahead at the endless succession of snowy sandhills that glowed an eerie shade of blue in the moonlight. Reasoning that the horses might be just over the ridge, he convinced himself to wait before making his plea to turn back.

A frantic Savanah drove over one dune, then another, and then several more, until they were somewhere in the middle of a trough within the two-story-high sandhills, going farther into the middle of a ranch that was roughly the size of Washington, D.C. In the middle of the Mescalero's wilderness, it felt as if they were on a life raft, caught between the waves, in a storm out at sea.

Asadi turned, searching in every direction, but nothing was familiar. And pretty soon the hoofprints were scattered as well. After a good fifteen minutes of driving, Savanah stopped. Any sign of the horses had disappeared. And all that was left were their tracks, which seemed to either zigzag in random patterns or morph into figure eights.

It didn't take long to determine that it wasn't only the horses that were lost. They were in just as much danger as the animals, if not a whole heck of a lot more.

16

I f Garrett had been awoken by Saint Peter himself, telling him he had moved on to the forever hereafter, it wouldn't have been much of a surprise. There were colorful lights, ethereal music, and he was even enveloped in an electric blue haze. But the dried blood on the floor from a boot to the back of the head was a pretty big clue that he'd *not* ascended to the Pearly Gates.

His second hint was the grungy hipsters surrounding him. If there was such a thing as cowboy Hell, it probably looked a whole lot like this.

Garrett was close to panicked at the thought of such a damnation when he sat up, looked around, and realized he'd been dragged into the Greyhound. There were no seats and the windows had been covered, leaving an empty rectangular shaft lit up by the purplish-pink glow of black lights. Low murmurs filled the air, along with the pungent stench of marijuana.

Groaning as he stood, Garrett looked around to find a dozen or so members of Cosmic Order's hit squad blocking a narrow path toward the front of the bus. Seemingly on their own accord, they parted like the Red Sea to reveal Kai Stoddard standing defiantly within the scrum.

Instinctively, Garrett reached for his pistol, but found the holster to be empty. "Oh, yeah," he grumbled to himself as the fuzzy images of the fight suddenly came rushing back.

Kai lifted Garrett's Nighthawk into the phosphorescent light. "Looking for this?"

Garrett was tempted to rush him but thought better, given the odds. "That's where I left it."

Kai took a couple of steps forward and the others moved farther to the sides of the bus. He stopped a good six feet away. "And that's where it'll stay for now."

Garrett smiled. "I've been met with some poor invitations in my time, but this one beats all."

"You weren't invited here."

Garrett held his grin to show that he wasn't rattled. "Guess we have that in common."

"*You* came into our camp," Kai chided. "Not the other way around. And you need to get it through your head that none of us were responsible for what happened on your land."

"Heard you before, Kai. Problem is that I don't believe you."

"Don't care what you believe," Kai bristled. "Fact of the matter is that you're wrong."

"*Fact* of the matter," Garrett countered, "is that you're holding me against my will at gunpoint. Doesn't exactly make you look innocent, now does it?"

In Kai's eyes flashed a hint of recognition that he was in the wrong. He looked to the others around him. "Okay, everyone out. I want to talk to him alone."

One by one, each member turned and drifted to the front of the bus. They dipped through a burgundy partition near the driver's seat and filed their way through the opening. As the last one exited, their leader turned back and marched forward, the pistol gripped tight in his hand.

Kai stopped a few feet away. "I want to know something, Garrett. And I want the truth."

Garrett took a quick glance at the pistol and thought about whether or not honesty was the best policy in a situation like this. "I'm listening."

Kai looked away for a moment and swallowed hard. "I want to

know if you really believe that I just left you all up on that mountain to die?"

Garrett let out a long sigh, taking a little time to come up with his answer. But it wasn't because he was making up a lie. It was because he wasn't. There were times when the simple truth was a lot harder to stomach. And this was one of those occasions.

"No, Kai, I don't believe that. Don't believe that's true at all."

Kai turned back. "Then why'd you say it?"

It was a great question, one for which Garrett still didn't have a ready answer. "Kai, I said that because I knew it would hurt. And I wanted you to feel some pain."

Kai *did* look hurt. "I don't understand. *Why?*"

"Because you hit a nerve. By pure accident, you reached way back into my past and brought up some bad memories. Maybe even regrets."

Kai looked at him curiously. "Seems like the world is your oyster. Got everything figured out. What could you possibly have to regret?"

If the guy only knew? Garrett was just now getting out from under a mountain of debt, dating a girl who was way out of his league, and fathering a teenager who was still dealing with the crippling loss of his family. The only thing that he had figured out was that he didn't know anything about anything. And the more he learned, the less he seemed to know.

Had he sold his soul by joining forces with Vicky Kaiser? *Probably.* But his attitude had been that it was better to *live to fight another day.* But he had only traded one problem for another. Now he was teamed up with people he'd once despised, men like Sheriff Crowley.

Garrett shook off Kai's assertion. "Man, we took different paths after the Army. But that's about where it ends. I've made more mistakes in my life than I care to admit. And as far as regrets go, that's a long conversation. Trust me. I've had my own dance with the devil. Still dancing with him, if truth be told."

Kai nodded, seeming to get some relief from the answer. "What about the other thing you said? About how you consider anyone you shed blood with to be a friend."

"Think you know that I don't mess around when it comes to loyalty. No matter where we stand on issues out here, you'll always be a brother."

There was a pregnant pause from Kai. "I consider you a friend too. How could I not?"

"Look, your outlook and mine might be different on all this stuff. But given our history, I thought we could knock down some walls, and come to a truce before more people get hurt."

"I know what you think, Garrett, but I promise I had nothing to do with those explosions."

"Maybe not you personally, but I aim to hunt down whoever is responsible."

"How do you know it was sabotage? Accidents happen. Could be as simple as that."

"Could be, but it's not. Not twice in a row." Garrett let a few seconds pass. "Remember back in the Panjshir Valley? Second time we got ambushed. What did we say?"

Kai cleared his throat. "We said there was no such thing as a coincidence."

"And it turned out we had a turncoat in our Afghan attachments. Reporting our every move."

Kai held up a finger. "But that's different. That was a war zone."

"Well, given all the explosions, it's sure starting to feel like one." Kai started to argue but Garrett cut him off. "This land is everything to me. And I won't let it be destroyed."

Kai let out a huff. "I want to help *protect* the land. And the people. Your ranch is a special place. Beautiful. Rugged. Wild. Not hard to see why you talked about it nonstop. All we're trying to do is stop the destruction of places like these."

Garrett couldn't help but chuckle. "I'm guessing that if we sat down and hashed it all out, you and I would probably see eye to eye on more than either of us would like to admit. But where we come to loggerheads is on *how* to do it."

No doubt their dispute probably all came down to the classic *environmentalism* versus *conservation* debate. Environmentalists wanted to set aside land so it could be protected from human abuse, while conservationists wanted to take care of the land so that it could be used by others in the future. There was probably some wiggle room on both sides, but they weren't going to settle that age-old argument in the next few minutes.

A slow smile rose on Kai's face. "You're right. I'm sure we could maybe find some common ground. But all that aside, I'm here to tell you that nobody in the group would resort to something like this. We advocate nonviolence."

It was Garrett's turn to smile. "Could've fooled me given the boot I took to the head."

"*Mostly* nonviolence." Kai raised the pistol, thrust the barrel into his left palm, and curled his fingers around it. Flipping the gun around, he handed it back. "Things just got a little nuts."

Garrett took the handoff and ran his index finger along the head wound. "Yeah, I'll say. I'm still seeing stars."

Kai nodded to the Nighthawk. "Just keep that thing hidden. With my military service, it was hard enough convincing these people I wasn't a narc when I joined the group."

Garrett tried hard not to laugh, given the fact that he actually was one. "Don't worry." He lifted up the back of his shirt and returned the pistol to its holster. "Secret's safe with me."

No sooner had he secured the pistol than he heard the roar of an engine outside the bus, followed by shouting. And it was at that moment he remembered his dad and Grace were supposed to be keeping watch. Seconds later, Butch came through the door, his stainless-steel Colt Python revolver leading the way.

Knowing that his dad was more than willing and able to do his part in thinning the hippie herd, Garrett yelled out, "Hold on, Daddy! Hold on! Everything's fine. We're just talking."

"Could've given us warning." Butch was clearly incensed. "You were standing there one moment and gone the next. We didn't know what the hell happened!"

"I know." Garrett looked to Kai, who was clearly unnerved by some old man he didn't know waving around a massive .357 Magnum. "Just lost track of time. That's all."

Butch didn't look like he was buying it. "Speaking of time. We're running short on it. Grace mowed over a couple of tents driving through and stirred up a coven of witches, I think." He jerked a thumb over his shoulder. "Come out screaming at us like we'd done spilt their brew."

Garrett didn't know what the old man was talking about. Didn't *want* to know. The bottom line was that it was time to get going before things somehow got worse.

"Be right there." Garrett turned to Kai. "I'm going out to the pipeline tonight to have a look. If I see anything out there that confirms anything, one way or the other, I'll let you know."

Before Kai could answer, he was interrupted by a blaring car horn. Garrett was about to inquire about the ruckus when Butch filled them in.

"And that would be Grace."

The old man spun around, Colt pistol in the vanguard, and made his way back up to the front of the bus. He dipped through the burgundy partition, presumably to check on his daughter, who had again laid on the horn again.

Kai furrowed his brow. "Mind if I go out to the ranch with you?"

"To the pipeline?" Garrett asked. "Why?"

"Because I've been thinking about something you said." Kai looked as if he was contemplating hard. "About Panjshir Valley. The ambushes. And the Taliban informant."

Garrett perked up. "Okay, you've got my attention."

Kai lowered his voice, looking a bit nervous. "There's another organization we're connected to. Group that provides our funding. Maybe there are some coincidences I can't explain."

Before Garrett could dig in, another blast came from his truck horn, which was followed by the unmistakable thundering crack of a .357. He turned and sprinted to the front of the bus, struggled to find a gap in the curtain divide, just praying like hell that Butch wasn't battling it out with hippies, carnies, or whoever the hell he thought was a witch.

17

Kim listened intently to their captors' voices, desperate to figure out who'd taken them at gunpoint from the warehouse and shoved black hoods over their heads. But beyond the road noise and an occasional honking horn, there was little to no clue who had them or where they were going. All she knew was that they'd busted into the wrong place at a very wrong time.

Given the particular neighborhood of Kunduz they were in, there weren't really any *right* places to be. Zadran's trepidation about this part of the journey was totally spot-on. He'd expected trouble and they'd certainly found it. And the longer they rode in the cargo hold of that truck, the more it became clear that they were being moved to a remote location. *Not good*.

The countryside around the city was teeming with drug runners, religious fanatics, and sometimes a combination of both. She suspected their kidnappers were heroin traffickers, which was actually a relief. They would want monetary reward, not vengeance. And the likely highest bidder would probably be the Taliban, who would expect a big favor for brokering her safe return.

A sudden stop of the truck preceded the zip of the roll-up door. Then someone grabbed her by the bicep and dragged her across the floor. With a jarring thud, she landed on her tailbone on the dusty ground and rolled to her side in order to work out the pain.

Resisting the urge to cry out, she bit her lip, and muttered quiet profanities that she desperately wanted to scream.

Fighting for composure, Kim gained just a little break from the throbbing in her lower back as the hood was ripped from her head. She squinted in the fiery blaze of a flashlight and looked around to find what she'd so desperately prayed for. Both Faraz and Bayat were thankfully alive. Jerked from her side to her knees, Kim looked around to see eight men fanned out before them. Half cradled Kalashnikov rifles. The others stowed either pistols or daggers in their belts.

Kim was about to tell Faraz to try to negotiate when one of the men stepped forward, dangling an UZI PRO submachine gun by his side. He leaned in close. "Who do you work for?"

Surprised with the revelation that he spoke flawless English, it took her a moment to answer. She didn't know where to begin or how much she should say.

The one who had spoken had short dark hair and was clean-shaven, looking younger than the others. He was sporting a Houston Astros cap and wore a black Ozzy Osbourne concert T-shirt. It was a stark contrast to the others, who were sporting thick dark beards and wearing turbans, pakol caps, and baggy traditional Afghan attire like *shalwar kameez*.

What they did have in common were looks of pure disdain. Their hatred for her was palpable.

Ozzy pulled up the UZI and pointed it at her face. "Stalling makes me think you're lying. And if you're lying, then you're wasting my time. We have ways of finding the truth."

"No wait." Kim made a conscious effort to be quick with her responses. "I've got no reason to lie because I've done nothing wrong."

Ozzy chuckled and then turned and translated to the others, who were equally amused. Whipping back around, he got serious again. "You shot your way into our warehouse." He dipped his head at Faraz, who had done the shooting. "You don't think that was wrong?"

Oh. That. Kim squirmed a little but again tried not to take a long time in her reply. "Look, we were ambushed on the street and went into your building because we were trying to escape. It was a total and complete accident, and we're really sorry."

Really sorry? Kim couldn't believe she'd just said that. Was this heroin trafficker really to believe that she had stumbled into their drug lair by chance? It sounded exactly like the kind of lie he'd just warned her about. Given his disbelieving glare, Kim figured she'd better start speaking the international language. If it had worked on Faraz, then why not this guy?

"Our safe return will guarantee you a sizable reward. No questions asked."

Ozzy looked amused by the answer and flashed a knowing smile. "A reward from who?"

"The American government."

"I'm well aware of that." He lost his smile, clearly no longer amused. "From. *Who?*"

Kim couldn't help but pause. A lie could get her killed. But so could the truth. She'd spent her life betting on the farce. For the first time ever, she decided to come clean. "The CIA."

Wrong answer. Before Ozzy could even make a move, one of the men yanked a dagger and came at her in a rush. She tried to rise but stumbled, hobbled with her feet bound. With a single burst of automatic gunfire, Kim looked up to find the leader had fired his UZI into the air.

His agitated cronies now kept at bay, Ozzy marched up and yanked her to her feet. He turned and gave a command to the others in Dari, who moved to Faraz and Bayat, still hooded, and jerked them up also. With the path now clear, she could see the walled structure behind them. It was a compound, the kind owned by someone with a lot of money and influence. The good news was they were alive. The question was for how long. They were in the middle of nowhere and no one was coming to help. And clearly her revelation about the CIA had generated a bad response.

Ozzy yanked a knife from its sheath, cut Kim's restraints, and shoved her toward the complex, which she determined looked like a tackier version of the Caesars Palace resort in Las Vegas. She also caught a glimpse of a tattoo on his forearm. In Islam, such adornments were forbidden. So, like the rest of his appearance, it was out of the ordinary. But it could just mean that he wasn't religiously devout. However, the emblem of the sword and shield was very familiar.

It took Kim a moment, but then it dawned on her that she'd seen that insignia before. In fact, she'd seen it quite often. Given the turmoil, her brain was a bit cloudy, and synapses weren't firing as they should be. But then it came to her in a flash. Same tattoo. Same place on the forearm. She knew that symbol so well because she'd seen the *exact* same one on Garrett Kohl.

18

Asadi didn't know how long they'd been traversing over and around the massive sandhills, only that with each passing minute he was growing more and more worried. In addition to his concern for the horses, he was anxious about their own safety. Once the blizzard moved in, they'd be trapped. And chances of rescue would be slim to none until morning.

Savanah eased up on top of the dune and jammed on the brakes. Turning back to Asadi, she asked, "See like a reference point or anything?"

"No. Nothing." Asadi leaned forward and looked over at Duke. "You got your phone? Maybe we could use the compass."

Duke shook his head. "Didn't think I'd need it since we don't get cell service out here."

Asadi gazed around at the darkness, which surrounded them on all sides. "Okay, I think we should probably keep going straight." It was only a feeling, but he felt like it was the right thing to do. Of course, his gut had been wrong plenty of times before.

Savanah turned to him looking nervous. "I was thinking just the opposite."

Asadi was about to second her suggestion when the drunk in the passenger seat spoke up.

"Dead wrong, Sacajawea." Duke glanced back at Asadi. "And so are you."

Savanah fired back first. "So, which direction do we go then?"

"Side to side," Duke replied coolly. "Run the length of the dunes. It won't take us back home, but it'll get us back to the landing strip. At then at least we'll know where we're at."

Asadi couldn't believe it, but Duke's idea wasn't half-bad. The Mescalero runway was long enough to land a 737, and the 120,000-square-foot hangar was large enough to park ten private jets. Aside from it being a huge visible landmark, there was a telephone inside the office. They could break in through a window and call for help.

"It's a big risk though." Savanah turned back. "If we miss it, we'll be worse off than now."

Asadi nodded, though he couldn't be seen in the dark. "Well, we can't keep going in circles."

She paused a moment, clearly pondering their options. "Should we give it a try?"

Asadi knew she was probably hesitant to make the official call since it was a decision that could doom them all. "Want me to drive? Let you have a little rest?"

There was another moment of silence where Savanah was probably debating whether she wanted to admit she needed a break. But she eventually looked ahead, and then pulled her bare hands from the steering wheel and shook them out. "For just a minute, maybe."

Asadi was happy to relieve some of that burden. He knew her pride would not let her admit she was feeling the effects of the cold. It wasn't the first time he'd given her an out to save face. And she'd done the same for him plenty of times. It was why they'd made such a good team.

Asadi strapped himself in the driver's seat and glanced over at Duke, who was seething. It was one thing to have Savanah at the helm. She was a ranch employee—as well as his chauffeur on occasion. Asadi, however, was an outsider, a *kid* no less. Given the injured horses and bad weather rolling in, things were about as grown-up as it gets.

Duke turned to Asadi. "Now where, smart guy?"

Asadi did his best to orient himself in the trough. "Try to find the runway."

Cutting the wheel left, Asadi pressed his foot on the gas, although a bit too hard. The 181-horsepower engine shot their Polaris into a violent lunge as the back wheels fishtailed through the snow. He adjusted pressure, pushed the accelerator, and eased them into a gradual forward momentum. Despite the cold and his anxiety, Asadi was exhilarated. It wasn't his first time driving a UTV, but it was his first time on one designed for racing instead of ranch work. It was all he could do to keep from cutting up the side of the sandhill and jumping over the crest.

Finding himself on a straightaway, Asadi pressed the gas harder. It was partially for the fun of it, and partially out of fear that time was ticking away, not only for the horses, but for them. In his note to Garrett, he'd written that he'd be gone no longer than two hours. It'd been about three.

Between the snarl of the engine and feeling of weightlessness as the Polaris launched over mounds, Asadi couldn't help but smile. The thrill was almost too much to bear. Part of him felt bad for his harsh criticism of Duke for doing exactly what they were doing now, but fun like this was impossible to resist.

Battling the urge to look back to see if Savanah was having a good time too, Asadi kept his eyes trained ahead, as far as the headlights would allow. But given their high rate of speed he doubted there was more than a second or two between the beam's reach and their front bumper. With the sobering thought of potential disasters, he eased his foot off the gas.

Unfortunately, the alarm bells in his head had not gone off quite soon enough.

Asadi didn't know what had caused the rise in the earth out ahead, only that it was probably man-made. Snow-covered, it blended so well with the surroundings that he couldn't hit the brakes before it was already too late. A sharp cut of the wheel to the right was enough to prevent a head-on impact, but the back left rear tire took the brunt of the jarring crash.

A painful jolt and the chassis slid right, sling-shotting the UTV sideways, completely parallel within the trough of two towering dunes. The skidding slowed, but then the wheels suddenly caught, causing the Polaris to roll over. They hung in suspension for a second, but the momentum carried them onto the roof, and in a sudden blur of motion they were upright again.

Asadi looked over to find Duke strapped in tight, a little in shock but seeming no worse for wear. With the motor now dead, it left only the haunting howl of an icy wind. A frantic turn of the head to check on Savanah revealed nothing behind him but an empty back seat.

19

Garrett flew out the side door of the old Greyhound to find that his dad's report of witches was not only true, but indeed a whole lot worse than he'd described. One was wielding an axe, another a baseball bat. With wild bushy hair and dark flowing robes, the five women surrounding the truck could have given anyone the impression of a paranormal threat.

Given the trench in the snow, and the tattered tent caught on the front bumper of the GMC, it was clear Grace had dragged the banshees' canvas domicile halfway across the encampment. The only good news was that Butch was pointing his Colt into the air, instead of at them. Garrett sprinted to the truck, yanked the back door open, and Kai piled in behind him.

Reaching over and jerking the door shut, Garrett shouted to his sister, "Go! Go! Go!"

As directed, Grace punched the gas and the wheels spun in the wet snow for a couple of rotations before catching with force and throwing them back into their seats. Garrett breathed a sigh of relief as they broke past the compound perimeter, cleared the bedlam, and then came to a stop in the empty pasture. Always happy to add insult to injury, his dad was the first to speak.

"What did I say?" Butch turned back to Garrett, looking somewhat amused. "Told you them witches were after us, but you didn't believe me. Thought I was crazy, huh?"

Although his dad was right, Garrett wasn't going to admit it. The old man was a monster enough know-it-all and didn't need any encouragement. "First of all, Daddy, those are just some poor ladies in their bathrobes. And they're right to be pissed. You demolished their damn tent."

Grace glanced back. "Well, that was my fault, you see. Hitting those witches was purely an accident." She jerked the steering wheel left and right a couple of times to prove her next point. "This big thing doesn't handle like my Mercedes. Turns slower than a tugboat."

"Handles just fine," Garrett argued. He could feel himself growing as agitated with Grace as he was with Butch. "And accident or not, you're both lucky that nobody was killed."

Of course, Garrett was only assuming that someone wasn't killed.

"Your dad's right." Kai turned to Garrett. "They are witches. Well, Wiccans anyhow."

Butch shot Garrett one of his famous *I told you so* looks. It was a second favorite to his *do you want to apologize* glare, which was probably coming up next.

Garrett refocused on Grace, who seemed to be enjoying the moment a little too much. "That still doesn't excuse you running over their tent."

Grace checked the rearview, where there was nothing behind them but twinkling camp lights, the bus, and a few dark outlines of makeshift shelters. "Just barely clipped the corner and the whole thing sort of came along with us." She smirked, clearly proud of her destructive handiwork. "Like I said, it was pure accident."

It could've been a lot worse, so Garrett let it go. On top of that, the idea of a little retribution for the earlier ass-kicking and what they did to his windshield sat quite nicely. Before he could relay the next part of their plan, Butch had chimed in again, this time throwing shade at Kai.

"You convince *Hanoi Jane* here to leave the cult and join us normal folks?"

Garrett looked over at Kai, nervous that the Jane Fonda comment might kill the positive progress. But his old friend was still all grins. Apparently he appreciated the old man's hijinks.

Garrett answered for Kai, "He's offered to help us."

"Help us do what?" Butch looked riled again. "Paint the Statue of Liberty red?"

Garrett threw up a hand. "All right, that's enough. Kai says he's not involved, and I believe him." Before Butch could respond, he added, "And enough with the commie jokes. He's against pollution, not capitalism. Whole different deal."

The reasoning seemed to appease Butch, who turned forward again. "Now what?"

"Now we go to the pipeline," Garrett answered. "See if we can gather any evidence."

"*Evidence?*" Grace turned and looked at him quizzically. "What do we look for?"

Garrett explained: "Saw plenty of explosions in war zones over the years. Causes can usually be pinpointed. If it's an accident, there's usually some telltale signs. If it's a bomb, then somebody was messing around out there that shouldn't have been, and there'll be a trail."

Garrett wasn't ready to reveal Tony's report about a trespasser at the Mescalero Compressor Station before the explosion just yet. Although he was warming up to Kai, he didn't know if he could really trust him. And until he was certain, Garrett wanted to keep his cards held close.

Butch turned his skepticism of Kai on full blast. "And what does Sherlock Holmes here have to offer? Gonna walk around smoking a pipe while he searches for clues?"

Garrett answered for Kai again. "Back in Afghanistan, he was one of our best trackers. Could figure out if we were dealing with friend or foe before anyone in our unit. It's a real gift."

Butch looked slightly impressed. "Take any help we can get, I guess." He cocked an eyebrow at Kai and gave a couple of head tilts toward Garrett. "This one couldn't trail a Sasquatch limping across the desert."

"Okay, that's plenty out of you for one night." Garrett pointed toward the caliche road leading back to the ranch. "Grace, get on that road up ahead there and drive east."

As she eased across the pasture, Garrett couldn't help feeling that something was off. His suspicions about Kai weren't fully resolved. But to this point, he had proved useful in a bind. It was the unease you felt when you forgot about a pot of water boiling or to turn off the stove. And then it dawned on him that his worry was less about who was there in the cab and more to do with who he'd left behind at the house.

Between getting shanghaied by hippies and whipped by witches, Garrett had completely forgotten to check on Asadi. He hated to wake him, but figured it was better to interrupt his sleep than to cause any worry. The boy might wake in the night and find that they'd not made it home. So, Garrett took the phone from his pocket and dialed the house.

The first unanswered call didn't worry him, nor did the second. But the third should've roused his son from even the deepest of slumbers, especially if he was camped out on the couch. And then it occurred to Garrett that Asadi might not be sleeping at all. The big question was where the boy might be this late at night, with a raging blizzard fast on the approach.

20

Kim glanced around their holding cell, which was actually a storeroom for an industrial kitchen. It was filled to the brim with enough canned vegetables and freeze-dried meals to comfortably feed a small army. A bullet to the head might be her fate, but she'd at least not die on an empty stomach. She took a stab at a little gallows humor to lighten the mood.

"Think we'll get a last meal?" Kim lifted a tin of fish in tomato sauce off the bottom shelf and stared at the label. "If we do, please God, don't let it be this."

She got a modest grin in return from Bayat, who took a seat, hung his head, and closed his eyes. He'd been dragging before their escape, but now he was completely wiped-out, on top of being injured. Faraz, conversely, wasn't amused by the joke at all. He leaned against a wall, slid down, and stared blankly at nothing ahead. His limbs were splayed like a dead man as he spoke.

"So . . . I never thanked you for rescuing me."

Kim didn't know if he was joking or if it was just a plain old sarcastic remark, but she laughed anyhow. She moved to him, sat down in front of his gaze, and leaned against a crate of canned chickpeas. For a fighting chance she needed an ally, which meant offering hope.

She locked eyes with Faraz. "Don't give up on me, okay. I know this looks bleak, but we have cards to play here. As I told you before,

Bayat and I are worth a lot, which means *you're* worth a lot. I promise I won't make any deal for our freedom that doesn't include you."

"Deal?" A slow smile crept up on Faraz's face. "There is no deal."

"These guys aren't religious fanatics," Kim explained. "They're just criminals. A bunch of money-grubbing thugs. Someone is going to realize how much they can make off of us and we'll be handed over to Kabul soon. Mark my words they're going to play ball."

"You speak Dari?" Before she could answer, Faraz continued, "Because I do. And I know what they said about us."

Kim leaned forward even more and lowered her voice, partially in case there was a guard outside their door who spoke English. "Well, what's going on?"

Faraz brought his knees to his chest and rested his forehead on them. His words were muffled but clear. "Said we were worth more to the Taliban dead than we were alive."

"You must've heard incorrectly. The U.S. will pay nothing for dead bodies."

Faraz looked up at her and smirked. "That's why you Americans lost over here. You had no understanding of the people you were fighting."

Kim's immediate response was to argue, but she wanted to dig deeper into what Faraz meant. "Can't say that I didn't try. But in the end, it wasn't enough. Did my best to help the people who actually wanted to make this a better place."

"With money?" Faraz asked.

"Sometimes money was the answer."

"It was *never* the answer."

"Then what was?" Kim asked. "What did you hear these guys say?"

"They said they worked for you."

Kim thought about Ozzy and his shield tattoo. "Look, I remember the name and face of every person I ran over here. Either you're wrong or they are. I've never seen these men in my life."

"Maybe it wasn't *you* personally. But they worked for the American spies. Maybe Green Berets?" Faraz shrugged. "Somebody recruited them. Trained them. And then abandoned them."

It was at that moment Kim realized why the tattoo she'd seen earlier was so significant. The *sword and shield of Afghanistan* were the elite units that worked with American intelligence and special operations. Garrett had become close friends with a few of these men, who had acted as scouts. Most of the soldiers in these elite Afghan attachments had been evacuated. But there were some, including their families, who were tragically left behind.

Kim had heard that those who weren't executed by the Taliban had had to swear allegiance or else risk reprisal on their families. Now many of the former soldiers were even on high-level security details for political leadership in Kabul. Others were plying their skills in the opium trade. It was a horrible fate for those who had dedicated their lives to improving the country.

Kim didn't have to ask because she already knew that they'd be turned over to the Taliban *after* being executed. "In terms of life and death, allegiance means more than money here."

"Now . . . you're getting it." Faraz smiled again. "Our beliefs may be backward and barbaric to you, but they mean something to us. Your dollars will someday be worth nothing, but our traditions and our culture will go on forever."

Kim was not only tempted to argue but to burst into laughter. Loyalties in Afghanistan switched on a dime. In fact, she'd probably seen warlords shift allegiances for even less. But that was neither here nor there. The men in this compound were trying to win back their lives. And the best way for them to do that was by showing that they were philosophically aligned. What better demonstration of that than to offer up the heads of some Americans on a silver platter?

"Okay, Faraz, we have no one willing to barter here. Means we'll have to save ourselves."

He raised his hands, palms up. "And how do we do that?"

"First." Kim held up a finger. "We'll need weapons."

Faraz picked up a can of evaporated milk off the floor. "This what you had in mind?"

Kim shook her head. "No, we'll need guns."

"Great." Faraz made a show of looking around. "You have any I don't know about?"

"Saw two Kalashnikovs and an M4 in the kitchen. Leaning against cabinets near the stove."

"Want me to call the guard?" Faraz tiled his head at the door. "Tell him to open up and hand them over. Maybe give us any extra grenades they have lying around."

Sick of wasting time with more tired jokes, Kim stanched his next quip with an obvious fake laugh. "Are you done? Because if what you're saying is true, then we might need to hurry."

Faraz lost the smile he'd worn while teasing and looked a little sick. "Yeah, I'm done."

"Good." Kim pointed up to a small window above the top shelves. "Think we can fit?"

A once-sluggish Faraz focused on the opening to the outside and sprang to his feet. He climbed the shelves, reached the window, and pushed it open. "Leads to the roof."

"Careful no one sees you," Kim warned.

Faraz turned back and looked down, his face lit up with excitement. "It's like a large balcony or something but nobody's around."

Kim's heart leapt, both by the fact that there was a route for escape, and because Faraz was in good spirits and focused. "Can we make it out?"

He gave the window another shove, allowing another inch or two. "Tight but we can fit."

Simultaneously they looked at Bayat, then back to one another. There was a mutual recognition that he would not make the climb. And he was too heavy to lift. Faraz turned back and pushed a couple of boxes aside to give them more room to maneuver around on the top shelf.

Kim rose and moved to the poor guy, whose eyes were barely open. "We're going to go through the window. But we'll return shortly. I promise." She looked up to Faraz. "Right?"

Faraz didn't answer, just turned to the window. His nonresponse didn't sit well. But that was a problem for later. For now, they needed weapons and transport. Whether she could depend on her partner to stick around was up in the air. With or without him she was coming back.

21

Asadi fought to stay calm, but with Savanah missing from the back seat of the UTV, it was hard not to panic. It was near pitch dark, and they were completely turned around on the far side of the ranch. A deep-seated guilt was building inside, and it sat in his stomach like a massive rock. While Duke wasn't without blame, Asadi knew that wrecking the Polaris fell back on him.

He unbuckled his harness and leapt from the driver's seat, scanning the area in a circular pattern around the wreckage. With his eyes to the ground, he yelled to her over and over until his voice grew hoarse as he frantically searched for her body. Asadi was widening the search when his foot hit a divot beneath the powdery snow and he stumbled to a knee.

Duke leaned over and offered a hand. "Watch where you're going, kid."

Asadi didn't accept the help or respond. He just got up and continued the frantic hunt. He was near giving up when Duke directed the beams of his flashlight on what looked like a snow-covered pipe, jutting up from the ground about three feet into the air.

"Looks like a riser." Duke ran his beams along the length of it. "Probably from one of the old pipelines that used to run through here years ago."

Asadi sprinted to the iron conduit and brushed the frost from the valve. Upon further inspection it was obvious why the back wheel of their UTV had been ripped off. This giant hunk of metal connected into an even bigger pipeline beneath the earth. Reasoning that the jolt and not the rollover was probably what ejected Savanah from the back seat, Asadi looked to the right, imagining their back left bumper taking the brunt of the riser and her flying left.

He had just come up with a theory as to where she might be when a moan came from the outer darkness. Before Duke had even pointed his light in the direction of the sound, Asadi took off in a sprint toward the bulge in the snow. Dropping to hands and knees, he scurried to find Savanah unconscious, her body half-buried in the powder.

Caressing her exposed cheek, Asadi spoke to her in his gentlest voice. "Savanah, wake up." He stroked her ice-cold face harder. "Come on, you have to get moving."

Duke scanned her body with the light, then looked to Asadi. "We have to get her out of this snow." He knelt beside them and brushed away the flakes that coated her jacket and blue jeans.

Asadi leaned in and whispered into her ear, "I'm scared to move you. But I'm scared not to. I don't know what to do."

Duke said, "Might be some old coveralls in the Polaris. Think I should get them?"

Asadi didn't know *what* to think. His only ray of hope was from the fact she'd cried out earlier, which meant she was alive. "Yeah, sounds good. We've got to warm her up."

As Duke sprinted off, Asadi leaned in again and cleared Savanah's mousy ringlets from her face. Anxious to get her moving, he racked his brain for something that would motivate her. "Savanah, the horses are still out there. They're cold. They're hurt. And we need to find them, or they're not going to make it. So, we have to get going. Okay?"

There was more than a little shame in what he was telling her, but Asadi reasoned that desperate times called for desperate measures. Had the guilt trip failed to work, he would've felt lower than he already did. But the slow rise of her eyelids had made it all worthwhile.

Before Asadi could help her, she was sitting upright. But with an attempt to rise to her feet Savanah gripped her side and cried out in pain. Asadi put a hand on her left shoulder to keep her still. "Hold on. Don't move. You might've broken some ribs."

Savanah nodded but didn't respond. They both knew the signs of that injury, as one of their buddies, Sam Clevenger, had taken a fall from a horse two months before and suffered the same fate. It was painful, not fatal. *Thank the Lord.* But hiking out of there over the snowy dunes would be way too much for her to handle.

"The horses?" Savanah asked in a groggy whisper. "Did we find them?"

Asadi could tell she was completely out of it, and he wondered if she had a concussion. "Not yet." He looked around at the towering heights surrounding them, not really sure why. "Too much ground to cover by ourselves. We need to go and get more help."

Savanah glanced over at the Polaris, which looked fine in the dark. "Let's go, then."

Asadi could hear the reluctance in his own voice. "We're not going anywhere in that."

The wooziness had faded, leaving her with a tone of exasperation. "*Why?*"

Her failure to recall the incident furthered Asadi's suspicion that she might have hit her head. There was a temptation to rejoice at the fact he'd not have to admit it was all his fault. But eventually there would come a time when he would have to tell her what happened. Fortunately, he could kick that can of truth down the road for a little while longer.

Duke ran up with supplies and laid them in the snow. "Found a pair of cloth work gloves too with the coveralls. They stink like hell but they're all we've got."

Asadi remembered a pair of tattered blue Dickies at the barn that Savanah's dog had birthed puppies on. He hoped they weren't the same ones, but they looked familiar.

"Let me see." Asadi grabbed the gloves from Duke and slipped them over Savanah's icy hands. "This will help some."

She gave him a modest smile of gratitude. "Better," she whispered.

Asadi doubted the gloves made that big a difference, but hopefully the coveralls would. They were stiff to the touch and smelled like a combination of dust, grease, and alfalfa hay. The material wasn't that thick, but it was better than nothing at all. Worried it would be too painful to get her into them, Asadi wrapped the coveralls around her like a blanket.

"Now, let's get you over by the engine. It'll keep you warm for a while."

An arm on each of their shoulders, Asadi and Duke eased Savanah to her feet and inched her over to the UTV. Although it wouldn't crank and the electrical system was shot, the motor was still burning hot, and the body of the Polaris provided good shelter from the blasting wind.

After getting Savanah as comfortable as possible, Asadi rose again and looked around. "I'm going to go for help."

"*Help?*" Duke wore a look of disdain. "Where you gonna go?"

"Same plan as before. Try to hike to the airstrip. I can use the phone in the hangar." Asadi looked down at Savanah, who was hunkered beneath the chassis, shivering. "Have to try something. She won't make it if we have to stay here all night."

"What if you miss the runway?" Duke turned in the direction that Asadi was facing and aimed his flashlight. At the end of the beams was only cold darkness. "There's nothing out there beyond it but wilderness for dozens of miles."

"I won't miss it," Asadi replied, mustering a voice of confidence for Savanah's sake. What he meant to say was *I can't* miss it. He turned toward the beams and then looked back. "If someone gets here first, just tell them where I went so they can find me."

Duke looked in that direction again and held his gaze as if pondering whether it would work. Then he turned back, clicked off the flashlight, and handed it over. "Good luck, I guess."

Asadi would've said thank you if Duke's gesture and his words had not been dripping with sarcasm. But he didn't care to waste any energy on that, knowing he'd need every bit of it for the journey ahead. Instead, Asadi knelt again by Savanah and kissed her on the forehead. He would've said something monumental if he'd had the words. But all he could think of was "Bye for now."

Getting only a slow nod in response, Asadi rose again, clicked on the flashlight, and marched to the top of a sandhill to try to get his bearings. He turned in a complete circle, hoping to catch a glimpse of a landmark, lights from the ranch headquarters, anything from which to draw a bead. But he found nothing but endless rows of snow-covered dunes.

22

After turning off the county road, Smitty put the truck in park and shut off the engine. He glanced over at the twinkling lights of the sprawling Cosmic Order encampment, which was bathed in a glow of moonlight, about a hundred yards in the distance.

Bo studied the site intently from the passenger seat, eyes narrowed, as if coming up with a plan. "So, how we wanna do this thing?"

"*We're* not going to do it." Smitty looked down at the backpack full of heroin in his lap. "I'm going to do this myself."

Bo looked somewhere between pissed and disappointed. "Then what the hell am *I* here for?"

Smitty didn't really have an answer. The truth of the matter was he felt that if they were going to do something this shady, then he wanted to do it on his own. After all, *he* was the boss, and the boss makes the hard calls. Practically speaking though, Bo might come in handy if there was trouble. Of course, he was infamous for generating a lot of it on his own. *Time for a lie.*

"See here now, you're a big ol' dude. Likely to get spotted. Whereas I can sneak in there undetected." Before Bo could argue, Smitty added, "Plus I need a wheelman. Once I plant the dope, there's a good chance we'll have to hightail it out."

After a moment of pondering, Bo turned back again, this time looking less agitated. "Where do I drop you off?"

Smitty studied the encampment where portable light towers illuminated the interior. But he noticed that the periphery was scantily lit. Between the cover provided by the mesquite brush, and the mechanical buzz of a few electric generators to mask his footsteps, he felt confident he could make a stealthy approach.

"Okay, Bo, pull up by that old frac pit to the east of the camp. There's a big berm where you can park and won't be seen."

Bo nodded in approval of their hideout. "Sure you can sneak in without getting busted?"

Great question. But Smitty knew he needed to keep Bo on board, lest he doubt the plan and want to come along. "Ah, hell, you know how them hippies are." He shot a grin. "Ones who ain't already asleep are probably stoned or tripping on acid. Hell, they see me strolling through camp, they're liable to think I'm the Mad Hatter or an Oompa Loompa. Won't pay me much mind."

Bo roared with laughter and slapped his knee. "Stupid hippies."

Smitty doubted Bo even got either the *Alice in Wonderland* or Willy Wonka references, but he could always count on him for a good laugh at the protesters' expense. With buy-in from his partner, it was time to psych himself up. While he hated the idea of framing anyone, even if it would all be swept under the rug, there was a part of Smitty that felt like he was doing a good deed by ridding the Texas Panhandle of the Austin interlopers, ecoterrorists or not.

Hardworking men and women around here needed the jobs that the oil industry provided them. Roughnecks, roustabouts, and even old dozer drivers like him had bills to pay. All the way down to the damn taco truck driver, lives depended on rigs running and the compressor stations and pipelines in full operation. But knowing that didn't remedy the lump in his throat.

Deep down, Smitty knew there was a good chance that he could ruin some lives if things didn't go according to the sheriff's plan. And one of those lives may very well be his own.

• • •

AS SMITTY SNUCK UP AROUND the backside of the encampment, he picked his approach carefully. It was dark, quiet, and peaceful as he tiptoed through the snow. The big question was where to stash the herion so it wouldn't be detected before the sheriff's raid. It had to be obvious enough to be found by a deputy, but not so blatant it would raise suspicion from a passerby.

Creeping closer for a better view, Smitty took cover behind a clump of mesquite, careful to keep quiet and stay low. He bent to a knee behind some brush, about twenty yards from the camp perimeter, did another sweep, and found a good spot. An Igloo cooler that was half-jutting out from beneath a nearby tent would allow easy access and a ready escape. He had just eased the backpack of dope off his shoulder when he felt the press of cold steel on the nape of his neck.

"Easy there, friend." Smitty eased his hands up. "I'm not armed." It wasn't a lie. Right before departing the truck, he'd stowed his Cabot Diablo 1911 pistol under the front seat. "Let me explain why I'm here," he continued. "Think we can work something out."

That was one of those things people just said because it sounds good and bought a little time.

In a quiet but commanding voice the gunman ordered, "Hand over that bag. Nice and slow."

Smitty dropped the backpack in the snow, careful not to make any sudden moves. Out of the corner of his eye, he saw the guy grab the backpack and unzip it. As he rummaged around, a lightbulb went off in Smitty's head. His only way out of this crime was to confess to a lesser one.

"Look, I wasn't forcing nothing on no one. Just have the stuff if anybody wants it, that's all."

The guy pulled the gun away, circled around, and stared at Smitty for a few seconds. "You work for Vicky Kaiser, right?"

Dressed in Marmot and Black Diamond cold weather gear, the gunman looked better suited for the Iditarod than a picket line. He had a bushy brown beard, barrel chest, and wide shoulders. And it was also obvious that the dude had some military training given the way he handled his gun, and how he'd snuck up without making a sound.

Big question was where he had received that training and why was he using it out there.

Smitty also noticed that the guy had a darker tinge to his skin and spoke with a slight French inflection. He knew it from having worked with French Canadians doing seismic work in North Dakota a few years back. He could even do a passable impression with just the right amount of booze.

Wanting to build on the confusion of the moment, Smitty doubled down with a little misdirection to take the focus off himself. "Look here, buddy, it was *your* people that came to us. Not the other way around."

"What people?" Frenchy looked stumped. "Who came to you?"

"A man and a woman." Smitty shrugged. "Didn't give any names. Married couple, I think. You got any of those around here? Ain't no biggie, man. Just some folks looking to party."

Frenchy didn't answer.

Smitty pointed at the backpack. "Told one of my ranch hands they were looking for something a little harder than what you got at the camp." The overpowering stank of some skunky weed wafting from the camp helped his creativity. "Ain't no judgment on my end."

"Your employee is wrong." Frenchy tossed a strap over his shoulder. "No one from here."

"Yeah, but they told my guy they were looking to score. That's why I came. Somebody's gonna be real . . . disappointed if they don't get what they asked for."

Frenchy glanced back at the camp, as if looking for the culprits. "Just stay the hell away or I'll call the law."

Smitty resisted a chuckle. If Frenchy only knew about *the law* around there, he wouldn't be making any threats. They'd be packing their asses up and heading back to Austin before they ended up in a West Texas gulag run by Sheriff Crowley.

"Don't want no trouble." Smitty feigned worry. "Just give me my bag and we're all good."

Frenchy stood firm. "Don't worry, I'll dispose of it."

Smitty could already feel Bo's wrath for having botched the operation. "Uh . . . that ain't exactly mine to give away."

"Time to go." Frenchy raised the barrel and aimed it at Smitty's head. "Am I not clear?"

Smitty didn't answer, just pivoted on a dime, took off in a sprint, and ducked into the brush. While he may have had reservations about Cosmic Order and their connection to violence, this encounter had him rethinking a few things. Between the explosions, bellicosity, and tactical Frenchy packing a submachine gun, something about this group sure as hell didn't add up.

23

Garrett didn't want to believe that his son was in any real danger, but the lack of response at such a late hour was one for the books. It wasn't unheard-of for Asadi to go out and check on the horses in the middle of the night, particularly with a storm coming in. But that would only take a few minutes. The fact that the boy wasn't answering meant that something could be wrong.

Garrett hated waking Lacey, but the good news was that she understood. It was a lot to ask if she could go to the house and check on him, but she loved Asadi just like he was her own. The mother hen in her would also want to make sure he was safe.

Meanwhile, Butch and Grace were busy blabbing in the back, and Kai seemed generally distracted in the passenger seat. He was probably trying to figure out how to explain to his cohorts that he had willingly left with the people who had torn down their tent and started banging away with a .357 Magnum before tearing out of their camp like a bat out of hell.

As Garrett pulled up to what was left of the pipeline, he wondered if they'd find any clues at all. There wasn't much left by the fire trucks but a smoldering crater. He parked the truck about thirty yards out, keeping the beams aimed at the twisted mass of iron jutting from the trench.

Garrett turned to face Butch and Grace. "Kai and I will run out and take a look."

Buch gazed out at the muddy disaster scene. "Take a look at what? It's a total mess."

"Truth be told, I don't think we'll find a damn thing now. But since we're here, might as well try."

Butch turned to his daughter. "Anything you want to see?"

Grace rose a little, looked out at the mud and the sloshy snow, and then scrunched her nose. "Christian Louboutin would *literally* kill me if I went out in that."

Garrett had no idea who Kristen Looney Tune was or why she'd care if his sister inspected the pipeline, but it was good news to him. He hopped out and slammed the door before anyone changed their minds. It was a lot better option than having Joseph McCarthy and Margaret Thatcher along for the hike, nonstop grilling Kai over why he'd joined the *Red Menace*.

As they marched in near lockstep to ground zero, Garrett turned to Kai. "Thanks for coming along. Appreciate any help I can get."

Despite his supposed willingness to assist, Garrett had to wonder if his old friend was there in order to keep an eye on him. Even worse, he wondered if Kai had only come along to lead him down a cold trail. He wouldn't be the first criminal in history to offer up his services with the intention of throwing off the investigation with false theories or by destroying evidence.

Kai lowered his voice. "Didn't seem like your dad or sister were too eager to join us."

"It's a long story with those two."

Kai gave a nod. "Had a falling-out, I take it."

Garrett wondered how Kai had nailed it on the first try. "How'd you know?"

"Oh, I just recognized the signs. It's clear they'd gone separate ways. Drifted apart. And now they're trying to find each other again. Me and my parents had issues when I got back."

Garrett didn't have to ask where he'd come back from because he already knew it was Afghanistan. And Kai wasn't the only one who was still struggling. "What was the problem?"

"Nothing I can put my finger on, really. It was just like . . . when

I got out of the Army everything was different. My time downrange was somewhere between the worst experience of my life and the only place I felt normal. Hard to explain."

Garrett couldn't help but smile. They were finding their common ground. "No explanation needed. Had the same situation at first. That's why I had to throw myself into something else. I went to college and started a new career. Stayed on the move for years and did everything I could to not look back."

"Lucky for you, there was something to take its place. Life in war zones is toxic but addictive. As much as I dreaded returning, I was just as antsy to leave the second I got home."

"I hear you," Garrett agreed. "Had to keep myself busy during the downtime. I was always hunting and fishing, riding horses. Idle hands and all that, you know."

"Yeah, well, I found a few less healthy hobbies."

Garrett needed no further explanation on that either. Kai wasn't his only old friend to turn to drugs, alcohol, or both. "What'd you do to turn it around?"

"Started doing exactly what you saw me doing earlier."

Garrett thought he'd take a stab at a joke. "*What?* Rioting?"

Kai coughed out what seemed to be a genuine laugh. "Environmental causes."

"Doesn't seem like a bad way to spend your time. Assuming everything's on the up-and-up."

Garrett felt like he was making progress with Kai and didn't want to kill the momentum, but if Cosmic Order was into some bad things, then he needed to know. Members of the group had damaged his pickup, attacked him outside of their encampment, and held him at gunpoint.

It didn't mean they were saboteurs, but they weren't sitting around making daisy chains and knitting *chullo* beanies either. They *were* dangerous. The question was *how* dangerous.

Garrett continued, "I guess what I'm getting at is that even if your organization wasn't responsible for these explosions, it condones violence."

"*Resistance,*" Kai corrected. "Not violence. There's a big difference in seeking to hurt others and standing up for what you believe in. Laying your life on the line."

"So, it's a *one man's terrorist is another man's freedom fighter* kind of deal. Is that it?"

Kai seemed to ponder a moment on his response. If he agreed, then he was essentially admitting that his group was capable of taking their actions to the next level. Which wouldn't necessarily help in making the case that they were innocent.

"Look, Garrett, these people found me when I was at my worst and gave me a purpose. You remember my love of the mountains. The outdoors. They helped me find that passion again."

"Nothing wrong with a passion for the outdoors. Guilty of that myself. Becomes another matter when innocent people start getting hurt."

"We never hurt anyone." Kai seemed to get lost in his thoughts for a moment before adding softly, "And who's really innocent anymore?"

Garrett empathized with his old friend, but he couldn't allow that last remark to go unchecked. "Well, you may not believe it but I'm glad you found meaning in your life. Just so long as your purpose doesn't conflict with mine. The whole *ends justify the means* thing goes only so far in my book."

Kai stopped a few feet ahead of the crater and turned to Garrett, looking exasperated. "Told you we didn't do it. Believe me or not, I don't care."

Garrett thought about pushing it further, but opted against it, lest he push Kai away and get no more intel at all. There was a temptation to ask how Cosmic Order had made it up there so fast. It seemed like somebody knew something in advance. Of course, groups like these were connected to environmental organizations with powerful lobbyists, who could've gotten wind of the pipeline expansion project through a sympathetic politician or environmental agency staffer.

For now, though, he needed evidence. But any that might have ever existed was buried under six inches of sludge. Garrett took out a flashlight, clicked it on, and aimed the beams out into the darkness. "Let's get a look at the perimeter. Maybe we can see some tracks coming in." He marched out ahead, hearing the quick squish of Kai's hiking boots in the mud behind him.

A rattle from ahead stopped Garrett in his tracks. He threw up his hand. "You hear that?"

Kai, who had immediately halted at the nonverbal command, didn't answer, just pointed in the direction of a second sound that was more of a metal *clank*. "Over there," he whispered.

Garrett turned right and shined his beams across a swath of dark pasture, resting momentarily on clumps of mesquite and then moving on until spotting a shimmer. A closer look revealed a white Dodge Ram, nestled to the side of a dirt pile that was nearly as big as the truck.

Garrett turned to Kai. "See anyone inside it?"

Kai shook his head. "Maybe it was just the wind rattling a can in the back bed or something."

Garrett stared a moment longer, focusing on the cab. It was difficult to make out anything in the dark, given the distance, which looked to be about thirty yards out. On any other occasion, he wouldn't have given the abandoned truck a second thought. It wouldn't be the first to break down in a pasture. But with everything going on, he figured that this one was worth a look.

They kept on the march, albeit more cautiously, taking softer steps and keeping their eyes locked on the truck. About fifteen yards from the pickup, Kai stopped abruptly.

"Hold up." He put his index finger to his lips. "Think I hear it running."

Garrett strained to hear it too, but between the howl of the wind and the ringing of his ears from years behind a gun, his hearing wasn't as keen as it used to be. "What you got, man?"

"It is." Kai leaned his right ear toward the Ram. "Engine's running, I think."

Again, Garrett didn't want to jump to any conclusions. Maybe someone from the emergency fire crew had volunteered to camp out to keep an eye out for reignition of the flames. With that reasoning playing out in his mind, he handed the flashlight to Kai, and then pulled the Nighthawk from its holster. "Wasn't it Ronald Reagan who said, *trust but verify?*"

He had just let the pistol dangle by his side when the diesel engine snarled and the truck lurched forward. Kai bolted right, just as the Ram sped up. With its massive grille guard dead ahead, Garrett set his stance, raised the pistol, and cracked three rounds into the windshield.

Despite the counteroffensive, the engine block still loomed larger and closer, and when the truck swerved right, Garrett dove left. The Ram raced by, narrowly missing him. He scrambled to his feet, took aim, but held his fire. The Dodge was already on the county road and tearing ass out of there. All that remained was the red glow of dust in the taillights.

Kai dashed up and ran the flashlight beams over Garrett. "You okay? You hit?"

Garrett looked down at himself. "Thank God, no. Missed me by an inch." He batted the powder from his coat and blue jeans and looked up at Kai. "How about you?"

Kai patted himself down too. "Nah, I'm good."

"Doesn't give me much." Garrett kept his eyes trained on the road. "But it at least confirms my hunch that something's going on."

Kai smiled. "And it *should* confirm something else."

"Confirms that it's not you, I guess."

"Also confirms that you need me around."

"Need you?" Garrett shot Kai a curious glare. "Why do you say that?"

A cocky smile rose on Kai's face. "Because I bet you didn't get that license plate."

24

Kim had expected Faraz to wait for her until she climbed out the window, but he was already way ahead, dashing across the flat roof to the ramparts on the far side of the balcony. She stopped to inspect her surroundings, nervous about what might be lurking in the night's shadows. But as far as she could tell there was nothing dangerous out there—so long as she wasn't counting the unmanned PKM belt-fed machine gun at an opening in the wall by the parapet.

There were a few scattered chairs against the iron railing to the left and a windowless wall to the right. The floor was littered with cigarette butts and dozens of spent cartridges that had certainly been a by-product of the PKM. Unfortunately, the crew-served weapon was way too heavy for a quick escape, especially with the 100-round ammo box attached to its tripod.

As Kim eased along the deck, she glanced at the inner walls of the desert fortress, noting that it looked exactly like the kind of place that belonged to a heroin trafficker. With this in mind, Kim took extra care to locate any guards atop the outside walls. What little illumination she could see by was coming from windows inside the mansion or from security floodlights.

Kim moved to Faraz, who was focused on something over the edge of the bulwark. She skirted around a pile of rolled-up prayer rugs and peered over also, finding five parked vehicles. There were two white Toyota pickups, a red one, and a black BMW X7 SUV. Given the remote location, on top of the fact that no one would be foolish enough to steal from a drug lord, she assumed the keys would be left inside and probably in the ignition.

Faraz's face lit up. "I'll get the wheels. You get the old man."

Spying an iron fire escape ladder, Kim began to move. "Come on. This way."

After making her way down the rungs, Kim gave a quick look around to find the courtyard empty. It was near sunrise, which meant most of the traffickers were still asleep. But there would have to be one or two on guard. She made a quick dash to the BMW to find the keys where she suspected, and what looked to be Ozzy's UZI PRO submachine gun lying in the passenger seat.

Kim opened the door, killed the cabin light, and grabbed the gun. "Come to mama."

Faraz zipped up from behind and eyed the weapon. "When do we go?"

Kim moved from the driver's seat. "Wait in here." She glanced at the compound. "Hopefully, I can sneak in unseen." She turned to Faraz. "But if I can't, you'll know pretty quick."

Faraz took her place behind the wheel and looked up. "What do you mean, *I'll know?*"

Kim unfolded the stock on the UZI, clicked it into place, and looked down at the Trijicon red dot atop the Picatinny rail. "You hear shooting, crank the engine, and put it in drive. Just be ready to haul ass the second you see us come out the front door. We'll be in a dead sprint."

Faraz just stared straight ahead. "And if you don't make it out?"

"Then disappear, Faraz. Get out of here as quick as you can and don't look back."

Kim wanted to say something meaningful, to tell him there was so much more in life. And most importantly, she wanted to remind him about Asadi. But she kept her mouth shut.

It wasn't just a factor of time. Which she was losing by the second. It was the note of finality. That message would be too close to parting words. And she wasn't quite ready for that.

Feeling dark desperation sweep over her, Kim jacked in a round, braced the UZI's stock to her shoulder, and sprinted to a side door. She tested the knob, found it locked, then moved on. Coming up to a corner, she peeked around to an open courtyard with an empty swimming pool. Kim pulled back immediately as a floodlight flashed on overhead.

Given the timing, she knew it was only triggered by a sensor, but that wouldn't matter to an inquisitive guard. Back flush against the wall, Kim held her breath and counted to ten, but the only sound that followed was the chatter and crowd noise from a televised soccer match. Another quick glance and Kim rushed to the next entrance.

A turn of the knob and this time it clicked. Ever so gently, she pushed the door and made her way inside, cringing as the hinges screeched and whined. With just enough light coming through the window from the beams outside, Kim brought the gun to her shoulder and eased down the dim corridor. A few twists and turns and she finally recognized a stairwell by the kitchen.

Kim moved through the staff dining area until reaching the storeroom. Breathing a sigh of relief that the area was unguarded, she moved to it and turned the dead bolt. Another quick listen yielded no detectable sound but the hum of a large refrigerator in the far corner of the room. Feeling her spirits rise as her plan was working, Kim lowered the barrel of her UZI before opening the door. She entered the storeroom, shocked to find that Bayat was actually standing.

"Come on," she whispered. "Faraz has a car. He's waiting for us."

Bayat shot her a weak smile and said in a raspy voice, "Knew you could do it."

"We have to move fast. Can you walk on your own?"

Bayat gave a solid nod, but his face told her otherwise. It would be all he could do to move at all, let alone quickly. Kim wanted to help him, but she needed to keep vigilant with her weapon as she led them through the house. She had just taken his hand into hers and got him on the move when the sound of voices echoed from the back entrance.

Kim closed and locked the storeroom door behind Bayat, then made an about-face and followed him. When she was certain he could keep up, she advanced ahead, leading them back out the same way she'd come in. When they'd finally reached the outside, Kim tripped the spotlight again by accident, triggering the sound of frantic voices.

"*Dammit!*" Kim pointed to the opening in the perimeter wall where the vehicles were kept, and whispered to Bayat, "That way! Through that entrance! Faraz is waiting on the other side."

"Wait." Bayat grabbed her sleeve. "Where are you going?"

"Just going to slow these guys down a little." With Bayat looking hesitant to leave her behind, she pulled away and gave him a gentle push. "I'm right behind you, now go!"

Reluctantly, Bayat shuffled off, stumbling the first few steps. He oriented himself with a quick glance around and then veered in the right direction. Kim turned back to the entrance to find the barrel of a Makarov pistol gliding past the threshold.

There was no waiting to see the whites of his eyes. She pulled the trigger and let her rip with a full-auto burst that tore into a gunman who crumpled to the floor. A quick left pivot and she took off in a sprint to the front of the compound. Every agonizing second covering the wide-open space she expected to take a bullet, but she made it to the wall without hearing a shot.

A swing around the opening to hook right and dash for the BMW was stopped short when she saw the empty parking place. Kim didn't know which was more heartbreaking, the fact that Faraz had abandoned them the second he had the chance or the forlorn look on Bayat's face.

Kim wanted to hate Asadi's brother for what he'd done but couldn't bring herself to do it. He wasn't born bad. He was just too far gone—a pure result of her failure to find him sooner.

25

bout a half hour into the trek Asadi realized he'd made a really bad call. At this point, he couldn't return to Savanah and Duke, but he felt no closer to reaching the Mescalero runway and hangar. The never-ending rows of snow-covered dunes had exhausted him completely. He trudged up one, only to find another. And then another. And then another.

There was at least a sensation of comfort and safety when reaching a peak, visible to the world again, versus the trough where he felt isolated. But neither crest nor valley provided any relief from the howling wind.

Ascending to the top of a mammoth hill, Asadi glanced around, realizing he had lost his sense of direction. He leaned over and massaged his aching thighs, wondering how much more he had to give. A part of him wanted to keep pushing, but Garrett had taught him enough about wilderness survival to know that doing nothing was sometimes the wiser option.

He was burning up his precious energy reserves, possibly for no good reason, and could feel the perspiration building inside his coat. Given the extreme cold, moisture was one of his worst enemies. On top of that, he was starting to feel the burn of dehydration. There was plenty of snow with which to hydrate, but his dad always told him not to eat it unless absolutely necessary.

Eating snow might quench his thirst but it would also bring

down his core temperature. At the moment, exposure was a much greater threat.

Asadi was tempted to stop and sit when a quick flash of light caught his eye. He drew a bead on the beam and was back on the move, dipping and diving, as he raced between and over a half-dozen more sandhills before finding only darkness again. He huffed and puffed, filling his burning lungs with more frigid air, wondering if what he'd witnessed was an optical illusion.

About to turn around again in another of what he suspected would be a useless search for anything but the nothingness of an icy wasteland, Asadi saw the flicker. This time it was much brighter, which meant he was getting close. He took off toward the light and ran down the hill. Ignoring the burn in his calves, he moved faster, and pushed down the incline.

Asadi was nearly at the bottom when his left foot landed in a divot, his ankle went vertical, and a sharp pain radiated through his body. Knocked off kilter, he tipped forward and somersaulted into the trough between the dunes. He rose and dusted off the snow, but a good bit of powder had found its way inside his coat.

A slow look up and ahead revealed some devastating news. The source of the light wasn't from the jet hangar as he'd hoped, or even a farmhouse. It came from an oilfield tank battery. It was at least a landmark, which gave him some comfort. But there'd be nothing there to help. So, Asadi pushed forward, favoring his right ankle just a little as he tramped through the snow.

Each step resulted in his boot tightening, which meant his foot was starting to swell. But he trudged on ahead toward the flood-light on the oil pad. A painful march onto the caliche pad revealed four tan-colored storage tanks, each about thirty feet high. An iron staircase led to the top, where a scaffolding ran the length of the battery.

In the middle of it all was a large pumpjack, stationary at the moment, and a few iron appurtenances on the outskirts of the site. Everything was covered in ice, or a frosty white glaze. A sign in front of the tanks revealed that it was a Mescalero Energy well. The fact that it was designated Boone 9-2H meant something to someone but certainly not to him.

Asadi moved to the stairwell and limped to the top for a better look around. Again, there was nothing to see but an endless sea of sandhills. Spying an oil field road coming in at the far side of the pad, he decided his best chance was to hike his way out. It was still a gamble, especially with a twisted ankle, but he'd at least have an end goal.

Psyching himself up for what was certain to be a miserable journey, Asadi took a deep breath, blew hot air into his hands, and latched on to the iron rail. The first three steps went fine, but on the fourth his boot heel hit an ice patch beneath the snow and sent both feet flying.

If the railing had been dry, he could've caught himself on the way down, but his momentum was too great. It ripped his hands from the bar and his body went into a free-fall slide. With each jarring step, he reached for the balusters, but they were just too slick to offer support. Asadi kicked out wide and his boots caught the posts beneath the railing and halted his descent.

The jarring stop saved him from tumbling but resulted in a loud *pop* from his busted ankle. His shriek was a combo of the ache of the injury and the terrifying plummet. If anybody had been there to witness the fall or especially the scream, Asadi would've been absolutely humiliated. But as luck would have it, he was alone.

Of course, Asadi didn't feel lucky at all. And his attempt to stand was met with an even harsher reality than embarrassment. The ache from his tailbone was surpassed by the throbbing inside his boot. A year or two prior and Asadi would have been tempted to cry. But Garrett had told him there was a time for *reflection* and a time for *action*. And with that in mind, he fell back on the wilderness survival training passed down from his dad, the former Green Beret.

Asadi's plan to help Savanah would have to be put on hold. Shelter, fire, signaling, and first aid were his priorities now. But knowing what he needed to do and actually doing it were two different things. The only resources he had to work with were a lot of rock, some tanks full of oil, and a whole bunch of steel. And with a blizzard approaching, he had to move fast.

26

Mario had made it perfectly clear to Kim that he would never return to Afghanistan. It wasn't that he was afraid, although there was much there to fear. It was a self-imposed exile, some derivation of the adage *you can never go home again.* Between his time as a SEAL and the CIA, he'd put down roots and made life-long friends. Many of which had not survived.

For the sake of his own sanity, Mario, like many others in the military and intelligence communities, had compartmentalized that part of his life. But not everyone had apparently sectioned off the desertion—hence the muzzle of a battered M4 carbine pointed at his face.

Mario had expected this might be a possibility and offered no reaction but an easy smile. "Well, that's a helluva greeting, Billy. Thought you said you'd help."

"Said we'd meet." Billy flashed a grin also. "Didn't say what would happen when we did."

It was a fair point. They had only agreed on a location and noth-ing more. Now, Mario was held captive within the crumbling walls of a bombed-out shack, in some dusty village near the Tajik border. But for a few bleating goats and some ancient-looking dirt farmers in filthy turbans, there was nothing in this lonesome outpost but the dark feel of a dying community.

Mario couldn't help but think that it was as good a spot for an ad hoc execution as it was for a secret rendezvous. And at the moment, it was about fifty-fifty as to which way it would go. He'd disarmed when he'd arrived, leaning his Noveske rifle in the corner of the room as a gesture of goodwill. The four former Afghan paramilitary officers surrounding him had not reciprocated.

The man aiming the M4 at him was named Hakeem Sarbani. But he was simply known to everyone as "Billy" because of the uncanny similarities in looks and demeanor to Billy Sole, the legendary Native American tracker from Arnold Schwarzenegger's 1987 action movie *Predator*. This former Afghan commando, with high cheekbones and muscled arms, basically still looked the same. But his long black hair was now streaked silver.

"Had you on the list," Mario replied quietly. "All you had to do was get on that *damn* plane."

"And leave my wife and kids behind?"

When the U.S. abandoned Afghanistan, Billy was left with two horrible options: get on a jet alone or stick around and hope for the best. For the specialized units helping the CIA, the option to Mario was clear. Get the hell out of there while you could and come back for your family later. But this was coming from a guy with no special attachments beyond drinking buddies.

Mario raised his hands to his sides. "I don't make the rules. If I did, there'd be nothing left of the Taliban but a bad memory. But I worked my ass off to get our guys out of here. And risked my life to do it. So did Kim. None of this was fair. But that's just the way it is."

Mario had known Billy to be a to-the-point kind of guy. As a leader in one of the most elite Afghan National Strike Units, known by their code name *Kiowas*, he had seen his share of combat alongside CIA paramilitary officers and U.S. Special Operations Forces. More than a few of these squads had a bad reputation for vicious night raids and civilian deaths.

This distinctive force, in tiger stripe camo like their forerunners in the Phoenix Program back in Vietnam, evoked terror in their adversaries. Acting as intelligence gatherers and assassins, these hit squads took a notable toll on the Taliban, Al Qaeda, and ISIS-K.

They were warriors to the bone, and vicious as hell, providing security in Kabul in the last days before it fell. But it takes a monster to kill a monster. And the Kiowas were the fighters the Taliban feared the most.

Billy's eyes blazed with hatred. "They killed my wife. My sons. My baby girl. They took *everything* from me. Even when I offered myself in exchange."

Mario didn't have to ask who he meant by *they*. Badri 313 had tracked down and murdered dozens of members from the Kiowa unit. The group was the Taliban's Special Operations Forces (SOF). While they were well trained and equipped like most traditional Western SOF units, operators within this group were only allowed to join if they agreed to be martyrs. They were even connected to the Haqqani Network, which meant strong ties to Al Qaeda.

"You want to find their killers, Billy? I can help you with that."

"Your broken promises are how I ended up in exile. Like a stray dog. Living off garbage."

Mario took a moment to gather his thoughts. "You want an apology?" With no answer in response, he continued. "Okay, you can have one. And you deserve one. I'm sorry for you and your family. And for what happened to your country. For everything. To be honest, I don't even know what *not* to apologize for at this point."

There was a moment when it looked like Billy might pull the trigger. But if Mario had learned anything about the man over the years, it was that he was not prone to rash decisions. The former team leader was calculating. Icy. He wouldn't make a move without a plan. And despite the abandonment, Mario knew Billy would never fully blame him for what happened.

They'd bled together and bonded over a mutual hatred of totalitarians. Although he'd never experienced it personally growing up in Puerto Rico, Mario's grandparents on his father's side had fled Cuba when Fidel Castro came to power. Stories of their imprisonment, torture, and execution of family members who didn't make it out were etched into every fiber of his being. And because of this, Mario knew just what to say.

"Look, Billy, I can't give you back what you've lost. And I won't pretend that I can. But what I can offer is a chance to reconcile. Put all this behind you."

"Are you kidding me?" Billy looked at him with an expression that fell somewhere between curiosity and rage. "Do you really think I could ever forgive the Taliban after what they've done?"

Mario shook his head. "I'm not talking about them. I'm talking about coming to an understanding with God."

It was clear that Billy was a shattered man. But he wasn't just beaten down by broken promises or authoritarian rule. He was a man who'd banked on the fact that *the Almighty* would reward the righteous, and now he felt betrayed. Mario's offer wouldn't bring back Billy's family or change a damn single thing. Working for the CIA again, however, would give him a significant advantage over his enemies. *Vengeance* was there for the taking.

"Don't need permission," Billy countered. "We can take revenge anytime we want."

"That's right," Mario conceded. "You don't need our blessing. But to make it count, to really make it hurt, you need our intel. Names. Addresses. Vulnerabilities. Travel patterns. We still keep tabs on all the high-level leadership. You help deliver what we need and it's all yours."

Billy gave a slow nod of understanding. "Okay then. We have a deal."

"Not so fast." Mario wagged his finger. "You have something for me?"

"Yeah, I know who took Kim. And I know where she's being held."

Mario resisted the urge to let out a sigh of relief. "Can we get her back?"

"We can," Billy affirmed. "But it won't be easy. A lot of people will get in the way."

Mario knew exactly what that meant. It was Billy's not-so-subtle way of saying that the toll of human lives would be a large one. It also meant that he was going to have to look the other way on how they got the job done. The Kiowas had barely followed rules of engagement before the Americans had pulled out. Now that the gloves were off, it was going to get ugly.

Despite the remoteness of their location, Mario could get weapons. "What kind of opposition are we looking at? Just tell me what we're up against and I'll make sure we've got the tools."

All of a sudden, it was starting to feel like old times again. He and Billy had planned so many operations together they could do it in their sleep. The problem was that they no longer owned the battlespace, which limited their movement. But there were ways around that.

Billy held up his cell phone. "Got a call from one of our old friends. Told me Kim and two others were taken to a heroin trafficker's compound."

Mario was tempted to ask what this guy was doing now, and how he knew that information, but thought it was better if he didn't know. Many of the guys they'd trained, once loyal to a fault, had found themselves in the drug trade or working for the Taliban. Some had even fallen in with violent Islamic extremist organizations.

Despite their differences, many of the members of the country's indigenous special operations community were still loyal to one another and maintained contact. Mario had always thought it a bit strange. But *that* was Afghanistan. The elite training they'd received from the Americans set them apart from the others. And they were fiercely proud of it.

"Is Kim okay?" Mario asked. "Is she hurt?"

"She and the others are alive, last I heard. Being held just outside of Kunduz."

"Heard from who?" Mario asked.

"Old team member. Guy you didn't know. Works for Akhtar Omar now. One of the biggest drug runners in the country."

"Will your friend help us get Kim back?"

Billy shook his head. "Said they already have plans, which don't include Kim or the others leaving Afghanistan alive."

"Makes no sense," Mario argued. "Why wouldn't they just ransom them to the Taliban?"

"There's a running argument among the traffickers," Billy explained. "Some want to kill them outright to show their loyalty to the regime. Others think they're worth more to the Taliban alive. And a whole other group just wants to sell them to the highest bidder."

Mario perked up. "No higher bidder than Uncle Sam. Call up your guy and tell him we're ready to make a deal."

"Doesn't work like that. Even if we used a surrogate to make the transaction, the Taliban would smell a rat. They look the other way on heroin trafficking, so long as they get their cut. But a deal with the U.S. without approval puts you on the naughty list."

"But you said there were other bidders?"

"ISIS-K. Al Qaeda. A few others who would love to torture and execute a few Americans and post it online. That kind of advertising is priceless."

Mario was confused. "But I thought nobody wanted to cross the Taliban. Wouldn't selling Kim to their enemies do just that?"

"You've been gone too long, my friend. You forget this land is full of zealots. Even some of the traffickers are living the life of jihad. For them, the Taliban is too . . . mainstream. They'd risk it all to make an example of an infidel."

Mario looked into the air for a second or two as he thought through the scenario. "Okay . . . how much time do we have while they make up their minds?"

"Not long." Billy looked grim. "If we're going to go, we need to move now."

Mario had counted on at least a day to get prepped and supplied but they clearly didn't have it. "Okay, I've got money if you can find weapons and transport."

"We already have everything." Billy's eyes went wide. "Been waiting for this moment for a very long time."

His revelation struck Mario in two ways. On the one hand, they needed to move, and Billy's guys were ready to go. *That was a godsend.* On the other, it dawned on him that he'd just recruited a band of well-trained, highly motivated foreign special operatives for his mission. And it was unlikely they'd be content with revenge against those who murdered their families once the job to rescue Kim was over. They'd be satisfied with nothing short of an all-out war.

27

As Garrett drove out to the compressor station with Kai, he was not only on edge after nearly being plowed over by the Dodge Ram, but Lacey's call about Asadi taking the truck to go see Savanah at the Mescalero Ranch didn't help matters any at all. The fact that his son went onto the highway without a driver's license meant that it had to be an emergency. Of course, the definition of *emergency* in the teenage mind could mean many things.

Given the approaching blizzard, there was a good chance that he had gone over to help with the horses, which was fine. But kids can be rash. And it wouldn't be the first time that good intentions had made for some bad mistakes.

For that reason, Garrett had dropped Butch back off at the ranch to tend to their own remuda, and asked Grace to go with Lacey out to the Mescalero barn to check on his son. Now he could focus on the more immediate threat with Kai. As they drove the dark roads, Garrett made small talk before transitioning into investigation mode, crossing over with some good-natured teasing.

"Couldn't help but notice that among the guys kicking the crap out of me earlier, a couple looked like they might've had some military service under their belts."

Kai stifled a snicker. "Three veterans. Served in Iraq and Afghanistan just like us. But no one from Group or Regiment. Just a couple of 11 Bravos from the 82nd who were Ranger qualified. There's also a former HUMINT guy from the 101st."

The fact that there were no others from Army Special Forces or the 75th Ranger Regiment wasn't that surprising. They weren't usually the friend of Mother Nature nonprofit types. But the fact that they had two infantry guys and an Army intelligence collector was interesting. Anyone who wanted to create their own little war could do some damage with skills like that.

Despite his enthusiasm to jump into some deeper questions, Garrett took a moment to stare out his side window at the nothingness of the dark, hoping not to seem too eager. "So, how'd you all find each other?"

Kai turned and squinted. "What do you mean?"

"Seems kind of . . . not so random, I guess."

"Not really. We're all passionate about our beliefs."

"Well, it's just that you're all Army." Garrett shrugged. "What are the odds?"

"Pretty good, I'd say." Kai sounded defensive. "Largest branch of the armed forces."

"That's true," Garrett conceded. "But it just seems like a really small-world kind of a thing since they went to Ranger School. Right? You didn't know them before now?"

"Nah, the Order just sort of discovered us."

"*Discovered?*" Garrett worried he sounded accusatory and tried to lighten the mood. "Kind of makes it sound like you were hidden. Like they found the Dead Sea Scrolls or something?"

"Not hidden," Kai corrected. "Just lost. Wallowing in AA meetings that weren't doing any good. I was living at a halfway house in Denver when they recruited me."

"Halfway house?" Garrett turned off the highway onto a caliche road and the whine of his tires was soon overtaken by the rumble of rock beneath his truck. "What was that all about?"

Kai looked a little sheepish. "Drug stuff mostly. Got busted for a couple of B-and-Es and resisting arrest. Judge took mercy on me since I served."

A single nod came from Garrett. "And the other guys?"

"Same as me. Lived in different places around the country but they were in similar situations. Most of the Order's members have a past. Runaways. Homeless. Mostly all former users."

Garrett didn't want to say it, but the organization sounded less like a group of shepherds and more like a bunch of predators. But who was he to argue with success? If it had taken an environmental cause to give these guys purpose, then good on "the Order."

"And who recruited you?" Garrett pressed, hoping he sounded more like a concerned friend and less like a DEA special agent.

"The guy who brought us on board was from Europe. Originally from France, I think."

"What the hell is he doing over here? Don't they have their own problems?"

"We're dealing with *global* issues." Kai sounded testy in his response. "The Order is based out of Switzerland but has an outreach that extends all over the world."

Before Garrett could follow up, Kai went back to an earlier question. "And we're not all Army, by the way. We've got foreign vets too. In fact, a Frenchman just joined our group. Foreign Legion, in fact. Second Foreign Parachute Regiment."

Garrett perked up, finding the military connection to be a huge point of interest but not wanting to give anything way. As he looked out in front of his headlights, he could tell by the curve in the white rock road that they were nearing the entrance to the Mescalero Ranch near the compressor station. He tapped the brakes to slow his speed, so they could talk a little longer.

"Well, how did this Legionnaire end up on your island of misfit toys? Get himself hooked on baguettes and chardonnay?"

"Nah, Cloutier's all right." Kai chuckled. "No real backstory other than that he's passionate about the cause. Got an email from headquarters a couple weeks ago saying that he was coming."

"Well, you've got the Airborne connection him with him then.

Anyone who willingly chooses to jump out of airplanes for a living is sure to gravitate to others who are just as nuts."

"You'd think, but he doesn't really click with the rest of us. Just kind of keeps to himself."

Garrett could chalk that up to cultural differences. The branches within the armed services were terrible about drawing negative conclusions about the others. Soldiers versus Marines was one thing, but institutional lines between countries was by far even worse. Of course, it was hard to trust a Frenchman under the best of circumstances, so he'd keep the guy on his radar.

Pulling up to the burnt-out Mescalero Compressor Station, Garrett aimed his headlights at the pile of rubble and put the GMC in park. Given the earlier incident with the Dodge Ram, he was fairly convinced that Kai wasn't responsible for the sabotage since the truck had nearly hit them both. But taking no chances, Garrett reached back and pulled the Nighthawk from its holster.

He flung the door open, but before getting out, he turned to Kai and grinned. "Wanna take point?" It was a subtle way of telling his passenger that he was still on probation.

"Sure." Kai smiled back. "I was always better at spotting danger than you were anyhow."

As his new partner marched out ahead, Garrett clicked on the flashlight and pointed it at the charred building. Inside was a hodgepodge of twisted metal and scattered debris.

Garrett panned the beam across the dark perimeter. "Let's hit the outskirts like we did before. Maybe our old friend is out there looking to finish the job."

Kai glanced back. "Do you at least believe it wasn't *me* now?"

Garrett didn't know exactly what to say, and quite frankly he was tired of beating around the bush. "Honestly, I don't know what to think anymore. Clearly, it wasn't you driving that truck. And if it was one of your friends, then he's not a very good one."

"But you still have doubts." Kai stopped midstride, and then turned back. "Why?"

"Because something about the Order just doesn't add up."

Kai let out a huff. "Like what?"

"If I had a clue, I'd tell you. But it's just a feeling that something's off."

Garrett hated to be so vague. And he knew it was frustrating his old friend. But he also knew that deep down Kai would understand. There's a sixth sense that you learn to pay attention to, particularly in war zones. And the former Ranger would get that if there was a *disturbance in the force*, then it was worth paying close attention to it.

"Kai, someone told you all to be up here before the explosions. Don't you find that strange?"

Kai looked frustrated. "Just proves something's going on behind the scenes. Things are happening at the top and they're not letting us in on it."

Garrett could tell Kai's earlier confession that someone somewhere was pulling strings revealed there were at least a few chinks in Cosmic Order's polished armor. "Okay, they're keeping secrets. Have any idea why they would do that?"

"Who knows? No different than when we served, I guess. Commands came down from the gods and we followed them. Even when they made no sense."

"How about the other military guys?" Garrett pressed. "They have the same concerns?"

"Garrett, I can tell by the questions you're asking that you believe there's a connection between the veterans, the Order, the recruitment, and the explosions. But there's not."

Garrett raised his hands, palms out. "But you have to admit that you've got some guys with real skills that can do bad things if they put their minds to it."

"It's *not* them," Kai argued. "They're not to blame."

"Then who is?"

Kai looked into the darkness, even though there was nothing to see. "The guy who recruited us. I don't know. Maybe there's something off about him?"

"Like what?"

"Just a weird feeling." Kai shrugged. "I don't know, man."

"Yeah, you do. What's on your mind?"

When Kai didn't answer, Garrett realized he'd better back off a little and let his friend draw his own conclusions.

"Look, Kai, you've got a Frenchman that joined the group and doesn't fit in. *Shocker.* They eat snails. But to the best of my recollection, it wasn't a Peugeot that nearly laid tire marks down our backs. It was a good ol' American Dodge. So, what else you got?"

Kai shook his head and laughed. "There's nothing else to tell you. I swear."

Garrett was about to ask what was so funny when the phone rang in his pocket. He fished it out to find it was Sheriff Crowley. He held up his palm to Kai, answered the call, and keyed the speaker function. "Got something for me?"

The sheriff sounded as if he was reading from a report. "Plates you gave me came back for a 2024 white Dodge 3500. Think that's your truck?"

Garrett looked to Kai, who nodded in confirmation. "That's it. Who's it registered to?"

The flutter of rustling pages preceded Crowley's answer. "A company vehicle belonging to an oil and gas company out of Odessa called Wolfpack Midstream. That ring a bell?"

In fact, it did strike Garrett as familiar, although he couldn't remember why. Since the recent boom, there were plenty of new operators snooping around the Panhandle. "Let me check."

Garrett typed in the company name on his phone and brought up the website. A quick glance at the home page revealed nothing of interest. It looked no different than any other pipeline company. But toggling over to Wolfpack executive's director's list revealed a potentially big piece of the puzzle. His sister's husband, Ryland Hobbs, was the chairman of the board.

28

Kim wondered if she should have just shot it out to the death. Given the alternative, which included interrogation and torture, there was a certain appeal in just letting the lights go out. But she still had Bayat's life to consider. And because she still maintained an inkling of hope that she could return him to his family back in Texas, she surrendered without a fight.

Kim walked down the concrete steps into the empty swimming pool and looked over at Bayat. It was clear by the look on his face that he had noticed the same thing she had. The drain at the deep end was plugged by a tarpaulin and covered in bricks. Glancing up at the dozen or so gunmen, who had their Kalashnikov rifles trained down from the rim of the pool, Kim shielded her eyes from the glare and spun around to find a video camera mounted on the diving board.

Kim swallowed hard and turned to Bayat, whose eyes were fixed on it too. "I have no idea what's going to happen, but I know it's not good."

Bayat looked down at the tarp and then back to her. "My son, Liam. You knew him well?"

At first, Kim was taken aback by the question, wondering if he was delusional. But then she noticed that Bayat's eyes were no longer empty, as they had been from his months of starvation and interrogation. He was oddly lucid, as if he'd perked up by coming to terms with his fate.

If these were to be their last moments on earth, Kim wanted them to be pleasant ones. "Yes, I did." For his sake, she forced a pleasant smile. "I visited him a few times. His farm is beautiful."

Bayat let out a weak chuckle. "My son is a lot of things. A great engineer. A science wiz. But a country boy, he is not."

Kim looked up again and glanced around the edge of the pool to find the gunmen were gone. She would indulge Bayat with stories of his son, for as long as time would allow. Which she suspected wouldn't be long. "I think Liam might surprise you."

"How so?" Bayat shot her an inquisitive look. "He's never been one for change."

"Well, he's made a few new friends since you were back home. My friend, Garrett, has been helping him get the ranch in shape and take care of the cattle. They even have horses now."

"*Horses?*" Bayat's eyes lit up. "That's my grandson, Wade, for sure. Takes after my wife's side of the family. Cowboys, all of them."

Kim detected a deep pride in Bayat's voice. "Oh yeah, Liam has jumped right in with both feet. Was even wearing a cowboy hat the last time I saw him."

Although Bayat was smiling, his eyes filled with tears. "Would've liked to have seen that."

Kim wanted to say *you still will* but knew better. "He's *made a hand*, I'm told." She shook her head. "Still don't really know what that means, but I guess it's a compliment in Texas."

"A big one." Bayat's eyes brightened. "Means he's come into his own. He's doing all right." A pause proceeded his next words. "Means I should be very proud of him."

"You have every reason to be," Kim assured. "Liam is a good man. A good father."

Sadness came back into Bayat's eyes. "And a good son."

Kim had just draped her arm around Bayat's shoulder when she looked up to find a fifty-gallon drum had been rolled to the edge of the pool. She immediately recognized the colors and markings on the side of the barrel, as belonging to a chain of national gas stations that were scattered about the country. Instinctively, she looked to Bayat, who was fixated on it too.

When a second and third barrel arrived, it was obvious why they were down there. It wasn't enough for them to die. The camera was to capture them being burned alive.

Whether it was supposed to be a warning to the West, homage to the Taliban, or a plain old act of cruelty, Kim didn't know. But her knees got weak as her mind swam in visions of what unthinkable horror and blinding pain was soon to come.

"Let's not go quietly." Bayat grabbed her hand and squeezed. "Let's make them earn it."

Kim gave a nod and turned to the gunman at the steps. "That's the only way out."

He seemed to have anticipated their thinking, shouldered his Kalashnikov, and barked something in Dari that neither of them understood. Kim suspected the traffickers had not gone to all this trouble for nothing, and any attempt to escape would be met with the butt of a rifle instead of a bullet to the head. But she'd prefer to be unconscious if consumed by fire.

Kim gave Bayat's palm a couple of squeezes to let him know it was time, but before they could move, a commotion up top grabbed her attention. One by one, the drums were laid over on their sides and the contents sloshed into the deep end of the pool. It only took a moment for the sweet benzene smell of gasoline to waft past, burning her nostrils. She had just turned for the stairs when the rattle of automatic weapons fire sounded out from above.

Kim expected to feel either the rip of bullets into her back or the blister of burning gas but was instead met with the *thunk* and *flop* of dead bodies on concrete, and the simultaneous *clang* and *clatter* of rifles landing inside the pool. For a moment, the shooting intensified, then dropped to an occasional *pop-pop* that echoed against the concrete.

Slowly, the moans of the dying subsided, and all that was left was a gurgle of gasoline as it poured from the last drum. Kim helped Bayat up the steps to find that any gunmen who hadn't been cut down and fallen inside the pool was lying around it. Their bodies were bloodied and twisted, riddled with bullet holes from head to toe.

Kim cupped a hand over her eyes, given the harsh light, and made a complete circle on the last step. Scanning the top of the mansion's roof, she stopped short at the sight of a man behind the trigger of the PKM machine gun—the one on the parapet she'd seen during their escape.

Kim thought for a moment that it might be the English speaker, Ozzy. But she was in for an even greater surprise. Their savior, in this moment, looked more like his brother than he ever had before. As it turned out, Faraz wasn't too far gone after all.

29

As Lacey Capshaw pulled her silver Chevy Traverse up to the Mescalero barn, she looked through her icy windshield at the horse training facility. At a glance, she saw Butch's pickup and a John Deere Gator, but Asadi and Savanah were nowhere to be found. Per Garrett's request, she had brought along Grace, who had sat mostly in stoic silence the entire trip over.

Lacey had only known Grace in passing from years ago, so she had welcomed the opportunity to get to know the woman who could potentially be her sister-in-law. It also gave Lacey a chance to do a little digging into why Grace had suddenly popped back up on the scene after all these years. Her woman's intuition had kicked into overdrive.

Garrett and his dad were fairly street smart, but they were too ready to forgive and forget. And something told Lacey that the return of their long-lost relative had more to do with a chance at making big money on a pipeline deal than it did with mending fences. But she'd not mention that to anyone, least of all Butch. She hadn't seen him this happy since Asadi joined the family.

Lacey squinted and craned her neck forward as she drove around the grounds on the periphery of the barn for any sign of activity. "See anyone yet?"

Grace gave it a passing glance, seemingly uninterested. "You know how kids are. Probably just lost track of time. I'm sure they'll turn up."

As a mother of two, Lacey wanted to tell Grace that the idea of kids just *turning up* wasn't all that comforting. But she kept that to herself for the sake of maintaining goodwill. At this point, she was just glad Garrett's sister said anything. She hadn't necessarily been rude on the car ride over but she did seem a bit cold, maybe even distracted.

Lacey made a U-turn and drove back up to the barn entrance. She pulled her SUV in between Vicky's white Range Rover and the Gator and put it in park. She reached for the door handle but stopped short before getting out and looked back at Grace. "Is everything okay with you?"

Grace turned to Lacey, looking a little startled. "Of course, why do you ask?"

There was that insecure part of Lacey that remembered how she had been ostracized by high society when her family lost all their wealth. Her dad was once a successful oilman who went bankrupt while she was in college. Overnight, she'd lost everything, including her father, who took the loss of his company so hard that he ended his life. In a way, Lacey's life had ended too.

The world of money and prestige that she had grown accustomed to was gone. She was a Tri-Delt studying art history at TCU one moment and a college dropout the next. And with that Lacey and her mother went from the elite inner circles to the bottom of the social barrel. It made her wonder if Garrett's sister thought she was beneath them.

Little did Grace know, nor anyone else with the exception of Vicky, that the Capshaw family retained the lower unexplored zones beneath their old ranch. They may have lost the surface property, but they'd retained mineral rights in the deeper formations. And Mescalero Energy had just made her a most generous offer, which included a multimillion-dollar oil and gas lease.

The tides had turned for Lacey and her mother. And that meant they had turned in a major way for Garrett too. She just didn't know how to break it to him. While any *normal* person would be thrilled with the news of impending wealth, she wasn't so sure that he would feel the same. Her boyfriend was wildly independent, self-reliant, and proud. It was a quality she both loved and hated about her man.

Garrett was doing okay financially, but he still owed Vicky for getting him out of debt. A joint operating agreement (JOA) between Savage Exploration and Mescalero Energy on the Capshaw field would be huge. And if she and Garrett got married, then he'd further benefit from her lease bonus money and royalties. The bottom line was that he and Asadi would be set for life.

Lacey mustered up the courage to lay her cards on the table. "Grace, I know we weren't really acquainted that well growing up. And it's probably a little strange to see me dating Garrett after all these years. But you've barely said a word. And I get the feeling you don't like me."

Grace frowned. "Maybe I'm just not in a mood for conversation right now."

"You seemed fine earlier around Garrett and Butch. But that all changed when it was just the two of us."

"Pretty big assumption there, Lacey. Maybe it's not all about you. Ever think about that?"

"Okay . . . sounds like I've either said or done something to rub you the wrong way. And if that's the case, then I'm all ears."

Grace stared back blankly without a reply.

Lacey continued. "If you have a problem with me and Garrett being together then we need to address it now. Because whether you like it or not, I'm here to stay. Got that?"

"Can we just go," Grace snapped. "Thought you were *so* worried about those kids."

Lacey felt the sting of a little guilt. The kids were missing, and they were wasting time. But something also told her that they needed to clear the air. "You're right. Just thought maybe I'd offended you." She was reaching for the door handle again when Grace clasped her arm.

"Hold on." Grace swallowed hard. "There is something. A couple of things actually."

Lacey turned back. "Okay, what's going on?"

"First issue is petty and I know it. But since I came home—"

Grace clamped shut suddenly, seemingly overcome by emotion. Lacey wanted to give her the time to gather her thoughts but then Vicky moved through the threshold of the barn door and frantically waved them inside.

"Since you came home *what*, Grace? What's the problem?"

She fanned the tears welling in her eyes. "Since I came home it seems that all anyone can talk about—is you."

When the drawn-out confession finally sank in, Lacey resisted the urge to smile. "Well, that's a good thing, right? Your dad and brothers are back together again, and I've done my best to help look after them. Everyone seems happy."

"They *are* happy." Grace said it in a way that made her seem less than thrilled.

"Feel like I would be grateful if the shoe was on the other foot. Am I missing something?"

"Yeah, that's all wonderful unless you're the one who deserted them. Now I'm the outsider."

Lacey shook her head. "I don't think your family sees it that way at all. I think they're just glad to have you back in their lives."

"Oh, they don't need me," Grace fired back. "They have you now."

"That's not true. You all have a history together going back to the beginning."

"Yeah, a tragic history." Grace rested the heels of hands on her eyes. "And everything going forward from here on out it's only going to get worse."

"*Worse?* Why would it get worse?"

Lacey stared ahead at Vicky, whose frantic waving intensified the longer they sat there and nobody moved. She threw up an index finger to her friend, but it wasn't working. Ignoring Vicky, who kept beckoning them inside, Lacey turned back to her passenger.

"What's going on, Grace?"

Grace removed her hands from her face, revealing tears in her eyes. "I've set some things in motion and don't know how to stop them."

"What on earth are you talking about?"

Grace was just about to answer when Vicky stormed out to the Chevy and banged on the driver's-side window. "What the hell is wrong with you two? It's freezing out here."

Lacey rolled down the window. "I'm sorry, Vic. We just got into something and—"

"Whatever it is, it can wait. The kids are still missing and so are several of the horses. I've been waiting out here a half an hour for them to return. There's no sign of Savanah or Asadi and Duke's UTV is gone. I think something's happened."

It was unlike her friend to worry, which set Lacey on edge. She turned to Grace, who had quickly dried her tears and was looking regal again. Lacey wanted to dig more into Grace's revelation, but it wasn't the right time. The matter, however, was far from over.

LACEY COULDN'T HELP BUT FEEL as though Vicky was showing them around the barn like it was a crime scene. The kids were gone and left no trace as to where they were going. Having grown up competing in steeplechase, Lacey fretted for the horses, but more than anything else she worried about Asadi, whom she thought of as a son. With enough time wasted, she finally interrupted.

"Vicky, have you called Savanah's dad yet?"

"Ray and Bo are out on an errand." Vicky held up her phone. "I've tried and tried, but no one picks up. Don't think they have any service where they are right now."

Lacey knew better than to ask where they were or what they were doing. The kind of *errand* Vicky had sent them on was anybody's guess, especially given the recent explosions. But it wasn't surprising they couldn't be reached. Cell service was still sparce in the hinterlands.

"Look, I think this is just a case of the horses being stirred up by the wind and not wanting to come back to the barn." Lacey turned to Grace. "Why don't you take my car back to help Butch batten down the hatches at the ranch. Once I find Asadi, we'll head back in his truck."

Lacey handed the keys to her Chevy over to Grace and looked to Vicky. "Want you to give Crystal a heads-up about what's going on. As a mother, I'd hate to worry her unnecessarily. But if her daughter is out there, then she has a right to know."

"What about Garrett?" Vicky asked. "Shouldn't he be in the loop?"

"He's out of pocket." Lacey checked her phone to see if there were any messages. Unfortunately, there weren't. "He's probably with Ray and Bo dealing with the pipeline issue."

"What are you going to do?" Grace asked.

"I'm going to saddle up and go look for the kids."

"*Saddle up?*" Vicky's face registered her disbelief. "It's below freezing and getting worse."

"That's why I want to get out there now. That is if you don't mind me borrowing a horse."

Vicky was clearly still dumbfounded. "Why don't you just take the Gator?"

"Because I want some height to look around. Plus, the engine might spook the horses." When it looked like Vicky was about to argue, Lacey continued. "I bet the horses are just bunched in a corner, and now the kids are just trying to coax them back. I've got a lot of experience with that."

"If you're good here," Grace interjected. "I'm going to head back and help Dad."

"We shouldn't be far behind you," Lacey said.

Sensing Vicky's worry, Lacey said: "I'm sure the kids think they'll be in trouble. So, I'll make sure they know you're not mad and that Smitty and Bo can finish up when they return."

Vicky looked as though she was forcing a smile. "Sounds like a plan."

"Everything's fine," Lacey assured. "They're good kids. Smart kids. We can trust them."

On that positive note, Grace took her leave. But Vicky stood there wooden, clearly harboring something that she wanted to confess. Once Garrett's sister was through the barn's front door and out of earshot, Vicky finally let loose with what apparently was making her so anxious.

"I'm not a hundred percent sure we *can* trust them, Lace."

"Why on earth would you say that? Asadi and Savanah are two of the best kids I—"

"Not them," Vicky interrupted. "It's Duke. He's out there too."

Lacey had heard the kid was a handful, kicked out of boarding school and all that. There were even some rumors floating around about drug abuse, but there was a genuine fear in Vicky's eyes. "What's wrong with Duke?"

"What's wrong with him is that he's just like his father." Vicky looked away before offering up the rest of her dark confession. "He's exactly like *Preston*."

It took a moment to process that Vicky was revealing yet another one of the Kaisers' very dirty secrets. Duke wasn't just some punk nephew. He was the offspring of a murdering sociopath. The bad weather was enough to make anyone sufficiently worried. But given the revelation about who was out there with Asadi and Savanah, Lacey was scared to the bone.

PART THREE

Never shall I fail my comrades.

—from the U.S. Army Ranger Creed

30

As Garrett drove back to the ranch to confront Grace about her connection to Wolfpack, he couldn't help but think of the old saying attributed to P. T. Barnum. If there was truly *a sucker born every minute*, then he was the biggest one on the face of the earth. What Grace had to gain by sabotaging their pipeline though was anybody's guess, but he didn't have her devious mind.

By all accounts, a deal between the Permian and the Panhandle was a win-win. She and her husband would make money on the investment, and the Kohl family would get wealthy too. Although she'd been missing around there for a while, Garrett knew that his dad wouldn't cut her out of any financial windfall or inheritance from the ranch. It's just the kind of man he was.

As they got closer to the house, Garrett could see that the lights were on out at the barn. Although he knew the conversation would be explosive, he hoped to get everything out in the open. The funny thing was that his anger over the whole ordeal had less to do with the damage to their property, and more to do with the heartbreak. He'd lost Grace all over again.

Garrett turned to Kai, noticing that he looked a lot less clenched now that the Order was off the hook. "Might want to stay here. Have a feeling this is about to get ugly."

"Happy to sit tight." Kai looked like a prisoner on death row getting a stay of execution. "Sounds like a family affair. Don't want any part of what I suspect is about to go down."

Garrett put the truck in park and hopped out fuming mad. With a well-rehearsed tongue-lashing for his sister playing out in his mind, he marched to the barn. He had just walked inside when he was stopped in his tracks by Butch's startling words.

"Asadi is still gone."

Garrett's anger was overcome by anxiety. "What do you mean, still gone? What happened?"

"He's helping Savanah put the horses in the barn."

"But he left hours ago," Garrett protested. "What's taking so long?"

"Don't know for sure. Think they were having trouble getting them corralled."

Despite the falling-out between Asadi and Savanah, Garrett knew that neither of them would hesitate to help the other in a crisis. "Think I should go out there and help?"

Grace stepped through a side door with a bucket of feed. Apparently, she'd been eavesdropping around the corner.

"Everything's okay, Garrett. Looks like they just didn't want to give up because of the storm. Just taking longer than they thought."

The logic was sound. Both Asadi and Savanah were tenacious as they come. Neither would rest until the job was done.

Garrett calmed a little. "Wind probably has the horses stirred up."

"Lacey said that too." Grace moved closer and then stopped a few feet away. "She went out to let them know it was okay to come on in. Vicky's going to have her men take care of it."

Lacey being out there gave Garrett an immediate sense of relief. "Her men?"

Grace looked up in the air as if thinking hard. "A guy named Ray, and a . . ."

Garrett filled in the blank. "*Bo?*"

Grace pointed her index finger at Garrett. "Yep, that's it. Said they were out running an errand but would take care of the horses as soon as they got back to the ranch."

The fact that Ray and Bo were on the task gave Garrett an extra dose of confidence. But until Asadi was accounted for, he couldn't relax. "Think they need an extra set of hands?"

"Can go out if you want," Grace said, "but it sounded like they had it all under control."

Butch took a couple of steps forward. "Maybe we should head out there, just to be safe."

Going out there to help his son immediately would've been a no-brainer for Garrett on any other day. But the revelation about his sister's husband had to be addressed. "Yeah, I'll go too." He turned to Grace. "First, I need to talk to you about something. Something that can't wait."

Grace stammered a little, sounding nervous. "About what?"

"I'm talking about that Dodge Ram that tried to run me down when we were all out at the pipeline earlier. That's as good as any place to start."

"What about it?" Butch asked. "You get Sheriff Crowley to run the plates?"

"Damn sure did." Garrett kept his glare on Grace. "Got something you want to tell me?"

The look on her face morphed from worried to offended. "How *on earth* would I know anything about that?"

Garrett followed up with a clear demand. "That's what you're about to explain to us. No more games. No more lies. Truth time. Who tried to run me over out there?"

Grace pointed to the door where his truck was parked. "Why don't you ask your friend? The one who seems to be around every time something bad happens."

"Because as you already know," Garrett countered, "that truck nearly ran over him too."

Grace put her hands on her hips. "Then maybe it was one of his cronies."

"It wasn't," Garrett fired back. "Got any other theories?"

"Well, you're pretty quick to jump on the side of a group of people who attacked you." Before Garrett could counter, Grace spouted with venom, "Twice I might add. And by the way, *I'm* the one who drove into that encampment to save you. *Remember?*"

"That's right," Butch snapped. "Why are you badgering her? She's your sister."

Garrett broke his focus on Grace and turned to his dad. "I'm badgering her because she's keeping a secret from us. A big one."

"What secret?" Butch tilted his head at his daughter. "She was right about them carnies. You looking to point a finger, then look no further than them. They're the ones making trouble. All Grace has done is offer us up a good deal."

"Yeah, about that deal," Garrett countered, turning from Butch to Grace. "What pipeline company will get that contract once we sign your offer?"

"No idea." Grace shrugged. "Would be a bid process for it just like any other project."

Butch interjected, his focus on Garrett. "What are you getting at, son?"

"What I'm getting at is that there's more to the story here. And I want Grace to fill us in."

Grace glanced at the door, looking as if she wanted to bolt. "I don't know what you mean."

"Let me help you then." Garrett smiled, knowing he was getting closer to the truth. "Tell me what Wolfpack Midstream has to do with all this."

"Nothing." Grace kept her gaze averted. "Just another pipeline company."

"No, it's not." Garrett wagged his finger at her. "Because your husband is the chairman of the board. And the truck that nearly ran me down is registered to that company."

Butch turned to his daughter. "That true?"

Grace didn't answer. She just stood there staring daggers at Garrett.

After a few awkward seconds of silence, Garrett continued. "Meanwhile, Grace, you're up here whispering in Vicky's ear about a secretive LNG agreement on the Texas Gulf Coast."

"So, what if I am?" Grace asked defiantly. "And that's not a secret. The news just hasn't gone public yet. There's no crime in being quick on the draw when a major opportunity comes your way. It's called good business."

The truth of the matter was that Garrett hadn't seen anything about the deal itself that sent up red flags. But with billions of dollars up for grabs, it could bring out the worst in people. He didn't think his sister would actually put a hit out on him over money, but her husband was as ruthless as they come. *Who knows what he is cooking up with his investors?*

"Grace, I've been doubtful from the get-go that anyone in the Permian Basin is jumping up and down to spread the wealth on this Trans-Palisade deal. And I can't help but think that maybe some folks down there would just as soon take us offline than share in the reward."

"Take you offline?" Grace marched forward, fuming mad. "You *can't* be serious. You really believe *I* would be a part of something like that? That I'd come after my own flesh and blood?"

"Not sure what to believe." Garrett shrugged. "But I know something's not adding up."

Grace leaned in and got in his face. "You must think the absolute worst of me to level an accusation like this."

Butch eased up and gently pulled her back. "Easy there, sweetie. Tempers are running hot." He shot a stern look at Garrett. "Now look, there's obviously some questions that need to be answered here, but you're taking a mighty big leap with that kind of claim."

Garrett couldn't help but feel a little guilty. He had basically just accused his sister of attempted murder. But something was going on, and she needed to start talking. Although Butch still had the temperament of a rabid wolverine, he had softened in his old age on matters of the heart. If the old man had learned anything, it was that family mattered most.

Now that he had his daughter back, Butch would not let her go without a fight. For once in his life, he played the part of the peacemaker. "Best way to cool down is to get everything out on the table. Just like your mother used to do."

Before either Garrett or Grace could argue, Butch spoke to them in his *dad voice*, which was how he spoke to the horses. It was lower and softer, and always had a calming effect. "Both of you go to the house. We're going to settle this right now."

AFTER DELIVERING A CUP OF hot chocolate to Kai, who'd opted to sit in the living room and watch television, Garrett returned to the kitchen and sat down at the table where his father and sister were blowing on their steaming cups. He took a sip and then looked to his sister, whose eyes were red from a good cry in Butch's arms. It was clear she had something to confess.

"Well, Grace," Garrett began, "I hate to rush this, but since we haven't heard anything from Lacey or Asadi, I'm a little eager to get over to the Mescalero and help. But before I do, you need to tell me what's going on. The fact that your husband is connected to Wolfpack isn't just a coincidence. Someone's coming after me from that company and I want to know why."

Grace nodded, seeming to understand. "Okay, look, the deal I proposed to Vicky is the exact same one I proposed to you. I swear it. What I didn't mention is Ryland's involvement."

Garrett didn't know much about Grace's husband, Ryland Hobbs, beyond the fact that he was extremely wealthy. She was his second wife, and they had tied the knot after a shockingly quick courtship. None of the Kohls had been invited to the private ceremony, held at an exclusive Caribbean resort. And their noticeable exclusion hadn't helped to strengthen family ties.

"What about Ryland?" Butch looked concerned. "What's going on with him?"

"Well, we're getting a divorce," she admitted. "And it's messy. Real messy."

"Messy how?" Butch asked.

"It's been bad for a while. I put up with it for years but just couldn't take it anymore."

"Put up with *what* exactly?" Garrett could feel his pulse race at the thought of abuse. "He didn't get out of line, did he?"

Grace threw up a hand. "No, nothing like that. In fact, it was quite the opposite. He showed no emotion at all. Ryland basically just checked out of the marriage. He'd leave for days. Weeks at a time. Go on a hunting trip or gambling in Vegas and never even call. I wanted to work it out, but eventually got served with divorce papers. He didn't even have the guts to face me himself."

Garrett felt bad for Grace, but her story wasn't unique. And it still didn't explain what it had to do with him nearly getting mowed over by a pickup. Things had gotten ugly for a reason. "Was he having an affair?"

She shrugged. "There were rumors, but nothing more than that. I think he just got tired of me. Treated me like a ghost, hoping I would just leave on my own accord, I guess."

Butch, still looking dumbfounded, turned from Garrett to Grace. "Sorry to hear all this, but I'm still not sure what all this has to do with us or the pipeline."

Grace looked a little embarrassed. "Well, when we got married, I signed a prenuptial agreement. A solid one. Basically, said that if the marriage didn't work out for any reason, I wouldn't get a cent."

"Don't tell Bridger," Butch scolded. "Your lawyer brother might drop dead on the spot."

"Well, I know that now. But Ryland was charming, and I was an idiot in love. Never thought it would end. And at the time I was making good money on my own. Figured I could always just go back to work if it came to that."

Garrett remembered that Grace had made a good living in the oil and gas business. She'd been rising in the ranks at a midsize exploration company before getting married. "Why can't you just go back to what you were doing before? You're bound to have a ton of contacts."

"Ah . . ." Grace held up a finger. "Because Ryland is a very powerful man in Midland-Odessa. *Vindictive*. Nobody wants to cross him. He put out the word that I was not to be hired."

"Damn petty," Butch spat. "Especially after what he did to you."

"Petty, I've learned over the years, is Ryland's middle name."

"Sounds like you're the victim," Garrett interjected. "Why would he come after you?"

Grace looked ashamed again. "So . . . I might've found a way to get back at him."

Okay, now they were getting somewhere. Garrett braced for impact. "*What* did you do?"

Grace looked down at her mug of hot chocolate as she spoke. "Ryland's bank was in line to finance the pipeline between here and the Permian. It'd be the biggest deal he'd ever done. Would take his operation to the next level."

Garrett filled in the rest. "But you found an alternative."

Grace looked up at him. "Vicky and a few others around here that I know from the old days have the means to bankroll it. This multibillion-dollar deal would put the Texas Panhandle back on the map. Would give those operators down in Midland-Odessa a run for their money."

Now it all came together for Garrett. The explosions weren't about the environment. They were about greed and vengeance. Grace's soon-to-be ex-husband and his Permian Basin cohorts were sending a clear and distinct message to the Kohls and the Kaisers. *Stay the hell off our turf.*

It was true that the Permian Basin was the powerhouse region of Texas oil and gas. And apparently, they aimed to keep it that way. But Garrett's competitors, three hundred miles to the south, were going about it the wrong way. All it did was make him want it even more. He was just about launch into about a million more questions when the cell phone buzzed in his front pocket.

Garrett held up a finger to Grace when he saw it was Sheriff Crowley calling. "Hold on a second. I need to take this." He stepped into the hallway, made a beeline to his room, and shut the door. "What you got for me, Ted?"

Crowley spoke on the other end, a little delight in his voice, "Well, I got your man here. Thought you might want to stop by and say hello."

The mysterious answer threw Garrett off a little. "You mean Dodge Ram? That man?"

"That's the one," Crowley confirmed.

"Great. I'll be up at the jail as soon as I can get there."

Crowley chuckled. "Oh, you won't find him there."

Garrett paused for a moment, unsure if he really wanted the answer. "Where is he?"

"We're out on your place at a drill site location." There was a momentary pause from Crowley. "Sign says . . . Erickson 45H. Derrick is still up but nobody's out here."

"Be there in ten minutes." Before Garrett hung up, he had to ask, "Why's he not in jail?"

"Thought it might be better we ask a few questions . . . unencumbered."

Garrett knew that was code for *without a lawyer*. "Who all is we?"

"Smitty and Bo are here too. Asking a few questions for Vicky about the compressor station. So far, this guy's playing dumb. But the angrier Bo gets, the more likely our boy will talk."

Uh-oh. Garrett figured he'd better get there before it got out of hand. He wanted to get to the bottom of what was going on too, but at the end of the day, he was still a federal officer, even if he was on leave. Despite the attempt on his life, he wasn't above the law. At least not yet.

"Don't let Bo do anything crazy," Garrett cautioned. "I'll be right there."

"I'll do my best, but he looks a bit unhinged. You know how he gets. Of course, he lives a little on the disturbed side. So, who really knows?"

The thought of what that behemoth psycho was capable of pushed Garrett into high gear. He ended the call, beckoned for Kai to follow, and raced to the door. It might not be entirely legal, but he wanted some answers. And it looked like they'd caught the man who had them.

31

Asadi couldn't keep his mind from racing as he searched around the old drill site for anything to help him endure the cold. With the pain in his ankle intensifying, there was a temptation to sit and rest. But a lack of movement would only make things worse. Needing a shelter from the wind, he found a canvas tarp covering some machinery that he could use for a roof.

On the periphery of the oil pad was a discarded five-gallon bucket full of sour-smelling deer corn. He dumped the contents and used the container to dig and move snow. In a matter of minutes, Asadi had constructed his lean-to behind a solid caliche berm, piling up powder and packing it down to make a three-sided structure, just large enough to fit inside.

He'd read lots of online articles and watched plenty of YouTube videos on primitive fire-starting methods but had never actually done it himself. And the idea of learning on the fly while he was freezing and injured didn't exactly sound like fun. But with a pile of old tumbleweeds and a dead mesquite tree nearby, he at least had the materials to give it a shot.

As Asadi bolstered the shelter's side walls, his mind drifted to other problems. The most pressing was Savanah. Despite the fact that they wouldn't be out there in the first place had Duke not sent the horses running, he kept beating himself up about the crash.

Asadi knew she wouldn't blame him for the accident, but it wouldn't stop him from blaming himself.

Going downhill fast, he took a momentary break from his snow scooping and sucked in a couple of breaths. Pulling himself together, Asadi finished up the walls of his shelter and draped the tarp over the top. After tamping down the sides, he crawled inside and almost immediately felt relief from the cold and the howling wind. Again came a temptation to sit and rest, but the longer he sat there the harder it was to move. Not only was his body starting to tighten but his throbbing ankle continued to swell. A little more time and it might not take any weight at all.

Promising himself he would return to convalesce once a fire was built, Asadi slid his foot back to the ground and crawled outside of his burrow. With the immediate *whap* of the icy gale, his first inclination was to climb back inside. But his need for a fire wasn't only for fighting off the cold; it was to send out a distress signal. Nighttime rescuers would need help finding him.

Aside from that, the long trek over the sandhills had left him with a dry mouth and burning throat, and while he wasn't nearly to the point of dehydration, the idea of melting a little snow to quench his thirst and warm his insides sounded like heaven. For that though he needed fire, and for a fire, he needed a spark. He had plenty of kindling but no catalyst to produce a flame.

Spying some equipment in the corner of the drill site, cordoned off by a wall of corrugated tin, Asadi ducked into the headwind and dashed toward the barrier. In the glow of the floodlight, he studied the massive engine with its jumble of piping, cylinders, and wires. He groped along the icy hunk of iron, feeling its edges for anything that would help, but unfortunately came up bust.

Turning back toward his shelter, Asadi contemplated retreat, fairly certain that he could survive the night without a fire if worse came to worst. But it didn't rule out frostbite. His hands and toes were already growing numb. A little while longer and he wouldn't feel them at all.

Another glance around and he noticed a toolbox at the base of an elevated diesel tank adjacent to the motor. Fighting the urge to wish for a miracle, Asadi darted to the metal chest and opened the lid. To his disappointment there was nothing of any real worth to him or anyone else but a ratchet set, ball-peen hammer, and set of jumper cables. He dumped out the contents and rummaged through the mess, hoping to find something among the junk he could use.

Asadi had just tossed the lines aside when a thought came to mind. Among the many things Butch had taught him on the ranch, truck and tractor maintenance was at the top of the list. From fixing flat tires, to changing the oil, he had pretty much done it all. Thankfully, among those skills was how to charge a dead battery from a live one.

Asadi grabbed the jumper cables and dragged them over to the motor, fixing the positive and negative teeth to the posts. With a little prayer that his experiment would work, he held his breath, brought the two clamps together, touched the ends, and they crackled and sparked. After setting the cables on the ground, he grabbed the empty toolbox and filled it with kindling.

Splintered boards from a broken crate were added to the mix of mesquite limbs and dry Russian thistle. As the cherry on top, he opened the drainage spout beneath the fuel tank and let it soak the tinder. What Asadi had also learned from Butch was that gasoline explodes and diesel burns. He didn't want to go overboard with his accelerant but definitely wanted enough to catch the flame in case he only got one shot with a battery that might be at the end of its life.

His heart racing with both anticipation and a little dread, Asadi dragged the metal box over to the cables, picked them up, and positioned them right on the top. Just as before, he touched the ends together, but nothing happened. He connected them again. Same thing.

Then again and again, but there was still no click or a spark.

A loud exhale of frustration, and Asadi banged the prongs rapidly until suddenly an orange licking flame leapt from the container into the air. Although the blaze wasn't large enough to scorch him, the sudden flash and *whoosh* sent him stumbling away, hands blocking his face.

After a quick pat-down to make sure he wasn't burning alive, Asadi staggered forward, amazed by the fact that he'd actually made fire. It was a move that in all reality was a miracle. Or as Butch would've put it: "straight off of *MacGyver*." *Whoever the heck that was.*

32

Kim winced as Faraz pulled the trigger again on the belt-fed machine gun, and grinded away with a full-auto assault, obliterating what was left of their would-be executioners. Since they were of little threat, she suspected his goal was to eliminate any witnesses. Of course, she wanted to live but Kim had yet to cross that blurry line between self-defense and slaughter. Fortunately, she didn't have to. Faraz made no distinctions. He killed everything in sight.

Their path of escape now cleared of any human obstacles, Kim grabbed Bayat's hand and dragged him around the dead bodies to the shallow end of the pool. In a frantic climb, they scrabbled up steps slick with blood, then clambered onto the patio. Sprinting to the front gate, partner in tow, Kim found the BMW exactly where she'd left it earlier.

She flung the back door open, shoved Bayat inside, and jumped into the driver's seat. About a half minute later, Faraz came sprinting up to the SUV, turning back every few steps to make sure that no one was following. By the time he got there, Kim had the motor cranked and the BMW in drive.

Faraz had not even fully closed the door when she mashed the accelerator, and they tore out of the compound down a narrow dirt road. Looking ahead, Kim felt a little hope at the sun on the horizon, a ball of orange fire that cast an eerie but beautiful glow on the surrounding farmland. She had just taken her foot off the gas to decelerate when headlights appeared in the distance.

"Uh . . . you see that, Faraz?"

"Of course, I do." Faraz huffed in air, desperate to catch his breath. "What now?"

Kim glanced over. "Should we try to blow past them or get ready to fight?"

"I—I don't know," Faraz stammered. "How should I know?"

Kim was preparing to veer around them, judging how fast she could go without raising suspicion and hoping like hell they'd not stop when the red Toyota Hilux skidded to a halt. The pickup pulled sideways, wedging itself between waist-high crops on either side of the road.

"Go around it!" Faraz pointed at the back bumper. "Before they reverse and block us in!"

With no better option, Kim punched the gas and nosed their SUV into a ditch. A muzzle flashed from the passenger-side window of the Toyota and three bullets raked across the BMW's hood. Jerking the steering wheel right, she aimed for the road and jammed her foot on the gas. Back on the path, Kim checked the mirror to find nothing but a trail of dust. She got them going to up over ninety miles per hour, praying like hell there'd be no sudden turns.

Leaning forward in his seat, eyes trained ahead, Faraz gestured to a sign on the road as he translated, "Straight to Tajikistan. Or right to Pakistan."

Kim doubted that's exactly what the sign said, but she appreciated her passenger's interpretation. With only a split second to make the call, she opted left for Tajikistan. Not only was it a lot closer, but the Taliban likely wouldn't expect it, given the fact that she was part of Omar Zadran's convoy, which was originally headed east.

AFTER HALF AN HOUR WITH no one in their rearview, Kim spoke, for no other reason than to break the awkward silence. "Think we lost them?"

Faraz turned fully in his seat and checked their six. It was as if he didn't trust the mirror or was worried that his pronouncement had jinxed them. "We're clear, I think."

Kim looked back also and said under her breath, "At least for now."

On her glance back, she noticed that Bayat's eyes were closed, and he was slumped in his seat. He'd been nearly comatose since they picked him up, but the latest exertion had clearly pushed him to his limit.

Faraz glanced back at Bayat also, then turned to her. "So, what's the plan, boss?"

Kim was surprised to hear him use the word *boss*. It was an oddly American thing to say, for one. But it also struck her as curious because of his earlier betrayal. She wanted to let that go but couldn't. She had to know what changed his mind.

"You left us there, Faraz. Abandoned us to die."

There was a pause while Faraz seemed to contemplate his answer. "Came back, didn't I?"

"You did," Kim confirmed. "But I want to know why."

Faraz stared out at the wheat field on his right. "Who cares about the reason?"

"I care because I want to know if I can trust you. That it won't happen again."

"You promised me money," Faraz said flippantly. "Can't collect if you're dead."

Kim shook off his answer. "Come on, you know what I do for a living, right?"

"You're CIA." Faraz looked a bit smug. "Told me already."

"And you know what that means, don't you?"

Faraz turned to her looking curious but he didn't say a word.

"It means that I've spent an entire career listening to people like you lie to me." Kim turned and met his gaze. "And I know what you're telling me is a complete load of crap."

Faraz broke eye contact and looked out at the wheat again. "What's the difference?"

"I want to know if I can count on you to get this man to his family."

Faraz glanced at Bayat again and turned back. "You don't need me. You need a miracle."

Kim thought she would feel more hopeful in the light of day. But the sunlight only put a spotlight on their desperation. No doubt, it *would* take a miracle to get out of Afghanistan alive.

"Maybe you're right," Kim conceded. "But I'm not going to quit. And I want to know your level of commitment. And don't give me that garbage about the money. Why'd you come back?"

Faraz kept his eyes fixed on the nothingness ahead. "You know why I came back."

"I think I do, but I want to hear you say it."

"Because of Asadi, *okay.* I want to see my brother again."

Kim stifled a smile. "That's what I wanted to hear."

Faraz closed his eyes and leaned his head back into the headrest. "You happy now?"

"Yeah, I am."

Kim didn't know why that mattered so much to her. Maybe, deep down, she thought they wouldn't survive. And if she was going to die, she wanted to die with a partner who wanted what she wanted. Uniting Asadi with his brother had become an obsession. But it also had to do with the failure of Afghanistan. If she could do this one thing, then maybe not all was lost.

Kim turned and asked softly, "Do you trust me now?"

He opened his eyes and wiped away a tear. "I trust that you can get me to my brother."

Kim gave a nod of confirmation, even though he wasn't looking at her. "Okay, then that's a start. But we need a good plan. And I think crossing into Tajikistan is our best bet."

Faraz looked over. "I don't know about you or the guy in the back seat, but I don't have a passport. And the last I heard, you still needed one to travel outside the country."

"Traditional border crossings aren't an option for us. The Taliban will be everywhere. And checkpoints are going to start popping up all over. We need to ditch this car and get off the grid. Find alternative routes to the border and a place to cross that isn't being watched."

"To do that," Faraz interjected, "we'll need help. Once word gets out about what just happened at the compound, they'll issue a bounty. Which means we're going to be hunted by everyone in Afghanistan." He turned to her to emphasize his point. "And I mean *everyone*."

Faraz was right. They couldn't do this alone. There were former assets who might help, but she had no way to contact them. As the town in the distance grew closer, so did the danger. They would have to take a chance and try to find a pay phone. But as soon as they were spotted, the clock would start ticking. And it was only a matter of time until someone called it in.

Kim shot Faraz a smile. "Don't suppose you have a satellite phone by chance?"

There was another moment of silence and then Faraz chuckled. "Left it with my passport."

Kim reported her answer in a way that sounded absurdly official. "*Mine's* in the helicopter."

Faraz's chuckle billowed into a full-fledged laugh. Apparently, her reference to his earlier sarcastic remark about the *CIA black helicopters* struck a chord.

As Kim approached the outskirts of town, she slowed and pulled to the side of the road, wondering how on earth they were going to drive through there in a drug lord's stolen BMW and find a way to make a call without alerting the local authorities. She had just framed another bad joke when a shaky hand passed from the back seat to the front.

Kim turned to Faraz, who looked equally startled to see that Bayat was leaning forward, slightly alert. More importantly, within his grip was a blood-spattered cell phone, which he must've taken from one of the traffickers that Faraz had gunned down. She took the handoff and eyed the phone, shocked to find it fully charged and with a good signal.

"Bayat, this may very well be what saves our lives."

"You actually have someone to call here?" Faraz asked.

In fact, there was *one number* she had memorized before leaving, hoping like hell she'd never ever have to use it. But Mario was their only real chance at ever seeing another sunrise.

33

Lacey tugged on the reins, pulled her horse to a stop, and glanced down at the Polaris tire tracks in the snow. Looking out at the darkness of the pasture, she stood in the stirrups and widened her eyes but could see no farther than about thirty yards ahead.

The palomino gelding nicknamed Surf, short for Surfer Boy because of his bushy blond forelock, was thankfully tall. But the towering horse still seemed timid about venturing any farther away from the barn on such a cold and gusty night. He turned back several times, resting a big brown eye on her that seemed both curious and troubled.

Lacey reached up and scratched Surf between the ears. "Don't worry, big guy. Just a quick ride to the back of the pasture and we'll turn around."

She couldn't help but feel that the comfort was more for her than him. But it wasn't just the foul weather that had her worried. Grace's ominous confession of "I've set some things in motion, and don't know how to stop them" had somehow superseded every other thought. Part of her wanted to go back and warn Garrett, but at this point there was nothing much to say.

Another bombshell confession of the evening was that Duke Newhouse was actually in fact Preston Kaiser's son. Vicky's disclosure seemed to be a warning. *But a warning of what?* Did she think he was a threat to the Kohls? Because Duke's real father, Preston, had been a next-level narcissist and a borderline sociopath, Lacey couldn't help but think that there was much more to the story. And she was determined to drill down on that later.

Lacey trailed the tire tracks and hoofprints to the back of the pasture and then stopped just short of the fence line. She could see a gap where the wires were snapped and tangled beside a splintered wooden fencepost that was busted in two. A *cluck-cluck* of the tongue brought Surf into a trot and her to the awful scene.

At the sight of the blood near the damaged fence, Lacey's first instinct was to think the worst. Her mind's eye envisioned the UTV ramming the fence and the kids ripped to shreds. But another glance beyond its tracks revealed a jumble of hoofprints where the horses broke through.

Leaping from the saddle, Lacey clicked on her flashlight and led Surf by the reins to the fence for a better inspection of the bloody snow. She knelt down and tried to move in closer, but the gelding planted his front hooves and wouldn't move an inch. Horses had keen intuition, and his nervous snorts and nickers were clear signs that he was totally spooked.

Scanning the area with her flashlight, Lacey pieced together the story and fully understood exactly what happened. This was a rescue mission, which explained why Asadi, Savanah, and Duke hadn't come back. She climbed back into the saddle and coaxed a reluctant Surf back into action. It took a little nudging to get him directed through the gap in the fence.

Once on the other side, Lacey felt it was *she* who needed motivating. Beyond the paddock were the open plains and the daunting sandhills that towered in the distance like giant frozen waves. Pushing past her trepidation, she rose in the stirrups for a better view, then eased back into the saddle and clucked her tongue.

As Surf's momentum built into a trot, it was *her* intuition that suddenly kicked in. She moved the reins right and looped the gelding in a full circle around the outside of the fence to see if there were any clues she had missed. But being beyond the safe confines of the pasture sent an immediate chill up her spine.

It was well known in the Panhandle that early settlers had made their way through the ranch on the perilous journey out west. And out on the property there were more than a few graves of those who'd not survived the trip. There were several ghost stories about the Mescalero she'd heard as a child, all of which at the moment she was desperately trying to forget.

Lacey pulled the reins, brought Surf to a stop, closed her eyes, and listened. A momentary gust filled her ears, and she concluded it was just her imagination. Between the howl of the wind and dancing shadows cast by the moonlight against mesquite, her senses were in overdrive. She forced a smile to ward off the dread, then gave Surf a little kick to get him into the next gear.

Lacey was going at a quicker clip, but not so speedy she couldn't follow the trail. She maneuvered between bushes until coming upon a mesquite thicket, then made a wide swath around it. To her disappointment, there was no great discovery or resolution around the bend. The tracks went on and on, seemingly endlessly, out into the dunes on the dark horizon.

34

The drive from the house to the Savage Exploration oil well gave Garrett a chance to think. He would've liked to ask his sister more questions, but he had enough intel for a good start. If Wolfpack was engaged in a sabotage operation, it wouldn't be the first one in oil and gas history. And this pipeline deal was like discovering Montezuma's treasure for everyone involved.

Garrett turned to Kai, who was sitting in the passenger seat. "Can't help but notice you look a bit relieved by Grace's confession. Were you starting to worry that your friends were involved?"

Kai shot a grin. "Can't imagine anyone I know personally would go to the lengths that these guys are, but I suppose you never know. Still not so sure about the ones at the top. The ones behind the curtain. Who the hell knows about them?"

Garrett batted the air. "Ah, there's always a mother ship somewhere, and the bosses are never the ones getting their hands dirty. Just like the old days. A lot of *good idea fairies*. Everything's easy when you're sipping hot coffee from behind a desk. We do the job. They get the credit."

"Yeah, we get a lot of attaboy social media posts from the higher-ups." Kai laughed to himself. "But not a lot of volunteers when we're freezing our asses off or sweating in the heat."

"Look, you've done what you came to do, Kai. Cleared your

name and all. Why don't you let me take you back to camp? Think I can handle it from here."

"Well, if you don't mind, I'd kind of like to stay. Least I can do is help after our misunderstanding back at camp." Kai pointed to the busted windshield. "And for the souvenir."

Garrett was tempted to call Kai out but decided to let it go since they were making progress. "After Grace mowed through your place with my grille guard, I think we can call it even."

"It's not just that, Garrett. Truth of the matter is that this feels good." Kai looked as if he was struggling for the right words. "You know—the investigation. The mission."

There was no need to elaborate. Garrett knew exactly what he meant. After leaving the Army there were a lot of mixed emotions. But one thing that wasn't cloudy. More than the job or the cause, he missed the soldiers. It was the camaraderie he longed for most.

"Well, if memory serves, Magnum P.I. was a SEAL, not a Ranger. If you think you missed your calling as a detective, then you better keep searching for a new line of work."

"Just like old times." Kai shook his head and laughed. "Always a smart-ass."

"I can't go changing too much." Garrett shot him a wink. "As you've seen with my dad and sister, it runs in the family. But to be honest, it's nice to have a friend along for the ride. Seems like more and more I'm all on my own these days. Gets lonely."

Kai just nodded, seeming to understand.

Garrett was content that the ice was broken and some mutual trust had been gained between the two of them. But he still didn't know exactly how to address the situation with Sheriff Crowley and their *detainee* out at the drill site. He thought he should give Kai an out.

"I'm not sure what I'm going to find out here, but I bet it borders on the legally questionable. If legal at all. You sure you want to be along for something like that?"

"Legally questionable?" Kai looked skeptical. "What are you going to do?"

"I don't know just yet. Guess it depends on the situation. But all indications are that Grace's husband and Wolfpack are trying to send us a message. A warning. And I aim to send one back."

Kai smiled. "You remember where I'm from, right?"

Garrett recalled that Kai was from Humboldt County in California, which was known as the *Emerald Triangle*—the largest marijuana-producing area in the country. There was even a place within it nicknamed *Murder Mountain* because so many people had gone missing nearby. Although Garrett obviously couldn't condone illegal trafficking, he could appreciate people who lived largely removed from the rest of society, fought for their way of life, and preferred to handle problems themselves. There were a lot of similarities between Kai's family and his own.

Garrett turned back toward the caliche road, right as his headlights met Crowley's Ford F-250. It was a good fifty yards ahead of the drill site, where the derrick loomed larger overhead. Just a day earlier, there would have been a dozen rig hands buzzing around the oil well. But they'd just finished up and were getting ready to move to a new location. Which meant there was nothing around but dark frozen wilderness for miles in any direction. It was the perfect spot for the sheriff's so-called *unencumbered* interview with a potential saboteur.

Garrett pulled up beside him and rolled down the window. "Where's our boy, Sheriff?"

Crowley caught a glimpse of Kai in the passenger seat. "What the hell is *he* doing here?"

Garrett tilted his head at Kai. "Well, he didn't take kindly to nearly being run down by that Dodge either and had a few questions of his own."

"All right then." Crowley looked pleased with the response. "More the merrier, I reckon." He tilted his head at the well. "Ray and Bo have him down there between the rig and the slush pit. Got the place to ourselves."

Garrett shuddered to think what those two were up to over there. "Any idea who this guy is?"

A single nod came from Crowley. "Ran his ID and it all checks out. Frank Baxter. Address out of Odessa. Just some oilfield hand. Originally out of Seminole. Couple of DWIs from years ago, but his record is clean. No warrants, unfortunately."

Garrett stared in the direction of the derrick. "He give us anything to go on yet?"

Crowley shook his head. "Obstinate little sumbitch. Bo's threatened to rip his limbs off, but he hasn't said a word about why he's up here. He's guilty though, I'm sure of it."

"Don't worry. Got a little information about Wolfpack that will help us get some answers."

Garrett pressed the accelerator, easing down the road and onto the drill site. Just as promised, their prisoner was standing there next to the reserve pit, a reservoir used as a repository for drilling muds and well cuttings. It's a nasty slurry with a petroleum odor that stank like hell.

Garrett brought his pickup even with Smitty's truck and got his headlights in alignment. Before Kai could open the door, he threw up a hand to stop him. "Do me a favor and sit tight. Want to have a talk with this Baxter fellow alone for a minute."

Kai smirked. "Got something in mind?"

"Depends on how stubborn he wants to be, I guess." Garrett grabbed a lariat rope from behind his seat, threw the door open, and stepped outside. Before closing it, he added, "If it doesn't work, I might want to see how you handle things out in Humboldt County."

Garrett slammed the door and walked over to Smitty and Bo, who were standing a few feet in front of their scruffy detainee, who was wearing only a white tank top and blue jeans. He was standing on the frozen caliche barefooted. Without a scrap of meat on his bones, he had to be cold, especially with his outerwear and boots off to the side of the reservoir.

Garrett chuckled. "Still not talking, huh?"

"Oh, he's got a lot to say," Smitty said pissed. "Just none of it you'd want to hear."

"Trash talker, huh? Dealt with plenty of them before." Garrett noticed that Smitty and Bo were unarmed. "How'd you coax him out here in the first place?"

"Sheriff done it," Smitty explained. "Told the guy if he confessed, we'd turn him loose."

Bo smirked. "Making him stand in the cold was my idea."

"Figured as much," Garrett replied.

Stifling a violent shiver, a defiant Baxter shielded his eyes from the glare of the headlights and yelled in a raspy voice, "Now, who the hell are you?"

"I'm Garrett Kohl." He took a few steps closer. "The guy you tried to run over."

There was a moment of shuddering silence while Baxter seemed to think. "You came at me with a damn gun. What was I supposed to do?"

That was true. And it occurred to Garrett that the guy had only been sitting there when he pulled his pistol. "Never mind that. What were you doing on my land?"

"Observing," the guy answered. "Ain't no law against that."

"No, but there is one against trespassing. Which was exactly what you were doing."

"Just got turned around in the dark, that's all." Baxter's teeth chattered. "Getting lost on a backcountry road ain't much of a crime."

"How about manslaughter?" Garrett asked. "That sound serious enough?"

"I told them," Baxter seethed, "that wasn't me. I *didn't* blow nothing up!"

"I don't know." Garrett took a couple more steps forward. "Little birdy's been telling me some interesting stories about Wolfpack. Seems all arrows are pointing to your boss."

"Well, you can take them arrows and shove 'em up your ass. I know my rights! And you can't hold me out here like this. You're in a hell of a lot of trouble."

"Trouble for what?" Garrett asked.

"It was *you* who shot at *me*! So, why don't you pin them charges back on yourself?"

The lawman in Garrett couldn't help but concede that Baxter was spot-on. The only hard evidence of anything were the bullets from his 9mm that were lodged in the Wolfpack truck. It was time to get some answers because he was losing leverage fast.

"Let's talk about what we do know." Garrett turned back to Bo and Smitty. "Give us a minute, will you?"

A shivering Smitty gave a nod. "Holler if you need us." Looking relieved, he turned and marched away with his giant counterpart in tow. "We'll be in the cab."

Baxter piped up again. "Here's the facts, Kohl. I've been kid-napped, threatened with torture, and now I'm freezing my damn ass off, about to get hypothermia. Which means you and them two rednecks are screwed! So, I suggest you let me go before you end up in more trouble."

"Not until you answer a few questions."

"Did you *not* just hear me? I said, get me out of here. *Now!*"

Garrett moved up to Baxter, then glanced over at the reserve pit. He shivered as a damp gust of wind came whistling over the swamp. "Damn it's cold. I can see why you're pissed."

"Oh, can you now?" Baxter took a few clumsy steps forward and finally took notice of the lariat in Garrett's hands. Sarcastically he asked, "You gonna hang me if I don't talk?"

Garrett looked down at the rope, then back up and raised his eyebrows. "Hadn't thought about that, but it's not a bad idea."

Baxter bristled. "Take me back to my truck. The one *you* shot full of holes."

Garrett threw up a hand. "Stop right there."

Baxter stopped and dipped his head in the direction of Smitty and Bo's pickup. "Yeah, try keeping me here now without that big-ass Rottweiler handy."

As he trudged past, Garrett reached back, grabbed the guy by the back of the shirt, and dragged him to the reserve pit. He let Baxter fight for purchase for a couple of seconds, then gave a hard shove. A fearful shout preceded the splash by only a second, which was followed by his girlish scream and some thrashing about in the ice-cold sludge. He got himself dog-paddling and then hacked out the nasty spew of drilling fluid and brine.

"What the hell's wrong with you, Kohl! Gonna poison me in this crap!"

"Don't worry." Garrett took a knee beside the pit. "You'll drown or freeze long before you have to worry about the toxins."

"Ah, come on, man! Help me out of here!"

"Only if you help me first."

Baxter's eyes were pleading. "Please, Mr. Kohl! I got kids at home!"

"So does my friend, Tony Sanchez. And now one of his is lying in intensive care."

"Told you! That wasn't me!" Baxter's teeth rattled and his body quaked with cold. "Now, will you pull me out of here?"

"If it wasn't you, then who was it?"

"I don't know!" Baxter dog-paddled to the edge of the pit and reached out a hand for help. "That's what I'm here to find out!"

"What are you talking about?"

"Just throw me that rope and I'll show you. Got photos on the phone in my coat. Same thing that happened to us. I'll show you the damn proof. Someone hit our pipeline two weeks ago."

Garrett widened the loop on his lariat, twirled it over head, and launched it at the quaking Baxter, who put the ring over his neck and shoulder and cinched it tight. It took a couple of seconds of hard pulling to get the trespasser through the frozen muck, but he made it back to the side. He clambered onto the caliche, huffing and puffing until he caught his breath.

Garrett let Baxter get upright before launching in. "Explosions here are all over the news. If the same thing happened down there, then why haven't I heard about it?"

Baxter looked up at Garrett. "You ever been to Reeves County, Mr. Kohl?"

Garrett had driven through Pecos on I-20. It was some of the most remote and desolate country that Texas had to offer. And that was saying a lot. "Been across it a few times."

"Then you know there ain't a damn thing in the world out there but scrub brush, cactus, and dirt. We took care of the problem ourselves and kept it quiet. With a big LNG contract on the table with the Europeans, last thing anyone wanted was bad press to squirrel the deal."

Garrett offered a hand to Baxter and pulled him to his feet. "Still doesn't explain what you're doing up here in our part of the world."

Baxter hugged himself tight, desperate to get warm. "We thought you were behind it."

The accusation took Garrett off guard. "Why *on earth* would you think it was me?"

Baxter looked a little squeamish. "Well, you know, because of what your sister is up to with Vicky Kaiser. And it ain't our first rodeo with that damn family. They play dirty as hell."

Garrett knew that teaming up with Vicky would one day lead to problems. "I can't blame you for thinking that way, but I've made some big changes in how they do business."

Baxter looked ready to burst. "In case you haven't noticed, Vicky's sheriff and them redneck goons done kidnapped me, and you threw me into this swamp. Grateful you pulled me out and all, but I can't say a whole helluva lot has changed."

Garrett shrugged. "These things take time, I guess."

By the look on Baxter's face, he didn't appreciate the joke. "Suppose you know from Grace about the divorce. About as ugly as it gets."

Garrett nodded. "So I heard."

"After the explosion up here at the Mescalero, they sent me up to do some investigating."

"If you had questions then why didn't you just ask? I'd have set you straight."

"Because of what I said," Baxter explained. "Your sister is conspiring with Vicky, and we figured she might be connected to that foreigner."

"What foreigner?"

"Some guy they saw out there at the Wolfpack Compressor Station before it blew up. Couple of our technicians were out doing a pressure test and caught him snooping around near a line close to Monahans. Lied about being at the wrong facility. I was sent here specifically to find him."

"You get his name?" Garrett asked. "Any information on him?"

Baxter looked disappointed. "Nah, soon as our boys called the law, he took off and they couldn't catch him. He was kind of a big dude. Heavy beard. Darker skin. They did say that he had a weird accent. Only thing that sticks out, but it helps me to narrow my search some. Thought maybe he was working for the Kaisers. They've been known to hire the shady type."

Garrett let out a sigh. Just when he'd thought he could rest the blame squarely on Wolfpack, he got blindsided by this. Given the revelation from Baxter about the sabotage in the Permian, it was clear this was no isolated incident. And now it looked like there could possibly be a connection to Kai's mysterious Frenchman who had just breezed into town.

35

Simon Cloutier moved around a thorny mesquite tree to the drill site location, uneasy with what he saw playing out before him. As a former soldier in the French Foreign Legion turned contract security consultant, he knew the look of a skilled operator. And Garrett Kohl carried himself with such comportment. There was clearly more to this cowboy than first met the eye.

Simon wasn't close enough to hear the conversation between Kohl and Baxter, but he saw that they were smiling. Despite their earlier run-in, there appeared to be a meeting of the minds. And that meant problems. His plan worked best when there was animosity, mistrust, and chaos. He needed Wolfpack, Mescalero Energy, and Savage Exploration tearing each other apart.

Ducking low, Simon moved through and around clumps of mesquite brush until coming up against a barbed-wire cattle fence that kept him on the periphery of the white caliche base. The looming oil rig cast a shadow in the moonlight that kept him comfortably hidden. He had just gotten close enough to hear the conversation between Kohl and Baxter when everyone dispersed.

If the collaboration between Wolfpack and Kohl wasn't bad enough, Vicky Kaiser's henchmen were now somehow involved. For a place like Texas with endless stretches of isolated ranchland, it seemed as though its inhabitants had an uncanny ability to find one another.

Getting caught down in the Permian Basin was a fluke—just a case of bad luck. But the entrance of Kohl sent up major red flags. Spending enough time in the espionage underworld to know a spy when he saw one, Simon couldn't help but reason that this rancher was going to be a problem. Kohl was tenacious, albeit reckless, but his skills were not to be underestimated.

Simon pulled the satellite phone from his pocket and made the call. When the other end was picked up on the first ring, he launched in with the bad news. "We've got another problem."

A clearing of the throat preceded the answer in French, "Let me go to the other room."

It was early morning in Lyon, which meant Jean Dumont was probably slipping out of bed so that his wife wouldn't hear. Simon couldn't help but be envious of his boss. He could envision a dark room in a luxurious flat, rumpled covers, with a beautiful woman beneath them.

A few seconds later Dumont spoke again, clearly agitated. "*Now* what?"

Although there was no reason to suspect their phone call would be monitored, Simon kept the conversation vague. "Some of the locals are going out on their own. Looking for a culprit."

"Fine. That's why we sent you there. Offer them up a perpetrator, redirect their mistrust."

Simon debated revealing the source of his concern, already knowing the response he would get in return. "It's not just the fire inspectors or law enforcement who are investigating now. One of these local cowboys is on the prowl. He's connected with the pipeline deal."

"So what?"

"So, he's suspicious," Simon hissed. "Convinced this was an act of sabotage."

"Good," Dumont answered. "Lead him down that path, so long as it does *not* lead to us."

Simon hunkered behind a mesquite brush, careful not to be

seen by Kohl and the others. "He's talking to someone from Wolf-pack, and I suspect they're putting their stories together."

A brief pause followed Dumont's string of curses. "How would they trace this back to you?"

"I don't know. But these rubes aren't as stupid as you think. They know everything about their land. And they know when something is off. When someone doesn't belong."

"Just give it some time. The coming pandemonium that will ensue after the next explosion is sure to take the heat off of you."

"And if it doesn't?" Simon asked.

"If you're worried about this cowboy then watch him. Make sure he doesn't become a problem."

Simon already knew the answer but felt that he had to ask. "And what if he keeps this investigation going and it leads to us?"

A sigh preceded Dumont's response. "There is no *us*. There is only *you*. Plausible deniability was part of the deal. Or did you forget? You will do whatever is necessary to keep him quiet."

Simon took a breath and battled to compose himself. "That was *not* part of the deal."

"We sent you there to shut down this pipeline," Dumont grumbled. "To make it look unreliable so that the EU will dump these Texans for our client. We left the details up to your discretion. Maybe that was a mistake."

"That did not include taking any lives."

"One man is dead," Dumont shot back. "And another in critical care. Your time for worrying about the toll of human lives has passed."

"That was an accident." Simon gritted his teeth. "No one was supposed to be there."

"I can assure you those Texans will not care. You either fix this problem, or maybe this cowboy fixes you."

Simon rose to find Kohl and the others getting into their vehicles. He'd already planted a tracking device on his truck earlier, but he would need to stay close by to observe. "I have to go."

Dumont continued in a more pleasant voice, "My sources tell me that bad publicity from the explosion is already taking effect. Exactly what the ones who are looking to invest billions of dollars into this LNG project will want to avoid. Just finish the job, tie up loose ends, and come on home. A sizable reward will most certainly ease that nagging conscience of yours."

36

Mario stared down at his satellite phone, in complete shock that he was actually getting a call. He was even more surprised that it was coming from a number in Afghanistan. There was only one other person in the world who had his contact info, which meant it had to be her. Billy's commandos, sitting around him in the cargo hold of the van, appeared to be equally astonished.

Hitting the talk button, Mario took a gamble and guessed, "Gotta be you, Kim."

There was a crackle of static followed by a female voice. "Mario?"

Had he been alone, Mario would've launched a fist into the air and screamed hallelujah at the top of his lungs. But he made a concerted effort to play it cool. "You calling for a reason or just to say hi?"

Kim offered up a short laugh that seemed forced. "Sounds like you're on the move. Please tell me you're close."

"Depends, I guess. Afghanistan is a big country. Where are you?"

"North of Kunduz. Sitting on the outskirts of a little town, trying like hell not to get noticed."

Mario felt a little relief in hearing that Billy's source of intel had been right. "Just throw on a burqa and find a place to hunker down. We'll get you. Only about an hour away."

Another crackle of static preceded Kim's reply. "Yeah . . .

hunkering down might not be an option. We're in a stolen BMW and left a pretty big mess behind at the last place."

For the sake of time, Mario didn't ask her to explain. In all the years he'd spent in Afghanistan, he'd never even seen a BMW. So already they were going to stick out. Given the fact that they had been held prisoners, he assumed the *pretty big mess* was a lot of dead bodies.

"Here's the plan," Mario began. "Border is going to be locked down going out, so traditional crossings are a no-go. I already assumed that when I arrived and got us a helicopter."

"*Helicopter?*" Kim sounded a bit stunned. "Over here?"

"Well, that's where it gets tricky. Called in a favor from a higher-up who owes me in the Tajik military. He'll allow one Black Hawk to come across the border, so long as it doesn't tie back to them. Dushanbe has enough problems with the Taliban, he said. Last thing they want is an international incident."

Before the fall of Kabul, the U.S. had managed to evacuate dozens of American-trained pilots, with their aircraft, to Uzbekistan and Tajikistan. And to this day, it's where many of their fliers have stayed and much of their equipment remained. The Taliban demanded the return of their property and personnel, but their neighbors had held their ground, sparking the rift.

Mario had done all he could to get all the Afghan pilots and their families out of the country, but in the end, they'd just run out of time. Individuals with that expertise were desperately needed, and the aircraft that went with them was not easily replaced. Which meant the Taliban kept their remaining pilots under careful watch. Given this fact, Mario couldn't blame the pilot for not venturing too far into Afghanistan. If caught, he'd be tortured and executed as a traitor.

"Okay, I get it," Kim answered. "Where does that leave us?"

"Pilot is on standby just across the border. He'll cross in, but go only so far inland, which means we've got to get close to him."

"Done," Kim replied. "Give me the coordinates and we'll make it there."

Mario looked out the window and surveyed the barren desert landscape. There was only one highway between them, and without a change of vehicles, they were going to get noticed. "Listen, if you think the heat is on, then ditch the beamer and get some new wheels." Having almost forgotten the purpose of her trip, he added, "You got what you came for?"

"Yeah, they're both here. Bayat is in rough shape though. He needs medical attention bad."

"Got it." Mario looked over at the guy whom Billy had designated their medic. He wasn't a doctor and didn't have much more than a first aid kit. "About all we're equipped to handle is a blister. There won't be any real help until Dushanbe."

There was a pause on Kim's end, which meant she was assessing. "We'll be all right."

"Then I want you to swap out vehicles and stay in touch. Call me as soon as you're back on the road and let me know what to look for. We'll find a place off the highway to meet up."

Mario noticed that Kim ended the call without saying goodbye. He could tell that she was worried, even if she didn't admit it. Of course, he was nervous too. The next couple of hours would be highly dependent on the Taliban's inability to mount an effective manhunt. But once a real search was underway, chances of escape were slim to none.

KIM STARED THROUGH THE WINDSHIELD of the BMW at the town in the distance and stifled a nervous laugh over the fact that she'd so casually agreed to steal a car. For a tier one special operations guy like Mario Contreras, hotwiring a vehicle and disappearing undetected came as naturally as zeroing in a sniper rifle or field-stripping an M4.

She was proficient in evasive driving and tactical shooting basics, but most of her training focused on tracking terrorists, catching American traitors, and the recruitment and handling of foreign spies. Although Kim had experience with a gun, she preferred to leave shoot-outs and grand theft auto to guys like Garrett and Mario.

Kim pulled onto a dirt road near the outskirts of the upcoming town and parked behind a dilapidated adobe-style building that looked like an old automotive repair shop. There were a few junk cars littered among tall weeds, with a gantry and chain hoist sitting out there in the open. There was even a rusted-out engine that for some reason was still suspended midair.

After a big breath, Kim turned back to Bayat. "Faraz and I are going to hike into town and get another car. We'll be back here as soon as we can."

Bayat didn't even try to sit up. He just gave a single nod. "And it's okay, if you don't."

Kim was jarred by his response. "What are you talking about? Of course we'll be back."

Bayat donned a weak smile. "You've already given me something wonderful."

Kim couldn't possibly imagine what that could be. Since the Iranians had turned him over, they'd been ambushed, imprisoned, and nearly executed. "What have I given you but misery?"

Bayat's eyes went glassy. "You've given me news of my family. Of my son on a horse." He shook his head as if still in disbelief. "Liam has found who he really wants to be in this world. And that brings more joy than you'll ever know."

"And you're going to be right there with him on one of those horses. Okay? Just one last leg of this long journey and we're home. Don't give up on me now."

Bayat gave another nod, this one so weak it barely registered as movement. "Almost home."

Kim handed the UZI over the seat to Bayat. "Keep this while we're gone."

Faraz piped up. "Uh . . . don't you think we might need that?"

In fact, Kim thought there was a good chance that they would. But she wasn't going to leave Bayat defenseless. Opting for something other than the truth, she explained to Faraz, "I want to blend in. Slip in and out unnoticed. That would just draw attention to us."

Faraz didn't respond. He just stared straight ahead. He clearly didn't agree with the idea of going in unarmed and likely for good reason. Beyond the fact that it would leave them unprotected, pretty much everyone in the entire country walked around toting a gun.

Kim lowered her voice. "I don't want to do any of this. But I don't plan on being in that town any longer than we need to be."

"Fine. Let's go."

Faraz sighed and then threw open the passenger door. He popped out and stomped around to the front.

Kim turned back to Bayat and was happy to see that he had the submachine gun firmly in his grip. Part of her felt like she should have some sort of parting words, but she just reached over the console and squeezed his skinny knee.

Unfortunately, Kim got the distinctive feeling that Bayat's warrior countenance was all for show. It was pretty clear that in his mind, and more importantly, his soul, he had already drifted on from this world into the next.

37

The little voice in the back of Lacey's head telling her that riding farther into the frozen wilderness was a bad idea had gone from a whisper to a scream. But there was an inexplicable drive that kept her pushing ahead. Maybe it was a mother's instinct? Or maybe it was just plain old pigheadedness. But she couldn't allow herself to give up on the kids just yet.

As Lacey summited one of the towering sandhills, she had a sudden, distinct feeling that she would finally find them. But the UTV tracks she was following seemed to go on endlessly. Cresting the top of another knoll, Lacey turned back and was struck with a sense of dread. She could no longer see the barn or the back pasture—totally adrift in an ocean of dunes.

Lacey was disappointed that she hadn't found Asadi and Savanah, but grateful that she'd at least located the Polaris trail following the hoofprints, which meant she could tell Ray where to look. But that nagging feeling to keep trudging on hadn't fully subsided. Making a deal with herself to scale another hill, she prodded Surf on to climb the next one.

Once at the top, Lacey noticed that the UTV tracks veered left through the trough of the snow-covered mounds. With this sudden deviation, she prompted Surf into a canter and followed the trail until arriving upon a sight that made her blood run cold. After making a couple of full loops around the wreckage, Lacey slid down from the saddle and moved closer for an inspection.

She clicked on the flashlight, looked inside the Polaris, then all around the vicinity. Finding no clues or evidence of value, in or around the vehicle, Lacey climbed onto the hull and scanned the surrounding area, desperate to make sense of the footsteps in the snow. A thorough study of the pattern of steps told her that they'd survived. But where they'd gone was anybody's guess.

Realizing the dire need to go get help, she leapt from the UTV and dashed back to Surf. After swinging up into the saddle, Lacey turned the gelding toward the highest sandhill she could find. Once atop the hill, she slowed the horse to a stop and looked in every direction. To the west though, on the horizon, a single light radiated in the dark.

Taking it as a sign of hope, Lacey strained her eyes and found that someone had built a fire.

DESPITE THE AWFUL CIRCUMSTANCE THAT had brought Asadi into the life-or-death situation, he couldn't help but appreciate the opportunity to put his survival skills to the test. He knew, of course, that enduring a couple of hours alone was a far cry from surviving in the wilderness for months on end like his mountain men heroes Jim Bridger, Kit Carson, and Hugh Glass.

He also knew that his jumper cable, battery, diesel combo wasn't exactly rubbing two sticks together or sparking flint to make a fire. But it was more than most teenagers he knew could've come up with on the spot. It was a sad state of the times. If it wasn't on social media, a podcast, or couldn't be ordered with an app, the kids he knew just weren't interested.

It was yet another reason Savanah was his best friend. She was one of the few he knew who longed to live in another era, to be alive when there was little technology available beyond a compass, black powder, and the spyglass. Asadi couldn't count how many times they'd talked about their longing to grow their own food, cook what they hunted, and live off the land.

Their wishes were in large part born out of shows they binge-watched on streaming services like *Homestead Rescue, Alaskan Bush People*, and *Building off the Grid*. They were basically interested in anything and everything that Bear Grylls had to offer. At the thought of their good times together, and the fact that they might be over, Asadi's spirits were sinking fast.

While he hated to dwell on negative thoughts, they were a distraction from the terrors of the dark. He was grateful for the tarp over his shelter, but it *whipped* and *snapped* with the gale in a most unsettling way. There was also a metallic *clang* coming from behind the pumpjack that seemed to sound off when his nerves were finally calmed and he least expected it.

Asadi was about to investigate when he suddenly heard the three-beat rhythm of pounding hooves. He glanced around, eyes keen, searching for some unseen threat among the dancing shadows and swaying silhouettes, then hung his head outside for a better look.

Forcing himself to rise, Asadi moved outside. Ignoring the pain in his stiffening ankle, he limped toward the inbound horse that he recognized as Surf.

"Over here! Over here!" he yelled.

Lacey slowed the horse to a trot as they came in from the back of the drill site and eased up until they were at a halt. "Asadi, thank God! Are you okay?"

He nodded. "Hurt my ankle, but I'm fine other than that."

Lacey looked at his shelter. "Is Savanah with you?"

Asadi swallowed hard. That was not what he wanted to hear. "No, we had a wreck." He pointed in the direction of the Polaris. "I left her and Duke to get help, but I—"

"I know," Lacey interrupted. "They're gone though. Nobody's at the crash."

Still hoping for the best, Asadi suggested, "Maybe Ray and Bo found them."

"Maybe. But I didn't see anyone else around. Think I would've spotted them if they were out in the Gator."

Asadi looked out at the horizon. "And you didn't see any sign of Savanah or Duke?"

Lacey stared out at it too. "I got as high as I could up on the sandhills for a better range of sight. But it was just too dark. The only thing I could see was the floodlight and your fire."

Asadi looked up to find that the stars and moonlight were beginning to get blocked out by black clouds, then looked over to Lacey. "So, what do we do now?"

"I'll have to get you up in the saddle with me." Lacey reached forward and gave Surf's bushy blond forelock a good scratch. "Sorry for a little extra weight, big guy, but it's an emergency."

"Wait. If you saw the fire, then maybe I can make a bigger one. Put it on top of the hill, so Savanah and Duke can see it too."

"I don't know." Lacey looked squeamish. "Think it's best we get you back to get your ankle looked after. Make sure things don't go from bad to worse."

"It's okay." Asadi made a show of walking around without a limp. Despite the excruciating pain, he refused to show it. "See. I'm fine. Just send someone out here when you get back to headquarters." He pointed to the sign. "Boone 9–2H. Ray will know right where to find me."

"I'll go back and tell Vicky what happened. Sooner they can get out there the better. You can stay here and keep an eye out for them. But *don't* go anywhere. Just stay by the fire and keep warm. Now that we've got a good landmark, everything should be fine."

Asadi smiled wide to help Lacey rest a little easier. "I'll be okay. Just send help soon."

Lacey returned the gesture and said under her breath, "Garrett's going to kill me." Without another word, she turned toward the road, brought Surf into a trot, and disappeared into the night.

38

The drive to his brother's house gave Garrett a chance to think about the investigation, which seemed to be stalled. It wasn't Kai. It wasn't Grace. Nor was it even her soon-to-be ex-husband and his wealthy Wolfpack cronies in Midland-Odessa. Only thing that *was* certain was that the explosions were not accidents, as referenced by the first act of sabotage down in the Permian. Apparently, the missing lynchpin was narrowed down to some *foreigner* who'd fled the scene.

Baxter's story about the other explosion in Reeves County had sparked Smitty's recounting of his run-in with *Frenchy* out at the encampment. A quick call from Kai to his friends revealed that Simon Cloutier had left camp in his Jeep earlier and hadn't been seen or heard from since. In a group of nomads that was hardly a crime, but it was certainly unusual and worth a follow-up.

It was especially interesting that the leadership of Cosmic Order had given *Frenchy* a ringing endorsement. According to Kai, their home office in Switzerland had given instructions to allow Cloutier some breathing room to come and go as he pleased. Which seemed a bit odd.

As Garrett turned off the highway and onto the county road leading up to Bridger's ranch, he reached over to the passenger side and nudged Kai awake. "Almost there, man."

Kai sat up stiffly and yawned. "How long was I out?"

"Half hour or so." Garrett chuckled. "You were sawing logs the second your eyes closed."

Kai smirked. "Funny thing is that I haven't slept that good in years."

Garrett turned fully to see if he was joking. "You serious?"

"Nighttime is the worst for me. Too quiet. Too much time to think."

It wasn't the first time Garrett had heard that from other veterans. Tony Sanchez had taken to the bottle for that very reason. "If you ever want to talk, you know I'll understand."

"What's there to say?"

Garrett shrugged. "I don't know. Maybe a lot."

Kai asked in a way that seemed genuinely curious, "Like what?"

The last thing Garrett wanted to do was rehash what happened in the Panjshir Valley, but there was a part of him that knew he had to. "Look, for a long time, I held you responsible for what happened over there. For the men who died. You know that, right?"

Garrett half-expected Kai to recoil in dispute and launch an argument. But he didn't do any of that. He just gave a solemn nod.

"But I didn't just blame you," Garrett continued. "I blamed the squids hanging around Camp Lion, intel weenies at Bagram, and the damn brass sitting on their hands at Bragg. Hell, I even blamed God. Shook my fist at Heaven until my arm got tired and then pointed back at myself."

Kai turned to Garrett looking shocked. "*Why?* You didn't do anything wrong."

"Yeah, I know that now. And neither did the SEALS, MI, or leadership. And certainly not you. What happened, happened. And no amount of blame will bring anyone back."

Kai looked reluctant to accept Garrett's words. He turned forward, stared straight ahead, and got quiet. Only the howl of the wind and *tick* of icy snowflakes pecking at the roof filled the air.

Garrett went on. "The guys on that mountain don't get a second chance but we do. And I plan to do something with it. Ride away from the past and keep on going."

Kai looked as though he was contemplating those words hard.

"You're talking about your boy, right?" He slowly turned back. "Asadi is your do-over."

"He's a big part of it," Garrett conceded. "But I've got a girl I plan to marry, and that's a big part of it too. We've got a lot to live for, you and me, and there isn't a friend of ours who'd want us to squander what we have. They'd want us to live life to the fullest. Every single moment."

"Yeah, I left a lot unsaid with my family." Kai looked a little more hopeful. "Wouldn't mind going back to California and setting things right. Won't be easy, but I'd like to try."

"The key is to find common ground," Garrett explained. "For me and my dad, it was saving the ranch. That it was our center of gravity. Something to fight for. To die for, if necessary."

"You're willing to die for a piece of land?" Kai smirked. "Always knew you were nuts."

"Probably am," Garrett agreed. "Hard to explain but it was like bringing a dying person back to life. And the land, the cattle, and those horses helped Asadi to heal in ways I never could."

"I get it, I guess." Kai smiled. "But I still think you're crazy."

"I'm sure a psychiatrist would have a field day. But the ranch is a tie to my past. Where my Comanche ancestors roamed. Hell, my own mother is buried on the place. It's like a time machine for me. I can go back into the past and be with her again. Or I can look out and see the future. Imagine my grandkids riding those same trails that Bridger and I used to ride."

"Worse goals in the world than saving the land you love. But the oil and gas stuff I don't understand. Just doesn't seem to fit you. Your vision for the future."

Garrett gave a nod. "Yeah, well, there's a story to that too. Less romantic. To keep the ranch afloat, I had to go into the hole. And after wildfire hit the place, I ended up near bankrupt. I made a deal with Vicky Kaiser to partner up on an energy venture and she paid off my debt."

"So, that's how you ended up working with her?" Kai's face seemed to register an understanding. "Given what our bosses told us about her and Mescalero, the partnership between you two seemed a bit odd. Especially knowing your values. But now it all makes sense."

"It was a deal with the devil," Garrett conceded. "But I lived to fight another day."

"If it was that or nothing, I get it. Did what you had to do to save the place."

"Yeah . . . but if I'm being truthful, there was more to it than that. My pride got the better of me. I was tired of scraping by. Wanted to prove I could hack it in business with the big boys. Prove I wasn't just some washed-up old gunslinger who had nothing else to do after the war."

Kai turned to Garrett, looking a bit curious. "Prove it to who?"

"Don't really know. My family. My girlfriend. Maybe even myself. But it doesn't feel like me." He turned to Kai and laughed. "Hell, I don't sleep much either. Usually up all night, just wondering what I'm going to do next. This oil and gas business has been a blessing and a curse."

Kai didn't respond but looked like he understood. After a few seconds, he added. "It *was* my fault, you know."

Dwelling on his own confession, that he'd mentioned to no one other than the man sitting in the passenger seat, Garrett was caught off guard by the comment. "What was your fault?"

"Panjshir Valley." Kai wore a blank expression. "I made the wrong call."

"A lot of bad calls were made that day," Garrett assured. "Wasn't just you."

"None as bad as my own. Platoon leader wanted to take the route over the ridge you gave us. But I wanted to go around. I thought we could make better time skirting the mountain than going straight up. And it led right into an ambush that took us out of the fight."

Garrett didn't want to push the issue given Kai's admission. But as long they were heading down this awful memory lane, then they might as well go all the way. "There was another QRF that could've come though, Kai. But they said you shut it down. *Why?* Why would you do that?"

"Battle of Mogadishu. Takur Ghar." Kai shook his head. "I

could go on and on with tragedies like that. To be honest, I thought
you all were doomed. And I thought we were too. Just didn't want
to be the guy who made one horrible situation a whole lot worse."

Garrett was tempted to keep pressing. He had a lot more questions than that. But what was the point? The Rangers had seen their
share of battles gone wrong. And the Black Hawk Down incident in
Mogadishu was one not easily forgotten. Kai's call in the Panjshir
Valley was a bad one. But it was an honest one. It was a decision that
had crushed more souls than actual death.

Garrett sighed with his concession. "Well, nobody's got a crystal ball. I've made my own bad choices. Can't fault you for doing
what you thought was right at the time."

"Against the advice of others." Kai stared out the window into
the darkness. "Thought I knew better. Simple as that."

Although it was Kai who was making the admission, Garrett
felt as if the burden was lifted from him. "Don't hold on to it anymore. If I can let it go, then so can you."

"Not sure I know how to do that." Kai turned back. "You found
your new path. But I'm still looking for mine."

"Not sure what that path is either." Garrett smiled. "But I'm
willing to help you find it."

With a solid nod from Kai in return, Garrett decided he'd better
change the subject, lest the conversation turn into a weepy full-on
confessional. Fortunately, they had just arrived at his brother's ranch.
As they rumbled over the cattleguard, he pointed out ahead.

"This is Bridger's house. Know I told you about him a time or
two."

Kai looked up as if digging back into the past. "Successful attor-
ney brother who could do no wrong. Am I remembering it right?"

As it turns out, Bridger *could* do wrong. In fact, only three years
before he had unwittingly gotten involved in a money-laundering
scheme with Preston Kaiser and a drug cartel. But Garrett wouldn't
muddy the waters. For now, they'd use his brother's analytical lawyer mind to help piece together whatever conspiracy the Order
might be involved in with Simon Cloutier.

39

The farther Kim marched away from the BMW the less she thought of Bayat's safety and the more she thought of her own. She'd ripped a piece of fabric from her chador, fashioning a headscarf that would conceal her blond hair, cover her face, and leave a slit for the eyes. It was a passable disguise at a distance. But an up-close inspection would be the end of the farce.

The idea was to sneak in from the back of the town, steal a car, and hopefully disappear without notice. Fortunately, the rural desert community was sparsely populated, with only a few scattered pedestrians seemingly on autopilot, moving lazily along the dusty streets. Women in burqas dipped in and out of shops, while men gathered in twos and threes outside them, smoking cigarettes and occasionally glancing around as a car or tractor puttered by.

As Kim made her way through town with Faraz at her side, it appeared as if nothing was out of the ordinary, until they came upon a crowd of about twenty men gathered on the main street of town. She was about to suggest to Faraz that they turn and go the opposite way when a couple of men, dressed in traditional Afghan attire of round-top *pakol* hats and flowing *shalwar kameez*, spotted them. They shot a suspicious glare at Faraz and beckoned him over.

Kim whispered, "Think we should turn around? Pretend we didn't notice."

He whispered back, "Then they'll assume we don't belong."

"We *don't* belong," Kim argued. "Nothing we can do about that now."

"Just stay behind me and I'll handle it."

Before Kim could persist, Faraz moved ahead and broke into Dari, little of which she could decipher. They gave her a couple of quick glances, but out of respect for Faraz, who they likely assumed was her husband, didn't let their gazes linger. As seconds turned into minutes, Kim was beginning to worry that they were hanging around too long.

Kim was subtly trying to get Faraz's attention when he abruptly ended the conversation and turned around. He spoke to her in Dari, and then waved her over. As she took a few timid steps toward them, he broke away from the two men and blocked her from their view.

Faraz leaned in and whispered, "Problem solved." He grabbed her by the arm and ushered her away from the crowd. "There's a place here we can rent a car. End of the street. Real cheap."

Kim glanced back as they moved down the sidewalk, finally feeling like they were a safe enough distance from the crowd to speak out loud again. "I hope real cheap means free. Because in case you've forgotten, they took all our money back at the compound."

"They just need someone at our destination that can vouch for payment."

"And you know someone who will do this?"

Faraz shrugged. "Don't worry. I've got it figured out."

Kim was tempted to keep pressing but when she turned back to the crowd, she noticed it had doubled in size since they'd first arrived. "Did you figure out what's going on over there?"

"Oh yeah, they're looking for us."

"*What?*" Kim looked back again and picked up her pace. "They said that?"

"Don't worry." Faraz tightened his grip on her arm and eased her back to a steady pace. "They don't suspect that it's you and me."

"Why wouldn't they? First thing you tell them is that we're looking for transportation."

"They're looking for three people. Not two. All of which they heard were Americans. The story was that a local merchant was robbed, his workers killed, and the thieves stole his car."

"*Merchant?*" Kim guffawed. "News is more skewed here than back at home." She looked up at Faraz. "How did you explain why we're here?"

"I told them that we came by bus, but we had to get off and rest because you're pregnant and feeling nauseous. Said that we're on our way to Shir Khan and need to be there by afternoon to visit your sick mother, who is in the hospital."

"And they believed that?" Kim asked.

Faraz smiled, clearly proud of his handiwork. "Every word."

He looked and sounded a little too cocky for Kim's liking, but she had to admit he was cool under pressure. Aside from that, the concocted story he'd made up on the fly was surprisingly pretty sound. If they made it back alive, she might have to offer him a job. Like any good CIA ops officer, he had that ability to lie with ease. *Maybe a little too easily.*

Kim felt her body tense each time they drifted near a passerby. But they never so much as elicited more than a passing nod. Feeling a sense of hope or relief had always generated a roller-coaster effect. The moment she felt secure was the moment she doubted her safety.

Approaching the end of the street, Faraz pointed up to a chipped painted sign with a poorly sketched outline of a car. "This is it. This is the place."

Kim hadn't expected a Hertz or Avis, but she'd certainly imagined something a little more reputable than this. Out front of the storefront were two white Nissan Sentras that could be described as jalopies, at best. One had a flat front tire and the other was missing an engine hood.

Faraz turned to her at the front door. "Just wait here. I'll be right back."

Kim wanted to argue, hating the idea of being left out in the open on the street. But she had no idea what would happen if the owner spoke to her directly. "Just hurry, okay?"

Faraz shot her a glare. Clearly that was the plan, and the admonition had rubbed him the wrong way. But before she could apologize, he turned and went inside. To anyone watching, the marital spat probably made their phony relationship look all the more real. But only a few seconds later she was under scrutiny, as three men spotted her as they came around the corner.

They watched her with looks of suspicion and contempt, possibly because of the shoddy quality of her homemade niqab and given the fact that she wasn't wearing the traditional blue burqa. Or maybe it was just due to the fact that she was unescorted. Averting her eyes, Kim lowered her chin, eased up to the wall of the rental shop, and tried to make herself small—not hard to do at five foot two and a hundred and fifteen pounds.

She had just felt a hand grip her shoulder when the door flew open and Faraz marched outside. He shoved the one who had grabbed her and sent him tumbling into the street. Another stepped up to help, but Faraz was already there, yelling in the guy's face. When a third moved in, Faraz turned his glare on him, jabbed a finger into his chest, and unleashed a fiery verbal assault.

Kim only knew a few words in Dari like *wife*, *insult*, and *honor* that were flying back and forth. When it looked as though things couldn't get worse, Faraz cocked a fist and mentioned the name Naji Zindashti, his drug kingpin boss, which stopped the attackers dead in their tracks. The crisis appeared to be averted, but the commotion drew the attention of the nearby mob.

As a throng of shouting men ran in their direction, Faraz held up the keys and said something to Kim in Dari that she presumed meant *let's get the hell outta here*. Unimpeded, they moved to the hoodless white Sentra and got inside. He cranked the engine, which surprisingly started, and he put the car in drive. As they pulled away, Kim sank into her seat and checked the rearview. Fortunately, it revealed that there was no one in close pursuit.

Kim looked over at Faraz, ready to thank him for rescuing her when she noticed his bloody knuckles. "What happened to your hand? That from when you pushed the guy?"

Faraz brought them to his face and studied them as if surprised. "Guess so."

"You guess so?" Kim asked. "You didn't feel it?"

Faraz kept his eyes forward, turning occasionally on side roads and down alleys, making a circuitous route away from the main street that would be difficult to trail. "I don't know."

Kim could tell he was being cagey. "How did you get the car keys? Did the owner agree to let someone else vouch for you in Shir Khan?"

Faraz looked a little guilty. "Not exactly."

"Then how did you get them?"

"I tried to reason, but he wouldn't listen." Anger flashed in Faraz's eyes. "And then *you* got yourself in trouble. So, I did what I had to do and then took the keys and left."

"You mean you knocked out some innocent person and stole them?"

"We needed a car and now we have one. Just be glad it only came to that."

Part of Kim knew that Faraz was right. Desperate times called for desperate measures, and given the impending danger and Bayat's weakened condition, it was about as bad as it could get. But in all her time on the job, she'd never asked anyone to harm an innocent civilian. Of course, this was a classic *ends versus means* scenario. It was literally life and death.

She had to remind herself that Faraz, in addition to being sweet little Asadi's long-lost older brother, was also a criminal. It was unlikely this was the first time he'd used physical violence to get what he wanted. But that was a problem for another day. They'd tipped off their location, which meant they were even worse off now than they were in the BMW.

As soon as she and Faraz picked up Bayat they could be on the road. And with a little lead time, they could safely link up with Mario undetected. With her CIA counterpart in mind, Kim pulled out her cell phone to make a call. She had just typed in the number and was about to press send when the rattle of automatic gunfire prompted Faraz to slam on the brakes.

Kim yanked the cover from her head and glanced around. "Where did that come from?"

Head on a swivel, Faraz jammed on the accelerator, sped down the dirt road, and nosed the car around the corner of the auto repair shop where they'd left Bayat. He was still there, as was the vehicle. But unfortunately, so were their old adversaries in the red Toyota Hilux.

The only good news was that the back-and-forth exchange meant Bayat was still in the fight and giving them hell. But the tit-for-tat wouldn't last long. She had left him with only one extra magazine for the UZI. Which meant in a matter of seconds, his ammo would be spent.

arrett could tell that giving Bridger a heads-up on the investigation had paid off in spades. His lawyer brother was busting to report a win for their case from the moment he opened the door. The former high school quarterback was still extremely competitive and was as aggressive in the courtroom as he had been on the football field. It was clear by his face that they were headed for victory, or at the very least that he'd scored a big touchdown pass.

In the short time he'd had to start his investigation, Bridger had put together a war room with maps, legal documents, and printed articles that were scattered about the den and the kitchen. After Garrett made introductions, his brother gestured toward a table in the dining area where there was a carafe of coffee, as well as a spread of bacon, eggs, and pastries laid out for them.

"Given the hour," Bridger began, "I feel like this qualifies more as a midnight snack than breakfast. But I thought you could use a little fuel to keep you running."

"Man, you have no idea." Garrett looked around for the pastry baker but came up empty. "Where's Cassidy? Wanted to see if I could grab a couple of her famous homemade cinnamon rolls for the road. Asadi hears that he missed out on the mother lode, I'll be in trouble."

"She and the girls hit the road this evening," Bridger explained. "Headed to Lubbock for some 4-H thing down there. Wanted to shake a leg before the weather moves in." He grabbed a couple of rolls and put them on a napkin. "And don't worry about taking a few rolls. *I'll* be in trouble if I don't save some for him."

"Looks like they barely missed the snowstorm." Kai took a bite of his cinnamon roll as he spoke. "Wind is picking up and skies are going dark."

"Gonna be a nasty one," Bridger agreed, scooping a healthy portion of eggs onto his plate. He turned to Garrett. "Eat up, Bucky. You look like hell."

"Feel like it too. Been a long-ass day and I've got a feeling that it's far from over."

Bridger poured Garrett a cup of coffee from a carafe on the table. "You smart enough to think while you eat?"

Garrett grinned. "Only if you dumb it down for me."

"No problem." Bridger shot Kai a wink. "Been doing that my whole damn life."

Kai chuckled, seeming to get a kick out of the teasing. "Well, Counselor, Garrett might've told you that I'm along for the ride to clear my group of any wrongdoing. Any luck with that?"

Bridger shook his head. "Afraid not. In fact, your organization has quite a reputation for civil disobedience. Mostly in Europe though. Record is pretty clean here in the States."

"Better update that record." Garrett cut eyes at Kai, including him in the playful teasing. "Witnessed some civil disobedience around here up close and personal."

Kai raised his hands in a show of mea culpa. "Man, I told you I was sorry about all that."

"I know. I know. And I'm also aware that blocking roads and blowing up pipelines are two vastly different crimes." Garrett looked to Bridger. "Seen anything like that over in Europe?"

Bridger looked down at his notes. "Broken windows. Graffiti. Disturbing the peace. But nothing that would land anyone in the hospital or the morgue."

Garrett felt a little funny defending the Order, but as a law enforcement officer he knew that there was a big disctinction between unbridled passion and extreme violence. He wasn't excusing the former. But he didn't want to waste his time going down any pointless rabbit holes.

Kai looked hopeful. "So, you're saying that you don't suspect it's us?"

Bridger took a sip of his coffee, seeming to buy time while he thought. "At this point, there's not any direct link to Cosmic Order. But I found something else." He spread several printed newspaper articles out across the table. "There were other incidents similar to what happened here, each one in a time span of about five years, at different places across the globe."

Kai took a minute to study the articles. "None of these mention the Order."

"Not specifically," Bridger agreed. "All different environmental organizations, each with names that are dumber than the next." He smiled and added, "No offense."

Kai stayed focused on the news stories. "Then what does that have to do with us?"

Bridger slid a stack of papers that looked like a report over to Kai. Each section was marked with yellow Post-it Notes. "Did some research on your funding, and that's where it all gets real complicated. Looks like you've got some skilled accountants and lawyers."

Garrett kept himself from laughing. His brother was a master of corporate shell games, largely because he'd done it with the best of them. "Okay, what are we looking at here?"

Bridger shrugged. "Nothing that out of the ordinary on the surface. Cosmic Order is funded by an environmental philanthropy called Earth Action Now. They're the face of the movement. Highly connected. Pretty big lobby all over Europe, Canada, and the United States."

"That's no secret." Kai seemed a little defensive. "Just look on the internet. You can find the connection there without a whole lot of searching."

"Oh, I did." A wry smile spread across Bridger's face. "But did you also know that Earth Action Now gets the lion's share of its backing from Ressource Absolue, an oil and gas company based out of Marseille, France?"

"*Energy* company," Kai corrected, as he clearly flew into protective mode. "Absolue is one of the good guys. They were founded as an oil and gas company, but they're aggressively moving toward renewables. You should look at what they're doing to promote wind and solar."

"Saw that too. Looks like they'll be fully transitioned to green energy in about fifty years."

"It takes time," Kai argued.

"Hell of a long time," Bridger agreed. "The company and all its executives will make billions on oil and gas between now and then."

Wanting to prevent an argument, Garrett intervened. "What are you getting at, Bridger? Hypocrisy isn't a crime. A lot of companies do that. Absolue is just playing the game."

"Yeah, it's a game for sure." Bridger pointed to an article with the headline that read "Activists Disrupt Pipeline Expansion." The lead paragraph identified Nature First as the face of the protests. "A little more digging," Bridger added, "and you find that Absolue was up for the bid on this particular project. Press got so bad for the rival energy company up against them that they ultimately pulled out of the running and slinked away in disgrace."

"Who ended up getting the pipeline project?" Garrett asked.

Bridger looked like he had just laid down a royal flush. "Well, who do you think?"

Kai, on the other hand, looked sick to his stomach. "When did this happen?"

"About two years ago." Bridger pointed to the other articles with similar headlines. "Wherever you go, there's a nexus between Absolue, Earth Action Now, and some frontline group of environmental radicals. And that connection is symbiotic. Relationship goes back with multiple vanguard organizations that all just disappear when something bad happens like a protest gets out of hand, or someone gets hurt, and investigators start closing in."

Garrett took a moment to process what he was hearing. "Okay, then it sounds like Cosmic Order might just be Absolue's next fall guy."

Bridger's research certainly married up with Kai's confession that Cosmic Order was taking its cues from overseas. But a corporate boogeyman was one problem. The bigger issue was that there was an operative on the ground. And there was a good chance he would strike again.

"If that's true," Kai said to Garrett, "then we need to do something. The question is what."

Garrett took a sip of his coffee. "First and foremost, we need to find that Frenchman."

"Frenchman?" Bridger asked surprised.

"Simon Cloutier," Kai answered. "He was sent in from our headquarters office in Switzerland. But it looks like he went missing from my camp a couple hours ago."

"Pulled a gun on Smitty," Garrett added. "Of course, you can't hold it against him. Guilty of that once myself."

Bridger furrowed his brow. "Frenchman on the loose around here shouldn't be hard to find."

It was true that the man would stick out, but only because he was about a couple of centuries too late. French pioneers were among the first to explore the area around the Canadian River. In fact, it was rumored that the name itself came from a group of French traders who'd noted the presence of Canadian merchants at the confluence with the Arkansas River.

Kai looked to Garrett. "What do you think finding Cloutier will prove? He's not going to admit to blowing anything up. Even if you throw him in that oil pit."

"*Oil pit?*" Bridger glared at Garrett. "What's he talking about?"

Garrett winced. "Trust me, Bridger. It's better you don't know." He turned to Kai. "You're right. But if Cloutier is the bomber, then there's a good chance that he's either scouted or will be scouting other locations to hit."

Kai gave an approving nod. "But how do you narrow the search?

There has to be a million facilities he can hit around here. And you said it yourself, pipelines are running everywhere."

"You can narrow it down like this." Bridger pulled up a map on his laptop of pipelines in the area. He pointed to an intersection of pipe. "Once the Mescalero Compressor Station went down, this one took up the slack. This one goes offline and we're sunk. We'll be down for months."

Garrett studied the photo. It was inside the perimeter of the Washita Game Ranch. The property, nearly three thousand acres, was surrounded by a fence that was ten feet high. Because of the whitetail trophy deer roaming the area, it was monitored closely for poachers. It wouldn't be impossible for someone to cut the wire or disable the locks, but whoever was coming in or out would no doubt be caught on one of the dozens of security and trail cameras.

Garrett looked to Kai. "I know the guy who runs the place. He'll give me the code to get into the front gate and office. Let's go see if Cloutier has popped up on his feed. If we find him snooping around by the Washita Compressor Station, then I think we've got our man."

Bridger perked up. "I'll keep researching on my end. Got a text into a law school buddy of mine in Houston with Baker Botts. His firm has done a good bit of work with Absolue. Maybe he'll have some intel we can use."

"Good deal. In the meanwhile, we'll do our best to find this Simon Cloutier, or whatever his real name is. I'm assuming that it's an alias. I'll get the sheriff to run it."

"You really think Cloutier's the guy?" Kai asked Garrett, looking a little squeamish. "That he's connected with one of these other groups that were working for Absolue?"

"Nothing's for certain just yet. But he's the best suspect we have now given what we know. And I think the quicker we find him, the quicker we get to the bottom of all this."

"Need anything else?" Bridger asked.

Garrett held up his coffee mug. "How about a to-go cup? Our work's just getting started."

41

Ike Hodges couldn't have been any more stunned had Crystal Smitty walked in dragging a dead skunk and smacked him with it upside the head. It was the first time she had returned to Crippled Crows after putting in her two weeks' notice years earlier. He would've been a lot happier to see the best waitress he'd ever had if it wasn't the middle of the night.

The hour of the visit, coupled with the serious look on her face, meant there was trouble.

Sliding from behind the bar, Ike made his way through the crowd and met Crystal halfway. But before he could playfully scold her for staying gone so long, she had him in a hug, generating a few cocked eyes from some drunk nosy patrons. Which meant it was time for some privacy.

Aside from the crowd noise and blaring electric guitar solo onstage from Comanche Moon's lead singer, he didn't like the idea of being gawked at by customers. It had taken years to build his reputation as a *not to be screwed with* owner of the *World's Trashiest Dive Bar* and he hated to think that the countless ass kickings dished had all been for naught.

Ike broke away from his guest and rested his forearm over her shoulder. He leaned in and whispered in her ear, "How about a little bourbon to warm you up?"

Crystal waved her hand at him. "Been on more of a chardonnay kick lately." She added with a smile. "Just a minute of your time will do. I can't stay long."

Ike looked at her askance. Crystal's time hobnobbing with the Kaisers hadn't just resulted in a different appearance. Apparently, it had altered her palate too. "Well, step into my office then." He pointed to the door behind his bar. "Let's get away from all this racket."

Crystal led and Ike followed her inside his office. Just like old times, he sat atop the floor safe while she eased in behind the desk. Had anyone walked through the door, they would've thought she owned the place. While he was happy to see this former party girl settle down and get focused on Ray and Savanah, it made him a little sad.

Turning down a drink was his first clue that she'd changed. And truth be told, he'd always been partial to bleach blond and skintight. But the darker hair, and business casual attire, showed that she'd really moved on since becoming Vicky Kaiser's assistant. And it suited her just fine.

Crystal picked up Ike's cell phone, which was buried under a mess of papers. "Guess this explains why you didn't answer my calls."

Ike felt a little guilty, but the damn thing was starting to feel like a ball and chain. "Sorry about that. Probably should keep it close since I got rid of my landline."

Crystal looked at him curiously. "Why'd you get rid of your phone?"

"Nothing but trouble on the other end usually. I've learned over the years that anybody who wanders into a place like this doesn't want to be found."

There had been plenty of wives looking for husbands, and sometimes the other way around. But with age he'd become more reclusive. Ike understood the need to drop out of sight, unwind with a drink, and just be left alone. Basking in the neon, whiskey in hand, with some outlaw country playing in the background for some folks was just what the doctor ordered.

As Crystal leaned forward, her smile vanished. "I needed to find you for a good reason."

"If you're here this late, I'm guessing it's kind of pressing. We can save the small talk for another day. What's on your mind?"

"Actually, it's two things, Ike. You're the only one around here who knows about one of them. Which means I gotta talk about it with you."

If there was ever a place in the world where terrible secrets were made it was Crippled Crows. But there was only one confided to him by Crystal that he swore he'd take to the grave. "This about Duke?"

Crystal swallowed hard and gave a single nod.

"What about the other issue?" Ike asked.

"Well, it's related to Duke in an odd way. Or I don't know. Maye it's not." Crystal was clearly flustered. "Sorry I'm not making much sense. I'm just stressed."

This time, Ike leaned forward. "What's going on?"

"Savanah can't be found for starters." Crystal paused, looking as if she was replaying the situation in her mind. "Well, not just Savanah. Asadi and Duke are missing too."

"*Missing?* Missing where?"

"Out at the Mescalero," Crystal explained. "They went out on Duke's Polaris looking for some horses earlier and haven't been seen since."

"And you're worried something happened?"

"We don't know at this point." Crystal teared up a little. "Vicky said Lacey rode out looking for them. But Ray and Bo are unreachable. Garrett too. They're off dealing with all that explosion stuff." She looked a little sheepish. "Guess I was hoping that maybe we could get up in your helicopter and try to find them ourselves."

"Crystal, I'd do it without a second thought, but my bird is still down for repairs. Thanks to the aforementioned gentlemen, I'm still plugging up bullet holes from my last favor to Garrett."

Crystal looked disappointed. "That's okay. They're probably already back at the barn anyhow." She looked at her phone again, as if expecting to get an update at any moment. "Just better safe than sorry, you know."

"Never apologize for being a worried mama. Happy to help if I can."

Crystal got up from the desk chair. "I should probably get back out there. We can discuss the other thing some other time."

"Nonsense." Ike waved her off. "My bird might be winged, but I still got Black Betty."

Ike was fiercely proud of his new Ford Raptor. Well, it was new to him anyhow. He'd won the agate black metallic finish pickup with twin-turbo 450-horsepower engine in a high-stakes poker game from a drugstore cowboy in Spearman. The losing party had inherited all the money and pomposity of his granddad, but not a lick of the old man's business sense.

"Think the kids might be lost out in the sandhills?" Ike asked.

Crystal nodded. "Vicky said Duke's UTV tracks were headed that direction."

"Then time's a-wasting." Ike jumped off the safe and waved her on. "I'm sure everything's fine but it won't hurt to go out on patrol." He winked at Crystal. "Just leave your car here and ride with me. It'll give us a chance to catch up."

THEY'D MADE IT ABOUT HALFWAY over to the Mescalero Ranch in his Ford Raptor when Ike inquired about Duke. He wouldn't have pried into the past if he didn't think it was important. But after they'd discussed the latest theories on the pipeline explosions and made a little small talk, it seemed an appropriate time to ask. After all, she was the one who'd first brought it up.

Ike turned to Crystal, noticing that she seemed nervous. And he suspected it wasn't just about the kids. "So, how's the Duke situation working out? Rumor has it he's back living with Vicky."

"He's back, all right. Just never thought I'd ever see him again."

"How do you feel about it?"

"Weird as hell." Crystal pinched the bridge of her nose. "There are so many things I want to say to him but can't. And even if I could, I wouldn't know where to start."

"Why can't you talk to him? I mean . . . who's stopping you?"

Crystal looked at Ike like he was crazy. "Really think Duke would want to know the truth?"

In all Ike's years he'd concluded that the truth was way over-rated. But he also lived with a *come as you are* mentality. It wasn't in his nature to be someone he wasn't, which sometimes meant that his philosophies contradicted. Of course, that's when life was the most interesting. And it's probably why a lawbreaker like himself had buddied up with a law-and-order DEA cowboy. With Garrett Kohl, the only thing you could expect was the unexpected.

Crystal looked forward and sighed. "I can't tell Duke anything because of the contract. I agreed to it. I signed it. And I took the money. Nothing more needs to be said than that."

"The *hell* it doesn't! Deals with crooks are made to be broken. And Preston and his old man are two of the biggest criminals I've ever met. And that's saying a lot!"

"I know, Ike. I know. But I gave my word. And when you grow up dirt poor, you got nothing else in this world but your honor. I made a pact and I aim to keep it."

Ike calmed himself. "If anybody knows that you're a woman of your word, I do." He gave her a playful nudge from across the console. "How many times did I try to get you to leave Ray when he was in prison and saddle up with me? But you never strayed once. Loyal to a fault."

Crystal grinned back. "Maybe . . . you're just not as good a catch as you think you are. And it wasn't because I was loyal to Ray. I just had higher standards."

Ike laughed. "You've always been about ten rungs above me, Crystal. No doubt about it."

"Well, when it comes to Duke, there's a cold hard reality that I don't like to think about."

Ike had never asked about her love affair with Preston Kaiser and didn't want to know. But Crystal had confided that she'd been in high school when it took place. Not only would it have caused a major scandal because she was a minor, but it would've landed that son of a bitch in jail. For the sake of protecting the Kaiser name, his father had covered it up with a bribe.

After accepting a cash payment of $25,000 and signing an airtight nondisclosure, the seventeen-year-old Crystal went away to have a child that she was never supposed to see or talk about ever again. Duke went on to live with an aunt, who he thought was his mother, and he was not to return to Canadian. But the High Plains is like a vortex that sucks back its kin.

Ike decided to cut the jokes, as she seemed to get more serious. "What cold hard reality are you talking about?"

She folded her hands and looked down at her lap. "People like the Kaisers don't really want anything to do with people like me. At least out in public."

"Crystal, he's not just some random Kaiser. He's your son. That changes things."

"Does it though?" Tears streamed down her cheeks. "What does it really change? All of a sudden, he realizes that his real father is dead and his mother is some trailer trash waitress."

"Don't you say that. God broke the mold when he made you. I mean it, now."

"But it's true, Ike. I'm not like the Kaisers. You know where I'm from. Where I've been."

"Well, here's some more truth. For all my joking, I would've married you in a heartbeat. Hell, you know I love Ray, but I'd have brained him with my billy club and buried him out behind the bar if I thought you'd run away with me." Ike nudged her arm with his knuckles. "I'd even let you visit him on holidays just to show what a good sport I am."

Crystal cleared the tears from her face and laughed. "Thanks, I guess." She turned and smiled. "Sounds . . . romantic?"

"I'm creative if nothing else." Ike gave her a solid nod. "My exwives will tell you that."

Crystal laughed. "They've told me that and a whole lot more."

"Look, Crystal, your secret's safe with me until the end of time. All I'm saying is that whatever you do, do it for the right reasons. It might be a shock to Duke at first, but he'd be lucky to know you as his mom. Won't take him long to figure that out."

Crystal smiled and looked ahead. "You're sweet to say that, Ike. But there's something else. Something that only I know. Now that Preston and his father are dead."

When it came to the Kaisers, there were some deep, dark secrets that could get you killed. Ike shuddered to think what this could be about. "If it has anything to do with Jimmy Hoffa or the Lindbergh baby, I don't want to know."

Crystal shook her head. "It's worse."

"How could it be worse?"

"Before I signed the contract with Preston's father, I wanted to make sure that my child would be taken care of. Mr. Kaiser, on the spot, took out some papers from a desk drawer and showed me where he'd amended his own will and testament to include Duke as an heir."

"Amended how?"

"Mr. Kaiser told me he wanted to keep the Mescalero Ranch with a male successor. Said it was built by a man and should be run by a man." Crystal rolled her eyes. "You might remember how old-school he was."

"Arrogant asshole is more like it. But sounds like him. Think this document was legit?"

Crystal shrugged. "I'm not a lawyer or anything, but it looked pretty official. Plus, he had no reason to lie about it to me. He seemed pretty proud of himself. Like he was getting away with something that had nothing to do with my situation. It was like he wanted to show it off."

Ike smiled with the realization of knowing why Vicky and her goofy sister Miriam hadn't been seen until after Preston died. They'd probably been given sizable trust funds to live off of, but the real Kaiser fortune was in the land and the businesses associated with energy exploration, which the girls had been cut out of until Preston's untimely death.

"What about the oil and gas?" Ike asked.

"All of the mineral assets too. According to that will, Duke is the rightful heir."

Ike couldn't believe his ears. "Does Vicky know about any of this?"

"I have no idea what she knows. I'm pretty sure she's aware that Duke is Preston's son. But I doubt that she knows about the will. And my guess is that if she does, she's not talking."

"Does she know that you're Duke's mother?"

"No, thank God." Crystal chuckled. "We get along okay as long as she's bossing me around at the ranch. But if she actually had the full story, I'd probably end up in a hole somewhere."

Suddenly, Ike thought back to his joke about Jimmy Hoffa and realized that he might've been closer to the truth than he ever imagined. He didn't think that Vicky was as bad as her father or brother, and he really didn't know that much about her at all. But if there was anything he'd learned over the years running a dive bar and serving multiple generations of patrons, it's that the apple doesn't fall too far from the tree. Kaisers were cruel to the bone.

"Whatever you do, Crystal, don't tell anyone else what you just told me. Big money makes for big crazy. Even a rumor of something like that is enough to get you killed."

"Believe me, I know." Crystal turned to him looking a little fearful. "See why I've kept all this to myself? Not even Ray knows any of this. Other than you, it's a deal that died with all the Kaiser men." As an afterthought, she added, "Except for Duke, I guess."

Ike reached up, massaged his bristly beard, and thought about what was at stake. It didn't take long to come back to his tried-and-true old philosophy. The truth was *way* overrated.

42

Garrett studied the video footage on the computer monitor in the Washita Game Ranch headquarters office, wondering if he and Kai were wasting their time. Other than the impressive trophy bucks, a whole lot of mesquite on the high ground, and a thick grove of oak trees down in the river bottom, the game and security cameras had captured nothing of value for their cause.

Sheriff Crowley's trace on Simon Cloutier had yielded no results, which was odd. Of course, there was no law against giving a phony name to his cohorts, but at this point there was no innocent reason as to why. If they could get some biometrics like fingerprints, a facial scan, or voice recording then they could run it through the databases with his friends at the CIA.

Garrett was about to go back through the video footage again when his brother called. "What you got for me, Bridger?"

"Couldn't find anything on Cloutier, but I got an earful on Ressource Absolue from my buddy in Houston. Couldn't get into specifics. Attorney-client privilege and all. But he told me that it's pretty well known that Absolue talks a good game on environmental issues but they're ruthless as hell. Operate like any of the other majors when it comes down to business."

"That doesn't surprise me," Garrett replied. "What else is new?"

"What's new is that Absolue is a direct competitor with Texas on LNG. In bed with the Qatari government to fill the order for the contract. Which they can. They're working behind the scenes to lobby the European Union to go with their suppliers over ours."

Again, that wasn't surprising. A deal of this magnitude would bring out everyone's cutthroat side. But the French were America's allies. Were it Russia, China, or Iran, Garrett wouldn't put it past them to engage in some kind of subterfuge. That said, unlike most Western intelligence services, France was fairly open about using its resources to engage in corporate espionage.

Is Simon Cloutier their spy?

Garrett continued. "Your friend think Absolue would get involved in something over here?"

"According to him," Bridger answered, "they wouldn't touch this kind of thing with a ten-foot pole. Too much backlash if something went wrong. But he told me about a consulting group based out of Lyon, France, called Solutions Globales. He said they're associated with Absolue and just *might* take things to the next level if the stakes were high enough."

"Global Solutions," Garrett repeated in English to himself. "Could they be any more vague?"

"Apparently, that's the way they like it. They're registered on Dun & Bradstreet, but that's about all I could find. No website. No articles on the company or interviews with executives. Just confirmation from my friend that they come highly recommended."

"Recommended for doing what?" Garrett asked.

"When I asked my friend, he got kind of uncomfortable. Said he didn't know exactly what they do. But they had access to high-level players. Focused on regulatory issues, corporate strategy, influence campaigns, and risk mitigation."

"You think your old law school friend might be covering for them?" Garrett asked.

"Nah, I don't think so. You know the old expression, 'If you have to ask how much something costs, you probably can't afford it.' I got the same impression with Solutions Globales. If you have to ask who they are, then you're not part of the club. My friend runs with a prominent crowd, but there's a whole other level of exclusive out there. And it has a lot to do with having the word *billionaire* by your name."

Over the years, Garrett had found that there were two sets of rules. It wasn't just the *haves* and *have-nots* anymore. Those at the very tip top of the food chain were playing an entirely different game on a whole separate field. For some reason, Jeffrey Epstein and his private island came to mind. That was an extreme example of corruption off the rails, but shadow systems and alternate rules for the world's most rich and powerful did exist.

Companies like Solutions Globales catered to individuals who operated in that realm. It was a world that Garrett didn't know. While there was nothing that particularly helped him right that moment, he couldn't help but think he was on the right track.

Garrett turned to Kai, who was still going through the video feed. "See anything yet?"

Kai looked up from the monitor and grinned. "You're not going to believe this, but I think we've got Cloutier. Looks like his Jeep, anyhow."

"How long ago?" Garrett pressed.

"He's here right now. West side of the ranch." Kai focused on the monitor. "This is the live feed from a perimeter security camera."

"What's he doing?"

"Just got out with a set of bolt cutters and walked up to the fence. Looks like he's about to cut the chain."

Garrett held the phone closer to Kai. "Bridger, did you hear that?"

"Yeah, I heard. That's the closest entrance to the Washita Compressor Station. Bet that's right where he's headed."

"Okay, we're going to stop this guy before he gets there. In the meantime, keep working on the link between Absolue, Solutions Globales, and the LNG deal with the EU. We've got nothing more than a conspiracy theory at this point. But we're connecting the dots."

Bridger asked, "Let's say we connect them, then what?"

Garrett spoke on the move. "The good news is once I have

something to go on, I can take this up to Conner Murray at the NSC. Can't mount much of a fight here at our end, but there's an American mission in Brussels. If we have evidence that a French competitor company is involved in corporate espionage and a potential sabotage operation, then the EU needs to know."

AS GARRETT DROVE TOWARD THE compressor station where they'd seen Simon Cloutier heading, he scanned the darkness on the periphery of his headlights but found no signs of life beyond the biggest mule deer buck he'd ever seen and a couple of fast-moving doe. If the Frenchman was still out there, then he had either gone the opposite way or was hiding down in the river bottom.

Garrett pulled up Conner Murray's contact info and pressed his number to make the call. Expecting to leave a message, he was shocked when the guy actually answered his office phone.

"Conner, this is Garrett Kohl. Sorry for calling so early, but it's important. Can we talk?"

Murray sounded groggy, like he'd pulled an all-nighter. "Yeah, what's going on?"

"Don't really have a long time to explain but wanted to give you a heads-up on a few things."

There was a pause on Murray's end before he asked, "You get a call from Mario?"

Garrett could detect a hint of worry in his voice. "No. Was I supposed to?"

"No, no. Sorry. Had something else on my mind. What's going on, Garrett?"

Garrett could tell there was a subject he needed to revisit, but given the urgency of the sabotage issue, he kept focused on the topic at hand. "Not really sure. We've got a pipeline deal going on down here in my part of the world and we've had a couple of explosions."

"Saw that in a situation report here." Murray had a tinge of sorrow in his voice. "Sorry to hear about the accident. Your family safe?"

"Yeah, we're all okay, thank God. But I'm not so sure it was an accident."

"The report said that—"

"Yeah, I know what the report probably said, but we think there might be something else going on. In fact, I'm chasing down someone right now who might be involved."

Murray's voice went from worried to eager. "What can I do to help?"

Garrett looked over at Kai, who was pointing to the right in a fork in the road. "Maybe a lot later on. But for now, I just need help filling in some gaps." He made the turn and stepped on the gas on a straightaway in search of Cloutier's Jeep. "You ever hear of the French security consulting company Solutions Globales? It might be connected to what's going on down here."

"Know of it, but don't know anyone over there personally. They've done some security work for people I've worked with in Europe. Founded by former members of DGSE."

Garrett had never worked with the Directorate General for External Security, the French equivalent to the CIA or British MI6. He'd heard they were a competent service but found it unusual that in addition to intel gathering, counterterrorism, and counterintelligence, DGSE had a more robust focus on economic spying than any of their Western counterparts.

He scanned ahead for Cloutier but saw nothing. "What do you know about them?"

"Very buttoned-down. Tight-lipped as it gets. Only take clients on referral. Highly connected with political leaders in the Middle East, Asia, and Africa. And my understanding is that they've got a lot of media influence. You want a story planted, they're your solution. If you want a story squashed, they can do that too. It's a one-stop shop for making problems go away."

Garrett thought about the concept. "What about creating problems? Any history of that?"

"Not that I know of offhand. But it doesn't mean they don't.

Covert action capabilities wouldn't be out of the question. Psychological operations. Influence ops. Why not?"

"What about a paramilitary component?" Garrett asked.

"Well, their personal security detail is made up of former DGSE Action Division. Basically, it's France's version of CIA Ground Branch. Former special operators from the armed forces and a few Foreign Legion guys mixed into the bunch. Why do you ask?"

Garrett pressed down on the accelerator on another straight stretch of road. The intel from Murray had his pulse racing. "Think they'd actually carry out a sabotage operation on U.S. soil?"

"Not sure. But the guys working for Global Solutions are some of the best in the business. From an operational perspective, they're certainly capable."

"Don't doubt they've got the skills," Garrett agreed. "But the stomach for potential blowback is another thing. Somebody would have to be worried to death about getting caught."

The sound of clacking on a keyboard preceded Murray's response. "Just did a quick search on the company and pulled up a report. According to a Defense Intelligence Agency source, Global Solutions was rumored to have aided in the Nord Stream pipeline explosion."

At the news, Garrett's pulse raced even faster. This lead looked promising. "Okay, now we're getting somewhere. They've got a history of this kind of thing."

"Don't jump to any conclusions," Murray warned. "That's only one account. There was more speculation and hearsay over that Nord Stream incident than any I've ever seen."

"You don't give it much credence," Garrett pressed.

"Didn't say that either. Just nothing was proven. But Global Solutions has the expertise and potentially the motive." There was a moment of low mumbling while Murray scanned the report. "Says here that their client, Ressource Absolue, made a fortune after the pipeline was destroyed."

Now with a suspect behind the bombings within reach, Garrett felt like they were getting somewhere. "Too many factors adding up. Has to be a connection to what's happening here."

"Would send you some help but your friends are tied up right now."

Garrett knew better than to ask where Kim and Mario were or what they were doing. He'd only get a cover story or a lie. Since hanging up his metaphorical guns he'd been left out of the loop, which was exactly how he wanted to keep it for the time being.

"Don't worry." Garrett looked over to Kai. "I'm getting some help from an old friend."

"Glad to hear it." Murray cleared his throat. "Just promise me you'll back off if things start looking dangerous."

"It's a deal," Garrett lied. "We're just going to keep an eye out. Do a little surveillance."

The phone call ended with Garrett feeling a bit more invigorated. With the input from Bridger and Murray, his investigation was coming together. If they could just catch this Frenchman in the act of sabotage it would be all but over and done.

Garrett pressed the gas and sped into a curve. "See anything, yet?"

"Not yet. But he's got nowhere to go. One road in. One road out. Once he gets up to the compressor station he'll be trapped. We may not catch him in the act, but I'd say he'd better have a damn good reason for being out here by himself in the middle of nowhere."

Garrett gave a confident nod. "Between what we know and what we suspect, it's enough to hold his feet to the fire. If we can get those guys who spotted the *foreigner* up here to identify Cloutier, then there's enough to start a real investigation. We'll see how cagey this Frenchman wants to be once we have a witness ready to testify and manslaughter charges on the table."

Kai chuckled. "Hope you're not planning on going back to that slush pit again. After what I saw earlier I—"

Kai had not gotten out the rest when the GMC's front end

lifted into the air and the pickup corkscrewed left, flipping first onto the roof, rolling to its side, and then turning over once more in slow motion until the truck was back on all four wheels. Several seconds passed as Garrett sat dazed, wondering if what just happened was real or imagined. Wondering if he was even alive.

His ears ringing from the blast, Garrett looked around through the shattered windows to find the truck engulfed in a cloud of pulverized caliche and snow. Instinctively, he mashed the gas to get off the X, but he saw that the hood was crumpled. His truck would be junked for parts.

Reaching right for Kai, Garrett felt before he saw that his friend was bleeding. In the chaos of the moment, his mind raced for answers. But the only conclusion he could draw since they were near the compressor station was that they'd arrived too late to stop the next act of sabotage.

As a suffocating waft of dust filled the cab through the busted-out windows, Garrett reached for the handle and kicked the door open. He had just stepped outside, gasping for air, when a bullet snapped by his ear. Diving to the ground, he rolled beneath the chassis and put his hands over his head as a flurry of rounds *tinged* and *thunked* against the back bumper and the tailgate.

In that moment it became obvious to Garrett that they weren't just collateral damage from an attack on the compressor station, but rather the target of an ambush. And it was no longer important that they were on to Cloutier. What mattered most now was that *he* was on to them.

43

K im watched frozen as two gunmen in the back bed of the red Toyota pickup unloaded with their AK-47s on the BMW below. Given the mayhem of the firefight, the shooters had not seen nor heard her and Faraz pull up in their Nissan. Before she could even suggest it, Faraz threw the car in reverse, jammed his foot on the gas, and backed behind the building for cover.

He pointed to a side door of the structure. "Can you get to Bayat through there?"

"Think so." Kim eyed the dark opening for a couple of seconds, trying to remember if their SUV was parked close enough to reach him without getting shot. "What's your plan?"

"I'll come in from behind. Distract them. While you get him out of there."

"And when they turn their guns on you?" Kim asked. "Then what?"

"I don't know." Faraz kept his gaze straight ahead. "But I'll think of something."

It was a horrible idea, but Kim didn't have a better one. "Okay, just be careful."

Without waiting for a reply, Kim flew out of the door and ducked into the building without even so much as a quick peek before going inside. She widened her eyes to utilize any light from a couple of broken windows. Navigating around some old equipment, she saw the plastic bucket about a half-second too late, tripped over it, and crashed to the floor.

Scrambling to her feet with a bloody knee, Kim dashed to the side door, discovering that two gunmen in the back bed of the Toyota were shooting almost straight down at Bayat. He returned fire from behind the BMW's hood with his submachine gun and caught one of them in the chest.

He shifted his aim on the next guy, but his UZI had coughed out its last round. With Bayat now defenseless, Kim stepped outside, picked up a rock, and hurled it at the gunman with hasty aim. It didn't connect, but it got his attention. He turned left and set his sights on her.

Kim hit the ground and covered her head with her arms as a flurry of rounds thunked into the wall. She was expecting the bullets to follow and braced for impact when a car horn sounded off, an engine roared, which was followed by a *bang* and a *crunch*. Looking up, Kim saw the smoking engine of their hoodless white Nissan crumpled beneath the back end of the red Toyota.

Sprinting to the BMW, she stopped at the back bumper and eased to the corner. Suspecting Bayat was out of ammo, but not knowing for sure, she didn't want to take the chance of falling victim to friendly fire. She dropped to a knee, eased up to the taillight, and whispered to Bayat.

"Hey, it's me!" She waited a couple of seconds and tried again: "Move this way if you can!"

After a few seconds of silence, Kim took a gamble, glanced around, and then withdrew immediately at the horrible sight. Not even bothering to stand, she clawed around the corner on all fours and collapsed atop Bayat. She didn't need to check his vitals, given the bullet hole, which was just slightly to the left of his sternum. Not unfamiliar with violent death, Kim was certain that given the placement of the round, so close to the heart, it was a near-instant death.

Reaching up to his face, Kim gently touched his eyelids and dragged them shut. She stifled a sob, remembering back on his earlier words: "Let's not go quietly," he'd said. "Let's make them earn it." True to his word, he'd done just that. Reza Bayat had fought like a lion to the very end.

Faraz walked up, his eyes fixed on Bayat, and said in a way that was oddly casual. "All the others are dead."

It took a second for Kim to notice the bloodied rock in his hand. It looked exactly like the one she'd thrown just moments before, but it could've been any of the dozens that were scattered around. Faraz was in a daze, no doubt a result of having just bashed in a man's skull.

Kim felt she should address it but didn't have the strength. "Can you help me with him?"

Faraz looked at her coldly. "Help you do what?"

It was a reasonable question. And it was one for which she had no answer. "We can't just leave him here like this. Out in the open."

Faraz dropped the rock in his bloody grip and it thudded onto the ground. He walked over, kneeled beside Bayat, and then reached out to Kim. "Can I have your scarf?"

Kim removed the material, which had gathered around her neck, and handed it over. Faraz took the covering and gently placed it over Bayat's face. Seemingly without effort, he scooped up the slight body and walked inside the repair shop, mumbling a prayer in Farsi that carried on the breeze. She tried to rise to follow, but her knees buckled, and she slumped against the car.

Kim gazed out at the horizon, thinking through one defeat after the next. This was supposed to be her do-over—a chance to make amends. She was going to leave *this time* having done something right for the people, the country, and God willing herself. But Afghanistan wasn't just the *graveyard of empires*. It was a place where any hope of redemption goes to die.

44

Powering through the pain of his sprained ankle, Asadi dragged mesquite branches to the highest sandhill peak he could find. Several trips up and down the dunes had left him winded, sweating, and a little disappointed with the size of his pile. But it was as good as it was going to get, and the fact that he had a fire at all was a feat worth celebrating.

Asadi used a few of his embers to ignite the brush, then did his best to block the blossoming flames from the raging wind with his body. As the flames grew, he moved closer and took comfort in their warmth. The blaze was nice, but still no comparison to the comfort of his nearby shelter. Longing for its protection, he turned back to it and stared. There was temptation to crawl back in his lodge and convalesce for a while, but he couldn't bring himself to abandon his post.

Tempted to cry at the thought of losing Savanah, Asadi threw a couple more mesquite branches on the fire and turned toward the rows of endless snow-covered sandhills. In the blink of an eye, he saw a shimmer. It looked like a flashlight about a hundred yards away. He waited a minute, then one more, praying that Duke and Savanah had seen his signal fire.

When another minute passed without a sign, Asadi did the unthinkable. He left the comfort of the flames to go after them himself.

• • •

LACEY GENTLY TUGGED THE REINS to slow Surf down as she raced up to the barn. Near the entrance by the corral, she leaned back in the stirrups and brought him to a halt. Stiff from the cold, she forced herself out of the saddle and slid to the horse's side. Her frozen feet radiated with a shock wave of pain when her boot heels struck the ground.

Vicky dashed up, looking frantic. "Oh, Lacey, thank goodness." She looked past Surf, clearly in search of the others. "Did you find them?"

Lacey's face was so cold she could barely get her jaw working. "Crash. Out there."

Vicky's hand flew to her mouth. "Are they hurt?"

Lacey nodded, before talking through the stiffness in her face. "Asadi's got a busted ankle. Made it to one of the wells. But Savanah's hurt, and she and Duke are missing."

"What happened to Savanah?" Vicky asked.

"Don't really know. Asadi said she might've broken some ribs. Hit her head, I think. But by the time I got to the crash, Duke and Savanah had left. So, she's at least up and moving."

Vicky looked only slightly more relieved. "I've been calling Ray, but he still won't answer."

Lacey held up her phone. "Been trying to call Garrett since I got a signal but he's not picking up either."

"I'll call Crowley." Vicky pulled out her phone and brought up the sheriff's contact info. "Have him put together a search-and-rescue team."

Lacey pulled out her keys. "I'll go back and get Asadi from that drill site."

Vicky looked back up and shot a skeptical glare. "You sure you can find him again?"

"I'll just follow the same road that brought me back here. Should only take a few minutes."

"Want me to go with you?"

"I can handle it," Lacey assured her. "Just stay on the phone until you get someone out here. We've got to find Savanah and Duke before that storm rolls in."

"Don't worry." Vicky gave a reassuring nod. "I'll have someone on the way out to help us by the time you get back."

THE ONLY GOOD THING ABOUT the cold, Asadi determined, was that his body was going numb. There was still a dull pain in his ankle but for the most part he couldn't feel a thing. No doubt he was doing permanent damage to the ligaments. And the farther he moved from the safety of his camp, the more uncertainty set in. He was starting to wonder if he'd even seen a light at all.

Asadi was about to turn back when he saw a beam of light two hills over. Without even thinking, he shouted and waved his arms wildly. "Over here! Over here! This way!"

When the beam of the flashlight swung in his direction, Asadi couldn't help but smile. Without giving a thought to the pain in his ankle, he careened down the knoll, careful to keep his own beam straight ahead so Duke and Savanah could follow it. He tried desperately not to show his overwhelming joy, which was difficult when he was nearly about to burst.

Asadi threw up a hand to shield his eyes from the harsh glare. "I was beginning to think I wouldn't find you. Was just about to turn back."

"Glad you didn't," Duke answered shivering. "I was headed the wrong way."

Asadi didn't know what registered first, the fact that Duke said *I* and not *we*, or the fact that he was standing there alone. Fighting to get his vision used to the dark again, Asadi moved ahead and scanned the length of the ridge above. "Where's Savanah?"

From behind Duke answered, "She was too weak, so I had to go on."

Asadi spun around and marched up to Duke. "You just left her?"

"Don't see her, do you?"

"You're not serious." Asadi turned to the ridge, then back to Duke. "She'll die out there."

"Oh, don't be so dramatic," Duke hissed. "She's fine. Just couldn't keep walking, that's all. So, I told her I'd go find somebody." He looked a bit smug. "Which as you can see, I did."

Asadi was tempted to be angry, but he supposed what Duke had done wasn't that different from his own decision to look for help. The difference was that he would have never left Savanah alone. But rather than dwell on that, he tried to focus on the good news, which was the fact that they were reunited. All they had to do was go back for her now.

Asadi pointed at the ridge from where Duke had come. "Okay, you ready?"

"Ready for what?"

"Lacey will be back to get us soon. So, we need to go get Savanah. Between the two of us, we can help her over the sandhills. But we need to hurry."

Duke shook his head. "I don't even know where I came from. For a while I was just going in circles, I think. Couldn't find where I left her if I tried."

Asadi couldn't believe what he was hearing. "Are you crazy? We have to go now."

"Told you already. Don't know where she is. We'll have to get a team out here or something to go searching. No sense in us going out there and getting lost again."

As Duke turned and started marching in the direction of the fire, Asadi took off after him. "Come back! Where are you going?"

"Freezing to death, dammit! Gotta get warmed up."

Asadi grabbed Duke by the shoulder and spun him around. "I can't find her on my own."

Duke shoved Asadi to the ground. "Well, you're going to have to! Because I—don't—know—where—she—is. Understand?"

By the time Asadi fumbled to his feet and was back in pursuit, Duke was already halfway up the hill. "Come back here! You have to help me!"

Duke didn't bother answering this time, just kept on trudging upward until he was a shadow at the top. He crossed without looking back and kept right on going until he disappeared. It left Asadi fearful and hopeless, even more so than before. But he could only imagine how Savanah was feeling—injured and freezing—out there alone in the dark.

Asadi panned his beam as far out as it would go to find an unfortunate sight. What tracks he could find were in fact going in circles, with no straight path to follow. Worse yet, on the horizon, the moon and stars were nearly blacked out by the clouds. *The blizzard was rolling in.*

PART FOUR

I have swept away your offenses like a
cloud, your sins like the morning mist.
Return to me for I have redeemed you.

—Isaiah 44:22

45

Simon scanned the area from behind the lip of the ridge, content with his destructive handiwork below. The GMC was inoperable, resting a few meters off the road by a thicket near the river. The roadside bomb had done the first part of the job. His weapon would do the rest. Then he could plant the heroin, destroy the compressor station, and finally head home.

Simon brought the FN P90 submachine gun back to his shoulder, wishing he had access to his SIG 553. At a little over fifty meters, he would have preferred the longer reach of his rifle and greater advantage from its magnified optics. But the bullpup firearm was much easier to conceal. Despite this minor drawback, his current situation could not have turned out better.

Kohl and Stoddard had unwittingly set their own trap.

The only thing left was approval from Solution Globales leadership and a little help from their covert influence team. They would alert the media, and their influencers within political circles would start whispering in the right ears. And once the Texas pipeline project was off the table, Ressource Absolue would be the clear frontrunner for the European LNG bid.

As images of a flight to France came rushing to mind, Simon cautioned himself about getting too far ahead. His cause for concern was timing. His adversaries were pinned down below, potentially injured, which meant he would have to wait them out. Given the remoteness, he wasn't worried about being discovered, although he'd been wrong about that before. But with a snowstorm rolling in and roads worsening by the minute, he didn't want to get trapped.

After fishing the satellite phone from his pocket, Simon made another call to Lyon. At least it was business hours now. On the first ring, Jean Dumont answered after clearing his throat. "Hope you have good news this time."

"Better than I thought. The cowboy I told you about just arrived at our next target."

Dumont sounded as if he was trying to restrain his anger. "*How* is this good news?"

"Because he brought Kai Stoddard along with him."

There was a pause, as Dumont tried to place the name. "The intel officer I recruited?"

"No. That one is from Portland," Simon reminded. "Stoddard was the Ranger. Drug history. Breaking-and-entering charges. Possible PTSD."

"Ah yes, the Californian." Dumont sounded pleased. "Family in the illicit marijuana trade."

"That's the one," Simon confirmed. "He and Kohl had an altercation earlier at the Cosmic Order encampment. Lots of witnesses. Possibly even recorded on video." Eyeing the demolished GMC below, Simon opted to keep most of the details to himself because time was running short. "I'm going to make it look as if this rivalry came to a very violent end."

Following a moment of silence, which was likely needed to process the plan, a snigger came from Dumont. "I like what I'm hearing. What do you need from us?"

"As soon as I take the Washita Compressor Station offline, I need you to direct the protesters over here immediately and alert the media. Get them here as soon as possible."

Simon looked beside him at the backpack of heroin he'd taken off the Mescalero yokel, who had earlier come into their encampment, claiming that a married couple from Cosmic Order had requested it. It was a poorly told lie, but that didn't matter. The drugs would come in handy for what he had planned next.

Simon continued. "They'll find what's left of these two and a little extra. Something to keep the media focused on Kai Stoddard, a former soldier with a criminal record, who has turned to environmental radicalism. This story of murder, drugs, and politics will keep the press talking about the scandal, which they will naturally trace back to Cosmic Order."

There was a distinct thrill in Dumont's voice. "It's all coming together, isn't it?"

Through the red dot optics on his P90, Simon scanned the area around the GMC, and then focused in on the busted back window, spotting movement inside. His answer was more to reassure himself than his boss. "Just one more step and I'm coming home."

46

Kim leaned against the BMW and dialed Mario's phone number, not knowing which horrible news to break first. The death of Bayat was obviously first on the list, but the next big issue was that they were no closer to escape. She wanted to ask Faraz why he'd crashed their car, but what was the point? It wouldn't help anything now.

Mario picked up on the first ring. "Any luck with some wheels?"

"Yes and no, I guess."

"More yes, or more no?"

Kim peered around the nose of the BMW and stared at the white Nissan. Its engine had quit smoking but there was no hope for it. "We're still in the beamer."

There was a pause on Mario's end, as he conversed with someone else in the background. "Billy just got off a call to his old buddies and the word is out about you guys. Kabul is sending Badri 313 out on the hunt."

Kim's heart sank. It wouldn't only be the Taliban or a drug lord on their heels; they'd be hunted by every religious extremist with an axe to grind against the U.S. from Kandahar to the Hindu Kush. Truth of the matter was that she'd rather die than suffer at their hands. But it wasn't just her own life at stake now. She had Faraz to consider too.

"Where does that leave us, Mario? Don't you spec ops guys have like twelve backup plans?"

"That's the Green Berets," Mario explained. "SEALs do it right the first time."

Kim wanted to laugh for the sake of keeping some levity but couldn't force it out. "Guess that was Garrett I was thinking about."

There was some talking back and forth on the other end, some of which was in Dari. Then Mario got back on the line. "You still at that old auto repair shop?"

Kim looked up as Faraz came around the back of the SUV and kneeled beside her. She tapped the speaker function on the cell phone, so he could hear as well. "Same spot. Why?"

Someone speaking Dari in the background preceded a translation from Billy, and then Mario's explanation. "Looking at some maps here. Show's a granary to the east." There was another muffled voice and then he continued. "Well, what's left of one, anyhow. Some Soviet-built grain bins and a massive storehouse that the Taliban used to use as a weapons depot. It's bombed mostly to rubble, they said, but the main structure is still standing."

"How does that help us?" Kim asked.

"Just an out-of-the-way place to hide, and a way to stash your car, so it won't be found. Longer the Taliban keeps searching for the BMW the better. Soon as they know you've ditched it, every vehicle on the road will be stopped and searched. We won't stand a chance."

Before Kim could counter, Mario continued. "From where you are now, there should be a farm road leading to the granary. Get on it and head east for about eight miles. Given the flat terrain, you should be able to see the silos to the north. We're about twenty minutes away from there. Should get there right behind you unless we hit a checkpoint."

Kim looked to her left at the route Mario was suggesting. It really wasn't much more than a bumpy old farm road, barely fit for a tractor. Traveling in the BMW would be slow. "Is it close enough for that friend of yours in the Black Hawk to come pick us up?"

"There's a chance. But the pilot was clear that he wanted to stay as close as possible to the Tajik border. Worried about getting shot down."

Kim would've liked to make the argument that the Taliban didn't have the capabilities, but the truth of the matter was that they did. The Afghan air force had severely degraded since the U.S. military's departure, but they were still capable of launching a wicked assault. Last she'd heard, their Russian-made Mi-17 helicopters were in good working order.

Also, there was at least one Embraer A-29 Super Tucano, a light attack aircraft, that was still operational. But even if their airplane wasn't in service, the MD 530F helicopters, equipped with miniguns and air-to-air missiles, were functional and more than capable of shooting down a Black Hawk or taking out any ground vehicles, which would put a quick end to their escape.

Kim hated their odds but had no better options. "We'll be waiting for you at the granary. Just get there as quick as you can."

"If we get held up, do you have any weapons to put up a fight?"

Kim looked around the front end of the BMW to the Toyota pickup. Just in front of the hood a discarded Kalashnikov was lying on the ground. "We inherited a few things along the way."

Hearing this, Faraz got up from where he knelt beside her and moved toward the Toyota, presumably to get the rifles and extra ammo.

"Good," Mario replied. "But do your best to lay low. Last thing we want is more attention."

It irked Kim a little to hear Mario relay the obvious. Clearly that was the idea. Now she knew how Faraz had felt earlier at the car rental place when she'd told him to hurry. Rather than make a big deal over it, she just agreed.

"Not planning on looking for any trouble, Mario. Gunfights are your department."

"Hoping there won't be any at all. Billy is glued to the maps right now. He thinks we can make it to the Tajik border through some back roads. As long as Badri 313 are on the ground, we can outflank them. But the second they get air support we're screwed."

Kim turned from the road back to Faraz as he came whipping around the corner with two AK-47s, one in each hand. He had a couple of MultiCam chest rigs, stocked with thirty-round magazines, dangling over his right shoulder. One of them was spattered with blood. She pulled the phone closer to her mouth when Mario's next sentence was choppy.

"You still there, Mario? It's starting to cut out."

Kim waited a few seconds for a reply, but the phone went dead. She hadn't even had the chance to tell him about Bayat. Of course, it wouldn't affect their plan any. The next phase of the extraction would still be the same. She looked over at Faraz to find that he had the weapons gathered, which meant there was only one more unfortunate task.

Kim didn't even have to ask. He'd already figured it out.

Faraz set the rifles and ammo at her feet and looked up at the repair shop. "You pack the guns. I'll bring Bayat."

Although his task was a dreadful one, there was something about his words in that moment that gave Kim a sense of peace. She hadn't had to direct him to retrieve the body. It seemed almost instinctive that they would not leave a comrade behind. Whatever the reasoning, it gave her hope, a reason to believe that Faraz might be the good man she hoped he'd be after all.

47

Lacey sighed with relief as she drove onto the drill site and saw Duke by the fire. She could only assume that Asadi and Savanah were inside the shelter, which meant they could now focus on the horses. She parked beside the pumpjack, jumped out of her SUV, and called out to Duke. When he finally turned back, he didn't just look rattled. He looked terrified.

"Sorry if I scared you." Lacey softened her tone. "Just thought you saw me drive up."

Duke stared at her blankly at first but then got defensive. "You didn't scare me." He just turned to the fire and went back to warming his hands.

Lacey didn't know how to respond. His reaction was not at all what she would've expected. She bent over and looked inside the shelter to find it empty. "Where's Asadi and Savanah?"

Duke kept his gaze fixed on the flames. "Still out there, I guess."

"Out where?" Lacey made a concerted effort to keep calm. She knew he might be injured, possibly in shock. But she also knew now that Duke was the son of Preston Kaiser, a full-fledged sociopath. "Asadi was just here a few minutes ago. Where is he now?"

A shrug preceded Duke's monotone response. "Looking for Savanah, last I saw him."

"You left her behind?"

Duke looked up and his eyes went fiery. "She was being hard-headed. Wanted to go a different way, so we split up."

The story was getting stranger by the second. Given Duke's odd behavior, he almost certainly had a head injury. "A different way?" Lacey asked. "What way?"

Duke pointed at the dunes. "Out there." He turned in a complete circle and arrived at the same spot. "Hard to tell where we were when we met up. But I'm pretty sure it was west."

Lacey looked up at the sandhill where Asadi had built a signal fire. Clearly, Duke had made no attempt to keep it burning for the others, as it was nothing left but a few glowing logs. "That's the opposite direction of the crash. Why would Savanah do that?"

"Runway's that direction," Duke replied casually, still warming his hands near the flames. "There's a phone in the hangar. Thought we could make a call from there and get some help."

Lacey took a moment to process the explanation. It made perfect sense, but something was off about his delivery. She didn't want to let Vicky's revelation from earlier color her perspective, but it felt like he was lying. "And you're sure about this?"

"That's what I said." Duke looked up from the flames and glanced around, never looking her in the eye. "Can we get the hell out of here or what?"

It was all Lacey could do to keep from laying into the brat, but getting back to ranch headquarters immediately was the right call. If she could get Duke in front of a map, then maybe he could pinpoint Asadi and Savanah's location.

"Let's go," Lacey ordered. "Get you in front of a map and figure all this out."

Duke looked confused. "Figure what out?"

"Where you saw Asadi and Savanah last. Vicky is working with Sheriff Crowley to get a team together. Need you to give them a good place to start looking."

"A team?" Duke perked up. "What kind of team?"

"You know, a search-and-rescue team. Volunteers with dogs. If we can get you to show us where you were the last time you saw Asadi and Savanah, it would be a huge help. It's not likely that they made it that far injured. Especially in weather like this."

Duke looked eager to move. "Yeah, no problem. Let's go then."

Lacey couldn't believe she'd return without Asadi and Savanah. But the key to finding them was narrowing the search. Regrettably, their fates were in the hands of Duke, whom she couldn't yet bring herself to trust.

ASADI LOOKED BACK AGAIN FOR his signal fire but figured by now he'd moved too far away to see it. It was doubtful that Duke had made much effort to keep it going, if any at all. But at least Duke knew that he was headed east, which meant he could direct rescuers right where to go. Unfortunately, as the clouds blocked out the moonlight, it was much harder to navigate.

Asadi pointed the beam of his flashlight on the ground behind him, shocked at how quickly the snow covered up his tracks. He took a couple more steps and then came to a sudden stop. There was no physical impediment in his way, but something rendered him immobile. It was as if an invisible force were urging him to turn back.

Feeling the horrible sting of guilt for failing his friend, Asadi reversed course and followed what little he could find of his previous trail. He trudged through the dark and cold, up one sandhill and down another, keeping himself motivated with thoughts of Savanah and happier times. He was so lost in the moment that he didn't see the lump beneath the snow.

Before Asadi could stop his forward momentum, he tripped and landed face-first in a snowbank. After fishing for his flashlight beneath the powder, he turned and pointed the beam back up the hill. There was the temptation to let out a string of curses for yet another thing that had gone wrong that night, but then a thought struck him like a lightning bolt. *Could it be her?*

He clambered to his feet, sprinted up the dune, and kneeled

beside the bulge in the snow. In his utter exhaustion, he'd nearly passed right by it. A few feet either way and he'd never have had a chance. But the joy of his incredible discovery was cut short by the fact that his unconscious friend was as cold as ice.

Savanah wasn't dead but there was a good chance that she was dying. And Asadi had no idea if he could save her. He had no idea if he could even save himself.

48

After taking a moment to make sure it was safe to move, Garrett crawled from beneath the chassis of his GMC and slithered back into the driver's seat, keeping low beneath the windows. Kai was slumped and leaning against the door. His eyes were open, but his chest was heaving, hand clenched on to a bloody thigh.

Garrett leaned over, keeping beneath the dashboard, and spoke to his friend in a low voice. "He's got us sighted in. We've gotta make a move for better cover."

Kai turned to him slowly. "Sure thing, my friend. You first."

Garrett was glad to see that Kai was in good enough spirits to engage in a little teasing, but that wouldn't last long. Despite what most people thought, being inside a vehicle during a gun battle wasn't optimal. The engine block could stop a bullet, but the roof and doors weren't as good a buffer as one might think. A shot in the right place would put an end to them both.

"First try was poorly executed," Garrett admitted. "But now I know where he's at."

Kai raised his chin above the dash and scanned all around, careful to keep most of his head below the busted window. He focused on a grove of leafless trees down on the banks of the Washita River. "Decent cover to our right. That's where I'd set up if I were him."

"Unless you have the high ground," Garrett countered. "Which he does. Right behind us."

"You saw him?"

Garrett shook his head. "No, but I heard the shots. Came from up on a ridge. Didn't sound like a rifle. Probably a submachine gun."

Kai winced as he strained to turn around for a look at the knoll. "Why don't we wait for Bridger? Didn't you tell him to meet us out here?"

"Be nice to stack the deck, but I bet Cloutier's going to creep up and try to finish us off."

"Seems risky to move if he's got the high ground. Maybe he'll just try to wait us out."

Garrett raised up a little, and looked out the back window, but saw nothing but darkness. "Don't think he's going to want to risk someone coming by. Sounds like he's made that mistake before. And I don't think he's going to want to sit around all night freezing his ass off."

Kai's teeth chattered. "He's not the only one."

Garrett looked down at Kai's left thigh, which seemed to be bleeding worse. Between the blood loss and the dropping temperature he wouldn't last long.

"We've got to tie that thing off." Garrett reached behind his back, grabbed a set of braided nylon reins. "Can you do something with this?"

A confident nod came back from Kai as he pulled out the Benchmade knife from his pocket, cut the reins for a makeshift tourniquet, and strapped it on tight. "That to your approval?"

Garrett couldn't have done it any better himself, but he scrunched his nose in a faux show of dissatisfaction anyhow. "Good enough for government work." He reached behind his back, pulled the Nighthawk from the back of his jeans, and handed it to Kai. "You've probably sworn off weapons of warfare, but I'm hoping you'll make an exception given our circumstances."

Kai ignored the barb and press-checked the weapon like the old pipe hitter that he still was. "Wanna jump outside and run around in circles again? Give this guy some more target practice?"

Garrett couldn't help but laugh. He had that one coming. "Well, what I'm thinking isn't much better than that, I'm afraid."

"What's the plan?"

Rising again, Garrett looked back in search of the shooter. "Plan is to take the fight to him."

Kai offered the pistol back. "Then you're gonna need this."

Keeping low, Garrett leaned over the console and reached down to the floorboard of his back seat. He fished around blindly until grasping the Shikari bow—a Christmas gift he'd had custom made for Asadi by a master craftsman named Rob Lee down in Cherokee County. He dragged it back over the console and removed an arrow from the attached quiver.

Kai eyed the hunting bow with skepticism. "Can't help but think that this is just another bad version of bringing a knife to a gunfight."

Garrett was longing for his Lone Star Armory TX4 rifle. Unfortunately, a stop by the house to get it would've taken too much time. But as former secretary of defense Donald Rumsfeld once said, "You go to war with the army you have, not the army you might want or wish to have . . ." That meant that his bow and five arrows would have to do.

"Not ideal," Garrett answered. "But it's going to get up close and personal once I'm in that thicket. Just need you to distract him while I make my way to cover. Think you can do that?"

"Just point me in the right direction. All I need is a muzzle flash."

"Well, you're about to get one." Garrett looked to the right and studied the grove that led up to ridgeline again. "Once I'm in the woods, I'm going to sneak around the backside of that hill along the riverbank and hopefully catch him by surprise."

"Doesn't sound like it's going to be much of a surprise attack once he sees you move."

"True," Garrett acknowledged. "But I'm betting on the fact that he'll think I'm trying to escape. Making a run for help. Doubt he'll suspect that I'm coming after him."

"Seems pretty risky." Kai studied the gap between the truck and the grove of trees that lined the river where Garrett would make the assault. "You sure about this?"

"Nope." Garrett smiled. "But I'm pretty sure that the only way we live is if Cloutier dies."

49

Mario was careful to keep low in the back of the cargo van, despite the fact that no one could see him. But even if they did, he wouldn't stick out from the others. With dark eyes and dark skin, he looked little different than the five other warriors that Billy had assembled for the mission. He'd even borrowed a turban and *shalwar kameez* to complete the disguise.

The drive along the highway had gone unimpeded and a quick raise up to look out the windshield revealed that they were in a breadbasket region of the country. There was agriculture equipment, grain barns along the road, and a gold-colored crop about knee-high that stretched as far as the eye could see. Mario assumed it was wheat, but what did he know? He was a beach bum from San Juan, not a farm boy from Texas. He'd have to ask Garrett if he made it out alive.

Snapping himself out of some bleak thoughts, Mario looked at his watch. Based on the length of time they'd been traveling, they were near the rendezvous spot. But a quick glance through the windshield showed nothing on the horizon but an endless stretch of cropland beneath an empty sky. It was colored a sickly yellow from the wafting dust that rose high into the air.

Mario glanced around at Billy's soldiers, kind of surprised that he didn't know a single one of them. Although they'd each served in different Afghan Special Forces and National Strike Units, there'd been a lot of mission crossover. Most of the men he'd known and worked with over the years had departed with their families. Only a few had remained behind.

Since none of his men spoke English, Billy relayed their backstories, each of which was more tragic than the next. The driver and the one in the passenger seat were brothers whose families had been killed in a NATO drone strike years ago. Fortunately, they blamed the Taliban, who had commandeered their home for one of their senior religious leaders.

Every tale was different, but they all had similarities. In some form or fashion these men were victims of the regime. Mario knew that what he was offering in terms of intelligence support for a vengeance mission wouldn't return their lost loved ones or right any wrongs, but it might provide some solace—if not for these old warriors—then at least for him.

Mario saw that Billy, now in the passenger seat, had perked up. "What you got, man?"

Billy waited a few seconds, then pointed ahead. "Looks like the granary. I think we're here."

Mario let out a sigh of relief. To this point, they'd met no obstacles. He wasn't complaining, but he'd learned over time that there was such a thing as *too good to be true*. "You see Kim?"

"No, I don't see anyone at all." Billy waved him up. "All looks clear."

As Mario made his way to the front of the van, he couldn't help but worry. Since the call had cut out earlier, he'd not been able to reestablish contact. It wasn't that surprising since they were in the middle of absolute nowhere. Unlike him, Kim didn't have a satellite phone. Which meant the farther she moved out into the country, the less likely it was she'd have any cell service.

Mario looked ahead to find the grain storage facility. He'd imagined some semblance of a modern depot along the railroad tracks like he'd seen while traversing the American Midwest. But the main structure was about the size of two basketball gyms, stacked one atop the other. The gray concrete walls gave it the drab look of an old Iron Curtain industrial slum.

Not only was the building dilapidated, but it had also been bombed and rebuilt about twenty times over half a century. The outside walls were pockmarked and the inner grounds cratered. There were piles of corn, wheat, and beans around the silos. A few of the commodities were stored beneath open-air sheds, with roofs or rotting wood planks and rusted corrugated tin.

The driver tapped his foot on the brakes and let the van coast before they eased to a stop at the entrance. And it wasn't hard to figure out why. It wasn't only that the place had an ominous feel. There were irrigation ditches on either side of the grounds and a fence along the back that would hem them in once they drove inside the compound.

Mario gave the command: "Go ahead. This is where we're supposed to meet them."

Billy confirmed the order in Dari and the driver toed the accelerator. With a turn of the wheel to the left, they drifted across the culvert over a wide drainage ditch into the facility, making a straight shot toward one of the bomb-ravaged grain storage towers.

The closer they drove to the silos, the more damage he could see. But the bullets and bombs had done less destruction than the years of neglect. Like everything else in Afghanistan, the facility had fallen into disrepair. It was the Soviet-era version of *The Land That Time Forgot*.

Billy turned back. "You see anything?"

Mario had a sinking feeling. She should've been there by now. But he had told her to hide the BMW, so maybe she was on the other side of the building. "Not yet."

Billy must have had the same thought because he nudged the driver and pointed to the rear of the massive brick storehouse. Another push of the accelerator and they were again on the search.

As they crept around the side of the structure, Mario glanced back at the others, who were looking fairly tense. "All part of the plan," he said in English.

Billy rolled down his window, hung his head outside, and studied the ground. "They're not here. Never were. If they had been, there would be tracks in the dirt."

The timid driver looked over, as if wondering if he should keep going. This time, Mario took the initiative to prod him on. He pointed to the back of the building. A few seconds later they were around the far side, empty-handed as expected. They were curving around an auger when Mario saw something back at the entrance that dashed all his hopes.

The appearance of an American-made Humvee would've once been a wonderful sight. The arrival of three would've been even better. But driven by the Taliban, and more specifically, Badri 313, a task force made up of the violent extremists, made it a harbinger of death.

In an odd twist of fate, Billy and his men were now face-to-face with the unit that had murdered their families. While Mario had been sincere in his promise to help them take their vengeance, he'd planned on being a hell of a long way away from there when it all went down.

50

S mitty looked down at the map of the ranch on his desk and then glanced around his office in the barn and caught eyes with the makeshift rescue squad. The fact that his darlin' girl had been missing all night and he'd been unavailable put a lump in his throat. And the thought of what frozen hell she could be going through had him so choked up he could barely speak.

Smitty swallowed hard, locked eyes on Duke, and asked in a way that sounded more suspicious than intended. "You're *sure* they went this way?" He tapped his index finger on an area of the ranch west of the drill site. "Headed for the runway?"

"Yeah, I'm sure." Duke nodded. "That was always the plan."

Smitty glanced around at the others, to find them looking as worried as he felt. As a whole, they weren't much of a search-and-rescue team, but until Crowley put an official group together, their makeshift posse would have to do.

Smitty looked to Lacey. "If you can go back out to the drill site and post up there, that'd help. Maybe they'll double back and find it again." He turned to Crystal and Ike. "I want you two to ride the roads. Nine times out of ten, if a lost person finds one, they're going to stay on it."

A look over at Bo, and Smitty ordered, "Go on over to the hangar and turn on all the lights, including the landing strip. They might see them if they're heading that way."

Bo looked concerned and Smitty knew why. He'd hinted at his plan on the way over.

"What about you?" Bo asked. "Hope you're not planning on something foolish."

"I'm gonna take the Gator and try to follow their trail out in the sandhills."

There was a collective look of dread from everyone, but Crystal spoke first.

"Babe, there isn't anything I wouldn't do to get Savanah back safe, but I don't want to lose you too. What if you get turned around out there?"

"I won't," Smitty said, although it was purely for show. "Know this place like the back of my hand. Can find my way around it blindfolded. Don't worry about me. I'll get good and bundled up. But that Gator is the only way we can maneuver through those dunes. And it's way too cold to take a horse. It's either this or I'll have to walk."

Smitty knew there'd be no further arguing from anyone. What he was saying was just cold hard facts.

Duke piped up. "What about me? What am I supposed to do?"

Smitty wanted to tell him to leave town and never come back. But he forced a smile and made up a job for him. "Want you to stay here and wait for Vicky. She'll be back once she's coordinated a rescue team. Tell her where we all went, so there's no wasted effort."

Before Duke could argue, Smitty looked around at the others. "Any questions?" He gave them a millisecond to respond and then clapped his hands. "All right, let's go."

IKE TURNED TO CRYSTAL AS he drove his black Ford Raptor down the oil field past the Boone 92-H. "You want to stay with Lacey? I know she's your friend. No problem to go back."

They'd seen to it that Lacey was set up for the wait at the drill site, which she'd do in her warm Chevy. Ike had her turn the headlights west in case the kids returned.

"I'd rather be on the move," Crystal replied. "Think I'd go crazy just sitting around."

Ike tapped on the brakes and pulled his truck to a stop. "Know exactly what you mean. Only really makes sense for one of us to drive these roads. Think I'm gonna try something else."

Crystal looked at him like he was nuts. "What are you talking about?"

Ike reached back and grabbed his thick coat from the floorboard. "Want to go to that crash site and have a look around. Even if it was the plan to head west toward the runway, I just don't think they could make it that far. Especially with both kids injured."

"Going on foot seems like a bad idea." Crystal's eyes were pleading. "What if you get lost?"

Ike held up his iPhone. "I've got satellite on here. Marked where the wreck was on the map. Then I dropped points at the drill site where we left Lacey. It'll be cold as hell, but I can find my way to the Polaris and back with navigation." As she was about to argue, he cut her off. "Plus Ray's headed out that way in the Gator. Chances are we'll find each other, anyhow."

Crystal stared out ahead through the windshield, looking a little frightened. Between the howling wind and swirling icy flakes that pecked at the window, it was clear this was no ordinary storm.

"You sure about this?" she asked. "You heard Duke. Seemed certain they were headed west."

Ike didn't know how much he should say about Duke. The kid was a scumbag for sure, but he was still her son. Still, his whole story seemed a bit too polished.

"I know what Duke said," Ike conceded, "but I also know it's easy to think you know something for a fact when you really don't."

She whipped back around, clearly offended. "So, you think he's lying?"

"Nope. Just confused, that's all. And when everybody's looking to you for answers, particularly when it comes to life and death, sometimes it's hard to say you don't know."

"I can see that happening." Crystal looked back out ahead at the headlights, which captured a vortex of swirling snow. "Hard to deliver bad news, I guess."

"Nothing harder," Ike agreed, thinking of his own situation, right then and there about Duke. Wanting to get the focus off her son, he pivoted back to the strategy. "Ray's right, you know. If the kids stumble upon a road, they're going to stay on it."

"Think so?" Her voice cracked and tears poured. "Because I can't bear the thought of—"

Ike reached over the console and gave her shoulder a squeeze. "I know, Crystal. I know. You just keep driving this road. Back and forth between here and the main barn. With me and Ray out there and you and Lacey along the road, that'll cover all our bases."

Crystal quickly wiped away her tears. "If you find our little girl, you take care of her, okay?"

Ike threw on his coat, zipped it up, and opened the door to face an immediate *whap* of frozen wind that nearly ripped it off its hinges. He pulled the stocking hat over his eyebrows and the hood over his head.

"Make you a deal." Ike thwacked his knuckles a couple of times on the dashboard and stepped outside. "You take care of my girl, and I'll take care of yours."

Crystal smiled as she slid into the driver's seat. "Black Betty's in good hands with me."

51

As Garrett prepared to make a move, it wasn't lost on him that this might be the last time he'd see Kai. The tourniquet seemed to be working, but it was only a Band-Aid. Of course, his own chances of survival were fifty-fifty at best. As soon as Garrett moved, Cloutier would open fire, having a clear advantage over him from the top of that ridge.

Garrett turned to the old Army Ranger and made a desperate attempt to drum up just the right words. In true Kohl family fashion, his first inclination was to lean more sarcastic than sappy. But at the last second, he changed his mind. Kai had lived the last few years spiritually broken. A wounded soul. If they died right then and there in the frozen Texas wilderness, then Garrett wanted to once and for all set things right.

"Kai, if we make it through all this, I want you to know that you're welcome out on the ranch. We've got a little cabin on the back side where Ray Smitty used to live. In exchange for some help with the horses and cattle, it's all yours until you figure out what's next."

Garrett knew that Kai had to be thinking what he was thinking. No matter what happened, the Order was a dead organization. Even if most of its members weren't connected to any wrongdoing, the name and its leadership were over and done.

Kai nodded. "I'd appreciate that." He turned and flashed a mischievous smile. "Think you might hear a few of my ideas? Ways to make your operation more environmentally sound?"

"Don't push it," Garrett chided. "My dad already thinks you're the second coming of Che Guevara. Going to be hard enough to convince him you're not setting up a fifth column as it is." He threw out a hand to shake on the deal. "But hell, I'll try anything once."

Kai took Garrett's hand and gave a hard pump in acceptance of the offer. "Well, before we take on Butch, we've gotta get past a Frenchman." He turned to the window and stared out at the dark thicket. "So, you just say the word, my friend, and I'll light up the night."

SIMON SUSPECTED THAT ONE OR both men had been injured in the blast, and now they were forging a plan. They didn't have the option of waiting around. No doubt, the two inside the demolished truck knew the same about him. He still had the compressor station to destroy before the sun came up. Fighting the urge to move in and finish them took the utmost restraint.

After panning the area with his optics, Simon returned to the truck and placed his red dot sight on the driver's side door. He'd just re-adjusted, rising from his prone position in the snow, when the side door flew open again, a figure leaped out, and sprinted toward the woods.

Simon dropped and took quick aim, having only missed a few steps on who he assumed was Kohl. A click of the selector switch to full auto and he pulled the trigger. But no sooner had the first few rounds left his barrel than the return fire came from the passenger side of the GMC. The bullets weren't close at first, but the sharp crack of the last one sent his chin into the snow.

In a lull in the firing, Simon raised back up to reengage, but the runner was already in the thicket at the bottom of the hill. Slithering backward off the ridge, he surrendered the high ground, then turned to find he was below the apex and out of reach of that pistol. He didn't like the odds of two against one. But he was, however, invigorated.

It was the feeling of knowing that he had a trick up his sleeve.

52

Kim knew little about Texas history beyond what Garrett had told her over the years. But there was one iconic image that stuck out in her mind. Although she couldn't see her would-be rescuers, who were returning fire from inside the granary, it was clear that Mario and his Kiowas were in the fight of their lives, against all odds, in their own South Asian version of the Alamo.

Looking at her phone for probably the millionth time, Kim saw that she still had no service, and hadn't since the highway. No doubt Mario had tried to call her many times to warn her about the Badri 313 fighters. But even if he had, she'd still be left with no better options. Their only chance of survival was to link up with the Kiowas and flee to the border.

Faraz tapped the brakes and rolled the BMW to a stop on the dirt road beside a massive concrete silo. Kim scanned the wheat field surrounding the complex, realizing they were completely out in the open on ground that was pancake flat. And there was only about fifty yards behind them and the Taliban forces, who were unleashing hell on her friend.

"Our guys are blocked in." Kim pointed at the back of the storehouse. "But if we can skirt around the perimeter, through the wheat field, then maybe our guys can sneak out the back."

"Then what?" Faraz shifted the SUV in reverse, but turned to her looking horrified, clearly in disbelief over the plan. "We hitch-hike from here to the Tajik border?"

Kim sighed, racking her brain for a better idea. They couldn't fit everyone in the SUV, and they were at least twenty miles from Tajikistan. Even if they evaded this Badri 313 unit, the Taliban only would dispatch reinforcements and air support to finish the job.

"Okay, Faraz, you're right. We wouldn't make it far. Only way we're getting out alive is by helicopter, which means that Mario will have to get that Black Hawk pilot to make a *huge* exception and get his ass over here. We'll just have to hold these guys off until then."

After a few seconds, Faraz gave a reluctant nod, shifted into drive, and punched the gas, tearing off the dirt road into the wheat field. As they hugged the outside perimeter, Kim saw the red check-engine light flash up on the dashboard. The BMW was overheating, likely due to a clogged air intake. The acrid smell of burning plastic blew through the vents.

Racing up behind the storehouse and out of the line of fire, Faraz slammed on the brakes, and they slid several feet to a jarring halt. Kim threw the door open amid the waft of dust and raced to the rear of the SUV. She had just popped the back hatch to start pulling Bayat from the bay when she heard footsteps from behind.

Kim turned glacially with her hands to her sides, praying the gunman wouldn't shoot her down, while part of her hoped he would. There was a damn good chance that a quick death was the better option. But to her joy, neither executioner nor dungeon master had arrived. For better or worse, it was the Puerto Rican ambassador to the *graveyard of empires*.

A STRAIGHT SHOT THROUGH A gap in the fence put Kim inside the granary and in the middle of the action. The place smelled like spent fireworks, mixed with dust and mildew. She turned to find that Faraz was right behind her. Billy and his crew were scattered about the second floor, firing M4s and AK-47s from open-air vents and portals in the walls.

Made of cinder blocks and concrete, the granary was providing great cover for the Kiowas, who'd shoot, reposition, and fire down again. Billy's men were good; in fact they were so good that it gave Kim some hope. But then came the unexpected *gung-gung-gung* from the .50-caliber crew-served weapon mounted on a Humvee, which meant they were woefully outgunned.

Mario pulled Kim close and yelled over the echoing gunfire. "It's that damn Ma Deuce that's killing us. We've knocked out three shooters from the turret, and they just put up another."

Kim looked around for anything that would help, finding nothing but pile after pile of moldy corn. "Any luck getting that Black Hawk?"

Mario shook his head. "Too worried about getting shot down. At least that's what he says. My guess is that he's less worried about getting killed and more worried about getting caught."

Kim grabbed Mario's sleeve and dragged him away from the shooting where she could hear. "Tell him we'll pay whatever he wants. Promise the keys to Fort Knox, I don't care. Just get him here now!"

"Think I didn't try that already? He said there's no amount of money that's worth it."

Kim had no argument, but there had to be some sort of incentive. Right then Faraz's words came rushing back. He'd said, "That's why you Americans lost. You have no understanding of the people you were fighting. Money was *never* the answer."

Kim still had no idea what the answer was, but it didn't mean she wouldn't try. "Your chopper pilot speak English?"

"*Zemar?*" Mario gave a nod. "Yeah, even speaks it with a southern accent. Lived in Alabama while he did a stint at Fort Rucker. Watches NASCAR for the love of God. He's one of us."

Kim held out her hand and gave Mario the gimme here motion. "Then get him on the line."

Mario keyed the number, said a few words, and handed over

the satellite phone. When another heavy bout of automatic gunfire opened up nearby, Kim put her palm against her left ear and ran down the stairs. Although she felt exposed, she snuck out to the back of the building.

Kim ducked behind what was left of a crumbling brick wall and yelled over the noise. "Can you hear me?" Getting no response, she yelled again, "You still there?"

A voice came back that broke with static. "Yeah, I'm here."

"Listen, Zemar, we're in big trouble. If we don't get you out here, it's over for us."

"I'm really sorry," he replied. "But it's just too risky. My answer hasn't changed."

"Then what would change it?"

Zemar paused before answering. "I need to know what's out there. What I'm up against. I'm not worried about the ground. I'm worried about the air."

Kim turned back and surveyed the horizon. Other than an endless stretch of wheat fields and dirt-colored sky, there was nothing much to see. "I can't tell you what's out there. Just no way for me to know. It would be a big risk. Probably the biggest of your life."

The words came out so smoothly, Kim couldn't believe she'd said them. For the third time in her CIA career, she'd actually told the truth. She waited for a moment but got no reply. If she was trying out firsts in Afghanistan, then why not another. "What do *you* think we should do?"

When he didn't immediately answer, Kim assumed he had either hung up or the phone went dead. She was just about to go back upstairs when Zemar spoke again.

"How long can you hold out?"

"Not long," Kim answered knee-jerk, having no real idea. She just knew that as soon as their ammo was out, they were done. And they had to be getting close. "Maybe a half hour. Tops."

"Okay, I have an idea. But it's a long shot. One-in-a-million chance it will work."

Before he changed his mind, Kim jumped on it. "Whatever it is, we'll take it."

"I don't have time to explain. Just be ready to go at a moment's notice. Understand?"

As the line went dead, Kim turned back to the stairs, wondering how she would explain to Mario that a plan was in motion, but she had no idea what it entailed. The only thing for certain was that she'd leave out the part about there being a *one-in-a-million chance it would work.*

53

Asadi rolled Savanah onto her back, careful to keep her covered in the nasty old Dickies coveralls that she'd somehow managed to keep wrapped around her this whole time. He rubbed the back of his hand against her icy cheek and moved the beam of the flashlight in for a closer inspection. Hypothermia wasn't the only danger. Frostbite was a major concern.

As gently as he could, Asadi pulled her left eyelid up to see if she would wake. Despite the bright beam, her pupils were wide. Rising from where he knelt, he whirled around in search of anything that could help. Within the trough of the massive sandhills, there was nothing but snow. But spotting a drift nearly three feet high, Asadi got the idea for a shelter. He grabbed the coveralls, dashed to the mound, and dug both hands into the powdery snow.

A shock wave of pain ran from the tips of his stinging fingers through the rest of his body. Pushing through the throb of his muscles and burning lungs as he gulped in air with each raspy breath, Asadi forged little walls that blocked out the wind. Convinced his dwelling was wide enough for two, he laid the coveralls over the dividers and covered them with powder.

Once it was tamped down, Asadi pulled what vegetation he could find in the near vicinity and mashed it down as insulation from the frozen ground. It wasn't perfect, and it wasn't nearly as comfortable as the shelter he'd made before. But it was the closest thing to a snow cave he could make with the resources at his disposal.

Now for the hard part.

Asadi knew it was dangerous to move Savanah. But he knew what would happen if he didn't get her out of that howling wind. He dashed back over, kneeled by her shoulders, and cupped his hands beneath her armpits. The first tug was unproductive, as her body was frozen in the snow. But a second swift yank, with a mighty groan, broke her free from the icy crust.

After a quick readjustment, Asadi got a better hold, and pulled again with all his strength. He was careful to keep his momentum at a steady pace as he dragged Savanah back to the cave. Letting her rest before entering, Asadi decided to do something that he'd been dreading, and would possibly regret. He took off his coat, put it on Savanah, and zipped it up to her chin.

Immediately he felt his loss of body heat and wondered if it was a foolish move. But there was no doubt in his mind that she was dying. And if he didn't do everything he could, he'd regret it forever. With what little energy he had left, Asadi pulled her into the cave and drew her in tight. Knowing that he should get her talking if possible, he struggled for the right words. But he didn't struggle long because Savanah slowly opened her eyes and spoke first.

It wasn't much, nor meaningful, it was simple and to the point. All she said was *thank you*. But if another word never passed between them from here on out, Asadi could live with that. Savanah would at least know that she'd not been abandoned, and he'd risked his life to save her.

SMITTY WAS BEGINNING TO WONDER if retracing the route on the John Deere Gator was a horrible idea. Despite his boast of knowing the ranch like the back of his hand, he hadn't anticipated the trouble he'd have traversing the sandhills in whiteout conditions. The machine handled both the terrain and the weather like a champ, but his failure to locate the Polaris was pure user error.

It wasn't just the storm or the emergency that was clouding his mind. It was the fact that he'd completely abandoned Garrett. But with the kids in danger, he'd determined that the investigation could wait. The only surprise was that the colder he got, the more motivated he was to keep on the hunt. If *he* was this frozen, then he could imagine how terrible it was for them.

Smitty was wondering if he'd gone too far south and should start searching east to west when a break in the snowfall revealed a most joyous sight. A quick count revealed that all the horses were accounted for. The only anomaly was the mysterious human within the middle of the herd. He killed the engine, so as not to spook the horses, but kept the light pointed in their direction.

The figure among them made a brisk jog over to the Gator.

"One miracle down," Ike reported, as he slid into the passenger seat. "Just one more to go."

"Glad for your good luck," Smitty answered. "I've had no such fortune looking for the kids." He shined his flashlight toward the herd. "Wish I knew how to find the horses again. Don't think we're gonna get them back to the barn without leading them by hand."

Ike held up his phone. "Way ahead of you, my friend. Dropped points as soon as I found them. They've got a nice windbreak down in this trough and some tall grass to munch on too. So, I think they'll be fine to ride out the storm here. We can come back at daybreak."

"Any of them injured?"

Ike winced. "One looks a little rough, but he'll make it. Couple are cut in a few places, but not too bad. We'll need to have a vet waiting back at the barn to patch them up."

Smitty hated the thought of the horses out there suffering but had to press on. "Didn't expect to find you out here, especially on foot."

There was a part of Smitty that was a little agitated at Ike for leaving Crystal alone when she was clearly distraught. But it was hard to be too mad at a man who was out risking life and limb to help save Savanah. And it wasn't the first time he'd done it. Smitty owed Ike a hell of a lot.

Ike shrugged. "Something didn't add up to me about Duke's story. Call it a hunch. But I don't think Asadi and Savanah are moving to the runway."

Smitty looked around, feeling slightly less helpless than before. "Any clue where to start?"

Ike raised the screen on his phone where they both could see it, widened the map, and pointed to a spot. "Let's start at the crash site and make concentric circles. The horses are within a half a mile of the UTV, so it's as good a place to begin as any, I'd say."

Smitty cranked the Gator and strained his eyes to see through the swirling snow. He imagined the hundreds of rings they'd have to make to cover the areas around the crash site. And the uneven terrain would only complicate the search.

"Circles aren't real easy in these dunes, Ike. Worried we'll miss a spot."

"I know, but we've gotta try. Can't leave a single stone unturned."

Feeling a bit hopeless, Smitty turned away so that Ike couldn't see his tears. "All right then, navigator." He pressed his boot on the gas. "Lead us the way to my darlin' girl."

54

As soon as Garrett hit the tree line, he threw his back against a thick elm and slid down until his butt smacked the ground. Chest heaving, he sucked in frigid air, straining to hear the gunshots, barely detectable given the shriek of the gale. Trying hard to slow his breathing, he glanced around the trunk, finding that his field of vision was even worse than before.

Thick wooded areas tended to be a rarity in the Texas Panhandle, with the exception of a few creeks and riverbeds, which were both few and far between. In a place as vast as his homeland, being surrounded by trees made Garrett a bit claustrophobic—maybe even unnerved. With the eerie darkness and soft falling snow, it reminded him of the hedgerow maze from *The Shining*.

Praying that he'd fare better than Jack Nicholson did at the end of the movie, Garrett struggled to his feet, took an arrow from the attached quiver, and nocked his bow. He gave another quick glance around on both sides then dashed over to a clump of cottonwoods. When no shots rang out, he rested a little easier, got his bearings, and moved to the banks of the river.

As Garrett snuck through what concealment he could find in the crumbling brush, he couldn't help but think of the area's tragic history. Only about thirty miles to the east was the Washita battlefield where General George Armstrong Custer led his 7th Cavalry troops against an encampment of sleeping Cheyenne. In actuality, it was more of a massacre than a fight, a truly sad affair that had ultimately boiled over after years of broken treaties, deep-rooted mistrust, and horrific atrocities committed on both sides. But such was the violent history of spilled blood in the region. And after all these years, they were still out there spilling more.

When Garrett arrived at the water's edge, he found that the river was little wider now than what most people would consider a stream. And what did exist was frozen across, with a thick layer of pristine white powder covering it, all the way to the other side, where the woods picked up again. He followed along the riverbank, careful to stay within the tree line for cover.

When he was nearly at the ridgeline, he saw Cloutier's tracks, and considered it a good sign. The guns hadn't fallen silent because Kai was down. They'd stopped shooting because the Frenchman had escaped. Keeping a careful aim on the thicket across the ice, Garrett backed away and turned to return to his truck. But he'd not even made it more than a few steps through the woods when gunfire opened up and rounds cracked overhead.

Ducking and taking cover behind a leafless pecan tree, Garrett took a knee and peered around the trunk. The woods were so thick he doubted Cloutier's rounds had made it past the first couple of bushes. He rose, kept low, and darted through the thicket, using what cover he could find in the waist-high tufts of brittle buffalo grass. Spying tracks, Garrett eased nearer to the river's edge.

Maneuvering through the dense thicket, he searched the opposite side of the riverbank. Spotting a little hunting cabin nestled in the woods, he dropped to his knees and threw his back against a felled tree.

A quick scan across the frozen river sent him diving for the ground, as the muzzle flashed from around a stack of firewood along the right side of the cottage, and rounds zipped overhead. Bullets shredded the top of the log, sending snow puffs and splinters raining down atop him, then stopped suddenly.

Assuming Cloutier was reloading, Garrett sprang from his hide, sprinted closer to his adversary, and dove behind a shredded stump.

He moved a few feet over and took a quick peek above the rim, but immediately regretted it. The machine gun rattled and bullets churned through the rotten wood.

Rolling right, Garrett rose, took hasty aim with his bow, and let loose an arrow at Cloutier, if for no other reason than to buy a little time. Now all he could do was wait.

SIMON COULDN'T BELIEVE HIS LUCK. The arrow that came at him had only clipped his left bicep—a flesh wound at best. Six inches over and he'd be lying there dead. His elation from having survived the attack was only short-lived, as the bad news was that he'd not a bullet to spare. Between the shoot-out with Stoddard and the battle with Kohl, his supply was nearly spent.

The key to taking out this cowboy was to lure him into his trap. And to do that meant taking a risk. It meant showing himself. He clambered to his feet, sprinted through the woods, dodging trees, hurdling downed limbs, and then veering back to the riverbank.

Dusted with fresh powdery snow, it took a moment to locate the detonator within the brush, but the wires were still connected to the bomb he had planted and it was ready to go. All he needed now was the hasty cowboy to make his move.

GARRETT TORE A PATH BACK to the Frenchman's trail and found the place on the river where Cloutier had crossed. Taking a calculated risk that the ice was dense enough to hold his weight, Garrett took his first timid step. But no sooner had he set his boot down than he saw a silhouette on the other side. He let loose an arrow that pierced the Frenchman in the right shoulder.

Although Cloutier went down without firing back, Garrett didn't rest easy. Craving a kill shot to finish the job, he threw caution to the wind and sprinted across the ice. He'd taken only a few steps when the explosion came from behind and rocked him forward. His knees hit first, the rest of him followed, then his forehead slammed against the ice.

Almost immediately he felt the water begin to soak through his sleeve. Gunfire erupted again but there was nothing he could do to counter. His bow had slid through a crack in the ice and, in all likelihood, sunk to the bottom of the river.

Garrett rolled to his back and looked up, watching and waiting as the dark figure approached. Singed, battered, frozen, he willed himself to rise, but his body would simply not obey.

55

Mario couldn't believe what he was hearing from Kim. There was a plan to get them out of there but she didn't know what it was, who was involved, or when it would happen. He didn't want to kill any hope, but he suspected the pilot had only told her what she wanted to hear so that she'd finally shut up and leave him alone.

"What makes you think Zemar will show?" Mario asked.

"Not sure." Kim looked uncomfortable being pressed. "Just think he'll pull it off, that's all. Got a feeling he's got an ace in the hole."

"An ace in the—" Mario did his best to calm down, which was hard to do with the near-constant rattle of echoing gunfire. "Now, tell me *exactly* what he said again."

"There's nothing to tell!" Kim went from uncomfortable to agitated in a split second. "He said for us to be ready at a moment's notice. And then he hung up."

"And that's it? Nothing else?"

Kim shook her head. "That was it. He needed to hurry, so he got off the phone."

"Okay." Mario let out a huff. "I'll tell Billy to get his team ready to evac." He pointed at Faraz. "Might give your buddy a rest over there. He's looking a little twitchy."

Faraz was taking cover behind the thick concrete wall, pock-marked from four decades' worth of bullets and bombs. He'd shoot around the corner in short bursts with his AK-47, then reel back again to avoid returning fire. The kid was holding his own, but he had that look of a soldier on the brink. There were only so many close calls and near misses a human could take.

As Kim dashed over, Mario held back, wondering what he was going to tell Billy. Because it sure as hell wasn't going to be the truth. Their best option was to fall back to the rear of the building and climb down into the irrigation ditch and try to escape. As plans go, it was a terrible one. But at the moment, it was all they had.

The problem with escape was that they'd be hidden for only as long as the Badri 313 unit thought they were still in the building. Which meant someone would have to hang back. The question was who. The obvious answer was Billy and his team since they weren't the ones leaving town. But Mario knew that he couldn't leave them behind—not again.

Certain Kim would never agree to him staying, Mario decided to keep that information to himself. He chuckled at the thought of what fate might be in store for the *Puerto Rican Ambassador to Afghanistan*. And he wondered if there was some old saying about an envoy going down with an embassy, the way a captain goes down with a ship.

If there wasn't one, then maybe they'd make one up in honor of him.

KIM LOOKED OUT THE WINDOW to find that things were a lot worse than she'd thought. Three more Taliban Humvees had arrived, another of which had a massive Browning M2 mounted on the cab. She was about to yell to Faraz when flames spit from the machine gun's muzzle.

It wasn't only Kim who hit the floor; one of Billy's guys dropped too. But he'd dived about a half-second too late to duck the .50-caliber bullet that took nearly half of his head. She clambered over to him and swapped her junky AK-47 for his Colt M4. After snatching four extra magazines from his kit, she got to her feet and threw her back against the wall beside a window.

Kim turned right in search of Faraz, to find he was gone. With the gunfire outside intensifying, she dropped the spent magazine from her newly acquired rifle, popped in a fresh one, and hit the bolt release. A quick count to three and she slid the barrel outside.

Almost immediately she withdrew as a round *thwacked* the wooden frame beside her. With a little pep talk to herself, Kim spun back around, put eyes to optics, and scanned the area below. It was at that moment when the old Alamo analogy became all too real. Dozens of fighters were surrounding them—blocking off their escape route—and would soon be inside the building.

With nothing to lose but her life, Kim held her ground. She locked on to her first target, a uniformed Taliban soldier leading the charge on their right flank. A pull of the trigger, and a spray of blood came from somewhere between his chin and body armor. As the fighter went down, she readjusted, took hasty aim, and fired two shots at the next in line.

Kim landed one in the carrier plate and another in his shoulder. It wasn't a kill, but he dropped his gun, turned, and fled. As a third ran up to help the officer, she set the reticle on him, and was just about to fire when the Humvee turret rotated the Browning M2 in her direction.

She had just ducked when the .50-caliber rounds screamed over her and sparked against the concrete ceiling. With the crumbling debris and shrapnel raining down, Kim dropped her weapon, hit the ground, and threw her arms over her head. Feeling someone grab her hand, she looked up to find Faraz kneeling beside her.

"Come on!" he shouted. "You have to see this!"

"Are you crazy? Get down!"

"You hear that?" Faraz smiled and pointed up. "Can you hear what's coming?"

Kim couldn't hear anything but the rattle of gunfire and the shouts from Taliban soldiers as they moved around the granary.

Given the ringing in her ears, it was hard to make out his words, much less distant sounds. But then it finally came to her. She didn't know if she as much heard as felt the pounding *thump-thump-thump* of helicopter rotors in her chest.

The others must've noticed it too. The shooting stopped and everything went silent. Kim gave it a few seconds, but then she couldn't resist the urge to look. She turned to Faraz, put her finger to her lips, and tilted her head at the window. Almost in unison they eased up along the wall and looked left toward the sound of the *whomping* blades.

Then the sorrowful words *oh no* slipped from Kim's mouth, as she spotted the hulking Mi-17 helicopter. It was leading the way for three MD-530 light attack helicopters, better known in the military community as *Little Birds*. They were all painted in Afghanistan's distinctive desert camo pattern and marked with insignias of the Taliban's fleet.

It was easy to see why the fighters were cheering below, pumping their fists, emboldened by the sight. The Badri 313 commandos now owned the sky, the ground, and everything in between.

56

Asadi wrapped his arms around Savanah and hugged her tight. He'd love to pretend it was so he could keep her warm, but it was growing nearly impossible to fight off the deep chill that had settled into his own bones. On top of that, he wasn't putting off much more body heat than she was. And with the lack of movement inside their little den, it was only getting worse.

Wincing as he readjusted, Asadi looked out the far end of his cave where his legs were hanging out in the open just below the knee. He did his best to wriggle his legs, and pound his boots, which were caked with snow, but the icy powder was fixed to the denim and leather. With those efforts a bust, there was not much else to do but lie there and freeze.

Asadi contemplated several options that could lead to their rescue, but every idea that he had seemed to come up short. There was no chance of lighting a signal fire, which meant his only other choice would be to create some other form of SOS. So, once the storm did pass, then helicopters would at least be able to spot them. There was a momentary thought that this option was better suited for body recovery than search and rescue, and it troubled him that subconsciously, he was already giving up.

Battling the urge to give in to defeat, Asadi rocked forward to give the rescue signal idea a try but Savanah gripped his arm and pulled him back.

"Don't leave me, Asadi." Her voice was just above a whisper. "Please don't go."

Asadi felt a deep-seated sadness at the thought of Savanah worrying that he might leave her behind. First, he'd left her after the crash, and then Duke had abandoned her when she couldn't keep up. It was only natural she'd fear that it could happen again.

"Not going anywhere." Asadi brushed the back of his hand against her forehead. "Just going to see if I can make a signal somehow."

Savanah pulled him closer. "I don't want to be alone."

Asadi untensed and leaned back, not really knowing what to say other than, "I'm sorry."

Although her voice was weak, it was rich with sincerity. "Sorry for what?"

Asadi shook his head and sighed. "Where do I even begin?"

He was sorry for stealing Butch's truck and going out to the Mescalero Ranch when he knew it was wrong. He was sorry for crashing Duke's UTV. Most of all he was sorry for failing to get her out of this situation. And now he was just plain sorry for giving up.

Somehow though, none of that mattered at the moment. But something else did.

Asadi turned to her and spoke about what was really in his heart and had been for a while. "Savanah, more than anything, I'm just sorry we're not friends anymore."

His words hung awkwardly for a few seconds and the pause in her response seemed to be intensified by the howling wind. "But we *are* friends." Savanah added with a touch of playfulness in her voice, "Just in a fight, that's all."

Asadi shot her a wink. "Then do you think we could at least stop fighting until we're rescued? Or you know—dead?"

He wouldn't have made such a grim comment with just anyone else, but jokes like that had always been their thing. Fortunately, it got a genuine laugh.

"Okay, but not a second longer." Savanah labored to smile. "Then we're back at war."

Asadi let out his own laugh, a more robust one than he thought he could give after all his exertion of the last few hours. "What can I do? How can I make you more comfortable?"

Another pause came from Savanah. It seemed as if she had to really muster the strength to speak. "You gave me your coat. Now, how about your pants?"

Asadi laughed again. The fact that she still had a sense of humor was a very good sign. "Don't think you'd want them. They're frozen stiff. And stuck to my legs, I think."

Savanah's brow furrowed as she gave her order: "You need to move then. Get up and walk."

He knew she was right. But honestly, he wasn't sure if he could. Aside from that, he wanted to relay something important. "If I never get the chance, I wanted to tell you about Faraz."

"*Faraz?*" she asked groggily. "What about him?"

Asadi could hear the genuine interest in her voice. "Well, he's alive."

A couple of seconds passed as Savanah seemed to be processing the news. "You're sure about this?" She looked at him skeptically. "Because we've been told that before and—"

"I know, Savanah. I know. But not this time. I actually spoke to him."

Asadi was tempted to be frustrated with her disbelief, but Savanah was just trying to protect him. She knew all too well the sorrow of false hope.

Savanah shot him another doubtful look. "And you're positive it's him and not some weird scammer or something?"

"He sounded a little different," Asadi admitted. "Older. But he used the word *Badih*. That's what he always called me. Nobody would know that but him."

Savanah's face brightened, as if nothing in their world was wrong, and he was her only concern. "If Faraz is alive, then you have to make it through this, Asadi. *You* have to live."

"*We* have to live," he corrected. "I'm not doing anything without you. Not again."

Savanah removed a glove and took his hand into hers. "But this is what you've been waiting for since you got to Texas. This is your dream."

"In the dream, you're right there with me."

Savanah squeezed his hand. "You can't just stay here. You have to get up and go."

Her skin was ice-cold. And the fact she was no longer shivering was a bad sign. It was clear that her body was shutting down. Asadi propped himself up and focused on his legs, willing them to move.

"Well, if I go, then you're coming with me." He turned to her and offered his hand. "We do this together or not at all."

Leaving was a risk, Asadi knew, but staying and doing nothing was an even bigger gamble. And if they waited any longer, there was a good chance that the cave would be their tomb.

57

Mario watched helplessly as the incoming Afghan helicopters maneuvered in sequence around the building, looking to be orchestrating a way to get their guns in position. He should've done something. Anything. But they were outnumbered and surrounded. In terms of options, there were none. Kim had been right when she warned that *this* might be their Alamo.

Looking over at the others, Mario saw that Billy and the Kiowas had stopped firing down on the enemy and were watching in amazement as the hulking MI-17 helicopter went stationary about half a football field away. Simultaneously, the light-attack Little Birds dove in from the sky, formed a line, and circled around back.

Mario covered his mouth with a keffiyeh scarf as dust floated into the granary and looked down at his vibrating phone. Which he almost didn't feel given the thundering *whomp* of the rotors. He hit talk and brought the phone to his ear, ready to lay into Zemar with a profanity-laced tirade for leaving them to die.

It took a few tries, but when the message from Zemar registered, it all made sense. *Get down! Get down!* Without even responding, Mario turned to the others, who were still gawking at the display of power like they were spectators at an air show. "Everybody hit the deck!"

As if on cue, one of the Little Birds cut loose with its gun pod on the uniformed soldiers down below. At a rate of fire of 1,100 rounds per minute, its .50-caliber FN M3P acted less like a machine gun and more like a chain saw. At least a dozen Badri 313 fighters, caught flatfooted in the open courtyard, were nearly cut in two.

The ones who saw it coming turned tail and ran but ultimately fared little better. The attack craft, still on the hunt, rotated in pursuit and opened up its barrels. A few wounded stragglers dragged themselves to cover, but there was no sympathy from the Little Birds, which kept unleashing hell. Chopper one banked right and climbed, while the next in line opened fire.

Mario knew he should have ducked and hid behind the wall, but he was too enthralled to move. What was left of the Taliban's best of the best dove back into their Humvees for cover, while others tried in vain to drive away. But the Little Bird simply shifted aim. And by the time its guns were empty, there was nothing left of the vehicles but smoking debris.

The third chopper in line hovered for a moment, floated over the wreckage, and then looped around the building. There were a couple more bursts of gunfire, presumably to finish off any stragglers who were trying to flee on foot. Then all that was left was the trailing-off sound of rotors in the distance, as it joined the rest of the Little Birds and flew away.

Mario knelt beside Kim and put his hand on her shoulder. "It's over." He was just about to inform Billy as well, but he and his team were already up and headed for the stairs.

Kim got to a sitting position and immediately searched for Faraz. After finding him only a few feet away, she turned back to Mario. "Zemar came through for us, huh?"

All Mario could do was shake his head and laugh. "How many times have we seen it over here? Allegiances change in the blink of an eye."

"Too many to count." Kim glanced back at the sound of the thundering *whump* of the Mi-17 and saw it flying toward them. "Now, let's get the hell outta here before they change again."

• • •

DESPITE THE URGENCY, KIM MADE it down the stairs slower than the others. It was out of fear, but also out of deference for Billy's men who'd want to get to the Taliban fighters first. A couple of shots rang out which were no doubt executions, then a few screams from those who weren't fortunate enough to get a bullet to the head. She turned back at the sound of footsteps.

Faraz rounded the corner and waved her to come. "You've got to see something. This way."

Following his lead, Kim took off in a sprint and followed him to the front of the granary. As expected, there wasn't much left of the Badri 313 fighters but a bloody mess. Severed limbs and headless bodies were scattered across the grounds of the complex. Their burning vehicles were nothing but twisted metal, spewing black smoke high into the air.

Kim looked at Faraz, who had stopped amid the carnage. "This what you wanted me to see?"

"No." He pointed beyond the smoldering wreckage of Humvees. "I'm talking about that."

About fifty yards out in a wheat field sat the massive Mi-17 helicopter.

Mario jogged up, holding his satellite phone. "Zemar said this guy is a friend. Will get us to the Tajik border. He's waiting there for us in the Black Hawk. We're good to go."

Kim glanced around at all the carnage. "How are they going to explain what happened here?"

"Air support is reporting back to Kabul that they engaged us, but we got away." Mario looked around at all the dead bodies also. "Clearly these guys don't have a chance to tell their bosses what really happened." He turned back to Kim and chuckled. "Afghanistan, right?"

Kim wanted to cry but held it together. "I'm sure there's a much more elaborate explanation but that can wait." She turned to Faraz. "Can you bring Bayat's body? We need to move."

Faraz gave a quick nod, sprinted over to the building, and disappeared inside.

Kim looked back at Mario. "How many can we take with us?"

"We've got room for everyone, but we don't have approval to bring anyone into the country but you, Faraz, and Bayat. Once we got the Kiowas across the border, there's a good chance that they'd be sent right back here."

"Nobody's getting sent back, Mario. And since when do you care about approval? I'll call Conner once we get to Tajikistan and explain the situation. He'll make it happen."

"But it's not just that." Mario turned around and looked at Billy and his men, who were turning over bodies, and dragging others from the Humvees and stacking them in rows. "Look at them, Kim. These guys aren't just off the grid. They've gone completely feral. I'm pretty sure Billy would've killed me when I got here if I hadn't offered him a bribe."

Kim shot him a skeptical glare. "What did you promise him?"

"He wanted revenge against the Taliban. So, I told him I'd help him get it." Before Mario said the rest, he winced, clearly bracing for impact. "Names and addresses of high-ranking officers. Whoever they held responsible for what happened to their families."

Kim let out a huff. "So, you sanctioned an assassination squad. Not in support of any U.S. strategic interests or security concerns. Just for good old-fashioned vengeance." She could tell he was searching his mind for a way to make it sound better. "And don't lie to me."

"Yeah." Mario shrugged. "That pretty much sums it up."

Kim shook her head. "Okay, well we've got to give them something. But we can figure it all out later." She turned and locked eyes with Mario. "This can go no further than us. Got it?"

Providing unapproved intelligence support was a pretty big no-no. If anyone found out, it would cost them their careers, and more than likely their freedom. But her outrage went only so far.

Without the arrangement, she and Faraz would be dead. She owed the Kiowas their lives.

"You got it." Mario gave her a solemn nod in return. "This stays between us."

"You really think they want to stay here? Just for revenge?"

"Billy said that's what they wanted."

"But they could have a new life," Kim argued. "A fresh start in America."

"Start over and do what?" Mario pointed at Billy. "Think that guy wants to trade in his rifle for a mop? Can you see him flipping burgers? Taking orders from some pimple-faced kid? He's a warrior, Kim. They all are. They want to die with honor and I can respect that."

Kim turned to the Kiowas and studied them for a moment, then looked back at Mario. "Go help Faraz get Bayat to the helo and tell the pilot to fire her up. We'll be right behind you."

Mario cocked an eyebrow. "Who do you mean by *we*?"

"All of us." A slow smile crept up her face. "This time, no one gets left behind."

58

Kai limped through a clearing in the woods, moving as hard and as fast as his wounded leg would allow. He looked back to see the trickle of crimson in the snow that followed, knowing all too well that his time on earth was running short. And given the explosion he'd just heard, there was a good possibility that the clock was ticking for Garrett too—if it was even ticking at all.

As Kai broke through the thicket by the river, he saw Simon Cloutier standing over Garrett's inert body, submachine gun raised above his head in what looked to be an attempt at one final savage knockout blow. Instinctively, Kai lifted the Nighthawk from his side and took quick aim. He pulled the trigger rapid-fire and watched Cloutier flinch as his bullets flew by.

Pistol empty, and no extra ammo, Kai dropped the gun and put one foot in front of the other until he'd built into a full-on charge where he met the Frenchman on the riverbank. As they squared off and locked eyes in the light of the moon, Kai saw that his adversary had a broken arrow protruding from his right shoulder and was gushing blood from his left bicep.

Cloutier growled as he lunged, swung the P90 like a club, and caught Kai in his hastily raised forearm, which had at least kept it from connecting with his head. A radiating pain shot through his body, and he knew that it had shattered the bone. Before taking the brunt of the gun once more on the backswing, Kai ducked. He felt the buttstock as it grazed across this back, but it was little more than a glancing blow.

As they crashed to the ground, the massive Cloutier shifted midair and maneuvered on top. Kai had just cocked a fist when the buttstock of the gun bashed the top of his head. After the second hit crashed down, he could feel his world going dark. But as Cloutier raised for a third blow, Kai grabbed the knife clipped to his pocket and flicked out the blade.

There was no way of seeing where he'd jabbed it into the Frenchman. And it didn't really matter. The only thing that was important was that he struck flesh. And he struck it deep. Then he struck it again and again. He plunged the blade over and over until his arm went numb.

As Kai pushed the massive body off him, he struggled to catch his breath. Between the last-ditch charge and the fight to the death, he was all but spent. Unfortunately, his mission was far from over. He still had to carry Garrett to an open area where rescuers could find them.

Kai rolled Garrett onto his back, hooked him under the arms for a fireman's carry, and raised up onto his legs. Bending low, he let out an echoing groan as he heaved the cowboy over his shoulders and bounced his body into place. Given Kai's head wound, a shattered forearm, and bleeding thigh, he willed himself forward, giving him the momentum to stay on the move.

Clomping through thick powder, while busting through a mesquite brush and traversing felled trees, made a hard job nearly impossible. And within the first couple minutes, he was tempted to sit down and rest. But he knew that if he stopped, he'd never get up again.

Kai looked out ahead, unable yet to see the edge of the grove, covering a lot less ground than he'd hoped. The dark woods had grown a bit hazy. He suspected it was partially because of the blood loss, and partially because of the falling snow. He ducked again, put eyes to the ground, and trudged on through the powder, calling out an old Ranger cadence as he marched.

Aside from his leg injury, Kai found it difficult to maintain balance, which sent him to a jarring knee more than a few times. But with a guttural cry and some primal strength from deep within, he found the will to rise, readjust his limp payload, and take a few more agonizing steps. With a smile, he thought to himself that Garrett, like all Green Berets, was mostly dead weight.

Kai was a little disappointed that his old brother in arms wasn't conscious for a clever joke at the Army Special Forces' expense, but it didn't stop him from a laugh. It was a distraction he needed to keep his focus off the pain in his wounded thigh. He'd lost his tourniquet along the way and now he could feel the blood running down his shin and soaking into his boot.

More than anything else, in that moment, Kai wished he could've thanked Garrett for the spiritual reprieve. The weight he carried now was nothing compared to the burden of his guilt for what had happened in the Panjshir Valley. Despite the agony of the task at hand, it paled in comparison to years of self-loathing and soul crippling blame. He was starting to feel at peace.

A quick look up revealed the edge of the woods. And with that image came a quickening of his pace. An even better sight was the flashing red lights on the approach that signaled help was on the way. As Kai broke out into the open and saw two silhouettes on the approach, his knees immediately buckled and he crashed face-first into the snow.

Kai rolled over and looked up to find a paramedic had scooped Garrett into his arms, while Garrett's brother kept on the move toward him.

Bridger knelt by his side. "What the hell happened?"

"Riverbed." As Kai fought to catch his breath, he pointed to the woods. "Frenchman."

"Is Cloutier still out there?" Bridger looked up at the thicket. "He still alive?"

There was no way he could be, but for some reason Kai didn't say it. "Don't know."

As Bridger helped Kai get upright, his gaze gravitated toward the wound. His eyes went wide. "We gotta get you out of here. I'll look for him later."

Kai just nodded and reached out to Bridger, who had offered a hand. But his legs had done all they could do. He had not even the energy to keep himself righted. As if the earth had reached up and pulled him back, Kai felt the pain go away. As his blood spilled into the soil, he was at one with the earth, a spirit connected. And for the first time, in a long time, he could finally rest.

59

As Smitty drove over the dunes through the swirling snow, he couldn't help but battle the deep-seated feeling that they just might freeze. Visibility was near zero and the temperature was dropping fast. He turned to Ike, who was leaning forward in the passenger seat, staring ahead.

"Starting to wonder if this is just plain stupid, Ike? Can't see a damn thing out there. And I'm thinking we might run them over by accident."

Ike was still dropping points on the map of his iPhone. They'd made concentric circles around the crashed Polaris and been careful not to duplicate their path. But it wasn't an exact science, given the rough terrain. They did their best to stay on course, but even if they were off by a few feet, it would be easy not to see the kids, especially if they were hunkered down in the snow.

Ike turned to Smitty, looking worried. "Think we might've missed them?"

"Hard to say. Anything beyond the headlights is a dead zone."

Ike turned toward the beams again. "Let me march out ahead and clear a path."

"That's going to be hard traveling," Smitty replied. "Let's take turns."

Snowflakes were moving nearly sideways because of the wind, creating something of an optical illusion. It was hard to get his bearings, to determine up from down. Not being able to judge the incline of the sandhills didn't help either. Having nearly flipped the Gator a couple of times, Smitty couldn't help but speculate it was the reason that Ike had volunteered to walk.

IT DIDN'T TAKE ASADI LONG to realize that he had masterminded a really bad plan. If he thought getting himself going was difficult after letting his muscles rest, it was nothing compared to getting Savanah on the move. In fact, it probably wasn't even safe. The only good thing was that he was so frozen, injured, and exhausted that the pain and misery no longer seemed real.

In what he guessed was about fifteen minutes into the journey, they'd only made it up a couple of hills. Worse than their speed was the fact that he had no idea which way they were going. In his mind, he was heading back toward the drill site, but he couldn't be sure. There was a good chance he was heading in the exact opposite direction.

Asadi had at first tried to keep Savanah talking, but the strain was just too much—not only for her but for him. Their breathing was ragged from huffing in frigid air, and it was getting harder and harder to satisfy their lungs. Then, at the peak of the third dune, he was certain that he was starting to hallucinate. Out ahead of them were headlights.

IKE STUMBLED TO A KNEE, labored to rise, and then turned back to Smitty. Maybe it was time to change their strategy. He knew the dad in the driver's seat was unlikely to call off the search, but they were literally just spinning their wheels. The thickening powder not only made it more difficult to walk, but it was getting jammed up under the Gator and causing it to stall.

Ike turned and walked back to Smitty. "What do you think?"

Smitty kept focused ahead, desperate eyes still on the hunt. "I'm ready to switch, if you are?"

Ike held out his phone to show Smitty their progress on the map. "Man, I kind of think we've done everything we can do. Should've seen them by now. No way they made it this far out."

Smitty looked panicked. "Then maybe we should circle inward? Take another pass?"

Ike grimaced. This was going to be harder than he thought. "Look, we haven't checked in with the others in a while. Why don't we head back and see if there's any updates?"

"If there were any, we'd have heard. Can't they get ahold of you with satellite service?"

"I think so. But with this damn weather, who knows?"

Smitty looked hopeful. "Think that's it? Maybe they got news, and we can't be reached?"

"Possible," Ike admitted. "Or maybe Crowley's got something going with a rescue team. More volunteers. Dogs and such." He held up the map again on his phone to make the case for going back. "If they do, what we've plotted here can help to narrow down the search."

The idea of working smarter, not harder, seemed to resonate. Smitty nodded in agreement, although it seemed begrudging. "Okay, maybe you're right. Hop in and we'll head back."

ASADI COULDN'T BELIEVE HIS EYES when the headlights that had been moving in their direction suddenly turned and went the opposite way. His scream for help came out a mousy little shriek. He was too dehydrated. But even at the top of his lungs it wouldn't have mattered. Any call into the night would have drifted away with the howl of the wind.

Invigorated at the thought of rescue, he leaned into Savanah next to her ear. "Someone's out there and they're looking for us. We have to move quick as we can."

His thoughts were that even if they couldn't catch them, if they moved fast enough maybe they could follow the tracks before the snow covered them up. Although Savanah didn't respond, he could feel her body stiffen and there was a pep in her step, unlike before. Although she didn't open her eyes, she got into a rhythm of stepping that was in sync with his own.

Asadi leaned in again. "We're doing it. I can still see them. Just keep it up." With every crown of a mound, his spirits rose. And with every trough, his terror set in. They had just crested another dune when he lost sight of the taillights, or any sign of the tire tracks in the snow.

Panicked, he pulled Savanah tighter and tugged her along. "Hurry, we're losing them!"

The quickened pace lasted a moment down the slope, but they soon lost their rhythm and fell out of step. It was she who tripped first and started the tumble, but Asadi lost balance and somersaulted down the dune. When he finally slid to a stop, he brushed the snow from his face and grasped around in the darkness for his friend.

Asadi was to the point of tears when he came up empty. He stood for a moment, took a couple of wobbly steps, then tripped over a powder bank, and went down on hands and knees. He was about to call for her when the beam of light traveled the length of his body until it rested just below his chest. Blinded, Asadi threw his hands in front of his face. But he didn't need to see to know who it was. He'd already heard the deep chuckle. And there was only one man whom he had ever met who never ever adhered to the expression *this is no laughing matter.*

Ike lowered the flashlight and smiled. "Well, if you were waiting on a Saint Bernard with a keg under his neck, I'm afraid you'll be disappointed." As he helped Asadi to his feet, he added, "But there's a half bottle of Cutty Sark in my glove compartment that might do the trick."

Too exhausted to even acknowledge Ike's bad joke, Asadi looked around in search of his friend. But there was no need to fret. Savanah was already with her dad, in his warm embrace.

60

Garrett awoke in the back of the ambulance, unsure of how he'd even gotten there. Given the hum and beep of all the lifesaving equipment around him, his assumption was that the paramedic beside him was in the full-swing process of trying to save his life. But when he fully came to and sat up in the gurney, he realized that other than a goose egg knot above the back of his head, and a few cuts and scrapes on his arms, he was fine—at least as far as he could tell.

Looking left, Garrett saw the body across from him was covered with a sheet. His muddled mind searched for answers not easily found. The last of his recollections was of someone coming toward him, who he assumed was the Frenchman. But then that desperate feeling all rushed back.

In his mind, Garrett saw himself clawing at the ice, grasping for his bow as it slid between the cracks and plunked into the black waters. His pulse raced at the thought of the hopelessness. But in a hazy fast-forward memory of events, he came to the sad conclusion of what happened on the banks of the Washita River. And he knew right then who was lying there beside him.

As if psychically connected, the paramedic turned from his equipment and eased over, looking a bit uneasy. The name Roberts was engraved on his ID badge.

"We did everything we could," Roberts reported. "But he'd just lost too much blood. Had a bad head wound and it looks like his arm was shattered too."

"So, he brought me in?" Garrett couldn't take his eyes off Kai. "All busted up like that?"

"Carried you the whole way and it's a good thing he did." Roberts smiled. "Given where you were by the river, and with the snow covering your tracks, we wouldn't have found you until daylight. With your core temperature as low as it was, I doubt you would've survived."

Garrett grasped for any inkling of a memory that could help him piece it all together. "He stared at the body beneath the sheet. "What about the other one? Big guy with a beard."

Roberts shook his head. "You're the only one who made it." He turned to Kai and added, "Your friend here was like the Terminator. Given his injuries, what he did was impossible."

There was genuine admiration in the paramedic's voice.

"Impossible for most," Garrett said. "But not for him. Not for that Ranger."

There was a temptation to really try to focus on the sequence of events, but Garrett was far too exhausted and his headache seemed to be getting worse. Aside from that, he knew that he'd be reliving that moment on the icy riverbank for the rest of his life. Although devastated by what happened, Garrett found comfort in knowing that Kai no longer suffered. There'd be no more climbing that mountain in the Panjshir Valley. After all these years, he'd made it to the top.

Roberts looked ahead, out the windshield, and then turned back again. "Just got to the hospital in Canadian. Your family is waiting. Of course, they were already here." He added as almost a second thought, "Because of your son."

Despite the sincere and adamant protest from the paramedic, Garrett ripped off the monitoring equipment, jumped out of the gurney, and flew out of the back of the ambulance before it even stopped. To his shock, it wasn't just his family but nearly everyone he'd known since birth. News of peril traveled fast in small towns, especially when kids were involved.

• • •

SMITTY SPOTTED GARRETT AS HE was coming down the hall and met him halfway. And he'd seen that dangerous look in his eyes before. Knowing that he'd better head him off before things got out of hand, he pointed to an empty room.

"Step in here, Garrett, and I'll tell you what's going on before you face the mob."

Garrett flipped on the light and closed the door after Smitty came through. "What the hell happened? Nobody at the front desk seems to have a damn clue."

"Everybody's okay," Smitty began. "Just know that from the start."

"Where's Asadi?"

"He's in surgery."

Garrett's eyes went wide. "Surgery!"

"*Ankle* surgery," Smitty explained. "Tore some ligaments out there, that's all."

"Out where? Last I heard they were bringing in horses at the Mescalero."

"They were," Smitty confirmed. "But they had a wreck on Duke's UTV out in the sandhills."

"Duke was driving?"

Smitty shook his head. "Asadi was at the wheel, but it wasn't his fault. Just a pure accident. Horses busted through the barbed wire, and the kids were doing their best to try and bring them back in. Just one of those hazards of ranch life."

Garrett took a moment before replying but seemed to understand. "Sorry about that. Don't know why, but I feel responsible since it's my son. What about Savanah? She okay?"

"Thank God, she'll make it. Broke a few ribs and is being treated for hypothermia. She'll recover though." Smitty smiled. "You know her. More worried about the damn horses than herself. Ike and Bo went out and brought them back to the barn."

"And Duke?" Garrett asked, almost as if it were obligatory. "He all right?"

Smitty cocked an eye. "The drunks always walk away unscathed, don't they?"

"Duke was drunk?" It was clear Garrett's dander was up again. "He the cause of all this?"

"In a roundabout way, yes, but he's not entirely to blame."

"Drunk on the job isn't a great start. He here? Because I've got a few questions."

Smitty caught Garrett by the shoulder before he could blast past him toward the door. "Hold on a minute. There's plenty of time for all that. For now, everyone just needs our support. We've had enough drama for one day, if you know what I mean?"

Garrett untensed. "You have no idea, my friend."

What Smitty wasn't going to reveal to Garrett now or possibly ever was Crystal's confession on the way to the hospital. He'd long suspected she was keeping a big secret from him, but he'd never imagined it was that Duke was her son. But that was a problem for another day. Another year. Or maybe never at all.

What Smitty did know was that the kid had major problems, and he couldn't help but suspect that Duke had lied about Asadi and Savanah's whereabouts for a reason. The fact that he had caused the whole thing by being drunk wasn't enough to make the average person fabricate a story that would result in the witness's death. But Duke wasn't your average person.

Smitty had worked for Duke's real father long enough to know that getting rid of an *inconvenience*, no matter how insignificant, was right out of Preston Kaiser's playbook. And he knew that because at one point, he had been one of those inconveniences. Of course, Smitty couldn't levy accusations in just yet. But it didn't mean he wouldn't watch that kid like a hawk.

Feeling the sudden need to shift the topic away from Duke, Smitty changed the subject. "Good news is that David is out of surgery and he's going to make it. Will be a tough recovery process requiring some skin grafts, but he'll be good as new in a few months."

"Glad to hear that." Garrett let out a sigh. "I'll go find Tony as soon as I can. Obviously, I've got a few irons in the fire right now with everything that happened out at the Washita."

"Yeah, Sheriff Crowley told me. I'm sure I don't know the half of it, but it sounds like we're at least done with all these *accidents* around here."

Garrett gave a slow nod. "I think we got our man."

"Anything I need to tend to on my end?"

Garrett shook it off. "Nah, Bridger has it covered on the big-picture evidence. Ones who were bankrolling it. I've got a contact who will take it up with the Europeans and deal with the Qataris. It's at the diplomatic level now. They'll handle the political and corporate ramifications. Not to mention criminal charges. Go after the company behind the sabotage."

"*Company?*" Smitty asked. "I've seen drug cartels that are more subtle than these people."

"You ain't kidding. But greed is greed. And the ones who are behind what happened here are going to pay for it. I've got a couple of friends who will see to that."

Smitty opted not to dive any further into Garrett's cryptic answer because he was already certain that it had something to do with the CIA. Over the years he'd learned it was better not to know. But a payback mission had Kim Manning and Mario Contreras written all over it. They were old pros at making problems, and sometimes people, just disappear.

"And Cosmic Order?" Smitty asked. "All the protesters?"

"They'll be gone soon enough. Once word spreads that one of their own was involved in the explosions, someone up high will pull the plug. Not exactly the kind of positive publicity that gets the big donations from the Aspen crowd."

At this point, Smitty had heard enough. It looked like things were about to go back to normal. He tilted his head toward the door. "What do you say we go check on our kids?"

61

One Month Later
Bayat Family Farms
Lefors, Texas

Kim stood side by side with Liam Bayat, staring down at the freshly turned soil where they'd buried his father beneath some cottonwoods. In only a year, the farm had gone from barely hanging in there to prosperous, mostly due to the ingenuity of its owner. Liam was an exceptionally gifted engineer who had pivoted from protecting WMD to bettering the earth. She didn't know a lot about the agribusiness or exactly what Liam was doing, only that he was melding old-world farming and ranching concepts with new ideas.

Kim turned to him and smiled. "Your dad would be so proud of what you've done here."

"Probably would've said I was too cheap to bury him in a real cemetery." Liam shot her a playful wink. "After lecturing me on the foolishness of giving up a steady job."

"Your dad was an innovator and so are you. I could hear it in his voice. See it in his eyes. He was proud of you, and the changes you've made in your life, Liam. He really was."

"Well, things are coming along out here, for sure. Wish Dad could've seen it."

"Something tells me he sees it now." Kim glanced over at the headstone beside Reza Bayat, which belonged to his beloved wife, Liam's mother. "And that he's finally whole again."

"Think you're right." Liam nodded. "Never believed I would feel so at ease with him gone like this. But I feel like I can finally let a lot of things go and just move on."

Kim needed no elaboration. She knew Liam's whole backstory, which included the tragic loss of his wife to cancer a few years before. He had been adrift since then, but now it seemed he'd found purpose in a new business venture. His latest experiments focused on regenerative agriculture, returning the land to native species, and a building project that focused on next-level aeroponics and hydroponics, which Liam assured her had nothing to do with growing marijuana.

He'd even been given a sizable grant by West Texas A&M to further his endeavors and was on his way to making a few major breakthroughs with some new patent-pending technologies. Liam's biggest problem was a shortage of help. With one kid in college and the other on the way out, he was trying to do it all himself. And there wasn't much labor near his secluded ranch.

That's where *she* came in.

Kim turned to the four men who were standing about thirty yards behind them. "You sure you can handle these guys?"

Billy's Kiowas were leaning against the fence. They had their baseball caps held over their hearts, in what they must've assumed was the appropriate show of respect near the grave.

Liam turned and stared them down. "Do I have a choice?"

"No. Not really." Kim winked this time. "You still owe me a favor. A *big* one."

Although she wouldn't have forced them on Liam if he'd really pushed back, Kim hoped that the situation would work out. These men needed a skill set in their new home country. They also needed to be hidden until all the details of their citizenship status could be worked out behind the scenes. And there was no better place than Bayat Family Farms.

"*And* you speak Farsi," Kim added. "Which is fairly close to their Dari. So, you'll at least be able to communicate. Or get close enough, sort of."

"I thought you said the leader spoke English."

"Yeah, Billy speaks English," Kim said. "Nearly fluent in fact."

"Didn't know there were a whole lot of *Billys* over in Kunduz."

"Hakeem Sarbani is his real name. But everyone calls him Billy." Kim laughed and shrugged. "There's a reason Mario told me about. Something to do with a movie. Arnold Schwarzenegger and an alien. Maybe Apollo Creed was involved? It was all lost on me."

Liam surveyed the group. "So, your Apollo Creed didn't want to be a farmer, huh?"

Kim winced. "Unlike these guys, who were desperate to get over here, Billy was a harder sell. I literally had to beg him to get on the helicopter."

"Helicopter?"

Kim batted away the question. "It's a long and classified story. I'll give you the sanitized highlights some other time."

Liam shook his head. "What the hell would make him want to stay over there with the Taliban running the show? Must have family over there or something."

"Well, that's not exactly the case anymore. Taliban killed everyone he ever loved."

A slow nod came from Liam in return. "Then I already know where this is going."

That was one of the things Kim always loved about Liam. He knew when *not* to ask.

"Billy's going to be staying with Garrett for a while. In a little hunting cabin on the ranch. I'll be back for him when I get things set up with something permanent."

Liam turned to her looking inquisitive. "Set up to do what?"

"He wants a job. And Mario has an opening. It's a match made in special operator heaven." Kim furrowed her brow. "Or hell, I guess. Depends on what side of the gun you end up on."

"So, this Apollo's got some skills?"

Kim looked over at the Kiowas. "They all do. But not like him. He's a one-man hit squad."

"I hope he finds what he's looking for then. Not sure he'll find it back in Afghanistan. But I wish him the best. Everybody has their own journey."

Over the past few months, Kim had delved into plenty of discussions on the subject of revenge. Knowing the awful things that the Iranians had done to his father, there was no lack of desire for retaliation. But Liam was also well aware that such an appetite was unsatisfiable. He'd chosen instead to let it go for the sake of his children. He'd chosen the future over the past.

Kim turned back to his house, where she was parked. "Guess I better get over to Garrett's."

Liam looked a little surprised. "What's the rush?"

The truth was that there wasn't one. She'd spent her whole life on the go, sprinting from one hair-on-fire emergency to the next. Something always propelled her forward. But for the life of her, she had no idea what that was—only that it was destroying her—body, mind, and soul.

"I guess there's not one. Just thought that I should—"

"Kim, there's nothing in the world you have to do over there that can't wait. All you have to do is just *be* for a while."

Kim looked back at the cemetery. "Don't you need a little time to yourself?"

"I've had enough time to myself." Liam gazed out of the open pasture. "Now that all this is behind me, it's time to move on." He looked back at her. "And it's time that you do the same."

Kim stared out over the plains too. She had this feeling welling up inside of her and didn't know if it would come out as laughter or tears. "Don't know if I can."

"I know you're hurting, Kim. Maybe from what happened to my father. From other losses over there. Maybe from something else altogether. But you can talk to me. I'll understand."

It was true that she'd been vague about what happened in Afghanistan. Part of her reluctance in telling Liam was that she didn't want to make matters any harder. His father had suffered because of her failure and she wasn't ready to relive all of that just yet.

"I guess I can stay a little while." Kim turned back to the Afghans, who were pretending not to notice this personal moment. "Maybe we can get these guys settled and go out for dinner."

Liam smiled. "Red River Steakhouse?"

She smiled back. "Their homemade rolls are my favorite."

Unlike the many times she'd been down to visit before, Kim felt no pull back to CIA headquarters, the National Security Council, or some foreign base or embassy overseas. She felt right at home there with Liam. She needed a respite from the next shadow war or global crisis, which was no doubt just around the corner. In the meantime, Mario could hold down the fort.

Staring down at the no-service indicator on her cell phone, Kim had to laugh. For the first time in a long time, she was glad to be off the grid and unreachable. With the help of a little solitude and some good country cooking, she felt as if she might actually be ready to talk about a lot of things that were heavy on her heart. Deep down she knew that the healing had just begun.

sadi had found that between their two injuries, his severely sprained ankle, and Savanah's broken ribs, they pretty much added up to a single person, capable of completing most jobs around the Kohl Ranch. Given the circumstances, Butch had given them a grace period of about ten seconds before he was barking orders about chores to do around the barn.

Luckily, whenever there were tasks that Asadi couldn't do on crutches, Savanah was around to pick up the slack. It was just like the old days. Since the accident, she'd spent a lot less time working out at the Mescalero. It supposedly had something to do with liability and insurance premiums, but Asadi suspected it had more to do with her wanting to avoid Duke.

Although the whole night of the blizzard was still hazy, Asadi couldn't help but suspect that Duke had purposefully left them out there to die. Garrett assured him that the crash, the injuries, and the bad weather had led to a level of confusion. And nothing more than that. He wasn't excusing the bad behavior that led up to the accident. But it was probably better to just let it go.

It seemed that after everything that had happened over the course of those few days had passed without much mention. The protesters were gone, the Mescalero compressor station was being repaired, and most importantly, thank God, Tony's son, David, was recovering nicely. The ones responsible for the explosion, Garrett assured Asadi, had paid for what they had done.

The only issue without resolution was the whereabouts of the poacher. Asadi was still convinced that Duke was a suspect, but since it hadn't happened again, he had decided to move on. Of course, that didn't mean that he wouldn't keep a close eye on his ne'er-do-well neighbor. Nothing between him, Savanah, or Duke would ever be the same again.

More than anything else though, Asadi was just glad to have Savanah back in his life. They were just friends and nothing more now, but somehow that felt right. It was the way their relationship had started. And if that's how it remained, he'd be perfectly content. What he wasn't content with was her shoveling out a horse stall—a job for which he was capable.

"Leave that alone," Asadi chided. "I just can't push the wheelbarrow. Can do all the rest."

"Not well by the looks of it." She stopped and glanced back. "Lucky you've got me around."

"I get enough grief from Butch about me loafing due to my ankle. Don't need you piling on."

Savanah leaned against her scoop shovel and shot him a playful smile. "Come on, you know you've missed me around here."

Lacey had always teased that he couldn't catch a hint if it was delivered with a mallet, but Asadi couldn't help but think Savanah was being flirty. He was debating how to respond when she dropped the shovel, clearly awestricken, and stared at the front door of the barn. A quick glance to the rear and he discovered why. Following behind Butch was an older version of himself.

Asadi gave in to his natural instinct and darted for his brother in a sprint. But his ankle wasn't as strong as his spirit, and it immediately gave way. The crash would've been more painful had he not the incentive to keep going. But he needn't exert any effort of his own. Just like when they were little, Faraz was right there to pick him back up.

For a few seconds, neither one of them could speak; they just held each other in a tight embrace. By the time Asadi let loose, he looked around to find Butch and Savanah had made themselves scarce. He fought to get the frog out of his throat with a couple of coughs. When the words finally came out, they came so easily in his native tongue, he even shocked himself.

"I had no idea you were coming today. If I would have known, I would have—"

Asadi wasn't sure how to finish the sentence. The fact was that he didn't know what he would've done differently. He'd imagined that very moment playing out in his head about ten thousand times. But somehow it never looked quite like this. It was different, but still perfect.

Faraz didn't even bother wiping away the tears. "Kim wanted it to be a surprise."

All Asadi could get out was "Well, it worked."

Faraz stepped back and took Asadi in. "You were just a kid last time I saw you. Now you're a cowboy." He chuckled and added, "Or a cow . . . *man*? Don't know what you call it here."

"Still cowboy." Asadi laughed and shrugged. "No matter how old you are. Not sure why."

Faraz shook his head. "Mother used to say that life never turns out like you imagined. But never in my wildest dreams did it end up with you and me on a cattle ranch."

Although it was nice to hear Faraz talk about their mother, it also put a damper on the occasion. Immediately, Asadi's thoughts drifted to their parents. Not since the first year he'd arrived in Texas had he yearned for them to be near more than now. But rather than dredge up any of those feelings with his brother, he tamped them back down.

Focusing on the positive, Asadi wrapped his arms around Faraz for another hug. Stifling a sob, he spoke with his face mashed into his brother's chest. "Gave up hope that I'd ever see you again. But now that you're here, I don't know if I can let myself believe it."

Faraz pulled back again and locked eyes. "Believe it, Badhi. I'm here for good. You can count on that, little brother."

Asadi didn't even know how to start catching up, so he decided to start with the beginning. "So, how did you escape? Where were you all this time? Is anyone else alive?"

Faraz laughed and Asadi immediately knew why. He'd not anticipated launching the rapid-fire questions himself. But once they started coming, it was impossible to stop. Although amused at first, his brother's demeanor seemed to change. His sadness was no doubt a result of the fact that his life after the massacre in their village had been much different than his own.

"Why don't you show me around first?" Faraz pointed to the horses noisily munching on feed in their stalls. "We have plenty of time to pick up where we left off."

As Asadi gave his brother a tour of the barn and told him everything there was to know about the horses, he couldn't help but notice that Faraz had changed. It wasn't only that the boy he once knew back in the village had become a man. There was an edge to him now. His eyes were different than they'd been a few years ago—darker and wary—always on alert.

Despite his earlier display of vulnerability when they'd first reunited, an emotional barrier had come back up during the course of their tour of the ranch. And it was as high and solid as any fortress wall. Kim had given fair warning that Faraz would need a little time to adjust. But something was different. His brother was not the same person he'd known back home.

Asadi was tempted to address it but decided to let it go. As Faraz had said, there was plenty of time to pick up where they'd left off. For the moment, he just wanted to enjoy the dream—to finally live out the fantasy of being united with his brother once and for all.

63

Garrett looked down from atop the Caprock and surveyed their house and the horse barn below. Knowing the reunion between brothers that was taking place inside it put a grin on his face that was sure to be there for a while. Bringing Asadi and Faraz together had been a long time coming. And a special debt of gratitude went out to his CIA friends for making it happen.

After taking Lacey's hand into his own, Garrett led her on a lazy stroll along the rim of the ridge. He looked out over the Kohl Ranch in all its glory. The ice-blue sky was the same color as his girlfriend's beautiful eyes, and the thaw of the snow had washed over the land, cleansing it, and nurturing his winter wheat fields into swaying waves of lush Irish green.

Garrett had his eye on the forty-five Black Baldy stocker calves that were walking the fence line on the way to the water trough for a drink; he was thinking of where his cattle operation was currently and imagining all that he wanted it to be. Despite the many setbacks in growing that part of the business, his plans now were even bigger and bolder.

Since his sister had returned home and taken over most of the duties of running Savage Exploration, he had the time to get back to his true passion, which one hundred percent centered on the cows and the horses. Despite the wrongdoing by Absolue Energy, the EU still went a different way on LNG, thus killing the Trans-Palisade pipeline. Which meant the Kohl family was still in the energy business but they would never get close to a deal that lucrative again.

Nevertheless, Garrett had made enough money to pay off his debt and keep the ranch afloat, with a little left over to buy a new GMC. But life went on, at least for him, if not for Kai Stoddard. And because it did, he would not waste a single moment of it. Wealthy or not, he would live each day like the Croesus of the Texas High Plains. Because in many ways, he was.

Lacey turned to him and locked eyes, wearing a look of pure contentment. "This is our place, isn't it? This is the spot."

The comment took Garrett a little by surprise. It wasn't that he didn't love hearing her say the words. He just didn't know exactly what she meant by them. He was fumbling for an answer when it dawned on him that they had walked that same stretch a year earlier, talking about where they'd want to build if they ever had the money.

"Yeah, this is it, all right." Garrett could feel his face radiating her satisfaction in the moment. "If we never left again, and this is all I had, I could die a happy man. Can't think of a single thing else I need when I'm right here with you."

"Same for me." Lacey let go of his hand, walked closer to the cliff's edge, and looked out over the ranch. "It's our little piece of Heaven."

If there were words that could've moved him more Garrett didn't know what they were. He'd been waiting for the right moment for far too long. There was always some issue, some obstacle, some reason he couldn't take that next step. Maybe the stars hadn't completely aligned in terms of financial security, but there was no question that he'd found the right partner.

"Lacey, I know awhile back I promised to build you a home up here. And I wanted nothing more than to do just that. But now, with the pipeline deal gone for good I just can't—"

"No, what you promised me was a house. Not a home. A *home* is what we build together. And I don't care if it's a mansion or a tent. I just want a life with you forever."

"That's exactly what I want too, Lace. I want to marry you." Garrett locked eyes and pulled her close. "We'll build up here one day, I promise. Just might take longer than I'd hoped."

"Of course, I'll be your wife." Lacey beamed in her reply. "But I want you to know something first. Something that will change everything. Course of our whole future."

Garrett pulled back and studied her face to make sure that everything was alright. But it didn't take long to figure out that whatever secret she was holding was a good one. In fact, she looked like she was bursting to tell him the news. "Well, what is it? Can't leave me hanging."

"You remember that meeting I had with Vicky a couple of months ago?"

"How can I forget? You and Bridger came back here grinning like a couple of fools. Thought y'all were cooking up a surprise birthday party for me at the Mescalero or something."

"Actually, it was about the minerals beneath the ranch my family owned. Turns out the seismic looks promising. Vicky offered a deal. And Bridger brokered the terms for me."

Garrett knew that the Kaisers had bought the surface to her father's property years ago and had built a solid infrastructure on the place, to include pipelines and tank batteries. So, it was only natural that Vicky would want to lease the lower unexplored zones.

"Well, that's great." Garrett was overjoyed to hear the news but didn't know exactly what she was trying to tell him. "But what does all this mean? How does that change our future?"

Lacey took his hand into hers again and smiled. "Means that you and me building a *home* together will take a lifetime. But building that *house* up here won't take long at all."

ACKNOWLEDGMENTS

To my beautiful wife, Diana, and wonderful children, Bennett and Maddie, thank you for all your patience, understanding, love, and support. I couldn't do this without you. To my parents, Robert and Holly Moore, and sister Allison Jensen, thank you for all you've done over the course of a lifetime. There are no better promoters of the series out there than you.

To my literary agent and confidant, John Talbot, thank you for being a great sounding board and a consistent voice of encouragement over the years. A huge debt of gratitude also goes out to Danielle Dieterich, who is an amazingly talented editor and an incredible partner in publishing. Thank you for helping me to take this novel to the next level.

To Jason Abraham, owner of the Mendota Ranch, I thank you for sharing your extensive knowledge of helicopters, hunting, horses, and pretty much anything to do with the great outdoors. To Joel Carpenter, (Fmr.) Army Ranger, 1st Battalion, 75th Ranger Regiment; Ian D'Costa, Director of Military/Law Enforcement, Lone Star Armory, thank you for providing technical expertise on weapons, tactics, and operational planning.

To Cade Browning, thank you for your legal expertise and equine knowledge, on top of being an amazing lifelong friend. A big thanks goes out to Klint Deere, Hospitality Manager, Mesa

Vista Ranch for providing great background on the area, as well as Milton Cooke, Proprietor, Stumblin' Goat Saloon and The Cattle Exchange, for help in promotion of the series.

I'd also like to thank Mark Erickson, Justin Garza, Ted Evans, and Joel Rhodes for all your help and advice. It's an honor and a privilege to call you friends. To the faithful readers of the series, thank you for your messages of support throughout this sometimes arduous process. They always seem to come at just the right time and mean more to me than you'll ever know.